BUNK.

ABOUT THE AUTHOR

A-P's short-lived breakout from the education system last century was followed by a brief career in a car-wash, a sideways move as a builder's labourer and an interlude as a bus conductor. He was recaptured and sent back to serve out his sentence in Bristol's greyest re-education institution, but then discovered love, which resulted in him running away to sea.

He is proud of having been made redundant five times - surely not a record, but a notable achievement nonetheless. Although digging himself out of life's plentiful chasms has involved a number of career changes over the years, eventually he found his way home, complete with a pocketful of stories and the chance to do what he always wanted.

Bunkeya

How Danny Rook left home, acquired a history, and failed to stop Mao getting the H-bomb.

A P Handley

THE REAL PRESS
www.therealpress.co.uk

ISBN (print)   978-1912119059
ISBN (ebooks)   978-1912119042

Cover illustration: 'WP198 at Ndola'
(A charcoal drawing by Jonathan Stockley)
https://www.jonathanstockleyart.com

To the one and only Rabbit

Studying history, we sometimes come to a point where the provable facts run out, and then pick up again on the other side.

The genre of *Secret History* – which is fiction, after all – invites readers to think about the previously untold story and perhaps to wonder whether it could be true.

In the end, who can disprove a story that has never been chronicled in the media or documented in the archives, when all other details appear to be established facts?

Acknowledgements

With my sincere thanks to the family of the late Dave Vande Putte, because it was Dave who corrected my French, Afrikaans and Swahili. To my great regret, Dave is no longer around to thank, or to treat us to the sound of his helicopter imitation.

Then there's 'Westie' – Pete West – who made sure the RAF chaps and the flying sequences sounded realistic. Nor let us forget Claudia Gould who helped me with my baby steps until I was able to write one word in front of another.

I must also thank The Rabbit for her encouragement, proof-reading and a thousand and one other services that gave me the time to get this and other stories down on paper after they had festered in my head, some for as long as 45-years.

I hope you like the cover picture too; thanks go to Jonathan Stockley for that, and to Cris Sharp for his design work.

Last, but not least, let me thank the team at the Real Press for more proof-reading, correction and support, and in particular David Boyle for giving me the chance to put forward an underling's view of Cold War history, and for recognising that (for some people) it is through the *story*, that history can reach the parts that kings and queens, endless dates and Acts of Parliament can sometimes fail to stimulate.

Contents

Team List & Map

In Africa – the Chinese and Angolans

Chan Weifeng	Special Revolutionary Guard
Hwang	Mining engineer
Jonas	Angolan revolutionary
and later:	
Guo	Railway engineer

In Africa – the Belgians and the mercenaries

Frédéric Vanderwalle	Belgian Colonel
Albert Liegeois	Belgian Lieutenant-Colonel
Mike Hoare	Major, in command of 5 Commando, Armée Nationale Congolaise (mercenary troops) (d. 2 February, 2020)
Jacobus Du Plessis	Mercenary corporal
Johannes Vermaak	Mercenary corporal
Daniel Rook	(Danny) Accidental mercenary
Anton De Witt	Mercenary trainee

In Africa – the CIA and the Marine Corps

Calvin Leitner	US Marine Corps Colonel
William Ferguson	('Flick') CIA agent

In Africa – RAF Servicemen at Ndola, Zambia

Peter Maxted	Squadron Leader i/c RAF Ndola
Tony Creswell	Flt Lieut. i/c Valiant detachment
'Noddy' Blyton	Flt Lieut. – pilot of WP198
Jonesy	Flt Lieut. – co-pilot of WP198
Ed (a.k.a. 'Nav')	Air navigator of WP198
Terry Hardaker	Flt Sgt, WP198

In Africa – RAF Servicemen on Beira Patrol

'Shorty' Longhurst	Flt Lieut., 37 Squadron, RAF
Alexander Baker	('Sandy') Navigator on Shorty
	Longhurst's Avro Shackleton
'Dodger'	Flt Lieut. Longhurst's co-pilot

In Africa – Others in Zambia

Kenneth Kaunda	President of Zambia 1964-1991
	(d. 17 June 2021)
James	UK Deputy High Commissioner
Sir Stewart Gore-Brown	Lieutenant Colonel; ex-pat
	(d. 4 August, 1967)
Robin Hunter	A junior trade secretary
Laurence Chipokwe	Zambian Minister of Police
Makondo	Zambian Police Inspector
Lionel Roberts	Colonel; UK military attaché

In Washington DC

John F Kennedy	President of the United States
	(d. 22 November, 1963)
Lyndon B Johnson	President of the United States
	(d. 22 January 1973)
McGeorge Bundy	United States National Security
	Advisor 1961-1966
	(d. 16 September, 1996)
John McCone	Director of Central Intelligence
	1961-1965
	(d. 14 February, 1991)
Ray S Cline	Deputy Director of Intelligence
	and head of the CIA's Directorate
	of Intelligence 1962-1966
	(d. 16 March, 1996)

US Atomic Scientists

Glenn T Seaborg — Chairman of US Atomic Energy Commission 1961-1971 (d. 25 February, 1999)

John S Foster Jr — Director of Lawrence Livermore National Laboratory 1961-1965

Norris E Bradbury — Director of Los Alamos National Laboratory 1945-1970 (d. 20 August 1997)

Ministers & Civil Servants in London

Duncan Sandys — Secretary of State for Commonwealth Relations 1960-1964 (d. 26 November, 1987)

Richard A Butler — ('Rab') Foreign Secretary 1963-1964 (d. 8 March, 1982)

Denis Healey — Secretary of State for Defence (UK) 1964-1970 (d. 3 October, 2015)

Sir Timothy 'Dickie' Purdham — A Civil Servant in the MoD Air Commodore

Inspector Dodd — Special Branch police officer

Charles Rook — (Charlie) Danny's older brother

Lewis-Williams — Charles Rook's boss

Galloway — Lewis-Williams's boss

In Beijing, People's Republic of China

Marshal Nieh	(a.k.a. Nie Rongzhen) Marshal of the People's Liberation Army, in charge of the PRC's atomic warfare programme (d. 14 May 1992)
Donald Hopson	British Chargé d' Affaires
Zhou Enlai	Premier of the PRC

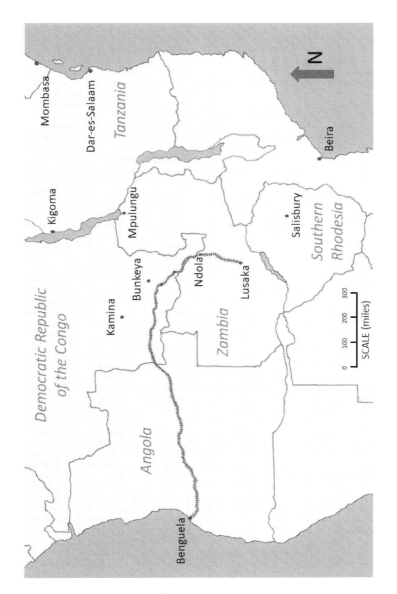

Africa in 1964

One

"Is there anybody there?"

Despite the haunting tremble in Lizzie's voice, Charlie still felt doubtful. This was just another stupid girly game. Then his fingers began to tingle.

His sister's eyes grew wider. "Who's there?" she murmured. The glass twitched in silent answer. She caught her breath, then whispered, "Do you have a message for us?"

Although it was warm outside, from somewhere a cool current penetrated the fly-screens, raising the soft hairs on the nape of Charlie's neck. He shivered with excitement. Slowly at first, the glass moved in an erratic spiral from the centre of the circle towards the letters arranged on the green baize surface of the card table. It hesitated for a few seconds before settling beneath the letter G. Next came the letter O.

"Go," breathed Charlie. The glass paused below the T.

Lizzie shook her head. "Got!"

Charlie ignored her. Another O. The toddler, Daniel, gripped his sister's free arm. Charlie couldn't tell whether the child wanted to get a better view, or was seeking reassurance. Lizzie only had eyes for the glass, flexing her arm until Daniel released his hold.

"Go to..." Charlie's next words rasped out, struggling to form in his dry throat. "It's telling us to go somewhere."

B... U... N.

"Go to bun?" Lizzie sounded unsure. The glass moved more strongly now. "You're not moving it are you?"

Charlie lifted his fingers until they barely brushed the glass, then tried to swallow. "No, it's not me."

K... E... Y... A.

His curiosity made him want to go along with it, but so far it wasn't making any sense.

W... H... E... R... E.

A real word; signs of a message emerging. Despite the light touch he could feel the glass vibrating. Lizzie gaped. Her eyes glistened. Charlie didn't know what to think. He knew he wasn't spelling out the message. The shock on his sister's face made him certain that she wasn't, either. Gone were their suspicions that the other was somehow manoeuvring the glass. Daniel clutched the edge of the table, hauling himself up on tiptoes, spellbound.

Y... O... U.

Then, footsteps on the stoep – Miriam, the children's nanny. "Master Charles," she called. "Miss Elizabeth? Where are you? It's time for Daniel's nap now."

E... V... E.

Charlie felt perplexed. Miriam might interrupt them at any moment. His desire for the glass to complete its message fought against his fear at what they had conjured up. What if they began to forget some of the letters? Half-choking with fright, he croaked the words that the spirit could not. "Go to Bunkeya, where you eve..."

The handle rattled and the door swung open. The glass had been sliding diametrically across the circle, away from the letter E, but when the African woman entered, it swerved and in an instant shot across the baize at speed, its rim colliding with the wooden lip of the table. The glass flipped into the air, arcing towards the wide stone hearth, spinning in flight.

"*Chenjerai!* Look out!"

Four pairs of eyes watched helplessly as the glass

glinted in a shaft of sunlight, dipped, and shattered on the stonework. Lizzie gasped. Daniel shrieked and burst into tears. Charlie, his face guilt-ridden, looked away from the diamond splinters, then directly at Miriam, afraid of what she would do or say.

The Shona woman rushed forward. She scooped Daniel into her arms, cuddling him, rocking him, almost smothering the frightened child. Then, catching sight of the cards, she turned away with a moan and made the sign of the cross on Daniel's forehead before crossing herself. Glaring at Lizzie she hissed, "You get the brush. Now, girl. You sweep all this glass away. You get every bit, you hear?" She scowled again at the circle of cards. "Burn these! And don't you mess with *Chipoko* no more, Missy. Bad spirits! Leave 'em sleep. You escape this time, but next time maybe not so lucky. Next time maybe hellfire burn your soul."

Lizzie fled, on the brink of tears. Miriam stroked Daniel's cheek to sooth him, then frowned at Charlie. "Evil magic, Master Charles! Never again, you understand?" Charlie put on a contrite face and nodded. "Don't make me tell," she said. "Promise you say your prayers tonight. Get out of here now." She pushed at his shoulder to force him from the room. "Go and help Noah in the garden."

After dark, Charlie contemplated what the next letter might have been. He had his father's dictionary open on his knee. From the direction the glass had been moving, possible letters could have been N or R. An N might have led to the word 'eventually'. Otherwise, it looked like 'ever after', 'everlastingly' or 'evermore'. He didn't like the thought of going anywhere under sentence of those timescales, let alone this unheard-of place called Bunkeya. It ought to be easy to steer clear of it though, now he had been warned.

As the house settled down for the night, the mystery remained to tantalise Charlie. What message would the glass have traced out and what had animated it? He hadn't been guiding it. It certainly couldn't have anything to do with Daniel – he could only manage baby talk, let alone spelling. It must have been one of Lizzie's tricks. But if so, why could Charlie hear her crying herself to sleep?

Enough! Served her right. Stupid game – wanting to get the cards to tell her how many children she'd have. If she didn't stop blubbing, their mother might hear. Then Miriam might be forced to betray what had been going on. He heard the boards creak as Miriam crept into the nursery to comfort Daniel, who was whimpering too.

Two

On Thursday July 25th, 1963, the representatives of the Soviet Union, the United States of America and the United Kingdom concluded their negotiations in Moscow over the Partial Test Ban Treaty. They initialled what they had agreed, then notified their respective governments.

Wednesday 31 July 1963

(1) The White House, Washington D.C.

A subtle change in the acoustics of his office made Ray Cline, Deputy Director of Intelligence, look up. The President was standing in the doorway. Cline stood up too.

"So, Ray. The *People's Daily* just decided to rain on our parade, huh?" Kennedy wasn't smiling. "What's made the Chi-coms come out against the treaty? They're not affected. Not yet, anyway."

Cline felt uneasy about the tapes recording in the background. These days, he spent too long choosing his words. The result often sounded pompous.

"Uh... You have probably been informed that there was a particularly bitter blast out of China yesterday, which we received today, saying, uh..." Cline glanced down at his notes, playing for time, before quoting the words that Kennedy must have seen already. "...In which the Chinese government officially said that the Test Ban Treaty was 'a big fraud to fool the people of the world'."

The President loosened his tie and slouched against the door frame. Cline continued to read from the newspaper article. "It was unthinkable that the Chinese government would be a party to this dirty fraud and that the interests of the Soviet people – of all the people of the Socialist camp, including the people of China, have been sold out by the Soviet Union through the policy pursued by the Soviet government in allying itself with the United States to oppose China." Cline set down his notes. "This is just about as strong language as –"

"– As they've ever used?" interrupted Kennedy.

"Sorry, Mr President. I meant to say, it's much stronger than they've ever used before."

"Look, Ray. I know you and McCone and half the agency think signing this treaty could be dangerous, but we can't afford another face-off like Cuba. It isn't even a year yet." He shook his head, as if to clear an unwelcome worry.

Cline thought Kennedy looked weighed down. "No, Mr President."

"You know the guys from the Livermore and Los Alamos are coming in this afternoon to tell me what *they* think." Kennedy pointed at the pages clutched in Cline's hand, then jabbed the air as he spoke. "But hell! Is this what the Chinese really think? The world needs them on board. And the damned French, too. I need to know why China's against this. I need to know before I see the scientists later. Get an analysis to me as fast as you can, Ray."

"I'll get on it directly, Mr President." Kennedy grunted, eased himself around against the chafing of his back-brace and, with obvious effort, limped away. Cline sat down again. The Chinese had escalated their anti-Soviet rhetoric well beyond the usual formula. The editorial was aimed more at Russia than the US, though. Cline mused, mentally drafting a memorandum for Kennedy about China's resentment over Soviet withdrawal of collaboration in building and testing a nuclear weapon. Possible phrases sprang to mind – 'the culmination of bitter recriminations...', 'the rising wave of ideological polemics...', 'a gulf that was not going to be easily bridged...'. Just the sort of political oratory that JFK loved.

Cline made sure he was loitering near the water cooler around the time the President's meeting ended. When they left the cabinet room, the tall guy, Seaborg from the Atomic Energy Commission, seemed less annoyed than the other two. But Foster and Bradbury were grim-faced. No surprise that they hadn't bought into Kennedy's vision. For those two, the bigger picture seemed to lie in building the ultimate, the most sophisticated, the most elegant hydrogen bomb that the American tax-payer could afford... and then some.

(2) Guerrilla and Political Warfare Academy
Nanking, People's Republic of China

Chan Weifeng, Special Revolutionary Guard, stood at attention outside the camp commandant's office. Normally, a sixth sense kept him one step ahead of trouble. Today, however, it seemed his talent had deserted him. He thought back over the past few weeks but couldn't recall doing or saying anything to feel guilty about. Guilt? Innocence? They didn't seem to matter in China these days. When somebody denounced you, fate took over.

Chan reckoned they had kept him waiting for at least half an hour already. The rigid pose was making his legs ache. He wriggled his toes inside his canvas boots and tensed his calf muscles, trying to pump the blood around. Whatever crime he had committed, it must be serious. He tried to quell the thought, but it only made him feel more nervous. It came down to two possibilities: When the People's Liberation Army sends for you, you can be certain either that you're in trouble – or they are. And placing any reliance on the latter would be a mistake. But if not, then what?

"Enter!"

In case unseen eyes were watching, Chan performed a drill move to come smartly out of the attention position. He froze his features into a mask, stepped forward with a stamp or two, opened the door and, through a process of more stepping and stamping, arranged himself, once again at attention, in front of the commandant's table. But it wasn't the commandant who sat behind it. By the look of this citizen's waistline, and from his style of clothing, which was indistinguishable from that of the Great Leader – 'the red sun in the centre of our hearts' – this was The Party.

The Party inspected Chan for several moments, clearly trying to crack his composure. Standard procedure. Chan kept his face blank, regulating his breathing, hoping that the official could not see the pulse in his throat or hear the thud of his heart. The visitor finally grew tired of his charade and picked up a thin sheaf of papers.

"Chan Weifeng, how come you speak Portuguese?"

There were worse sins. "I had a job on the docks in Macao, Comrade. They put me in charge of a gang of workers. The Portuguese thought I was good at it, so they gave me more to do. I needed to understand their language so I could carry out orders from the imperialist boss-class." It wasn't a secret. Chan hoped he hadn't already condemned himself.

"You made trouble."

"I worked in secret as an agitator for The Party, Comrade. I did what they wanted."

"But you ran away."

"There must have been an informer." Chan blinked a couple of times to mask the brief flicker as he stole a glance at the figure behind the desk – solemn, inquiring, non-judgmental.

"One morning I spotted a police squad getting ready to raid the wharf where I worked. I escaped in time and the Party helped me get out." The interview seemed to be going better than Chan had feared. Of course, it could still be a trick to get under his guard, but he felt justified in adding a word in his favour. "My position here at the Academy is down to the Party."

"How did you avoid the police, that morning?"

Surely this was already covered in his file? "I escaped through the back of the go-down and persuaded an old bird-seller to change clothes with me. There was a line of railway boxcars heading out of the docks. I jumped on board and hid behind some rice sacks. I was lucky."

"A man makes his own luck. Resourceful, not lucky."

If this was trouble, it didn't feel like it. Chan relaxed half an inch, then jerked into the attention position again, acknowledging the slight compliment and emphasising his commitment to the cause.

The official gestured towards an open newspaper that faced Chan across the table, forcing him to bow his head. "Have you seen a copy of *Renmin Ribao* today?"

Chan needed to know how the land lay. He tried his luck by offering an oblique answer, meaning to suggest that a loyal examination of the paper, absorbing the wisdom of his superiors, was an unvarying daily habit. "Not yet, Comrade." If the official suspected this was a pretence, his face didn't show it.

"Sit down. Take some time to read this article about the proposed Test Ban Treaty."

The newspaper's editorial accused the Soviet Union of a massive fraud, a filthy deception, a betrayal of Socialist people worldwide. Khrushchev had thrown in his hand with the Yankee capitalists and the war-mongering British imperialists, to further isolate China. It was very stirring stuff. Somebody somewhere must be hurting badly.

Chan looked up from the article and, although seated, stiffened to attention again. His fear of being in trouble receded further. "Thank you for drawing this to my attention, Comrade."

The official smiled. "What do you know about these atomic weapons?"

"I only know what I've learned at the Academy. The Yankees used them to crush Japan and end the war against the Axis. The Soviet Union, Britain and France also possess them. But I don't know much more than that." Chan had noticed that the newspaper called for a world summit to discuss disarmament. He had enough sense to leave political matters for others and answer only the question that had been asked. In due course, if it was important, someone would tell him what to think.

"You saw that China has called for a conference?" Chan nodded. "This is clearly impossible. The nuclear powers have too much at stake to agree to our agenda." The official paused, then spread his arms wide. "So, what is China to do?"

It looked like a direct question. Chan knew he was being tested rather than consulted but he had no idea what the official wanted to hear. He felt that a shrug would be wrong. To gain time he narrowed one eye and peered upwards, gripping his chin.

"Come on, Chan. You're a perceptive man. China's already in this position. What are our options?"

This was better. Discussing the options would put off the need to make a choice until the real agenda became clear.

"This is still only a political battlefield, Comrade. So, it depends on why China proposed a disarmament conference in the first place. At the Academy we learn that in political negotiations one should always start with a reasonable impossibility. A refusal makes your opponent seem obstructive and, if the dialogue breaks down, it allows you to pursue the policy you had in mind all along." The official studied Chan, declining to interrupt. "Disarmament is logical: everyone wants to live in peace. But trust is lacking, so it's impossible. When the powers reject the suggestion..." The fog began to lift and one possible motive became clear to Chan. "...I can see one option: Our leaders can now insist that China has been forced to develop its own atomic weapon to protect the People from foreign aggressors who refuse to disarm."

The official leaned back and looked pleased. "Go no further, Chan." He cleared away the newspaper, shuffled the paperwork aside and made a wide, encompassing gesture with his right hand. "Did they teach you anything here about the Soviet offer to help China build our own atomic weapon?"

"We learned that the Soviets are not to be trusted. Khrushchev told us he would help, but in 1959 he withdrew his promise."

"Correct. Since then, the reasons for our country to possess its own bomb have kept getting more important. We can't go on being threatened by the Soviets, Chan. All nations must learn to treat China as an equal. We must continue developing our own bomb – despite the problems." The official raised one eyebrow and stared at Chan from underneath it. "One problem is resources –

how to supplement our stock of uranium. We need more." He paused as if to imply that he expected a reply from Chan, but Chan knew nothing about uranium. The risk of saying something irrelevant or stupid felt too great so he simply rocked forward, nodding in gentle, silent agreement. The official took a deep breath, perhaps disappointed not to have trapped Chan into an unguarded comment, then he sighed. "However, we predicted this problem and planned around it."

Chan's talents lay neither in science nor planning. He couldn't see a role for himself yet, or why the official had shared such knowledge with him – certainly not out of friendship. Chan stayed silent. This was not the time to overstep any boundaries. In an equal society it pays to know who is master.

"Tell me... The world's richest source of uranium is not in China but...?"

Chan had no idea. The official seemed amused, inclined to toy with him for a few moments, expecting a guess. Chan obliged. "Soviet Russia, Comrade?"

"The world's richest source of uranium lies in the Belgian Congo."

"Africa?"

"Correct. The Belgians discovered it before Hitler's war. When Germany overran Europe, the Belgians in the Congo refused to capitulate. They loaded their stocks of ore into railcars, sent it down the Benguela Railway to Lobito and secretly shipped it to a warehouse in New York." The official leaned forward across the desk and lowered his voice. "Later, when the Yankees discovered that the ore was already in their country, they bought it from the mining company and paid for the mine to be re-opened. Like us, they had discovered they needed a great deal of uranium to make their bomb." The official paused again, as if waiting for Chan to catch up.

"You said we need more... A lot more, then?"

"Yes. A lot more." He tilted his head to one side and peered at Chan as if trying to make a decision. "But only a year after Khrushchev broke his promise to us, the Congo became independent. It was a bloodbath. The Belgians knew they could never hold the country. They had to get out fast."

Chan now saw the point of the lecture. "So, the capitalists no longer control the mine?"

"Correct, yet again. And this is our opportunity. We plan to re-open the mine in secret. Perhaps we'll even transport the ore the same way the Belgians did – rail to Lobito, then ship it out from under their noses. When the Yankees hear about this, maybe it will teach them to respect us."

Chan had been taught that battles gained against imperialism were of no value unless others could be won over to the Socialist cause by seeing the failings of the capitalist system. His suspicion strengthened that The Party was about to order him to join this operation. Perhaps his previous work on Macao's waterfront would be put to good use.

"Chan, the Benguela Railway runs for over thirteen hundred kilometres from Katanga in the Congo through Portuguese West Africa – Angola. It reaches the Atlantic coast at Benguela, then heads north to Lobito. You speak Portuguese. You've studied political philosophy and guerrilla warfare here at the Academy. Now you have the chance to put it into practice by volunteering..." here the official paused, and performed the same trick again of speaking to Chan from beneath his lowered brow; "...volunteering for a mission in Angola, to perform work of the greatest importance to our country." He beamed at

Chan. Chan understood immediately that he was now expected to leap to attention and express his patriotic devotion unto death. It seemed worth volunteering, if only to quit the classroom and escape the endless political lectures and discussion groups.

He realised he had become bored with learning about the theories of Chairman Mao. He had become stale. The best remedy for making his pulse beat faster again was the thrill of adventure. But for an orphaned former street urchin there was also the honour of being chosen. Chan composed his face, rose to stand at attention and saluted. "You can depend on me, Comrade."

The official's smile widened still further. "Excellent! I'm sending you to Angola. I have a contact in one of the local independence movements. Get to know this man. Advise me of his organisation's merits. If they are rightly suspicious of the Soviets, they may be open to a new approach from China."

The official halted, giving Chan the impression that the verbal briefing for his political mission was over. Chan saluted again.

"I haven't finished, Chan. My contact will act as your guide. You will walk the length of the Benguela Railway to assess whether it's a dependable route for our uranium supplies. If it's in poor condition, or vulnerable, you will advise how easy it would be to disrupt the railway. You will travel to the Congo with a mining engineer. You will assist him to re-open the Shinkolobwe mine, recruit native labour, and ship vital ore samples back to China." The official paused again. "Any questions?"

Chan could see this was much more than organising a gang of coolies to discharge sacks of rice. His mission was political, but with a military slant to it. But the military mind also concerns itself with practical matters.

"Just a small matter, Comrade... Supplies. Will your contact have organised caches of food and other supplies along the way?"

"I'm sure he will have thought of that."

But whether the contact had or hadn't, here was an ideal opportunity to experience the practical application of revolutionary Marxism – weapons, explosives and the excitement of covert action. This was the perfect time for a change. Contact with Angolan revolutionaries, possibly blowing up the Benguela Railway and stealing uranium from under the noses of the capitalists – that was the life and the excitement he craved. Chan saluted for a final time.

Friday 22 November 1963
At sea, 55 miles northwest of Cabo de Santa Marta,
Angola

Chan waited for the crest of the low swell wave, then stepped neatly off the pilot ladder into the bottom of the workboat. With his left hand, he grasped the safety line dangling from the rail above him. Placing his feet wide apart to brace himself against the gentle rise and fall, he watched as, six metres above him, Hwang, the mining engineer, began to clamber down the pilot ladder that hung against the hull of the factory-ship *Dong Hua 5*. Clearly, even after the voyage from China, the engineer remained uncomfortable at sea. He paused to gather his courage before each deliberate step, moving a single hand or foot, then clinging on again for several moments to regain his nerve. Hwang looked down after each effort. He appeared to be trembling. Chan could not resist offering some advice to his colleague.

"Don't look down." Then, provocatively, "If you fall,

you'll have a soft landing. Wet, but soft!"

This failed to dispel Hwang's fears. Several minutes passed before Hwang was close enough to Chan's steadying hand for him to risk stepping off the pilot ladder.

"One, two, three – now!"

The engineer delayed for half a second, launched himself bodily by detaching all four limbs from the pilot ladder at once, and landed in the workboat. Prepared for a fall of perhaps half a metre, his mistimed fall of three times that height caused his knees to buckle, and he crumpled into a heap in the bottom of the boat. Whilst Chan regarded Hwang with disappointment, the sailors turned away in contempt. In silence they sculled their craft across to the small fishing vessel that would take Chan and Hwang into Benguela. Once alongside the trawler, the man at the tiller called out for a heaving line to be lowered so they could secure a loop under Hwang's armpits as a precaution during his anticipated lubberly climb aboard.

In the late afternoon, Chan leaned on the deck rail, trying to gain an impression of the first foreign shore, other than Macao, that he had ever encountered. There were no proper harbour facilities at Benguela, just two concrete wharfs, about a hundred and fifty metres long, protruding seawards from the low sandy beach. Chan glimpsed the remnants of a couple of collapsed wooden jetties, with the occasional barnacle-encrusted pile peeping above the surface. No deep-sea merchant vessels came here, just the odd shallow-draught coaster and, of course, the fishermen. A single-storey customs building squatted at the landward end of the quay. At the seaward end, a lone child had spread out a net and was removing strands of seaweed from it. To the east, the marshy coastal plain stretched inland for maybe four or five kilometres. Beyond the old colonial town, a distant crescent of dry, sandy-brown cliffs glowed flame-red in the setting sun.

Now that the heat of the day had passed, made bearable by a recent refreshing shower of tropical rain, Chan straddled the ship's rail and jumped down onto the jetty. He stuffed his hands into his pockets, killing time by ambling half way along the wharf and peering into the water for no obvious reason other than the seafarer's overwhelming need to get away from the incarcerating vessel once in a while. Then he crossed to the other side of the jetty, moved a little farther from the trawler, crouched and spat into the water.

A solitary official stepped outside the custom-house and lowered himself onto an upturned packing case, facing west, his face full of pleasure, lit by the sunset. At that moment a battered truck bumped on to the wharf and drew up alongside him. The African driver leaned out of the space where once his door had been, and called: "*Olá, chefe! Boa noite!*" The officer acknowledged with a simple wave.

"I want to see if these fishermen will sell me some fish – or trade for this tobacco and fruit." The driver glanced over his shoulder, gesturing backwards with his thumb to indicate the goods on offer. He then raised a hand, rubbing his thumb and forefinger together, to indicate a cash deal. A wide grin spread across his face, and he winked at the official, who rose to his feet with a grunt. The officer peered over the tailboard of the truck.

"What's this? They won't want any of this rubbish." He stepped back in disgust. "Been thrown out from the market, has it?"

"There's nothing wrong with the tobacco leaves, at least." The African appeared affronted. "A man has to make a living."

"Don't let me stop you, but this stuff is just shit. If you poison these Chinese, don't blame me if they come looking for you with a knife." He waved the driver forward onto the wharf. The trader grinned, tipped his fingers to his forehead and drove the truck alongside the fishing boat. Chan, meanwhile, thrust his hands back inside his pockets and trudged back towards the vessel, following the lorry.

The African eased himself out of his cab, then called out in Portuguese to two Chinese crew-members, lolling on the rusty rail. They ignored him. He stepped back towards the flatbed and unfastened the single toggle that secured one raised wooden side of the cargo deck. With a great show of salesmanship, he play-acted the uses to which tobacco and fruit might be put, all the while keeping up a strident commentary. Chan rested one foot on a bollard to watch the performance. When the Portuguese language failed to have any effect, the trader tried again in French, then English. Chan sidled across to the truck, peered at the fruit and screwed up his face in distaste. Enhanced by much lively gesticulation, he let out a string of Chinese oaths, then turned on his heel and climbed back aboard the vessel.

From the quay, the African pleaded with Chan, who stared back as coldly as a stone lion. New tactics would be required if a deal were to be struck. An idea seemed to occur to him. He reached inside the cab and extracted two bottles of beer, which he brandished above his head. Chan remained stock still, considered the matter for a moment, and then held up four fingers. With an anguished expression and hands raised to the heavens, the trader made it clear that he was already down on the deal. Clearly defeated, he collected a further two bottles from the unseen hoard. Satisfied, Chan motioned the vendor to come on board. For his part, the African turned to face the customs official, waved the bottles above his head and, as if to demonstrate his unshakeable confidence in the eventual success of his marketing campaign, shouted out: "*Todo mundo gosta de cerveja!*"

Yes. All over the world, men can be persuaded by free beer.

Chan needed to make certain that the long-standing plan still held good. He, Hwang and the trader had begun their meeting in the fishing boat's mess room, a small utilitarian cabin at the aft end, next to the rope locker. Because cooking and eating went on in the same space, a squadron of local insects buzzed around in anticipation of attacking the next meal. The African sun had made the un-insulated steel bulkheads hot to the touch. The scorching surfaces radiated an oppressive heat, which the open scuttles had little chance of dissipating in the motionless evening air. The trio needed to find somewhere less like a furnace.

The only other secluded space in which to conduct a secret meeting was below deck in the fish-hold. The climate there was quite the opposite. With the freezer equipment chilling down the day's catch, this place proved more suitable for a brief discussion. By contrast the small group now had to wear duffle coats to avoid being frozen along with the cargo. But at least by this stage of the voyage, even Hwang was used to the smell of fish.

"Look here, Jonas," said Chan to the African, indicating two large ice-blocks. "You see these lumps of fish? Well, our assault rifles, the Geiger counters and the Yankee dollars are already frozen right at the centre. They were all heat-sealed in heavy-gauge polythene before we left China, so there shouldn't be any damage."

"Good. The customs officer's shift finishes at eight o'clock. You'll need to get a derrick rigged so we can hoist this stuff onto my truck just before then. We'll make it look good by letting him see the tobacco coming on board in exchange. Hopefully, the relief officer won't want to inspect the cargo when he sees it's only frozen fish. If he does, I'll just drop him a little *gratificação* and he's sure to let us get on our way." Jonas thought for a few moments, then asked: "How long will it take to thaw, so we can get the equipment out and get moving?"

"That'd take too long. We'll just hammer it apart with iron spikes. That'll be much quicker. You can find spikes, or something to split open the blocks, can't you?"

"Yeah – easy, man! Then tomorrow I'll sell the fish at Kasseque market, and maybe buy some beer and visit a *beeeg* woman, before we leave!" He laughed, anticipating both pleasures. Under Chan's guidance, Hwang's Portuguese had improved to the point where, assisted by Jonas's gestures, he was able to grasp the African's meaning and he chuckled too.

In an effort to avoid drawing attention to their departure, the skipper had confined the rest of the crew inside the accommodation. Although there was little danger that he would be overheard, the skipper withdrew into the shadows at the top of the gangway and softly wished good luck to Chan and Hwang. Then he turned towards Jonas and bowed his head, in respect.

"Okay, Hwang!" Chan needed the engineer to understand completely, so he flipped out of Portuguese for his next few words. "No waving. No farewells. Don't do anything that might make it look like we're not coming back." Hwang was no actor. Previously he had only looked nervous. Now he looked shifty. Chan saw the problem and turned to Jonas.

"Help me, Jonas. If the customs officer looks surprised

to see two Chinese going ashore, I'll leave the talking to you. You can give him a wink and tell him you're taking us to meet your sister..." Chan cupped his hands in front of his chest and jogged them up and down lewdly. Hwang smiled. Chan relaxed, pleased to have overcome Hwang's trepidation, and encouraged by the hope that it might soon be possible to hold a three-way conversation in a common language.

The two Chinese clambered into the cab, trying to put the minimum possible weight on the corrugated cardboard that was the sole fabric covering the passenger seat. It made a poor job of preventing the rusty springs from pricking and pinching their flesh. Jonas started the motor, and began to ease the truck forward.

Chan had timed their departure perfectly. The customs officer's relief arrived a little late, even by local standards. The newcomer appeared flustered, ignoring the departing truck. His words to the first official must have made his colleague anxious too. The officer threw up his hands in alarm, and dashed back inside the shed. In moments they were both hunched over a transistor radio, plainly visible through the lighted open windows.

Jonas eased the truck forward, a feeble puddle of light spilling from its one working headlamp. Neither of the two officials seemed to notice as the vehicle rolled alongside their window. Jonas reduced speed to a slow walking pace, offering eye-contact to the officials, but they were too engrossed in the radio programme to notice. It seemed safe to drive right on through. With a wholly un-African degree of care for machinery, he applied a gentle pressure with his right foot. The truck bumped off the wharf and out onto the open road.

"Must be listening to a football match, eh?"

"Maybe," Chan agreed. Silently, he thanked bygone

legions of unknown ancestors for helping him to get away without being stopped by customs.

Jonas accelerated the truck along the dock road, flashed a gleaming white grin at his companions and shifted up to second gear. Consequently, the three of them were ten seconds too late to hear the radio announcer's shocked voice relaying details of a broadcast from Radio Lisbon.

"Acabamos de ouvir da Rádio de Lisboa que o Presidente Kennedy morreu. A polícia de Dallas ainda não prendeu o assassino."

President Kennedy was dead. The Dallas Police had not yet captured his killer.

Three

Wednesday 1 January 1964

(1) The Old Admiralty Building, London

In a Foreign Office ante-room, beneath the nicotine-blackened portrait of some long-forgotten father of the Empire, Duncan Sandys, Secretary of State for the Colonies, eased his left cuff aside, glanced at his watch and sighed. He envied the Scots, still under their eiderdowns, taking advantage of the bank holiday north of the border to recover from the revels. Butler! If he had known that the Foreign Secretary would be this late, he could have had another hour's sleep. The fellow only had to waddle across The Mall from Carlton Gardens.

In time, the faint sound of a flat-footed shuffle penetrated Duncan's slight headache, then stopped abruptly as a bowler-hatted figure halted in the doorway. A tweed overcoat lay across one arm. A battered leather briefcase hung from the other.

"Happy New Year, Rab!

"And you too, Duncan. Not the beginning I would have wanted."

Duncan had waited long enough. "You ready to start?"

"Sorry old chap. The PM wants an appraisal of how our transatlantic cousins are going to react. You'll have to handle this on your own."

Inwardly, Duncan sighed again and rose to leave.

"Mr Charles Rook, Minister." The Principal Private

Secretary ushered in the junior civil servant and then added, "Twenty minutes only."

The young man looked nervous. "Come in and sit down," said Sandys with a vague smile. His tongue felt like a doormat. He yearned for another coffee. "It's only going to be you and me, I'm afraid. You'll have gathered that Southern Rhodesia's broken away from the Federation. The Foreign Secretary's having to deal with the international end of it. Left the Commonwealth stuff to us." The minister turned to his PPS. "Ready to kick off?"

"Certainly. Mr Rook is an economist, Minister. Clearly, we need to know a little about the economic wealth of the late-lamented Federation." The PPS turned to face Charles. "We need to remain – ah – nimble, to ensure that future relationships in the region continue to favour the United Kingdom. I'm sure you'll tell us everything we need to know." The PPS then put on a serious expression and tilted back his head expectantly.

Charles looked down at his sheaf of notes. "I've got a lot of material here, Minister. I'm only wondering how much background I need to give you. I mean – if we've got less than half an hour..."

"You could always condense it into a short briefing paper," said the PPS. "...If we feel we need it. The minister's time *is* very precious, you know."

But in the light of his re-planned New Year's Day and a lassitude fuelled by over-indulgence, Sandys was prepared to make small talk for a moment longer. It required less mental effort, too. "I believe I detect an accent. Where do you call home, Charles?"

"Southern Rhodesia, sir. My family has a farm near Bulawayo."

"Ah! Facts, figures and local knowledge all rolled into one." At this compliment, Charles flashed a nervous grin and Sandys made an instant decision. "Look, if we run out of time you can always scribble the figures in a memo. First, tell me what the African colonies are likely to think about all this. What'll they do?"

"Well, signs of resentment are everywhere, sir. Some of the blacks look at you now like a leopard looks at a tethered goat. To the north and west you've got the example of the Congo. It's always been brutal but the mood seems to be spreading." An anxious look crossed Rook's face, as if he regretted his reference to 'blacks'. He pressed on, perhaps hoping to cover his clumsy choice of words. "Lusaka doesn't want that kind of disruption. They've got too much to lose. But what happens in the Congo is the key to all this."

"The Congo isn't part of our brief, Rook," said the PPS.

"But you can't ignore it, Sir. Cuba and the USSR haven't. Most of the Congo's borders are shared with countries that take a strong lead from Moscow or Havana. The net's tightening. The outlook for whites is changing fast. You hear stories of revenge killings – atrocities! The longer the West and the mining companies try to influence matters, the more we'll be made to pay for trying to keep control. Britain can't avoid becoming involved. Northern Rhodesia is demanding independence now, but the country is almost cut in half by the huge Katanga bulge. That border is too stretched-out to ignore. And that's where all the trouble is going to start, courtesy of Castro or Khrushchev... or Mao."

"I feel you're being a little alarmist, Rook. I believe what the minister intended was for you to say a few words about local loyalties, future trade – that sort of thing. Accidents of geography are irrelevant. You should leave the global politics to those with more experience in such matters."

Charles turned away from the PPS and appealed to

Sandys. "Minister, I know today's meeting with Mr Butler was supposed to last all morning. And I'm grateful that you've re-arranged things so I can have a few minutes of your time, but I've sort of lost my chance... I mean it's all about the mineral wealth. I was hoping to impress that on the Foreign Secretary."

"Why are minerals relevant?"

"Minister, when the Belgians granted independence, they baled out as fast as they could. It took Britain and America by surprise. We had no time to develop a strategy for stopping uranium from the Shinkolobwe mine falling into the wrong hands."

"You're saying a single Congolese mine threatens the cohesion of colonial Africa?"

"In the sense that it's a big prize in a chain of circumstances, yes." Sandys didn't move a muscle. Charles had no option but to continue. "What's going on in the Congo today is bad enough – endemic corruption, violence, oppression, political instability. But the whole place is a powder keg, waiting to go up. If it blows, it's likely to take half of Africa with it."

Sandys looked amused and slipped into mild sarcasm. "Is that all?"

"Not quite, Minister. Under Resolution 1885, the UN's final deadline for pulling out of the Congo is the 30th of June, this year. Right now, the country is in the middle of a power struggle. Whoever emerges on top might, if there's a miracle, use Katanga's wealth for the good of the country. But if the top man is a Russian puppet, he'll use it to incite violence. He could support underground movements across half the continent." The PPS tutted but Charles had regained the minister's attention.

"Even if he turns out to be just another despot, sir, there's a thousand ways he could make himself as rich as

Croesus. But the angle that worries me is if he starts selling vital minerals to our enemies. He wouldn't worry about selling uranium to any black, brown, yellow or white mafia or man that can pay the price. The Russians and Cubans are infiltrating Katanga right now, and the Chinese won't be far behind."

The PPS stepped in. "Mr Rook, political oppression and instability in the Congo are a fact of life that we can't do anything about..."

"Forgive me sir, but what I'm saying is we need to prevent uranium falling into the wrong hands. If the Congo falls apart, it'll drag the colonies of the old Federation down with it. And as to preventing a massacre – well, even if there wasn't any uranium wouldn't that be the right thing to do?"

The PPS replied using the tone that he might employ to reassure a child. "We don't see any sign of Congolese cut-throats spreading into the Rhodesias."

"And the uranium?" asked Sandys.

"We have other sources, Minister."

"No – I mean stopping the stuff falling into Communist hands."

"Well, Africanisation is unstoppable, Minister," said the PPS. "With our own election coming up, I don't believe there's the money or the appetite here for a policy based on military intervention in the old Federation... And particularly not the Congo. After all, Britain's experience in Kenya wasn't very pretty. I'm sure we wouldn't want to repeat it."

The PPS glanced pointedly at the clock, closed his diary with finality and rose to dismiss Charles as quickly as possible.

As Charles Rook trudged back to his empty office, he felt

that he had performed poorly, that his card had been marked, that his reputation would remain blemished for all time, and that any prospect for advancement of his Civil Service career had probably sunk alongside his reputation. The government's African policy would now be confirmed as non-interventionist and the Congo could be ignored, just as long as nothing serious happened before the general election.

(2) 'Thornhill', near Bulawayo, Southern Rhodesia

"Daniel? Are you in there?" Silence. "Can I come in?"

The youth hung his soldering iron on a hook, and opened the door a finger's width. "Yeah, come on in, Dad."

It was rare for his father to visit what had become known to the family as 'the shack'. Perhaps he felt that this was now another man's territory, even though Daniel was barely seventeen years of age. He peered about him in the gloom. A reading-lamp stood angled on his son's desk, highlighting an assembly of wires and dials. From a rack of equipment on the far wall, there burst a sudden chirruping of Morse.

"What's that, son?"

"Cape Town W/T station. He's receiving a ship's weather report."

"Good signal. What are you making?"

"Well, it was going to be a remote alarm circuit that triggered a klaxon. It was supposed to warn us straight away if *Tembo* trampled the fence to raid the maize again. But the transmitter isn't powerful enough."

"Why bother with radio? You could just string out a long telephone wire."

"Anyone could do that. It wouldn't be much of a challenge. Besides, the cable would cost too much and the next time the herd came this way, they'd just barge straight through it."

The older man fell silent. He clasped his hands behind his back and gazed around as his eyes got used to the lack of daylight. No-one in the family had much idea what all the gadgets were for. Daniel's father surveyed the general chaos of the untidy room and the particular jumble of circuit diagrams and technical manuals littering the desk before him. He made an encouraging noise through his teeth.

"Well, son, this is the start of a big year for you. Off to college in London and all. Electronic engineering, eh? Who'd have thought it?" He forced a brief chuckle. "You won't need a very big spanner for that, will you?"

"Guess not, Dad." Daniel wasn't making things easy for his father.

A deep breath and another try. "Well, look... Your mother and I have had a bit of a chat. You're obviously not really interested in farming, and I imagine you could use some extra cash when you get to London."

The conciliatory words drew Daniel's attention away from overcoming the gremlins in the stubborn alarm system. He rotated his swivel-seat to face his father. Rook, senior, thrust his left hand into his pocket, half turned away and reached towards a shelf, as if for support. Idly, he examined a circuit board peppered with colourful electronic components. None-the-wiser, but a little more at ease after stealing those few seconds, he continued. "Anyway, I phoned a couple of people I know in Jo'burg and I've got you the promise of a short-term job on *The Star*, if you want it, on the advertising desk. Really easy. Money for old rope. I expect you could take some of this kit with you, and play with it in your spare time if you wanted."

Daniel experienced a moment of regret. His father really didn't understand his feeling of achievement at discovering more about this new world of electronics. He let his voice fall then rise again to stop it from sounding like a rebuke. "I'm not playing, Dad. It's really interesting." He looked into his father's well-meaning face, lined and weather-beaten, the eyes now permanently narrowed from squinting day-long against the bright sunlight. But not all those lines came from a life spent outdoors. He knew that his father was worried. Already Charlie was safely packed off to London. Later in the year he would be following. Perhaps that wasn't soon enough. Escaping to a job in Johannesburg – money in the pocket. That could be useful.

"Sorry, Dad. This job... What would I have to do?" He allowed himself to smile and moved forward out of the gloom into the half-light so that his father could see his appreciation.

"Just follow orders, eh son?" Farmer Rook grinned to reflect Daniel's change of mood. "You'll pick it up in no time."

(3) Somewhere in Angola

"Now, tell me, Hwang. What do we learn from the time when the Soviets supplied missiles to Cuba, and how America forced Khrushchev to take them away again?"

Hwang shuffled, betraying his discomfort. He gazed up at the southern midnight sky, with its myriad multi-coloured points of light, blinking silver and gold, red, white and blue.

"I'm sorry, Weifeng. I only claim to be an engineer. It's filled up my whole life. And I know it's wrong, but it seems to leave no room for Party matters to take hold." Squatting there, Hwang clasped his arms around his raised knees and refocused on Chan. "I remember reading about it, and I know we had lectures about it, but I forget such things after a while. There's just too much that I need to know about mining." However, the lure of the night sky was too strong. It drew his gaze upwards again. "When I see a sky such as this – well, sometimes I can't see the significance of political battles. I'd rather leave it to others, and just do what I'm told."

Inside the circle of thorns, the flickering firelight picked out the prone figures of Jonas and a couple of the guides, already asleep. The other escorts huddled together on watch, listening to the night sounds, alert for the cough of a prowling leopard or the yip of lurking hyenas, as the wild beasts tried to work out how to breach the thorns and carry off a man.

Maybe Hwang was right. It was certainly brave of him to confess such thoughts. For three months, all Chan's efforts to educate him in political philosophy had failed. Hwang had proved a poor pupil. Lately, Chan had felt obliged to explore the concept of how the untrustworthy Soviets had squandered their advantage. He felt a duty to help Hwang understand why Africa had become the centre for anti-colonial struggle, and how the time had arrived for national revolution on a broad united front. But now he realised he had been wasting his breath. Perhaps he ought to tuck away the *Thoughts of Chairman Mao* for a while.

"Yes, maybe you're right. It's a beautiful night."

Four

Throughout their six-week trek beside the railroad tracks, Chan's party had rarely seen more than two or three trains a day. However, spaced among the rolling stock, those few all included a couple of open wagons from which armed troops mounted guard. Sensitive to the risk that the unexpected sight of two Chinamen might cause the commander to halt the train for a second look, the travellers kept a precautionary lookout in both directions. Since the trains travelled at no great speed, advertising their arrival with a huge plume of smoke and plenty of noise, the foreigners had ample time to step aside into the long grass and lie concealed until the chance of discovery had passed.

On this morning the typical dry red earth, low scrub and thorn bushes had given way to a welcome strip of taller trees with lush, sap-green vegetation. Chan, Hwang and Jonas stood on the western abutment of the Cuanza River rail bridge. The steel girder bridge spanned the divide in four sections, resting on three piers set into the riverbed. Its site had been well-chosen. A looping bend in the river between good surface rock on both banks narrowed the Cuanza to less than a hundred metres as it flowed north-westward, bright blue and clean. The bridge appeared to be in good condition. Its coat of grey paint looked fresh. The rivet-heads and sharp corners showed few signs of rust.

Jonas made a loose left-handed fist and gestured the

thumb over his shoulder. "This is as far as these men will go," he said. "We need to wait for another party of guides to come back down the line to join us."

"How long?" It was clear Hwang was impatient to start his real work.

"A day. Maybe two. This is Africa, man... We need to wait. They'll be bringing us more supplies."

"No hurry," said Chan. "Not on my account. I want to see how strong the bridge looks when an engine goes over it. If I were a guerrilla, this'd be one place I'd pick to sabotage. Easy to escape afterwards. A long way from any engineering facilities – the Portuguese wouldn't be able to repair it quickly."

"Bad idea, Weifeng. Our country needs that ore. This way is fastest. Why destroy it?"

Chan answered with a shrug. "I've got my orders too. Beijing needs to know."

"Look. If the revolutionaries blew up this bridge, how do you suppose we'd get all that rock back to China?"

"I'm beginning to think this whole line is too hard to defend. There might be more value in helping one of the independence movements to blow it up. You know – buying them some credibility. Even without the railway, we could still shift the ore by road, or perhaps go east instead of west." Chan turned to face Jonas. "Like the death of a thousand cuts – one bridge makes little difference, but each act that weakens the economy brings the day closer when Angola falls back into the hands of the people. What do you think?"

"Think? Well, first of all I think I might do some fishing," said Jonas. "As for sabotage, I'd rather you blew up something else." He cast his gaze across to the opposite bank. "About a hundred kilometres up ahead there's a little town where they know me. My father used to be the

stationmaster. So, please Weifeng, pick another bridge."
Contemplating fish for lunch, Jonas jumped off the
concrete abutment and scrambled down the riverbank.
Several weeks' exposure to Chan's Maoist doctrines had
come to a head that morning and upset his normal
composure. After some ten paces he spun round, planted
one hand on his hip, and raised an accusing finger.

"But just be careful about supporting the wrong set of
freedom fighters. You've got people round here that are
crazy enough to think these locomotives are fire-breathing
dragons, with white men riding inside their heads. I'm not
fooling. They worship your dragon-trains as gods. Some of
these tribes are still cannibals. You wreck one of their gods,
and they'll hunt you down, catch you and eat you. I'm
serious." His eyes widened, and he showed his teeth. "Eat
you alive, raw and screaming!"

Ominous swishes from down river made Jonas wary of
wading into the water. He returned half way up the slope,
clambered onto the upstream side of the structure, and
began to traverse sideways along the outside of the girders.
When he reached the first pier, he lowered himself down
and sat cross-legged on the broad concrete step. From two
metres above the water, he began idly casting his line. In a
while, with nothing on the hook, no locomotive in
apparent prospect and the sun directly overhead, he
stopped fishing, wriggled into the shade of the bridge deck
and fell asleep.

Jonas awoke to the sound of Hwang shouting an alert in
Chinese from farther up river. He sprang to his feet.
Hwang was right to call out – no doubt about it. Maybe a
kilometre away, the rhythmic clanking and snorting
sounds of an approaching westbound train had disturbed
the local birdlife, which squawked angrily in alarm.

Hwang flattened himself down in the grass. Jonas yelled out to Chan, emphasising Hwang's warning. "Hey, Weifeng! Now's your chance." Chan raced to the riverbank and crouched beneath the first span.

Jonas reached both hands above his head and gripped a horizontal girder. Lifting himself bodily off the concrete pier, he swung his legs up onto the metalwork. A well-built man, he began swaying his body from side to side under the girder. At the end of each swing, he inched his right hand higher, grasping for a fresh handhold until the moment when he could use his strength to bring his left arm alongside it and scramble through the ironwork onto the bridge deck. With the erupting cloud approaching from the east, Jonas sprinted to the western end of the bridge, then veered into the long grass, to stand beside the Angolan guides. Panting, he turned to face the bridge.

The articulated locomotive had a distinctive outline, with its boiler and footplate slung between two tenders. The water tender, bearing the letters 'C F B', came first, perched above one set of driving wheels. A second set of wheels supported the fuel bunker, piled high with logs. The relief-valve hissed as the driver vented steam to reduce speed. A military wagon followed the fuel tender. An awning at one end presumably sheltered a native corporal, dozing under the fierce afternoon sun. Four African soldiers slouched back-to-back on wooden packing cases, disinterested, failing to keep a proper watch over the essential river crossing. Jonas raised his arm in a slow wave.

The locomotive continued for perhaps four hundred metres, until the last of the wagons had crossed the bridge, then it picked up speed again. The powerful snorting resumed, and the column of smoke ballooned into the air as before. In time the screeching from the forest died down and calm descended once more to partner the oppressive heat. A combined scent of steam, oil and burnt eucalyptus wood lingered to tantalise the senses.

Chan emerged from beneath the bridge and strolled up the bank towards Jonas and Hwang.

Jonas grinned. "So, Weifeng – did you learn anything?"

"Indeed. It's obviously still a very strong bridge. I couldn't see a single design flaw. No sagging or rocking at all – no obvious weak spot where I'd choose to place explosives." Chan was enjoying the moment too. "Could you see anything shaky from over there?"

"Nothing."

"I agree," said Hwang. Jonas and Chan looked at him curiously. "It's a good piece of engineering. A heavy train like that and no signs of strain. It's the way the girders in each section spread the load."

"I thought you were supposed to be a mining engineer," said Chan.

"Holding the roof up and stopping the rocks falling on your head is only the same as supporting a train and stopping it falling in the river."

"I see..." Chan seemed amused. "I'm glad you came."

"I think you'd better pick another target," said Jonas. "It's only what I expected."

"Expected?"

"Well, the whole line – locomotives, workshops, stations, cuttings, bridges – everything – was designed by the British."

"The bloody British," Chan muttered. "I wondered when we'd come across them."

"Yes. The same firm designed the Sydney Harbour Bridge. This bridge is as strong as a buffalo. It'll never fall down on its own. You'd need a lot of dynamite."

Chan kicked at a rock, dislodging it, and watched as it

rolled down the bank.

"Tell me then – are you going to blow up my bridge, Weifeng?"

"I don't think so, Jonas."

"Because?"

Chan made an open gesture, spreading his arms wide. "It's pointless. We'd just be making life difficult for ourselves. This country isn't at the political tipping point yet. It'll take too long to get a revolutionary government in place. Until then, your country can't collude with China to export secretly-mined Congolese uranium."

"Agreed."

Chan shook his head. "Like Hwang says, we need that ore now. In a few months, not a few years. But to get the Portuguese out, the liberation movements would already have had to weaken the regime by blowing up the railway – and a lot more besides. It won't work. We need another route out."

"To the east?"

"I don't know, but I don't think we can rely on the Benguela Railway for transport." Chan mulled it over for a few seconds while his decision took shape. "No. Even if it was still intact, once the Americans found out what we were doing, they might blow up a couple of bridges themselves to stop us using the railway."

"Any other reasons?"

"Yes, one more – you've asked me not to." He grinned. "China doesn't want to make an enemy of the man who could be the first Socialist president of Angola."

Monday 30 March, 1964
West Bank of the Kasai River, Angola

The small group of men stood with their backs to the

setting sun. In the foreground their lengthening shadows stretched out over an easy descent through tall grasses and leafy scrub to an undistinguished river. Rust-brown rocks peppered the slope and lay haphazardly in the stream bed. Both sides of the river appeared undecided about their true character, changing every fifty metres or so from a three-metre-high bank, undercut and liable to collapse, to a copse of trees, to a flat muddy beach, to patches of reeds and back again.

Jonas broke the silence. "Well, Weifeng. I know it doesn't look much, but we've reached the border. That's Katanga over there. Shinkolobwe is about five hundred K ahead of you. You don't need me any longer, so I'll wish you farewell and *boa sorte*. We've got to go back home and start a revolution."

Jonas's words hung in the evening air. Chan turned towards him, searching his face for signs of any deeper meaning. In the stillness that descends as tropical daylight rushes away and before the night-time predators begin to haunt the darkness, there seemed no urgency for either to make the next remark.

Chan took a slow, deep breath that pushed his head back and made him grow by a hand's breadth as he straightened to his full height. "I've got a better idea, Jonas."

"Go ahead."

"Why don't you come to China with us? Let the MPLA do the fighting for a while. Mao's got friends in Tanganyika and Zanzibar, so we'll get out from there... Could be the best route out for the ore, too."

"China? Why do I need to go there? My place is here, booting out the Portuguese."

"Yes, I know. But maybe the time isn't quite right. Once my friends in Nanking see what sort of a man you are, I'm sure they'll back you. We can help you plan your revolution. Today your band is weak, but what if you could launch a movement with strong support a year from now?"

"Weifeng, you take a long time to let your thoughts reach your lips." Chan could hear the warmth in Jonas's voice. "Look – if I'm coming with you, I'll need a few minutes to say goodbye to my men... To tell them the new plan... Then we should get going in case a border patrol stumbles across us."

Chan squared his jaw, nodded once to acknowledge the new bond between them, then relaxed. "Not to mention more damned flies finding us." It wasn't the cleverest of responses so he flicked his hand in front of his face, as if to emphasise it and dismiss it in one gesture. All the same, he felt encouraged that Jonas hadn't needed much persuading. Clearly, his decision to accompany Chan to China had been reached well before he was asked. Nanking would be pleased.

Thursday 9 April, 1964
Shinkolobwe Mine, Katanga Province,
République du Congo

A new country now: Chan's instinct to protect the mission by avoiding unnecessary contact with officialdom had grown stronger. Accordingly, they had marched east for three days, bypassing the border town of Dilolo, then headed north to join the Jadotville highway. Within an hour of reaching it, they had secured a lift. Jonas's technique was simple but effective. He scrawled a dollar sign on a piece of board, and brandished it to every Mercedes truck heading east. Two passed by. The third stopped, the temptation to acquire hard currency proving irresistible.

The truck dropped the three men a few kilometres west of Jadotville, where Union Minière had constructed a good tarmac road into the hills to haul out the priceless ore. With the departure of the Belgians, the side-road had fallen into disuse, its destination now of little importance. However, that also meant their presence attracted no unwelcome attention, so their climb from the road junction to the mine became a lonely all-day foot slog.

≈

They reached the abandoned mine an hour before dusk. Although the expected pit-head winding gear, the ore-crushing machinery and the engine house had all gone, they could tell from the devastation that they were in the right place. Where the assay office had stood was only obvious from the broken sign, half-buried in a pile of rubble, along with the doctor's surgery. Union Minière had left few clues to the site's former function. The company appeared to have used a grader to obliterate all evidence of their occupation, giving the site the appearance of some vast, insane parking lot, abandoned in the bush. Only an undulating grimy landscape of crushed stone-chips and coarse black dust remained, with inky, mirror-like puddles lying in the depressions. Here and there, weeds and saplings forced their way through the carpet of grit, as nature attempted to reclaim this unpromising corner of the planet and turn it green once again.

The three explored onward, arriving at the top of an incline, an opencast scar driven into the mountainside by the pioneer miners. A fortress wall of pale irregular rocks, leaning back from the vertical, buttressed the shaft. In forty years, no cracks had developed in its mortar of battleship grey. Chan's impression was of an imposing stone entrance to some secret underground African military bunker.

Hwang started forward down the slope. "Let's take a closer look," he said. Chan and Jonas followed, granting him the moment that he had waited six months to experience. A hundred metres down the slope, the surface became flat.

"Concrete," said Hwang. "They've capped it with concrete."

"How thick do you reckon it is?"

"Not very." Hwang looked around, taking a fresh perspective on his surroundings. "See? It's only damp – not flooded. The rainwater must be soaking away into the mine."

"How long to cut through it?"

"We couldn't chisel through this concrete cap. There'll be steel reinforcement. If we start at the edge, we can probably excavate round the side of it. Say a couple of weeks."

"You reckon we're in business?"

"Yes. Just as soon as Jonas hires some native labour to do the digging."

By early August, Hwang's team of Congolese workers had demolished part of the retaining wall, exposing the edge of the concrete slab. They had undercut the cap, collapsing it piece by piece, to locate the buried entrance to the mine. Working by the light of flickering tallow candles, the miners had begun to fetch shards of yellow rock to the surface. Hwang tested the rock with the Geiger counter. This was what they had come to Africa to obtain.

Chan had spent a lazy day inspecting the heavy sacks of rock that were beginning to accumulate at the surface. The operation had progressed well, but the growing stockpile reminded him that they needed to get the radioactive ore home to China. After dark the three gathered in Chan's tent, listening to the portable radio for news. Jonas first tuned in to the broadcast from Elisabethville, translating it for his Chinese friends.

Tshombé had replaced Adoula as Premier. The former *République* had awarded itself a new name to reflect its 'democratic' credentials. The bulletin went on to say that a few days earlier, Simba rebels had taken Stanleyville, capturing over a thousand western hostages, including a handful of officials from the US consulate.

"That sounds serious," said Hwang.

Jonas agreed. "Yes, it's bad for the prisoners. These Simbas believe their witch doctors can conjure up special magic that turns them into lions on the battlefield – magic that changes the enemy's bullets into water." Chan puffed contemptuously at the notion. "Yes, but they drug themselves before battle," said Jonas. "They dance into a frenzy. Then they're oblivious to fear. They place no value on human life – including their own. You're right. For the whites it'll be pretty grim."

"In that case, maybe we should enlist some Simbas for our own safety," said Chan, making it sound like a perfectly reasonable idea.

"That's not funny."

"I know. But it's already turned to anarchy in Stanleyville. If that spreads, we're going to need some protection when we start moving the ore shipments overland."

"Maybe you're right."

"You agree?"

"Weifeng, you can't begin to imagine what it'll be like in Stanleyville right now. They'll be raping the white women for sure. Maybe they'll just beat up the white men and try to ransom them. Any Congolese officials, like teachers or policemen – they'll be slicing them up alive, as painfully as possible, maybe even using their teeth." Hwang looked both disbelieving and disgusted. Jonas continued. "I don't know if it's possible to solve the Congo's problems with a combination of whisky, hemp and the machete, but they'll certainly give it a try."

"For an African you don't seem to have a high opinion of your fellow men."

"Just being realistic, Weifeng. And these are the people you think might protect us?"

Wednesday 2 September, 1964
"Small Ads" Desk, Johannesburg Star

The street door squeaked and the bell gave its dull, comical 'tonk'. Some inventive soul had moulded a wedge of chewing gum around the clapper to dampen its former strident clang. At the sound of the muffled bell, Daniel looked up from his electronics magazine into the clear blue eyes of a lady. She was some ten years older than him, and had the shape, air and dress of as *fatale* a *femme* as he had ever beheld.

Normally, Daniel was keen to run errands, the longer the better, just so he could spend time away from the front desk. He preferred the more technical sights and sounds of the newspaper business – the hum as the presses began to roll, the clatter of the typewriters. On other days, even the grime of type-setting appeared more attractive than a spell on the small ads desk. But today was definitely one of the compensations.

"I'd like to put an advertisement in Friday's *Star*," she cooed teasingly. "I believe you call it 'Situations Vacant'." Daniel managed to choke off a gulp.

"Do you have it written out, or shall I take it down for you?" He instantly regretted what he had said. He had worked his stint on the public desk for several months and never let slip such an obvious *double entendre* as this.

The lady cocked her head on one side, pursed her lips – Daniel had never been so close to such lips – and fluttered her eyelashes, clearly amused. He realised that there were now 99 chances out of 100 that he would blush from embarrassment. He took a deep breath, feeling from total lack of experience in such matters that extra oxygen might control the problem.

"I don't think I'd better let you take it down."

The lady leaned forward and placed her elbow on the desk, cupping her chin in her delicate fingers. Daniel desperately wanted to glance down below that peach-perfect chin to check that everything else was in order.

"...As the actress said to the bishop," she whispered.

Failed! Daniel felt the colour spread over his cheeks. The tips of his ears began to glow. He took a biro from behind one radiant ear, straightened the pad in front of him, and transferred his attention away from those eyes.

"Sorry. Hot in here, isn't it?"

This vision of desire then placed her handbag before him on the counter and tipped out half the contents – sunglasses, a pack of menthol-flavoured cigarettes, a set of car-keys with a Jaguar medallion on the fob. A couple of lipstick tubes rolled towards him.

"Ah! Here it is." Her hand moved with the grace of a ballerina towards a piece of folded pink paper. Daniel noticed the crimson fingernails. "Any fit young man looking for employment with a difference, at a salary well in excess of £100 per month should telephone 838-5203 during business hours. Employment initially offered for six months. Immediate start." She paused. "Let's go for

Saturday's paper as well. I'm feeling... lucky today."

Daniel took extra care printing the words into the boxes on the pad, in the hope of buying more time. Even his scalp felt as if it were alight. He counted the words and leaned back from the counter in a lazy way, daring himself to meet her eyes on the level.

"For two entries, thirty-four words'll cost five rand forty-four, if that's okay?" He smiled. It felt like a game of cards. She smiled back, a queen to his knave. He couldn't hold her gaze, looked down and rotated the pad so she could see what he had written. "As you can see," he mumbled, trying to make it sound like he was doing her a great favour, "I've counted the phone number as one word. Hyphens normally mean two." She floated two 5-rand notes on to the counter, inviting him to reach towards her.

"I'll just need your name, and address, please."

"I'll bet you say that to all the girls!" She pouted; then: "Molloy. Put it down to Mr Molloy. Keep the change... er?" She dangled the last word in front of him, then raised her eyebrows, an unfinished question in search of an answer.

"Er... Daniel."

"Keep the change, Danny." She could have left, but seemed in no hurry.

"Thanks, uh... Mrs Molloy. That sounds like good money. I could use a hundred a month. What line of work is Mr Molloy in? What would I be doing?"

"Well, I'm only his secretary, not his wife." The idea seemed to divert her for a second or two. "I shouldn't be saying this, but I understand he's got a short contract to help the Congo government with a few little problems."

"Perhaps I'll give him a call." He offered the scrap of paper back to the lady.

"Keep it, Danny. I'll be waiting by the phone..."

Well in excess of a hundred a month... Daniel realised

the lady would probably not be working in the Congo. Although she had easily found out his name, he had failed to discover hers. He needed to improve his technique. Over a hundred a month...

He pocketed the slip of pink paper.

Friday 16 October, 1964
0702 GMT: Peshawar Airbase, West Pakistan

Late morning: A rising torrent of static 'mush' in the radio watchman's headphones wiped out reception on the 14-Megahertz US Air Force channel that he had been monitoring. Damned Soviet interference. He switched up to 18 Megahertz but the result was the same. Perhaps it wasn't the Ruskies. He checked that his aerial connection had not come adrift, flicked down to 4 megs, then rapidly up through the wavebands but it was the same everywhere. Possibly the receiver was on the blink. He shuffled across to a different stall but had no better luck. Could be an electrical storm – sunspots, maybe?

"Sergeant Summers, sir! Can you come over and take a listen?"

The sergeant listened. It was no accident that he and his specialist radio detachment were there, less than a thousand nautical miles from the site where the Chinese had been preparing to test their bomb. A sudden radio blackout like this – well, it could be sunspots but more likely it had a more sinister origin.

"Can you get a rough fix on it, son? How far up the waveband are you reading it?"

"It's strongest in the northeast, Sergeant, and it's all the way up the h.f. band."

"Okay." He thought for a moment. "Look, contact the radar boys – see if they can bounce a signal off whatever's out there. Get a range on it." Then he picked up the telephone.

"Operator? Get me an urgent call over the landline to NORAD."

0320 Eastern Daylight Time;
White House Tactical Alerts and Operations Center

"You're sure this isn't another test explosion to calibrate their equipment?"

The officer of the watch hunched over his desk, pressing the telephone handset tightly to his ear, absorbing every word of the reply. "Cheezus! At least a hundred times bigger, you say? Any doubt about the location?" A pause while he listened to the answer, then: "Okay, let me copy this down. Takla Makan desert... Estimated twenty kilotons... Seeking CIA authorisation for Taiwanese U2 flight... Got that... Yes sir. The President will be informed."

The officer swivelled his chair round to face his colleague at the other desk. But the latter had turned his chair round too, and had some news of his own to impart.

"While you were talking with NORAD, I had London on the other line. Looks like there's going to be a Socialist government in Downing Street before the day's out. And guess what? The guy who's favourite to get the Ministry of Defence used to be a card-carrying Communist!"

"On top of that Russian thing, we're going to have to wake the President."

"Nope. We're going to speak to Bundy first and see what he says. Then if anybody's going to get the President out of his bunk, it's going to be him."

"Mr Bundy, sir? Urgent call. Can you press your red button for me?"

The watch officer switched his own scrambler into action and took a deep breath. "You still there, sir?" A pause to verify, then, "Thank you, sir. I regret it's my duty to inform you that the Chinese appear to have successfully triggered a nuclear device on their proving-ground at Lop Nur..."

Clearly, the National Security Adviser was not one of those people who took time to figure out where he was, when woken at 3 a.m. He was full of questions.

"Approximately Hiroshima-sized, sir," said the officer. My partner's trying to reach DCI McCone right now. NORAD has already requested a U2 mission from Taoyuan Airbase to sample the cloud... But that's not all."

The officer glanced across at his colleague and continued. "Apart from the fact that Britain appears to have elected a left-wing government, we've just learned about a coup in Moscow. Khrushchev has been ousted from power. Brezhnev and Kosygin are in charge now." The two officers' eyes met again. They both raised their eyebrows. "Yes, sir. Once we get through, we'll get him over to the White House... Yes, sir. And Mr Cline, too... We'll be ready, sir."

The officer took the handset away from his ear but the telephone earpiece chirped one more time as Bundy voiced an after-thought.

"No sir, I'm sorry. No change over the hostage situation in the Congo. The rebels are still refusing to acknowledge either our telegrams or those from the UN or the Red Cross."

The officer put the phone down and spoke to his colleague. "Got through yet?"

"No. McCone's hotline is still engaged."

"That'll be NORAD hogging the circuit. Call him on his home phone. Bundy wants him in here, fast. No need to give any details. He'll already know why."

"Was Bundy okay? What did he say?"

"He said to get McCone and Cline into the Ops Center as fast as possible." The officer smiled. "He said, 'Tell Ray to drive the Chevy like he stole it.' Or something that meant pretty much the same."

Five

Cline: 'Mac' Bundy always adopted a logical approach. Between them, he and the Director of Central Intelligence, John McCone, monopolised the meeting for a quarter of an hour. Cline listened as, progressively, they put each security matter on hold. Before they could be sure about the Chinese bomb, they needed an analysis of particles in the upper atmosphere. Before they could be sure whether Brezhnev would prove a present danger rather than a future threat, they needed to recall the ambassador from Moscow. Next, he and McCone agreed that the British election result was a lower priority than the other matters, and left it pending.

Cline appreciated the value of good timing, but maybe his boss was leaving it a little late to get round to their number one problem. Then to his relief, though without understanding quite how they had moved from discussing the very important to considering the very urgent, they began talking about the Congo.

"Guys, I've been thinking about where this Stanleyville thing could finish up," said McCone. "Losing the consulate is —"

"— Real bad," interrupted Bundy. "I don't think the President's getting the best advice from Harriman. I know LBJ trusts him, but —"

"— Right." McCone leaned forward, cutting Bundy short. "Harriman's maybe seventy-two, seventy-three now. I'm worried about him. He isn't seeing what's obvious to you and me. He just isn't co-ordinating policy properly. I don't think he's grasped what's at stake."

"Or maybe who's pulling the strings."

"You said it. The Congo Working Group is hog-tied by the State Department, which suits the President fine. Right now, he doesn't want to worry about a bunch of missionaries who've got themselves in a fix and should've had the sense to quit the country three or four years back. As far as he's concerned, they all headed out into the wilderness looking for Jesus Christ, so they've got nobody else to blame if they end up finding Him. But *we* know what we're up against, right?"

"I guess so, John," said Bundy. "This 'staying friends with the non-aligned countries' shit just isn't working. The OAU mission is obviously playing for time. Kenyatta's not mediating properly. He's stalling until Russia and China can deliver their arms shipments. God-damned tin-pot British colonies. Nyerere's as bad, forming this pact with Zanzibar... Having to pussy-foot round a whole squad of Maoists in his new coalition."

Cline decided to weigh in. "The way I read the situation, the State Department's determined to sit tight for a while longer. Seems like they won't believe the Simbas are serious until there's a credible threat to the hostages' lives."

"By then it may be too late to do much about it."

Bundy: Once you'd gotten to know McCone you could time the moment he would make his strike to within a few seconds. It was pretty clear he was trying to manoeuvre a particular subject into the discussion. Okay. Cline's words had provided a hook. Time for a little mutual co-operation.

"You know, when you dig right down, my guess is you'll find a Cuban angle on this." Bundy knew he was on safe ground here with the CIA. Once you brought Cuba into the frame, or used the word 'Communist' you could see them mentally reaching for their holsters.

"True enough," said McCone. He held eye contact, enforcing a pause. "You know... American lives are one thing... Consular lives are another." He then flicked a glance at Cline. "And that's bad enough, but..."

"But none of it's as bad," said Cline, seizing his cue, "as having the Commies discover what's hopefully still locked in that safe in Stanleyville."

Sooner or later, once things got serious, something close to the real truth generally came out. "Maybe you'd better tell me what you've got hidden inside it then, Ray," said Bundy.

Cline took a deep breath. "That was a good guess about Cuba, Mac. I reckon you probably know the half of it already." The stilted language that he used for the tapes was gone. "You remember when the Cuban exiles started running wild after the Bay of Pigs?" Bundy nodded. "Things got a helluva lot worse when they started using US ports to raid Cuban shipping. We had to act. We figured the smartest move was to get them as far away as possible..."

"Sure – Katanga. We gave them some guns and packed them off. Glad to go, as I recall. Happy to support Tshombé's mercenaries against the Congolese rebels."

"It was more than just a few guns, Mac. We gave the exiles some boats and obsolete aircraft, too. Used 'em to get even with Castro's guerrillas. Revenge is sweet, they say."

This was just unnecessary history to Bundy. "I remember the 'who, why, where, when and how' well enough," he said. "My guess is it's the 'what' that you guys are concerned about. So, what's buried in that safe?"

"If we're lucky, our guys will have already burned the

whole kit and caboodle. Otherwise, there's the names of all the agents, the officials, the payoffs, the dates, the weapon shipments, the occasional rubbing-out, all traceable back to Langley. The whole thing amounts to a complete side-step around the Kennedy-Khrushchev pact." Cline looked worried. "If we're not so lucky, the Simbas got into the consulate before we could finish the job. Diplomatic status won't mean a thing to them. In the wrong hands those files would be dynamite."

"Does LBJ know?" McCone and Cline shook their heads. "So, priority one is to regain control of the consulate, yes?"

"But like we said, there's no way we can depend on Kenyatta and his crowd to come up with a political solution," said Cline.

A hissing sigh escaped over McCone's tongue. "But if it comes down to the use of force, from what I've seen, it isn't just Harriman. Even the Joint Chiefs don't seem to be taking this seriously."

Bundy noted the skill with which the CIA had turned their difficulty into his problem too. Their joint frustration at State Department blindness, the incompetence of the Joint Chiefs and the vacillation of the African peace mission left only one organisation that could rescue the situation. And there they sat – opposite him. But they needed support.

"As I see it," said Bundy, "we need to set ourselves some objectives: First thing – get into the consulate and destroy all the evidence about CIA-sponsorship of the Cuban exiles."

"I guess that puts the Vice-Consul and the other CIA staffers at even greater risk?"

"I'm afraid it will, Ray. That's number two. If we can get them out alive, that's what we've got to do. But destroying the files comes first. If word gets out that we haven't stuck to our side of the pact, it'll sink our Africa policy for decades."

"And if we can't get our guys out?"

"Other factors come into play – timing for one."

"But Mac, if we lose the chance to get those guys out in one piece, then as well as losing the files we risk the Simbas using US citizens as political pawns."

McCone interjected. "The staff in the consulate knew what they were signing up for. They'll have already worked out our priorities. Mac said it: Destroying the files comes first. But I'm sensing there's more than one agenda here. If that has implications..."

Cline seemed unwilling to abandon his colleagues in the consulate to the mob, but remained focused on Bundy. "This is starting to sound like there's a political agenda here too. Mac, I guess if you know something we don't know, now would be a pretty good time to spill it."

"Okay Ray, John. Look... If we know one thing about LBJ, it's that he doesn't like making decisions until they're cooked and ready to eat. Right now, he can't make space in his head to spend even two minutes listening to Harriman bleating about what's going on in Stanleyville." Bundy shrugged. "Now with this Kremlin coup and the Chinese bomb, there's just no way. So with the election three weeks away, he's not going to want to grab-a-hold of this Congo mess..."

"Three weeks!" Cline rolled his eyes, dropped his hands onto the arms of his chair and craned his neck forward. "Three weeks? In three weeks even the dumbest of those Simbas is going to have worked out that it's best to split up the hostages and move 'em to new locations. In three weeks, we'll have totally lost the initiative. Lost the element of surprise."

"But we're not going to be sitting around idle, Ray. Point is, I see our duty right now is to protect the President. We've got to keep LBJ corralled in the White House for a couple more days. We've got to stop him from heading out on the stump, no matter how much he wants to get out there, rallying support. He's got to stay here and handle these two crises – China and the Soviets. If the American people haven't already worked it out for themselves, they'll have to be persuaded that this is what they expect him to do. We need him to look presidential. If he goes out on the stump, he'll look like shark-bait."

"Maybe so, but three weeks?"

"This caper could blow up in our face, Ray. If we act too fast and the whole thing goes belly-up, just imagine. A couple of dozen dead US Marines, or worse still – prisoners; a failed mission and then someone discovers what's in that safe. The whole world would see the rescue for what it is – an ass-covering exercise. They can all add two and two by now."

"But Mac..."

"No Ray, LBJ would be finished. We have to wait until after the election." Cline made to speak but Bundy held up his hand. "There's too much riding on this. Think. If we can rescue the consulate staff, the papers *and* get any other US citizens out of Stanleyville as well, that's only going to bring benefits to the President."

"If it's not too late."

"Maybe there's a way."

McCone and Cline exchanged glances. "The floor's still yours, Mac," said McCone.

"Well, I hear at least General Adams has started working on it," said Bundy. "Hatched some damned fool plan to stage a US rescue attempt through Wheelus Airbase. Just one problem. That base is slap-bang in the middle of Tripoli for all to see, for Christ's sake. There can't be a better way of completely blowing the security of any rescue mission wide open. So, guys, we need to help him find a better idea."

The mention of security seemed to dispel some of McCone's misgivings. "Giving away the element of surprise. It's the worst sin, Mac. But it still sounds like a military solution. So far those guys on the JCS haven't shown they could plan their way out of a wet paper bag."

"You haven't heard the idea yet. We need to get this new British government co-aligned right now, before they've had time to think."

McCone sounded disapproving. "What do we need a bunch of Limeys for?"

"John, with all that's happened, we'll obviously need an emergency meeting of the National Security Council this morning. Afterwards, I'll have a quiet word with McNamara about something that's been on my mind since 3:00 a.m. See if you agree." Bundy leaned back in his chair. "Pretty soon, this new British government's going to find out they've got nothing left in the bank. They're bound to cut spending across the board, and as they're Lefties, cut their armed forces heaviest of all. I just want to remind them who their friends are and get a little help out of them before they close everything down."

McCone looked sceptical.

"Guys, the State Department's got its faults but it's right about one thing," said Bundy. "They want Adams to plan on using Wideawake Field on Ascension Island, not this base in Tripoli. Ascension is British territory. In the South Atlantic, a thousand miles from anywhere. Population? About five or six hundred, half of them scientists. Perfect for blanket security. And we've got an interest there already – NASA's new tracking station."

McCone and Cline began to nod gently as the merits of Bundy's theory became clearer.

"So," continued Bundy, "if you old soldiers approve, I'll wake the President, reassure him that everything's under control, keep him calm, keep him statesmanlike." McCone put on a wise expression and nodded with more emphasis. Clearly, he preferred Bundy, rather than himself, to disturb Johnson.

Bundy placed both forearms on the desk and lowered his voice. "Then, after the NSC meeting, I'll take McNamara aside. Suggest a strategy to him. Show the new Kremlin regime that we're serious. Maybe increase the B-52 airborne alert program flights from eight to, say, twelve a day." He spread his hands, palms upwards. "Then, all McNamara's got to do is persuade the British to buy into our plan to stage the hostage rescue through Wideawake."

"Do we know if it's serviceable as a forward base?"

"Not yet. But since it's their territory and hardly anyone lives there, I guess it won't attract too much attention if the British trial a few V-bomber sorties down to Ascension and their other African bases... I want McNamara to get the Limeys to recce the airfields for us. If it's half-way workable, I'm with the State Department on this. Mount the rescue airlift through Wideawake, at the same time as a Special Forces raid on the consulate to deal with this little problem you guys have been keeping quiet about."

"That sounds ten times better than Adams's feeble scheme, Mac," said Cline.

"So, Ray, what I need you guys to do is work on the undercover plan and figure out how to insert a small ground force into Stanleyville, so they're already hiding in the bushes at the consulate when the paras jump on the airfield."

Cline squeezed his chin and the DCI coughed politely.

They alone knew the extent to which the CIA had supported the 'friendly' forces in the Congo and the potential damage to their country's reputation if word got out. They had few options and could not afford failure.

"Guys, we can handle the Kremlin," said Bundy. "Khrushchev was finished anyway after his foul-up in Cuba. And we can handle Mao's new bomb. It had to happen some day. Socialists in London? Who the hell cares? All this is just bad news from faraway places." He lowered his brow and looked intently from McCone to Cline and back again. "But from what you say about those files in the Stanleyville consulate, they're different. If we can't regain control of that stuff or completely destroy it, the President's credibility, yours, mine, everybody's just goes up in smoke." Bundy paused for effect. "If he's re-elected, and if it all comes out, LBJ would face instant dishonour – and not just before the American people. His whole foreign policy would come crashing down, including Vietnam and probably Cuba. I know you don't want that." Bundy focused his gaze directly on McCone. "We can't let him down, John. There's no hiding place on this one."

For a man who had just got what he wanted, McCone did a good job of looking grave. He grunted his agreement. "Okay, Mac." He turned towards Cline. "Ray? Let's get busy on putting together an insertion plan that'll work. We'll update Mac a week from now."

Cline touched his right forefinger to his forehead.

"Thanks, John," said Bundy. "I'll get back to you when I've spoken with McNamara." Bundy glanced at the clock on his office wall. It showed 5:48 Eastern Daylight Time. "Time to wake the President. It's going to be a long day."

≈

Daniel was getting used to the fact that, as a mercenary, the price of his hire and the nature of his new trade required him to set aside a few scruples. At his recruitment, his familiarity with radio systems was regarded as a valuable asset. They promised him a pay rise, which certainly helped him to deal with the moral dimension of his current employment.

Along with those new recruits who had never before served in the armed forces, he was now drawn up on parade in the shade of an aircraft hangar, built by the Belgians to house elements of a non-existent Congolese air force. The weapons instructor filled his lungs with a generous volume of the stifling tropical air and announced in a penetrating voice what was about to happen.

"You men ..." Here he paused to survey the raggle-taggle bunch of youngsters, using a practised stare that conveyed the impression that never before had he been presented with such unpromising material. "You men will shortly begin your trainin' with the FN 7.62-millimetre self-loading rifle, or 'SLR' as we call it." He pronounced the abbreviation '*esslar*'. "First of all, I'm goin' to demonstrate the safety drill. Then I want each of you to step forward and draw a weapon, so we can get started."

Doing his best to use what he assumed to be the correct military procedure for such occasions, Daniel took one pace forward and came to attention.

"Sergeant-major, sir?" The weapons instructor fixed him with an incredulous look.

"What is it?"

"Well, sir. I'm here as a signaller, so I'll be using a radio, not carrying a rifle, sir."

Since he already wore a fearsome look of disbelief, there was no escalation of facial expression available to the instructor. Short of using physical violence, this circumstance forced him to express his feelings using speech alone. He began his reply in the *basso-profondo* register, his voice trembling with emotion. Slowly the pitch of his roar began to rise, losing none of its volume, clarity or passion, sweeping through the bass and on into the bass-baritone, whilst abandoning not one whit of its impact.

"Signaller you may be, but when the fuzzy-wuzzies are runnin' towards you wavin' their machetes, your precious radio won't be a lot of use to you. You might want to hang about and take a chance on shovin' it up one of em's arse, but the rest of your mates here are goin' to be shootin'. That's what they'll be doin'. And they'll feel a shaggin' sight happier about the whole business if they know that you'll be right alongside, pottin' Simbas too, and stoppin' 'em from getting close enough to fillet the thunderin' lot of you. So! You'll be drawin' a rifle along with the rest of your mates. I trust I make myself clear!"

Sunday 18 October, 1964
US Embassy, Grosvenor Square, London

"So you see, Sir Timothy, the United States remains highly suspicious of Soviet intentions at this time, which is why we've increased the number of B-52s permanently in the air, on alert. I know that for the RAF this strategy isn't a normal course of action, but Mr McNamara has asked me to approach you personally to suggest a pilot program – no pun intended – of dispersing British nuclear warheads, to preserve a minimum remote retaliatory strike capability, in the event of... erm... a Soviet first strike against ground-based weapons located in the UK."

Though the US defence attaché had just outlined a most unwelcome scenario for England's green and pleasant land, he allowed a winning smile to spread across his face. At any rate, Sir Timothy assumed it was meant to be a winning smile. He thought it looked a little desperate. Perhaps the attaché hoped that its effect, coupled with a Sunday lunch during which a perfect Vosne Romanée had been served, would bring about the desired effect. Sir Timothy, however, had learned long before that there was no such thing as a free lunch and remained unconvinced.

"I'm sure that as a defence attaché, one of the first things you discovered was that here in Britain, we're set up rather differently from yourselves. I applaud you for trying, but really, as both you and Mr McNamara know already, compliance with a request of this sort requires ministerial authority. What you ask is not impossible, but Mr McNamara should be making an official approach to the new government... Unless, of course, this personal approach means you're sounding me out first?"

The attaché leered across the table. Sir Timothy assumed this was perhaps his interpretation of a roguish smile, a salesman's gambit, an attempt to gain support from a man-of-the-world by means of a locker-room smirk.

"I guess maybe our Secretary of Defense didn't want to overwhelm your new guy on his first day in the job."

When on business, Sir Timothy was immune to smiles of every description. He ignored the wisecrack until the grin had slid from the defence attaché's lips.

"Let's be realistic, please. What's really on Mr McNamara's mind?"

"You mean apart from Brezhnev, Southeast Asia and Mao's new bomb?"

"One, it's still the same old Kremlin. Two, we can't help you in Vietnam. And three, Hong Kong's too useful to you, us *and* Mao. If the US really wanted to put pressure on China, the President would already have spoken with Chiang Kai Shek... And you wouldn't have been plying me with this delightful Burgundy. What's the real reason?"

The attaché turned in his seat and signalled to the steward who had served the meal. "Shall we see if Sir Timothy would like to finish up with a vintage cognac?" Once the waiter had set off on his mission to rummage through the embassy's wine cellars, the attaché put forward a suggestion. "How about the Congo?"

"What about it?"

The attaché glanced over his shoulder. "Sorry, Sir Timothy. For your ears only. Maybe you knew already, but Harriman's been spending a lot of time lately talking with the Belgians. McNamara's going to need a secure site in a friendly country so he can mount a hostage rescue mission. We're really interested in checking out some of Britain's bases in Africa and the Middle East. Aden for instance."

"Spot of local difficulty there, I'm afraid."

"Salisbury?"

"Same."

"What about Ndola or Gan?"

"Northern Rhodesia's on the point of independence. Surely Gan's too far from Stanleyville?"

There followed a period of quiet reflection. The attaché's former animation subsided into apparent cogitation, leading Sir Timothy to conclude that the man's next inspired suggestion would contain the solution preferred by McNamara all along. He was about to consult his watch when the attaché burst into life again.

"Hey, listen! Aren't we building a satellite tracking station on Ascension? We could reach the Congo in one hop from Ascension."

"Now, there's a thought."

"But it's perfect. Assuming that the RAF doesn't need ministerial approval for every flight that takes off, how about fuelling-up a V-bomber that isn't part of the front-line strike force, drawing a couple of nukes from the obsolete reserve to make it a realistic test-flight – if the nukes haven't already been dismantled, of course..."

"You make it sound so simple."

"Yeah, but think about it. You'd have tried out the dispersal of a couple of nukes, so McNamara gets the cover story he wanted. And if we could squeeze a couple of extra passengers on board to check out the facilities..."

Sir Timothy shook his head. "I don't know. You're asking a lot."

"All we're asking is to survey Ascension and maybe Ndola as potential staging bases to liberate the hostages. Listen – how many Brits and Commonwealth citizens do you think are prisoners in Stanleyville right now? Fifty? A hundred? We're not asking for British troops, just a usable runway and a cover story. You'll be a hero. It's perfect!"

Six

Sir Timothy was clear about one thing – the need to act quickly. Overnight the US attaché's words had bitten into his conscience and convinced him of the perilous plight of the hostages. In the morning, it took only a couple of phone calls to narrow down the officer who seemed to hold the most useful cards in current circumstances, and secure a meeting with him. Installed in Air Commodore Purdham's office, Sir Timothy described the previous day's American request, finishing with a shake of his head and a hounded look.

"I'm in your hands, Air Commodore... As are all those hostages."

The air commodore puffed out his cheeks, allowing a gentle trickle of breath to escape his lips. Already he appeared much pre-occupied with the difficulties. "It won't be easy," he said.

"I know." Sir Timothy blinked, looked down at his lap, then back into Purdham's eyes. His air of persecution now incorporated an element of pleading. He waited. It worked.

"Okay... Appreciate you've come here for a solution, not a set of excuses." For a few seconds Purdham cast around for a starting point before alighting on one. "You've probably noticed this about our transatlantic cousins... They spend a lot of time talking and not much time listening." He cocked an eye at Sir Timothy. "Here's the problem. They seem to find it hard to understand that other people do things differently. So, from time to time, they tend to assume things about the RAF that aren't quite pukka." Purdham stretched, rocked his chair back on two legs, and continued. "Dispersing atomic weapons for instance. If we're talking about loading an obsolete weapon like the 'Yellow Sun' into a Valiant, it's strictly one per aircraft, I'm afraid. Damned thing is twenty feet long and four feet across, so we can only fit one in the bomb-bay. If McNamara wants us to fly a couple of bombs out to Ascension, that means two aircraft and at least one tanker. Just thought I'd make that clear."

"I take your point."

"We're getting a bit worried about the airframes, though. They need some money spent on them." Purdham grounded all four legs of his chair again and leaned across his desk. "With this new lot in power, what are our chances, do you reckon?"

"Your guess is as good as mine."

"Well, the Valiant's been around for a good ten years. Vickers designed it for high-level missions but anti-aircraft missile technology has come a long way in a short time. Had to change our tactics. High level approach, drop down low to fox their radar, pop up over the target, dump the old tin can, and get out as fast as possible. But all that low-level stuff puts stresses on the aircraft that it wasn't built to take. We've down-rated the performance, but..."

"I thought you said you could manage a trip to Ascension."

"Yes, yes. As an exercise. For a demonstration of warhead dispersal, I could certainly find you a couple of Valiants. But I can't pull any Vulcans off NATO's front line." Sir Timothy acknowledged this with a flick of the hand. Purdham then added: "May I assume the Yanks don't want us to do any seat-of-the-pants stuff – no hairy flying? If that's the case, the Valiant definitely isn't for you."

"Just a quick flit, as far as I can tell. McNamara simply wants a cover story as a way of checking out a possible staging airfield to help rescue the Stanleyville hostages."

"Had to ask, old chap."

"You mentioned solutions, not excuses," said Sir Timothy, floating a subtle reminder.

"Yes, I did. But half a mo... Before I trot off to arrange this so-called exercise, I have to mention a couple of technicalities."

The co-operative words left Sir Timothy feeling optimistic. "Please – carry on."

"I imagine you know this already, but when the US Air Force flies a nuked-up B-52 round the Pole, they're technically in breach of a treaty with Denmark for flying weapons of war through Greenland's air space. The Danes pretend they don't know anything about it, and the Yanks hope nothing goes wrong. Hear no evil, see no evil, if you like."

"We're all on the same side, after all."

"That's my point. From here to Ascension, no problem. But between Ascension and Ndola and then on across Africa, we're going to be flying over some rather touchy non-NATO countries. We could be in serious breach of International Law. Just thought I'd mention that..."

"Accepted. You said a couple of technicalities."

Purdham gave a stifled cough. "Yes, well." Both hands jerked in time with the words, emphasising that there could be difficulties. "Getting hold of a bomb... It isn't like toddling down to the stores and drawing a pot of paint or something. There's such a thing as security."

"What about the normal NATO dispersal exercises? They're a regular thing, aren't they? There's bound to be one planned soon. You must have a procedure already, surely? Effectively, we'd just be holding another joint exercise with the Americans."

"Almost certainly, yes."

"And the Yellow Sun isn't front line ordnance any longer, is it? So all we'd be doing is using some time-expired kit to test procedures for dispersing weapons to foreign bases in times of tension. You wouldn't want it to get any more tense than it is now, for God's sake."

Sir Timothy left Northwood with a further worry unexpressed. Over the years he had learned that, sometimes, dealing with Uncle Sam was anything but simple. Disclosures were not always what they seemed. Honesty could be in short supply. His concern was that somebody in Washington might be trying to paint the United Kingdom into a corner. Maybe this was an attempt to establish the precedent of relocating atomic weapons to the far south in times of crisis, before the new administration had time to get its policies into line.

B-52s maintained continuous patrols over the North Pole, the Pacific and the Mediterranean, surrounding the USSR on three sides, though leaving a great gap to the south. Without doubt, the Russians had realised this. They now performed much of their secret research and testing in the southern republics. Perhaps someone in Strategic Air Command had finally realised the implications of this. Could the US be planning to get the RAF to cover this breach, by rehearsing a wide-field flanking attack from the south? And would that be such a bad thing? The Cold War threat demanded a Cold War response, not appeasement. For the time being, he felt he might pretend innocence and play along with McNamara's request. He could always defend it later as a humanitarian response to the hostage crisis.

"I knew you'd want to see these as soon as they came in, Sir." The officer oriented two facsimile images on Cline's desk, for comparison.

"Thanks for bringing them straight up."

"This one dates back to January." He then laid a finger on the second photograph, pushing it towards Cline. "And *this one* is just a day old."

Cline craned forward to study the second image. Three arrows and three accompanying labels had been stuck to the ten-by-eight, pointing out the features of interest. The photo-interpreter had also included a brief report suggesting that illicit workers had broken through the concrete cap that plugged the Shinkolobwe mine. Cline examined the relevant part of the photograph showing where the workers were thought to be dumping spoil against the cutting's retaining walls. At the top of the cutting, the interpreter had marked an area where he believed the gang was piling up sacks of rock. The scale seemed tiny but the experts had probably worked from a much larger image. Of course, it wasn't proof, but...

Cline thanked the officer, dismissed him and picked up the phone.

"John – you remember we asked for a satellite pass over Stanleyville and some of the strategic installations in the Congo? Something's come up. Intelligence reckons that somebody's re-opened the Shinkolobwe mine."

Cline listened for a moment or two.

"No, they don't figure it's South Africa or Israel. It's only small scale. Three or four tents, one vehicle, no obvious mining machinery. So it could just be some local guys doing a bit of prospecting..." It was clear that at the other end of the line McCone shared Cline's doubts. "No –

it's the preparation work that made the analysts suspicious. We know roughly how much concrete the Belgians poured. It's taken these claim-jumpers several weeks to break through. Somebody must think it's worthwhile. The best bet is it's a small operation backed by China or India to prove the concept – assay some ore, and see if it's worth the effort."

Clearly, McCone was thinking on his feet. Cline made a few notes on the blotter.

"Agreed. We need to take a look, John. No question. But you know, we don't have anyone there who's able to move freely on the ground. It's not safe for any white man to go wandering around alone in the boondocks, so Task Force Leo, COMISH, the guys in the embassy and our agents in the other missions are – uh – effectively confined to barracks. The only other whites who aren't prisoners or missionaries are a handful of Belgian colonels advising Tshombe and a couple of hundred mercenaries under this guy, Hoare."

There was a further pause as McCone voiced his thoughts to Cline, who began to smile. In the CIA, there was nothing the old-timers liked better than action.

"I'm with you all the way on that, John. Best part is, like you say – if it all goes wrong, no dirt sticks to LBJ or us!"

Wednesday 21 October, 1964
Kamina Airbase

As the C-130 Hercules touched down from Leopoldville, US Marine Corps Colonel Calvin Leitner peered through the window to his left. Kamina was no bush strip, although the grass in the centre of the airfield had begun to resemble a hay crop. Way out at the perimeter of the airfield the flat scrubland began. Occasional low trees and anthills shimmered in the heat-haze beyond the steel fence. Inside the wire, concrete watch-towers stood guard. Through the windows on the other side of the aircraft, Leitner glimpsed a DC-6 with an attendant fuel bowser, close to a maintenance hangar. The colonial architecture of the administration block and the control tower spoke of an all-but-extinct desire to dominate the country, its resources and its people. The Hercules swung off the runway and taxied to a pad in front of the tower. Its turbo-prop scream died away, leaving Leitner's ears ringing. The colonel's Marine bodyguard stepped forward, opened the exit-hatch and ducked through the doorway. A moment or two later he reappeared, pronouncing himself satisfied. Leitner reached into a shirt pocket, unfolded a pair of Ray-Ban Aviators and joined the Marine on the concrete pan, as if stepping out onto a movie set.

Inside the office, the air-conditioning had long since failed. Outside, the occasional armour-plated insect bounced against the wire-mesh fly-screens, whilst a collection of others, large and small, crawled about, jeering through the latticework at Leitner and a Belgian colonel.

"As you asked, Colonel," drawled Leitner, handing over a medium-sized manila envelope. "I've come to deliver the United States government's request in person, and in writing."

Grim-faced, Colonel Frédéric Vanderwalle took it without a word and deposited it in the centre of his desk. He removed his beret and, as if following some secret ritual, he folded the left and right sides underneath, reverently displaying the gleaming cap badge at the front, facing Leitner, its rampant lion pawing the air. He then placed the rolled beret at the corner of his desk, aligned fore and aft, equidistant from its front and left side.

Leitner imagined this elaborate procedure was for his benefit – a reminder to the US Marine Corps of whose country this used to be. Vanderwalle then shuffled his seat closer to the desk, waved Leitner to take the seat opposite him, reached into a drawer and extracted a steel letter-opener reminiscent of the World War II commando dagger. It proved to be sharp. Displaying no emotion, he sliced open the envelope and extracted the contents. As if he realised that this would annoy Leitner, Vanderwalle tamped the sheaf of papers to neaten the edges, curled his lips into a disagreeable scar, smoothed the pages so that they would lie even flatter and began to read.

While the Belgian digested the US government's message, Leitner remained expressionless. The man who sat before him was below average height, grey, gruff, very properly dressed and perhaps not as old as he seemed. He looked rather like a small-town shopkeeper.

By the time Vanderwalle had finished reading the contents of the envelope, he had sorted the paper into piles. There was the official request; appraisal of the situation; proposed mission objectives; outline plan of execution and recommended manpower numbers; supporting information (printed); supporting information (photographic); arms, rations and equipment requirements; transport arrangements; a communications schedule and an appendix of radio frequencies.

"I must now find the man who can 'elp you," stated Vanderwalle. "I shall return in one hour." With that, he unfolded his beret, placed it upon his head, adjusted it without recourse to a mirror, surprised Leitner by throwing him an unexpected salute and left the room.

The platoon sergeant spotted Vanderwalle's trim figure heading in their direction in time to alert the major.

Without turning round, as the sound of approaching footsteps grew stronger, Major Hoare called the group of youngsters to attention. Perhaps by accident, but with a certain enthusiasm they managed this manoeuvre with a greater degree of unison than hitherto. They liked and respected the major. He was their champion. Hoare performed a textbook about-face and saluted just as Vanderwalle halted next to the sergeant.

"Major, I see your new recruits are beginning to look a little like real soldiers. At last."

"Thank you, Colonel," said Hoare. "I'm sure they feel more like soldiers, too. We'll have them up to the required level by the end of the month, as I promised."

"Can they shoot straight, yet?" It was a fair question, though somewhat brusque.

"Indeed so, Colonel. One or two of them are better shots than some of our time-served men."

"And will they fight?"

Hoare twisted round to face the recruits. "You men! Are you ready to take the fight to these Simbas and give 'em a good kick in the goolies?" The answering roar might not have met with approval in the Brigade of Guards, but Major Hoare looked pleased with the spirited response. Vanderwalle, however, remained tight-lipped, appearing neither angry, intimidated nor impressed by this ferocious demonstration.

Major Hoare appreciated Vanderwalle's hidden qualities. He knew that beneath the off-putting exterior could be found a graduate of the Advanced War Studies course from l'École de Guerre in Brussels, a man possessed of as sharp a military mind as anyone from Douala to Dar es Salaam, or from Stanleyville to Salisbury. Colonel Vanderwalle had the reputation of a military perfectionist, planner and tactical genius, *par excellence*. Clearly, the colonel would have preferred to command disciplined, regular troops. But here, all he had at his disposal was a bunch of mercenaries.

However, as a commander in the field, Hoare knew he had to fight his battles with what was available there and then. Realising that Vanderwalle's regimental formality and his petulant expression would get him nowhere with these young trainees, he felt a gentle nudge was necessary.

Hoare lowered his voice. "This isn't a regiment of lancers, Colonel. These young men aren't like that undisciplined rabble fighting for Mulele or Olenga. *Oui, ils sont mercenaires, mais ce n'est pas Waterloo. C'est le Congo!*"

"*Ah, oui. Vraiment. C'est le Congo!* As God is my witness it has given me everything, but it is – as you say – the bane of my life!" Hoare's reminder began to take effect. The corners of Vanderwalle's mouth twitched a little. "Major, if you will kindly accompany me, I 'ave someone whom I would like you to meet." The colonel raised his voice so that at least the nearer soldiers might hear his words. "I propose a little military reconnaissance – an exercise to give your recruits a better idea of the ground they may soon 'ave to defend."

Shinkolobwe Mine, DRC

Jonas, Chan and Hwang were squatting in a loose circle around the radio, listening to a news broadcast. It had left Chan feeling quite morose.

"Look Jonas," said Chan. "I'm really worried about the state of this country. It's time we got some of this ore on the road to China, and *you* along with it. It's bad enough here right now – nothing works." He shook his head and waved his right arm in a gesture towards the horizon. "But once control of the roads falls to the rebels, we'll be pinned down – no way of moving safely."

The African had been sharpening a knife. He looked across into Chan's eyes, with his usual calm, amused expression. "The Belgians have a phrase for that. '*C'est le Congo*', they would say. It explains everything, from murder to monsoons."

With so much on his mind, Chan had no time for a discussion about colloquialisms. "How far do you think we'll get in this old pickup? I reckon we need a second lorry."

"If you still trust me with your dollars, I reckon I could drive this wreck into Jadotville, bargain for a while and probably get a good German truck. If you're worried, Hwang and I could go today – now, if you want."

Jonas's response raised another worry. "These Simbas you've hired," said Chan. "With you two away, would I be safe here?

"For a while. I reckon they assume I'm the chief. If I left you on your own for too long though, they'd probably rob you and leave."

"Or kill me..." From the way Jonas failed to deny it, Chan reckoned it was probably true. "Will they stay loyal to us once we get on the road?"

"As long as we keep the *muganga* happy, yes. If we feed him plenty of whisky, he'll make sure his men keep believing in his spells and potions."

Chan shook his head again. "I just wish it wasn't like that. These people seem to believe in no cause except killing each other. And they've got no discipline either. How are we ever going to get them to take enough interest in their own future so they unite and overthrow the regime? This isn't a revolution. It's just anarchy."

"I see your time here hasn't been wasted."

Chan shrugged. "I just didn't want to believe what you kept telling me."

"Don't get depressed about it," said Jonas. "You can't change it. Remember – *C'est le Congo*. A Chinese-style revolution should work well in Angola, but it won't work here. You'll have to persuade Mao to tackle things differently."

"Not me... I can't go against Mao's doctrine. With the training I've had they'd see me as a threat." Chan waved a finger at Jonas. "You're an educated man. Local knowledge, too. The leadership would take it from you." He looked away despondently.

Jonas picked up a couple of small stones and tossed them gently into Chan's lap. "Hey, Weifeng – didn't you hear what I said? I'm on your side. By the time you and I are standing in front of Mao, he'll have no option except to believe us... The newspapers will be full of pictures of massacred Europeans and stories of mercenaries taking revenge."

"But if they don't want the whites here, with all their money, why would they let in the Chinese, with none?"

"I told you – Angola and the Congo are different. Revolution stands a better chance of leading to a stable government in Angola. For this place, maybe Mao just has to wait so that rather than *wanting* the Chinese, the Congolese have no option. Eventually they'll *need* you."

Hwang switched off the radio and stood up. "Enough politics, you two," he said. "What we *need* is a truck. Come on. Let's go and see what's on offer – all three of us."

Thursday 22 October, 1964
Wideawake Field, Ascension Island

As Valiant WP198 sank beneath the cloud base at 14,000

feet, lining up for its south-easterly landing at Wideawake, the co-pilot allowed himself a brief expletive. The volcanic origins of Ascension Island would have been apparent to a half-wit. The main summit was surrounded by a profusion of secondary cinder cones and craters. In a fit of fiery fervour, nature had outdone herself, and it was clear that she had not known when to stop. Stretched out before them lay the single runway. It occupied possibly the only available area of flat ground of sufficient length for its purpose, for a thousand miles in any direction. Even then, the military engineers had been obliged to squeeze this strip of concrete into the space between two immense volcanic peaks.

Once the Valiant was on the ground, the 'follow me' jeep pulled in front of the milk-white aircraft to guide it to the area of hard-standing allocated for its brief stay. Five crew members eased themselves out of the port-side door, stretching their limbs after the long flight from home. With little to divert their attention, they hung about to wait for the tanker aircraft and the second bomber to land, some ten minutes behind them.

After staring pointedly north, south, east and west, the electronics operator delivered his verdict on Ascension Island. "Eeee, shaggin' hell, boss! What God-forsaken fookin' hole has thee brung us to this time?"

Kamina Airbase

In the end, the only workable plan that fitted into the time available was to persuade Colonel Leitner to ferry the ten recruits, two NCOs and two Minerva Land Rovers to Elisabethville in the C-130. Driving almost 500 kilometres from Kamina to Jadotville over roads that might have been washed away in places, or barricaded in others, appeared less feasible than a brief flight to Elisabethville, followed by a 120-kilometre drive back to Jadotville.

Hoare picked two NCOs who were old Katanga hands from the earlier post-independence fighting, and who consequently knew the territory around Elisabethville. He briefed the men himself, making it clear that they were to carry out the reconnaissance to Jadotville and onward to Shinkolobwe as if under real combat conditions. Weapons would remain loaded at all times. Stand-to would be observed at dawn and dusk and sentries posted at night. Photographs of the entry to the mine and samples of what was being dug out of the ground were essential. If possible, a couple of prisoners should be brought back to Kamina for interrogation. Departure would be at 05:00 the next morning. But the Hercules would not wait. The return journey would have to be by road.

Seven

Friday 23 October, 1964
Ndola Airfield, Northern Rhodesia

Squadron Leader Maxted approached the green-painted door of his temporary office in the cluster of whitewashed, single-storey buildings that had once served as RAF Ndola's administrative headquarters. Although a large empty hangar still remained elsewhere on the airfield, the majority of the sheds and out-buildings had been rented to bush pilots, air taxi firms, photographic surveyors for the mining industry, or fledgling airlines with a twenty-year-old Dakota and a workshop full of salvaged engine parts.

The one thing Maxted regretted was that for weeks on end there was nothing to do. In this fading remnant of Britain's imperial past, each new day plodded along in the same aimless fashion as the one before. Since Monday however, he had managed to escape boredom by preparing for the arrival of a detachment of Valiants, diverted from normal duties to mark the country's forthcoming independence with a fly-past. Maxted turned his key in the lock, twisted the shaky bakelite door handle and pushed. A small gecko, late to retire, scurried away and hid behind the tea caddy. He left it undisturbed. The first mug of chai could wait a little longer.

Needing to get hold of the local weather report, he picked up the telephone receiver and cranked the handle to call the tower. The earpiece crackled in annoyance.

"Morning, chaps! Maxted here. Could you send Thomas round with the weather synopsis? Much obliged."

≈

Clap-clap-clap! The airfield messenger stood in Maxted's doorway. Since most African dwellings lacked both a solid door to knock upon and a doorknocker to knock with, 'No-Weather' Thomas had never got into the habit of rapping on the door, but always announced his arrival by clapping his hands. Maxted enjoyed the daily weather ritual. As a one-man operation, he valued every human contact that came his way.

"Hello, Thomas. Come on in. Only one day to go now before Independence!"

"Good morning, Massa!" Somewhat excited, Thomas could not restrain his feet. They shimmied for a short distance, stamping out several rhythmic dance steps.

"Celebrating already? Is there any weather information today?"

The barefoot shuffle came to a halt. Although a civilian, Thomas had adopted certain military ways. As he puffed out his chest, his open yellow shirt rippled above a pair of grimy shorts. He flung out his right arm, which quivered for a moment at its maximum extension. He then retracted it violently in a formal salute, before taking one pace forward and handing a single sheet of paper to the squadron leader. Maxted's fingers brushed lightly across some faint marks at the top of the page, which he took to be the date. He had once given Thomas a new ribbon for the typewriter but, in all likelihood, it had ended up at the local market, as no improvement in readability resulted from this generosity. The page was otherwise blank. But, futile or not, Thomas always obeyed his instructions to the letter.

"There is no weather today, Massa!"

Maxted thanked Thomas, who then retreated to

prepare for his next assignment, wearing the joyful smile of a man who is happy in his work, bolstered by the knowledge of a vital job, well done.

≈

Maxted's telephone rang at the arranged time. After a few pleasantries and an apology for having no official weather forecast, he launched into the next best thing.

"Well, I'm afraid it's a take-it-or-leave-it situation really. October's definitely the hottest month. It's not too uncomfortable today but the humidity's starting to rise. It'll be worst about February time. We don't get much rain at this time of year, so the visibility should be good – say around fifteen miles at ground level. Most days it's just light airs from the west, well below ten knots. Later in the afternoon it might gust up to twenty knots, but the runway faces into the prevailing wind, so I can't see there being too many problems."

There came a brief acknowledgement from the other end, then Maxted again:

"What's your likely flight time from Ascension, so I can have the kettle on?"

Westminster, England

Carried upwards in an erupting tide of humanity, Charles Rook emerged into the fresh autumnal morning mist outside Westminster tube station. Breaking with habit, he took a short diversion towards the Victoria Embankment, and sat on the first unoccupied wooden bench beyond Westminster Pier. He reached into his breast pocket and extracted a letter. Although he knew its contents well enough, he unfolded the single sheet and re-read it.

The letter was brief. It provided no comfort at all:

we received a letter from Daniel two days ago and your father has not slept since. It was already a fortnight old when we got it. I couldn't read the postmark, but the envelope had South African stamps on it. Daniel wrote to say he was just about to fly off to the ex-Belgian military base at Kamina. I still cannot believe it, but he has joined the mercenaries. He has left no forwarding address, so it is impossible to get in touch with him.

I'm afraid I know the answer without asking the question, so I will just say this in case you get a chance to do anything. Daniel is supposed to be staying with you in London, attending university, not risking his life in the Congo. Darling, if there is anything you can do to get him out of there safely, I beg you to do it. We love you both too much to lose you.

Charles peered about him at the constant surging stream of bowlers, brollies and businessmen. His mother was right: what could he do? Contemplating her letter, he felt helpless. He glanced down again at the tutored handwriting, the strokes of the fountain-pen and her closing melancholic words. '*We love you both too much to lose you.*' He felt ashamed. This was his brother, after all. Although capable of swinging between youthful irresponsibility and mature gravity in an instant, and although deeply unfathomable, Daniel was still just a bloody teenager, his mind and body at the mercy of a toxic brew of hormones and self-doubt. Charles shook his head. Whatever his feelings, he was powerless. What on earth could he do?

C-130, en route to Elisabethville, DRC

Although this was only supposed to be an exercise, the expense of staging it had left Daniel impressed, but uncertain. Ten recruits, two corporals, two jeeps and most of all, a C-130 Hercules. For his first experience of basic training, he had assumed he might suffer a couple of days getting hot, sweaty and tired, tramping through the bush to attack an imaginary enemy. Training patrols, he imagined, rarely ran to this sort of lavish expense. There could be only one conclusion: this extravagant show was not for practice. From the foldaway webbing seat on Daniel's left, Corporal Du Plessis squirmed sideways to face him. Pitching his voice to penetrate the scream of four turbofans and the bass growl of the propellers, Du Plessis roared out his conversational opener.

"Well then, Sparkie! If we're going to be mates, my name's Jacobus, but if there's any sergeants or officers about it'd better be 'Corp' – Okay? Over there is my good friend, Corporal Johannes Vermaak. Lesson one – look out for your mates!"

"I'm Daniel," he replied, taking the offered hand. "Someone's gone to a lot of trouble, for a training exercise."

"Hey, Danny! Pleased to meet you. Nah! The Congo's a big country, man. This is the fastest way of getting around. Just a quick recce to give you new boys a taste of soldiering before we start the main push. Lucky the major was able to borrow a Hercules, eh?"

Though inexperienced, Daniel remained unconvinced. After all, what sort of exercise was it where basic trainees set out armed with live rounds rather than blanks? On the other hand, maybe the risk of encountering a party of Simbas was greater than the trainees suspected. He glanced around the cabin. If similar thoughts were troubling his colleagues, it wasn't obvious.

"Let's have a look at your kit, then." Du Plessis took the liberty of reaching over Daniel's left leg to take hold of his back-pack, which was wedged between his feet. He lifted the whole pack, one-handed, over the young man's leg, dumped it before him and began to rummage through the contents. Daniel had stowed everything the way he had been shown; Du Plessis murmured sounds of approval. Unbuckling one of Daniel's pouches, he extracted the two spare loaded magazines, tested the springs and peered into the narrow spaces behind the rounds to see whether they had all been lined up with military precision. He blew a puff of air into the magazine.

"Bit of fluff," he explained. "Could have jammed your weapon." In the dim light of the Hercules cargo compartment, Daniel reckoned the fellow would have needed X-ray vision to spot any fluff. He assumed he was being shown who was top dog. Du Plessis replaced the magazines, and pointed at Daniel's rifle. "Might as well check that, too."

Daniel had been gripping his SLR tightly since takeoff, the butt resting on the cargo deck. He lifted the gun onto his lap, made sure the safety lever was in the proper position and unclipped the magazine. Then he worked the slide backwards and forwards to show that there wasn't a round 'up the spout', before passing the weapon to the corporal. Du Plessis rattled the slide a couple of times on his own account and squinted into the breech, inspecting the freshly-issued rifle. There was not a mark on it. He removed the gas plug, peered at the pristine perfection that confronted him and replaced it.

"Just keep it looking like that, eh?" It seemed the corporal didn't want to leave the conversation there. "Listen – d'you know much about side-arms, Danny?"

"Hardly anything."

Du Plessis leaned over to his left, making space to reach with his right hand for the canvas holster hanging from his belt. He jerked open the flap, closing his hand around the grip of a blue-steel handgun, then withdrew the weapon with obvious affection. Relaxing into a slight slouch, he held the revolver in both hands between his legs, the barrel pointing downwards, as if he were making some deliberate sexual comparison.

"See that? Smith & Wesson model 29, that is. 44 Magnum with a five-inch barrel. Not so short that you lose accuracy, not so long that you can't get it out fast enough. Powerful too. It'll stop a car if you hit the cylinder block side-on."

"Not too long, not too short," said Daniel with the flicker of a grin. "Just right, eh?"

"It's a dangerous world out there." The corporal thumbed the catch and broke open the weapon, leaning closer towards Daniel to show him the ammunition – six brass, centre-fire rounds nestling in the cylinder. He took one out and handed it across.

Daniel took the metallic cartridge. It felt heavier than he had expected. The flat-nosed bullet had a much greater diameter than the streamlined 7.62-millimetre bullets loaded in his SLR. "Is this what they call a dum-dum?"

"Nah, this is a hard-nosed bullet – non-expanding. See, man, if you're out in the bush and you suddenly find you've got a lion or a rhino charging towards you through a thicket, this is your best defence." The magazine from Daniel's rifle still rested on top of his kit bag. Du Plessis twisted the magazine round so that the opening faced Daniel and then jabbed at the ammunition inside. "See, with that long pointy NATO round, if you fired a snap shot at that rhino there's a chance you'd miss. Every time your SLR bullet glances past a twig or a branch it gets deflected just that little bit more. With this baby, your flat-nosed bullet just keeps flying straight ahead, takes out that old rhino and carries on out the other side of him. Saved the life of many a hunter, the 44 has. Here – feel it." Du Plessis handed the firearm to Daniel, who accepted it with a degree of reluctance. The corporal leaned against him, pointing out the safety catch, encouraging him to spin the cylinder, to feel the weight and balance of the gun and to cup his fingers around the barrel with its full-length under-lug. Meaty.

"Do we all get issued with one of these?"

"No, man. It's my own. But I'll tell you this: Nobody in this game comes back for a second tour without a sidearm of some sort. You need to get one as soon as you can."

"I thought I was supposed to be operating a radio."

"Especially signallers, Sparkie. There's no room to be waving an SLR about in the back of a jeep or inside a radio tent. Only one thing. If you get yourself one of these and have to fire it at a buffalo or a Simba, just make sure I'm not standing anywhere behind him, will you?"

Daniel promised to remember that advice, and handed back the artillery.

Elisabethville Airport, DRC

The C-130 stood at a far corner of the airfield. Leitner watched in silence, with obvious growing exasperation as

Du Plessis first marshalled the new recruits into line for inspection, and then attempted to sort out some mix-up over who would carry what piece of kit. With limited success, Corporal Vermaak was attempting to un-lash the Minerva Land Rovers. The US master-sergeant in charge of the aircraft's cargo-bay asked him to stand aside, explaining, as is the tendency of sergeants, that he couldn't jolly well wait all day.

"You boys know what you're doing?" queried Leitner. Unanswered, he let it ride for the best part of a further minute, then led Du Plessis aside.

"Come on, Corporal. This ain't a Sunday School outing. It don't matter a pinch of shit if Phyllis can't sit next to Gertrude." The implied criticism was obvious in Leitner's face. "Get their asses loaded up and shipped out of here. You boys got a job to do."

Du Plessis looked crestfallen. "First-timers, Colonel, sir." He tried to brighten-up a little. "We'll have them out of here in a couple more minutes. They'll be fine once we've got a few miles under our belts."

As the aimless recruits milled around, a thick-set sandy-haired farmer's son called De Witt, with a lot to say for himself, jabbed his elbow into Dan's ribs. Without moving his lips, like a uniformed ventriloquist, he hissed at Daniel. "Things'll be a bit different when I'm section leader. Can you shoot straight yet, Rook?"

De Witt had already become a comedy character to the rest of the platoon. Whenever the trainees undertook any new foot-drill or weapons practice, De Witt made a point of asking a question. Because the instructors had seen and done it all before, the scope for inserting an intelligent query into their all-encompassing routines was often limited. Consequently, De Witt had quickly attained a reputation for unnecessary interruptions, if not for complete stupidity. His self-promotion as deputy section leader sounded to Daniel like the delusion of a falsely-confident idiot.

Daniel decided on an offhand reply. "I can normally hit what I'm aiming at."

"Well just remember – if there's a bullet out there with Du Plessis's name on it, I'll take command of this section. You'll be taking your orders from me."

"If that's what Corporal Vermaak says," Daniel growled out of the corner of his mouth. "Let's hope Du Plessis stays lucky, eh?" He turned his head slowly away from De Witt and although nobody could see his face, he mouthed a single word. "Prat!"

WP198 Cockpit – Approaching Ndola Airport, Northern Rhodesia

Flight Lieutenant 'Noddy' Blyton's calculations showed that for a sea level airfield he would have needed a threshold airspeed of just 118 knots. However, Ndola lay 4,000 feet above sea level, which would be as high a landing as he had ever undertaken. In round terms, in this thinner air, the Valiant would generate about fifteen percent less lift, requiring a higher landing speed to avoid the stall.

On final approach:

Despite Maxted's earlier 'average day' weather forecast, one or two thunderstorms lurked in the neighbourhood. As the airspeed sank below 150 knots, Noddy directed the co-pilot to increase the flap setting to forty-five degrees, to maximise lift. Flight Lieutenant Jones, in the right-hand seat, leaned forward and depressed the spring-loaded lever until port and starboard flap-position indicators showed the required value.

Noddy throttled back, reducing to his planned safe threshold airspeed of 135 knots. Jonesy carried on calling out altimeter readings. From what Noddy could see, they sounded accurate. There appeared to be no problem with the local setting that they had been given – the indicated height agreed well with Noddy's estimate of height above ground. Bit of a headwind, no sign of wind-shear or turbulence – looking good. Crossed the threshold, lined up nicely – easy does it.

"Bugger!"

At the very last moment, the gusting headwind fell away to nothing. Deprived of adequate lift, the Valiant smacked down with a wallop, accompanied by an expensive rending-sound, as if the whole aircraft had fallen into an elephant trap.

Over the intercom: "What the hell was that?"

"Felt like we've just been hit up the arse," replied Jonesy. "We haven't grounded the tail skid, have we?

Noddy began to apply the brakes. "Hey, Nav," he called. "What the hell was that thump? Is there any damage back there?"

"Agree with Jonesy, boss. Sounded like it came from aft of the equipment crate, and low down. Could be right. Maybe the tail skid took a bash."

"Get your head up inside the sextant dome. See if the fin and the tailplane look okay, will you? Fast as you can."

"Wilco, boss." The air navigator unbuckled his safety straps. Stiff from being hunched in one position for much of the flight, he eased himself out of his parachute harness and swung into position below the Perspex bubble, scanning left and right.

Noddy braked the Valiant to a slow roll. With two aircraft still some distance behind him, he felt it better to clear the runway, rather than occupy it. He kept the aircraft moving until he reached the next turnout, then brought her to a halt. Over the intercom the navigator called back with his report:

"Fuselage, fin and tailplane look fine, boss." Then with more familiarity, "You'll be glad to know I couldn't see any bullet holes, so we probably weren't shot down. Tell you what, though – if we did take a shunt up the arse, whoever did it has already buggered off."

"No damage to the wing?"

"Well, I dunno. Not as far as I could see."

"Roger that, Nav." Then Noddy addressed the local controller. "Ah ... Ndola tower, this is oscar three-six-two, over."

"Oscar three-six-two, this is Ndola tower, go ahead, over."

"Ah, Ndola tower ... oscar three-six-two cleared runway, but I'm showing two red lights on the wheel-brake temperature indicators. Do you copy?"

"Roger, oscar three-six-two. That looked like a heavy landing. Do you require assistance, over?"

"Ndola tower, it's probably a burst tyre, but request Rescue Services to come out and take a look – check for smoke and hot spots. Requesting clearance to maintain current position until we get the okay from Rescue, over." Noddy released the press-to-talk switch, and looked at Jonesy. "That ought to stall him for a mo."

"Oscar three-six-two; calling out the fire-tender now to take a look. We'll put a tug on standby to come and give you a tow to a safe location if required. Maintain position and listen out on this frequency."

"Roger tower, wilco. Ah – as a precaution, request clearance to shut down engines, over."

"Oscar three-six-two; affirmative clearance to shut down engines. Out."

Then, in another aside to Jonesy. "But you know what I'm dreading, don't you? It's a repeat of Taffy Foreman's fractured wing spar – that's what this is. I'm going to take a look."

Noddy switched back to the intercom. "Hey, Nav, listen. There's a tender on the way out to us and a tug on standby. As you're on your feet, open up and we'll take a quick walk around. See if there's any obvious damage. I'll join you in a minute." Then to Jonesy. "If the tower comes up again, feed him some excuse. Tell him the warning lights haven't gone out, so there's probably a hydraulic fluid leak in the brake circuits. Tell him it may not be safe to taxi the aircraft so we'll need a tow to the hangar." He jerked his thumb backwards over his shoulder. "With that nuke on board we need to get out of sight. We don't want anyone coming anywhere near us till we know what's what. You have control." Noddy unclipped his harness and headed for the exit.

Once outside the aircraft, the pilot and navigator walked aft around the tail to the starboard side to discover that, as expected, one tyre had suffered a blow-out. They looked up into the undercarriage recess. They could see no other obvious damage, but if the rear spar had buckled, they probably wouldn't see anything from underneath. The bomb doors remained shut tight, so they inspected the underside of the fuselage to their rear. They found no scratched paintwork or scored metal to suggest that the rear of the aircraft had scraped on the runway during landing. The officers walked thirty yards in front of the nose and turned to face the aircraft.

"Wings look true to you, Ed?" The navigator grasped his bottom lip between thumb and forefinger, to help consider the matter. He cocked his head from side to side, as if hanging a painting at an exhibition. The fire tender drew to a halt behind them.

"Looks fine to me. Straight and level, I'd say, boss."

"Afternoon, Captain." The officer in charge of the fire tender loomed up behind the two airmen. "Everything okay now?"

"Hi. Thanks, yeah. You'll want to check around, but we think that the burst tyre on the starboard side has damaged the hydraulics, so we can't rely on the brakes. Best thing would be to get the tug out here as soon as possible, and get him to tow us inside the RAF hangar, so we can fix it. How's that sound to you?"

"You're de baas, Captain." The fire officer strolled over to the starboard undercarriage for a quick check but, with Noddy's decision already taken, he seemed disinterested.

The RAF hangar at Ndola had been disused for some while. Once spotless, the floor was now soiled with a light dusting of eggshells, feathers, bones, second-hand nest material and other assorted avian waste products. Inside the corrugated iron walls, safe from prying eyes, the four bomber pilots clustered around the port undercarriage leg. Squadron Leader Creswell, the detachment commander, asked Blyton to brief them about the heavy landing. Noddy explained how, having crossed the threshold, the final descent to the runway was going according to plan. The windsock had been visible. He estimated that he was flying into a headwind of about 20 knots. At the critical moment, maybe 20 feet above the runway, the breeze had died away to nothing. In the thin air, he could do little about the loss of lift and the sudden increased rate of descent. His option of throttling up, overshooting and lining up again for a less risky landing was practically non-existent, offering no way to avoid the heavy landing.

"What worried me was this ruddy great bang from the

arse end. I haven't spoken to Taffy for a while, so I don't quite know what it feels like to damage a wing spar. But that's what I thought, straight away."

"Couldn't have been a clunk from a stalled compressor, could it?"

"Sounded too heavy for that. It shook the whole aircraft. The crew said it was aft of their compartment. Ed, my navigator, said it felt low down."

Creswell intervened: "Right-ho, chaps. Let's not jump to conclusions until we've got some evidence to go on. Now look... I haven't asked the tanker pilots to join us because we're facing a potential security situation here."

In operational circumstances tanker and bomber pilots lived separate lives. The requirement for security meant that tanker men knew very little about nuclear arms or the training for their use. For this mission, one seat had been vacated in each aircraft, making space for a total of three extra passengers. They had brought an officer from operations to survey Wideawake Field, an armourer to look after the bombs and a ground engineer, lovingly referred to as a 'flying spanner', to provide first-line aircraft maintenance.

Creswell continued. "The flying spanner seems like a bright kid, but I want to do a close inspection of the aircraft before we ask him to roll his sleeves up. I suggest we look at the mainplane between the wing roots, first." He looked about him, noticing a wheeled inspection platform in the corner of the hangar. "That's what we need. Let's bring it over here, and give the old girl the once-over, eh?"

Ten minutes later, the four officers agreed that the alloy skin of the fuselage had an unusual ripple in its upper surface, between the wings. A few rivets had also sprung from their normal flush positions. A fractured rear spar seemed to be the most likely cause. WP198 would be going nowhere.

"You're a lucky blighter, Noddy," said Creswell. "If that had happened at 45,000 feet, you'd have had to bang out and hope your crew could get into their 'chutes quick enough to float down and join you in lion-country! Let's have a look up inside the bomb-bay and see if there's anything obvious from underneath."

Noddy edged away from the group and climbed back inside the aircraft to operate the bomb doors. Once inside the cockpit, he eased himself into the left-hand seat and closed the two battery switches, listening as the rotary transformers began to whirr up to speed. Reaching forward to the far left of the central pedestal, he clicked the bomb door switch into the open position. He noticed the distant whine as the anti-buffeting air deflector rose. When it reached the end of its travel, a deeper sound took over as the heavier bomb-door motors tripped in. Then he heard shouting. Thinking 'safety' he knocked the battery switches off again, rolled out of the seat and grasped both sides of the cockpit exit port as he dropped through into the electronics cabin, heading for the outer door.

The three remaining pilots had been standing a little way behind the port wing, waiting for Noddy to re-join them. As the bomb-doors began to open, Jonesy, attracted by an unfamiliar silver tinkling sound like frozen rain on a tin roof, turned to find a strange sight. A cascade of seemingly thousands of ball-bearings was pouring from the whole length of the opening bomb doors, bouncing on the concrete floor of the hangar and scattering every which way, like small shiny insects startled by the light. For a moment, he stood open-mouthed, transfixed by the scene, apparently mystified by what was happening. But he was not long in that state. As the bomb doors opened wider, the tail fin of the obsolete Yellow Sun bomb, or 'instant sunshine' as it had come to be known, dropped to the floor, tolling a single, deep, funereal, metallic, ringing death-knell. Not one of the party had dared to imagine that the hard landing could have shattered the bomb-release mechanism. Yet here, for an instant was an atomic weapon with the rear crutch-hanger sheared off, suspended from its single forward attachment point. All eyes now stared in horror at this vision of doom. But worse! A second later, the twisted forward release clip fractured like a whip crack under the five-ton weight and the complete bomb clanged down onto the hangar floor. Somebody screamed in terror, a fitting match for the sound of its fall.

Fragments of each man's lifetime flashed before him. In shock, nobody moved. Here were men who had grown comfortable with the idea of setting out at the dead of night to obliterate their allocated personal target, a closed industrial city in the Ukraine or a missile site in the Russian Arctic. Yet no amount of training could have prepared them for the trauma of finding their own bomb landing right at their feet. But Creswell's training told him one thing above all else – something far more distressing. The bomb's Heath-Robinson failsafe mechanism had failed. Jonesy broke away, but his legs had the strength neither to step nor to hold him upright. He would later maintain that he had merely lost his footing on the carpet of ball bearings.

"STAND STILL!"

Time duly stood still. No-one stirred. Noddy's limbs locked solid, leaving him five feet above the ground, half in and half out of the oval hatchway. Creswell panned around, taking in the scene, drawing the others' eyes back towards him.

"Nobody move!" The words came in a low growl, a stage whisper that only heightened their effect. "There's nowhere to run to. Just think for a second. If she blows, she blows, and we won't know a thing about it." Someone breathed in, and then another.

And then, as if he were about to tell some comic anecdote in the officers' mess, Creswell's voice lightened. "Chaps, did I ever mention they sent me on a week's course a couple of years ago? 'Yellow Sun Appreciation Course' I think they called it. Thought I was off to Cannes for a holiday, but I only got a rail warrant as far as Basingstoke. Spent the week at Aldermaston instead. Any of you done the course?" His eyes swept around the stark faces. "No? Thought not. I suppose the damned bomb's been out of date for a while. Well, the boffins had come up with a wizard wheeze to avoid a premature detonation... That's premature *detonation*, lads. They filled the cavity with ball bearings." He cast his eyes down to the concrete floor. The others followed his gaze. "That's them there now. The idea was that even if the charges went off accidentally, the bomb couldn't implode more than a gnat's nudger, 'cause you couldn't crush the ball bearings. Simple really." Pleased with this explanation, he smiled at the crew. "All you've got to do is remember is to empty them out before you get to the target."

As he still had everyone's attention, Creswell continued. "Until a few minutes ago, if I've got my numbers right, there were precisely one hundred and thirty-three thousand two hundred and fifty-seven ball bearings filling the core of that bomb over there. And now there aren't any. To make things worse, they've discovered lately that the Yellow Sun's clockwork timers and the pressure fuses are vulnerable to an electrical surge. Quite simply, if the charges ignite, we shan't be around to help the world unravel a puzzling little megaton mystery. So, might I suggest that now is not the time to be thinking about having a cigarette? And if anyone feels like praying, could he arrange with the Almighty not to send along any thunderstorms for the rest of the day?" He paused, to make sure that the full effect of his words had penetrated the shroud of fear that enveloped his colleagues.

"Look, I know this may only be a feeble proposal, chaps, but you're most welcome to it. I can't remember anything in the book that covers a situation like this. So we're going to be big boys about it. We're going to chuck out normal procedures and work out how to fix this mess on our own. But what goes on in here stays in here – right?" He looked around, and found no dissenters. "For starters, I suggest that we roll the bomb so the drain-hole is facing up, then chock it so it doesn't roll back again. After that we'll sweep up every bit of this FOD, tip it back inside the core, hammer the bung back in, and finish off with a mug of tea while we decide what to do next." No better plan existed.

The normal spring in Noddy's step appeared to have unwound. He sidled up to the squadron leader. "That's a hefty piece of kit, Tony. We're going to need a bit of help here. Why don't you send Jonesy off to fetch Maxted and the rest of the boys?"

"Good man, Noddy." He called the co-pilot over. "Here, Jonesy. Stuff your hands in your pockets. Look as nonchalant as you can, and stroll over to find Maxted, will you? Don't tell him what's happened – walls have ears. Then get the tanker crew and the teckies over here without any fuss. No panic. Ones and twos. Walk, don't run. Talk about cricket or something. Everything's got to look normal."

Flight Lieutenant Jones acknowledged by tipping his right forefinger to his forehead. He then moved off into a corner of the hangar, retched and heaved up his lunch, aiming into a grating as accurately as any man could under the circumstances. He coughed once, spat a couple of times, shook his head and set off to find the station commander.

Creswell turned to Noddy. "Poor bugger!"

"Yeah. Look, just so I know we're on the same wavelength here, tell me – are you planning to use the aircraft destructor packs?"

"Good heavens no! Makes a frightful mess, and there's only one thing we've got that'll destroy that bomb... The bomb itself!"

McGeorge Bundy's Office, The White House

Cline was reaching the end of his briefing update for McCone and Bundy.

"Finally, when that satellite data came through on Monday it seemed like pretty strong evidence that the Chicoms were conducting some sort of operation. We had a word with General Adams's people and they sent a Marine Corps colonel straight down there to liaise with the Belgians at Kamina to see whether we could piggy-back on the mercenary situation. We're hopeful of further news shortly."

Bundy seemed unsure whether this was a good idea. "Don't we need to keep the military at arm's length on this for a while longer?"

"Agreed, Mac. But there's no substitute for having your own set of eyes and ears right there on the ground. Sending in military advisers is all very well, but... well, they're not very mobile, not very flexible – that's all I'm saying." It was clear that the CIA preferred a dependable American presence in Katanga, free to roam and free to act. Cline and McCone exchanged amused glances.

"What's so funny? What have you boys come up with?"

"Relax, Mac," said Cline. "We figure we've got that one covered. Remember Bill Ferguson?"

"Flick Ferguson? You bet your ass I remember Flick. I thought he didn't work for us any longer. Some big bust-up."

Cline put down his cup of coffee and sniggered. "Well, it was a good cover story. We figured this was just the sort of mission where we could use him. That should just about answer your mobility and flexibility requirements."

"I'll say. Just make sure he keeps his nose clean this time. At least till after the election."

"Sure thing, Mac." But Cline omitted to mention that, so far, ex-agent William 'Flick' Ferguson had not been located. Whilst the notice on his apartment door gave a clue regarding his current activity, there was no indication where he had actually 'GONE FISHING'.

Jadotville Highway, DRC

Crammed into the rear of the leading jeep with three other volunteers, their arms, supplies and radio equipment, Danny was trying not to notice that he was feeling both tired and hungry. The jeep's canopy had been left unfurled, giving a perfect all-round view, but leaving everyone exposed in the event of a rebel attack. Other than their destination, there had been no briefing about what to expect, making him also a little apprehensive. Ahead, in the front passenger seat, Corporal Du Plessis directed his driver to slow down. He then raised his arm to execute a contorted whirling signal that finished with a jerky movement to the right. Following this, the driver slowed the vehicle to a walking pace and steered it off the highway. The second Land Rover drew up right behind.

Du Plessis grasped the windscreen to haul himself to

his feet, then stepped on to the seat to survey the men in both vehicles. "Okay guys, jump out. Stretch your legs for two minutes and listen up." He sprang down and stood between the two trucks, beckoning the young soldiers to gather round.

"Orders:" He consulted his watch. "It'll be dark in less than an hour. There's about 60 kilometres to go, so we can't make it to the mine in daylight. Because we don't know what we're going to find when we get there, I plan to move in at first light, rather than risk getting ambushed by arriving there in the dark." He paused to make sure that his words were sinking in. One or two nodded. Some of the others appeared to be experiencing the first realisation that their new careers as gun-toting mercenaries could prove hazardous to their health.

'Ambushed?' thought Danny. He had been right; this was not quite the innocent training exercise that they had been led to believe. Beside him, De Witt's nonchalant, wide-legged stance indicated that he knew what he was doing, and that the corporal could depend on him in a crisis.

"We'll find a clearing somewhere up ahead," announced Du Plessis. "I don't want to be noticed from the road. Two men on watch at all times, relieved every two-hours during the night. If you've already got a buddy, sort yourselves into pairs before we make camp, or I'll have to detail you off into pairs, myself. Stand-to at 4:00 a.m. and we'll be on the road by half-past. Now mount up! Let's get going!"

"Shouldn't we cock our rifles?"

"Cock? You leave your bloody change-lever in the safe position, De Witt, unless I say different. I don't want you tripping over your feet and shooting me in the arse."

Danny noticed a few smiles. But, always reserved in any new situation, he had not yet got close enough to call any of the other recruits his buddy. De Witt's manner, alternating from tactless and brash to a cool aloofness, had managed to repel the rest of the section. Danny suspected the annoying fellow might be without a mate too. He hoped that if it came to being detailed off, Du Plessis would double him up with somebody – anybody – other than De Witt.

RAF Hangar, Ndola Airport

To re-ballast the bomb's hollow core with its full cargo of ball-bearings and reduce the risk of a premature explosion, Creswell suspended the normal rules about re-using foreign objects that fell to the hangar floor. They cleaned the steel pellets as well as they could, picking out such things as feather-down, barbs, filaments or grit that might choke the device as they flowed into the cavity. As a precaution, the armourer went barefoot and repeatedly earthed his hands to discharge any static electricity before dribbling the tiny balls back inside the bomb.

Dusk had long since fallen before the aircrew had gathered up the carpet of escaped ball bearings and inspected them. As the last components of the primitive safety system trickled back into the Yellow Sun, this brought a sense of relief to all. Now that the first phase of their problem-solving response was drawing to a close, Maxted began to wonder how he came to find himself in that position and what to do next.

Clearly, the arrival of these nuclear-armed aircraft was less about putting on a show for Zambian independence and more a cover-story for some secret mission. The risk of them becoming incapacitated on foreign territory had been discounted or, worse, whoever was in charge of the mission had not considered the possibility in the first place. Maybe there had been too little time to arrange proper security using specialist guards from the RAF Regiment or the Military Police. The consequences of this foolish omission now haunted the group. Alone, unarmed and dog-tired, how were they supposed to defend the two bomber aircraft and keep their lethal payloads secure?

Maxted arched his back, placing his hands behind his hips, stretching to ease the tension in his spine. The original plan had been for the three aircraft to depart for Gan on the following day. En route they would mark Independence Day by making a scheduled low pass over Lusaka, in formation. That was now impossible. Around him, the pilots and crew of all three aircraft made a sorry sight. Weariness had replaced fear, as the exhausted flight crews sank to the concrete floor, their faces pale from physical and mental fatigue. Some sat with their arms wrapped around raised knees. Others covered their faces. Two had already collapsed into sleep, too exhausted to sense the pressure of bone on cold concrete.

"Congratulations," said Maxted to Creswell. "We've prevented a major disaster."

Creswell seemed beyond speech. Hanging his head, then shaking it slowly, he simply inflated his cheeks and gave a prolonged heavy puff.

"I was thinking," Maxted continued. "That's just chapter one. Brilliant, but all we've done so far is stuck a finger in the dyke. Now we need to send for help."

Creswell seemed to know this well enough. He snorted with obvious contempt. "Contact Whitehall, you mean? Contact the maniac who got us into this mess?"

"For a start, yes. Only it won't be too easy. There's no secure phone lines here at Ndola."

"It just keeps on getting better and better, doesn't it?"

"Okay then," said Maxted. "How secure is the Valiant's

h.f. radio?"

"On a scale of nought to ten?"

"If you like."

"About two, I should think. Northwood reckons the Russians can read not only the scrambled voice traffic but the ciphered stuff, as well. We've got a one-time pad and a Morse key, but that takes forever."

Maxted nodded with resignation. "Unless you've got a better idea then, I think I need to see if I can contact the High Commission in Lusaka." Creswell seemed unwilling to argue.

Letting himself out of the hangar through the corrugated iron door, Maxted felt relieved. He breathed deeply but the feeling was brief. The scale of the disaster that he had helped avoid seemed to dominate his thoughts, clouding his judgement. For this to have happened, someone somewhere way above his own head must have made a right royal balls-up. Back home, somebody in the MoD or some ponce here in the High Commission would be looking for a convenient third party to blame. There seemed no way out. This was one of those military situations from which the man on the spot can never emerge unscathed, since all options appear to result in dishonour, dismissal or worse.

But Maxted was not prepared to accept such a fate. Some part of his mind, at least, refused to enter this predictable spiral of recrimination. He draped his 'number 6' tropical uniform jacket loosely over his left arm. The gentle night air felt refreshing, if not yet cool. A soft breeze enfolded him. He took another deep breath.

As he stepped out of the shadow of the hangar into the moonlight, his eyes were drawn to the two-and-a-half bars on the jacket's epaulet. 'Snap out of it, Maxted,' he thought. 'You didn't get those for sitting around, hoping someone else would solve your problems. There's got to be a way out of this.' But what problems! What were his options?

Could he remove the problem entirely? No, he could not – not in the short term. The risk of discovery seemed to affect every scenario. But if the accident to WP198 could be concealed for a few hours, they might reduce the impact of the problem. This might allow the other two aircraft to leave Ndola, make the expected courtesy flight over the capital and fly at least one bomb out of the country, perhaps minimising any potential diplomatic row between Britain and the new government. In just over an hour, it would be October the 24th – Independence Day. He wondered at what time Independence actually took effect. Was it one minute after midnight tonight? Was it perhaps at sunset, a full eighteen hours later when the Union flag was to be hauled down at Government House and the new Zambian flag raised, with the bands playing and fireworks bursting overhead? Not that it made much difference. There would still be hell to pay.

There was at least one other option... Certainly the single serviceable bomber should escape to Gan with its own bomb. A fully fuelled Valiant could make it that far without tanker support. But what if the tanker aircraft stayed behind, or doubled back after the display over Lusaka? Was it possible for them to quickly re-convert the tanker's bomb-bay by removing the hose-drum unit at the heart of the refuelling system? If the tanker's strong points were still in place, maybe they could still get the remaining bomb loaded up and flown out before some airfield official made the inevitable embarrassing discovery. Only WP198 would be left behind with its broken back, and no evidence that the bomb had ever been brought into Zambia. And even if they couldn't convert the tanker, provided that word of the bomb hadn't leaked out, it might be possible for the fleeing bomber to make a quick return from Gan and take away the second bomb.

As Maxted paced the deserted airfield in the moonlight, he knew the clock was ticking. They had to contact higher authority without delay or else suffer the consequences at a court martial. The scientists at Aldermaston, the diplomats, the boys on the squadron and probably the airframe designers at Vickers needed to be rousted out of their beds, stuck in a room and made to work out a solution. But no matter how much he might want to make direct contact with the Ministry of Defence in Whitehall, this insecure option was too risky. It was almost eleven o' clock now. In this part of Africa, the possibility of there even being an international telephone operator on duty seemed as distant as the stars overhead. Even had there been one, calls needed to be booked well in advance and were monitored avidly by the operators 'for technical purposes'. News of the disaster would spread like a locust swarm.

The Morse key and the one-time pad? Ridiculous. You couldn't have the necessary two-way technical conversation if you had to code up what you wanted to say, check it, send it, wait for a reply, decode it and then reply in the same laborious fashion.

Although he and Creswell had been too busy earlier to contact the High Commission, it was now imperative. Should he phone, or make a midnight dash? With a good start he could be on the steps at daybreak. But his jeep only had a quarter of a tank of petrol – far too little for the 200-mile journey. The likelihood of finding fuel at night between Ndola and Lusaka was about as remote as locating an international operator. They needed initial contact fast. It would have to be the phone, but Maxted knew that the instrument in his office would be no use to him. It was simply a remote extension, wired into the airfield's antique telephone switchboard, through which all outgoing calls had to be manually connected. But surely there was the solution. He should have thought of it before – that same switchboard in the airfield's control tower operated as a local exchange, and he knew it had long-distance trunk lines to Lusaka. Maxted abandoned the walk to his office and headed back towards the tower.

Keeping to the shadows and feeling like a thief, Maxted was not surprised to find the tower locked. However, the key to the outer door – the only locked door in the building – lay, as usual, behind a large terracotta pot in which a display of proteas normally blossomed. Maxted turned the key in the lock and crept into the darkened building. Except for a few late-night returns to Cranwell as a cadet, he had not made much of a career of midnight burglary. Now, on this formerly inauspicious night, he felt that his luck might just be changing for the better. Surely the risk of discovery was slender. The African night watchman would probably be off site, celebrating Independence with his friends. If, by chance, he was still somewhere within the airport perimeter, the odds were that he would be curled up asleep.

Maxted managed to creep upwards to the control deck without stumbling over any furniture. Moonlight striking through the panoramic windows lit the console and the silent radio equipment. His eyes had already adjusted to the light level, but the back of the room still lay in shadow. He still could not make out the lettering on any of the engraved labels underneath the controls on the telephone switchboard. Using the electric light was out of the question. It would be seen for miles.

He sat down at the switchboard, fumbling until his

fingers found an operator's headset. He fixed one earpiece over his left ear, leaving the other ear free to listen for the sound of any intruder, official or otherwise. Leaning forward, he peered at the museum-piece before him. A vertical bank of jack sockets confronted him, each labelled. These would be the local lines to the phones on the airfield. He peered more closely, but still could not read any of the labels.

Nothing for it. He struck a match and held it aloft, taking in the array of plugs, sockets, lamps and switches. The lettering on the vertical board leapt into life as he recognised the line to the fuel depot, the customs office, the fire station, and his own line. He didn't need to plug in a local termination, though. Below the vertical matrix of jack sockets wired into the local extensions lay a fearsome tangle of patch cords. He hoped he would not need those either. Somehow, he had to connect the operator's headset to a trunk line so that he could contact the High Commission. He located the switch used by the operator to monitor calls already patched in. The match flame was about to singe his fingers. He blew it out and struck another, examined the circuits available, then struck a further match before he could be certain how the operator switched into a trunk line. 'Simple when you know how,' he thought. 'Lusaka, here we come!' Crossing his fingers in the hope that there would indeed be a distant operator on duty at the High Commission, he chuckled with nervous anticipation and began dialling.

British High Commission, Lusaka, Zambia

Lieutenant Colonel Sir Stewart Gore-Browne, DSO, an honoured guest at the British High Commission reception, was holding forth about the rights of the African in his native land. He had championed those rights for virtually thirty years. Although he now lived quietly at his estate, a slice of England transplanted into Africa, Sir Stewart was widely recognised as a founding father of the new nation. A respectful audience had gathered around him, hoping for the chance to plagiarise any pearls of wisdom that might be sprinkled before them.

Elsewhere, the dinner-jacketed musicians of a 1930s-style quartet rendered standard numbers from their wartime repertoire, as High Commission staff, guests from the Commonwealth, esteemed ambassadors from friendly nations, prominent settlers, their wives and assorted ancient relatives, together with members of trade delegations, squeaked in patent leather footwear around the parquet dance floor. The socially pretentious hoped to encounter Mary, the Princess Royal, who was representing Her Majesty the Queen. Those who had met that lady before hoped to be spared from repeating the experience.

Younger members of the High Commission staff had gathered into an energetic flock that spilled out on to the lawns. Their conversations revolved around the exquisitely shocking music that had begun to erupt from the city of Liverpool. The whole reception had started to gain an uproarious life of its own, and a din to match.

Somewhere a telephone was ringing. Although there were several direct private telephone circuits terminating in the communications room, the High Commission's public telephone system was operated from an obscure cubby-hole, not quite under the stairs, but inadequately ventilated, and inferior in every other way. The duty telephone operator, somewhat deafened by the music and the growing volume of the conversations in progress, had excused himself and wandered out into the gardens for a cigarette.

For the first ten or fifteen seconds, most of those within range failed to hear the clamour of the bell, whilst those who did hear it ignored it. For the next ten to fifteen seconds, they were divided between indifference, expecting the operator or some other servant to answer the instrument, and distraction. After all: 'it could be important; shouldn't one answer it, or something?' Eventually, the pressure became too great. A junior trade secretary – a grammar school chappie from Ipswich or somewhere – detached himself from the group and headed for the telephone room.

"Uh – hello? British High Commission here..."

"Thank God for that. I was beginning to think there was nobody at home. Squadron Leader Maxted here – RAF Ndola. I need to speak to the governor-general, urgently."

"Oh, well, he's rather tied up at the moment handing over to the new High Commissioner. There's an official reception going on. I daren't interrupt him. There's royalty here and everything. Government delegations – the lot!"

"Look, I don't care if..."

"Sorry, you'll have to speak up; it's getting terribly noisy here. Could anyone else help?"

"All right – unless you're the senior air attaché yourself, you'd better go and find him for me, right away."

"We don't have an air attaché any more, if that's what you said. There's a military attaché though." The youngster had begun to raise his voice. "I'm only a junior trade secretary. Maybe you'd better tell me what it's all about in case we get cut off. It might take me ages to find him."

At the words *military attaché* a near-by Chinese railway engineer assumed a devoted expression, fixed his eyes upon Sir Stewart, stopped listening to him, and strained to pick up the junior trade secretary's words.

The conversation was not going quite as Maxted had

pictured it. Maybe the midnight dash would have been a better option in the first place. Much against his sense of discretion, he over-rode his self-imposed security constraint and decided to give the trade secretary an expurgated version of events.

"Okay – first things first. What's your name?"

"I'm Robin Hunter."

"Right, Robin, this is top secret... This is what I want you to tell the military attaché: A Valiant took a heavy landing at Ndola... It can't fly out again... It's damaged something called a Yellow Sun... It's very very serious... We need help... We need to guard the aircraft and the Yellow Sun... Now, who's the military attaché?"

"Colonel Roberts."

At the other end of the line, Maxted's heart was sinking fast at the thought of involving the army. This Colonel Roberts probably wouldn't understand anything about aircraft or nuclear weapons.

"Right. Go and find Colonel Roberts, and don't breathe a word of this to anyone else."

"Let me see if I've got this right." But Maxted's 'shut-the-fuck-up!' was drowned by massed jollity from the lobby outside the telephone room. "Squadron Leader Maxted, Ndola, Valiant, damaged Yellow Sun, need guards, top secret, right?"

On hearing the phrase '*top secret*', the railway engineer's characteristic inscrutability suffered a severe momentary lapse. He became goggle-eyed, looked at his watch, apologised to a Zambian transport-minister-to-be who had helped him to gatecrash the event, then excused himself from the festivities.

"Just get Roberts!" In the control tower at Ndola sat a man with his head in his hands.

In the lobby at the British High Commission, Robin

Hunter set off to find the colonel. Less than a minute later, the line went dead. Maxted tried to re-connect the call. His repeated attempts failed to have any positive outcome.

Ndola Airfield

Maxted knelt on the hangar floor, shaking Creswell's shoulder and hissing in his ear. "Look, it's a complete balls-up."

"Uh?"

"I spoke to the High Commission, but even if the message gets through, I don't think this Colonel Roberts is going to understand it properly."

Creswell rubbed his eyes and groaned. "Typical..."

"We're running out of time. Someone's bound to come looking."

"Okay – we'll fling a tarpaulin over it for the time being, then." A pause, while Creswell's senses returned to him. "Are you going for 'Plan B'? The midnight dash?"

"Right now, I don't see another option. If we could siphon a few petrol tanks, I might make it to Lusaka in the Land Rover by breakfast time. Then I could speak to the governor-general and this Roberts pongo, contact the MoD on a secure circuit and get things moving."

"Okay then. Give me your office key and I'll take charge at this end. Listen – when you get through to the MoD, make sure you speak to Air Commodore Dickie Purdham." Creswell waved his hand at the bomb. "He's the brainless wallah whose idea it was to send us here with this bastard on board."

"Purdham, yeah. I won't forget that name in a hurry." Maxted shuddered. "Only one thing, Tony – I hate the bloody taste of petrol..."

"You've tasted worse on mess nights."

Eight

Early Saturday Morning, 24 October, 1964
Cape Town Harbour, Republic of South Africa

The elegantly-named *USNS Pvt. José F. Valdez*, abbreviations, dots, accents and all, had arrived in Cape Town harbour on the 22nd. Just over 6,000 tons, no seafarer could ever have mistaken her for anything other than American-built. With her small wheelhouse squinting through circular portholes from beneath the shade of the full-width monkey-island and with her profusion of derricks, she was a time-traveller from a bygone era. But although she looked every day of her twenty years, she was well-maintained, and many a first mate would have given a month's leave just to have charge of a vessel with so few signs of rust.

But the *Valdez* appeared to suffer from a split personality. Whilst between the bridge-front and the stern rail she gave the impression of a true American merchantman, for'ard she posed rather a puzzle. Where, in a vessel of this size, one might expect to see the coamings of perhaps four or five hatches standing up above the main deck, here there were none. There were instead a couple of deck-houses and a large number of ventilators. And set into the ship's sides were several round portholes. It seemed that people were living and working in the places where one might have expected to find her cargo stowed.

Officially, the *Valdez* was an atmospheric research vessel. Then again, sometimes the story went that she conducted hydrographic surveys. But you didn't need all those whip aerials and a hundred US Navy Communications Technicians below deck on either a cargo ship or a hydrographic survey vessel. Though it was an official secret, she was a spy ship, a gatherer of radio signals traffic, a processor of electronic intelligence. However, with the *Valdez* visiting Cape Town about once a month in full view of merchant ships from every quadrant of the globe, it was a fairly open secret. The other give-away, of course, was that from stem to stern everything was painted navy grey.

But just because she was in port, chained to a buoy inside the breakwater and the time was now after midnight didn't mean that all was quiet on board the *Valdez*. No sir! Down below, radio watch-keepers tended the banks of scanning receivers, searching for suspicious transmitters to become active. It could be Cuban revolutionary soldiers infiltrating the Congo from the east. It could be Soviet aircraft already in the Congo or on their way there. It could be the Soviet embassies in Kampala or Cairo. It could be the Chinese legation in Lusaka or Lourenço Marques. It could even be the bloody British.

So, when a known Chinese frequency somewhere in the 9-megahertz band began to tune up, the auto-scanners alerted one of the CTs. He located a vacant monitoring position, spun the tuning control to match the target frequency and flicked the tape machine to record. He listened, fine-tuning the receiver to sharpen the signal. An oriental voice began to go through the process of locating the right person at the far end of the radio circuit. The CT plugged his headphones into the piped channel monitor to see whether he could find the mainland Chinese end of the conversation, hoping to strike it lucky. Maybe it was one of those channels that the *Valdez* monitored permanently and was recording already. Now he had the oriental voice in one ear and the piped channels in the other.

Still with the other end of the circuit un-discovered, the

CT heard a word – a non-oriental sort of word – the word 'valiant'. The voice halted. Somebody must have asked the speaker to repeat it because he said it again – 'valiant'. He went on for a while, then used the words 'yellow sun'. Wow! Curious! Now the CT had found the paired channel where speech on one circuit matched silence on the other. He noted down the exact time, together with the paired frequency, and called for an interpreter.

"Put it on tape for me, buddy," said the interpreter. "I'll take it away and review it. Oh, and dee-eff that channel to give us a clue whereabouts it's coming from."

"Pretty sure it's the Chinese embassy in Lusaka."

Once the recordings had been delivered to him, the interpreter lined up the two tape-decks and listened in to the 9-megahertz voice channel, noting down the timing breaks between transmit and receive. He didn't pay full attention to what was being said. The first job was to check the periods of speech and silence for the responding channel, to make sure the two were an exact match. There had been quite a long lead-in while someone tried to locate a military expert in China. That was fortunate; it had made it easier for the CT to pick the right channel from the many that were being monitored. Once the interpreter was sure that the tapes were synchronised, he tee-ed up the two tape decks again, marked the starting positions and began editing a composite tape with both halves of the conversation correctly interleaved. It was at that point that his pulse-rate stepped up a couple of gears. It wasn't what the Lusaka gook was saying, but what the Peiping end of the circuit was asking him to do.

In Chinese: "We think that 'valiant' is an English bomber. You also mentioned 'Ndola'. We know it's got a big airfield. Did it sound like the plane had crashed or was it just some engineering problem that meant it couldn't fly? How did it sound to you?"

"I don't think it had crashed. That would have been big news. We'd have heard about it. But an aircraft with a technical problem? That makes good sense. Yes, it could easily be that. I heard the Englishman say 'top secret' and then I guessed there was something they needed to guard."

"You said 'Yellow Sun'."

"That's what I heard."

"Can you put the political secretary on the line?"

A pause, then some verbal fumbling as the military man in China and the communist party official in Lusaka began their exchange.

"There's a strong possibility that an English aircraft has arrived at Ndola with a nuclear weapon on board. The railway engineer heard the gweilo at the embassy use the words 'Yellow Sun'. That's a codename for an obsolete atomic bomb. Do you understand?"

"Yes, I think so. Keep going."

"Maybe you've heard? A week ago, our scientists tested a fission bomb for the first time."

"Yes. It was reported in the newspapers here."

"But what we need to do now is to learn how to build the more powerful fusion bomb – a hydrogen bomb. Without it, the world will still take little notice of China. We think that at the heart of the English Yellow Sun is a hydrogen bomb. And right now, a Yellow Sun is sitting at Ndola. And we know it's virtually un-guarded because the English are panicking. If we can get a look at it – maybe even copy parts of the design, it could save us years of research... Do you see how important this might be?"

"Do you want me to get a look at it?"

"No – we need an engineer. There's too little time, so unless you can think of somebody else, it will have to be the railway engineer."

"Mister Guo – the one you were speaking to?"

"Yes, him. Listen... We need to get an hour or two to examine that bomb without being disturbed." A detectable change entered the voice of the speaker in China. From its initial deep urgency, its timbre now rang with the higher notes of both hope and anxiety. "My first thought is this: Do you know any Zambian officials who could persuade someone like a local police inspector to either provide a guard for the aircraft or arrest the aircrew, so they're out of the way? Is there somebody in Lusaka that you can trust? Someone we are... er, looking after, like a senior policeman, an army officer, a government minister?"

"One or two. There's a junior Minister of Police who's greedy for power and anxious to please. He's nobody, but his wife is the daughter of a tribal chief. That's how things are still going to work here for a long time, I'd say."

"That sounds ideal." The interpreter noticed a sigh from China, audible relief that with time so short, the speaker would not have to think up an alternative plan. "As long as he has the weight to give orders to the local authorities." Then a new thought: "Can we trust Guo?"

"I'm sure we can. This whole thing is happening because he took the initiative."

"Fine. But the English won't stand still on this; there's no time to lose. You've got to get Guo and this minister to Ndola right away."

"Yes. As soon as we've finished talking."

"I'll be quick. Unless you have a better idea, you need to get a car as soon as possible. Get somebody to fix that. Then you need to contact this junior minister. Bribe him if necessary – whatever it takes. What time is it over there?"

"It's just after midnight."

"And how far will you have to drive?"

"It's over three hundred kilometres. But there's a chance we could make it before dawn."

"Good. I think you and I are done now. Just put Guo back on the line. I'll make sure he understands what he needs to do."

04:30; Jadotville Highway, DRC

Nobody had slept well. At odd times during the night, a leopard had come close to the camp, making its rasping grunting cough. The whole idea of lighting a fire for safety, or of collecting thorn bushes to make a circle within which to sleep had become impossible in the total darkness. Collecting firewood was something one did in the daytime, not at night. At around 3:00 a.m. the leopard approached again, making a sound like a carpenter using a heavy saw in a timber yard. Du Plessis called everyone into action to move the jeeps closer together, top and tailed, engines running, with their lights shining in opposite directions. They heard no more from the leopard. As the first glimmer of dawn light began to disperse the clouds in the eastern sky, he gathered half the troop into a token stand-to, then ordered the remaining men to load up the kit.

Breakfast was a depressing affair. Du Plessis briefed the platoon about how the two jeeps were to stay in radio contact until he said otherwise. Then he tried to describe the objective to them. Intelligence said the area consisted of a wide area of open ground surrounding the mine entrance, with some slightly higher tree-covered rocky outcrops half a kilometre behind. His intention was to overwhelm any personnel at the mine using the two Minervas in leapfrog fashion. One party would provide covering fire for the other if they came under attack; but only if. They needed a live prisoner.

Creswell had had the good sense to station a crew member outside the hangar. Not that he thought it would do much good to have an unarmed man on sentry duty but, certain now that he faced a court-martial, he needed to prove that he had taken the obvious precautions. As an unintended consequence, the presence of Flight Sergeant Hardaker outside the hangar door also helped the travellers from Lusaka to locate the place they were looking for.

"Are you in charge here?"

Fatigued beyond measure, Hardaker had been slouching against a stack of wooden crates. He might even have dozed for a second or two. He looked up into the eyes of a well-dressed African civilian, perhaps thirty years of age. The fellow had the air of someone who was accustomed to enjoying the deference of others. Behind him stood a uniformed police officer, slightly older. At a respectful distance waited a group of policemen in a variety of incomplete uniforms. At least two of them had ancient rifles slung over their shoulders.

"No." He appeared to think better of his response. "No, sir."

"Then I've no wish to seem jocular, but would you take me to your leader?"

A look of resignation spread across Hardaker's face. Out-gunned, out-numbered and with few apparent alternatives, he flipped the latch and tugged the door outwards.

"Follow me, sir."

The two Africans picked their way into the hangar behind Hardaker. Deeply asleep, Creswell lay slumped against one of the main undercarriage wheels. Hardaker knelt in front of him, placed his hand on the officer's arm, and half shook, half massaged it.

"Two gentlemen to see you, sir," he murmured in a low voice.

"Terry? What's up? Oh God, I thought I'd told you to let nobody in."

"Didn't have a reet lot of choice, sir; they've got guns. I hoped it'd be all reet. I think maybe Squadron Leader Maxted's got through."

"Uh – okay." Creswell squirmed to his feet, smoothing his hands over the creases in his tropical gear, to little effect. His uniform cap was nowhere in sight, but he saluted nevertheless. "Squadron Leader Creswell, sir."

"Squadron Leader – good morning to you. I'm the Minister of Police here in Zambia – Laurence Chipokwe – and this is Inspector Makondo. We're here to help." He turned from the waist to survey the scene. "Your men seem very tired. Perhaps we should start by taking them to an hotel to sleep or eat or clean up? I've got a squad of policemen outside who can stand guard, now."

"Er … thank you, Minister. I'm grateful for the offer. It's most welcome, but I'm not sure I can allow that to happen."

"I'm sorry, Squadron Leader. You're obviously very tired too. Let me explain and set your mind at rest. I've come from the High Commission. Your squadron leader – Maxwell, Maxted or some such? – has reported what's happened. I'm not party to all that's been said, but your government and mine are keen to avoid any further diplomatic embarrassment. The British government has recognised that what they asked you to do was quite reckless. Not your fault, I know." Chipokwe paused to add weight to his next remark. "But with good will on your part, I'm sure we can find a way to smooth things over… And to keep you and your men out of jail." Without taking his eyes from Creswell's the minister nodded towards the Valiant and the device lurking close by. "I presume that object over there must be the bomb – the Yellow Sun?"

Creswell already suspected that he had no worthwhile cards left to play, but he felt uneasy about having to extend his complete trust to a stranger after an acquaintance of a mere couple of minutes. However, as the fellow clearly knew so much about the mission already, there seemed little point in denying it. All the same, his sense of caution urged him to remain reticent for a little longer, to see how much more Chipokwe would volunteer.

The African had another question. "Is this the aircraft that's been damaged?"

"She needs a thorough going-over, I'm afraid."

"And what about the other two outside? Are they loaded with bombs too?" Creswell stayed silent. Chipokwe raised one eyebrow, and served him a grin from beneath it. "Name, rank and serial number, eh? I don't blame you."

Creswell looked down at his feet and the minister's chin rose by a couple of millimetres. The bottom of the corrugated iron door scraped on the concrete floor as one of the African policemen pulled it ajar to peer inside. Scattered around the hangar floor, one or two aircrew stirred. If he was as smart as he sounded, it would take the minister no more than ten minutes to confirm how many bombs there were. This was not the sort of information that could remain secret for much longer, especially from armed men.

"Two bombs, Minister. The other aircraft is a tanker."

"Well, we need to get to work, Squadron Leader. *Tempus fugit!* Let me make my proposal again: Your men deserve proper rest if they're going to perform the flypast at Lusaka later today. I suggest an hotel straight away. What do you say?"

"Minister, please don't misunderstand me. I mean no disrespect, but unless you're carrying orders addressed to me personally that relieve me of my command and place me under yours, I believe I remain in charge here. What happens to my men, my aircraft and anything inside them is my responsibility. I'm sure I shall have to answer for it pretty soon, but that's my position."

"Very well said." Chipokwe appeared to consider matters for a moment, then reached inside his tailored jacket and took out a metal card case, stainless steel or perhaps even silver. He handed a visiting card to Creswell and gave him a few moments to inspect it. "Please give me a little credit, Squadron Leader, but I hope you'd agree with me on one thing at least... It would be a tall order for a confidence trickster to rattle off a few visiting cards at dead of night in the middle of Africa on the off-chance of running into an RAF officer with a couple of atomic bombs that he'd prefer to keep quiet about."

Creswell felt quite overtaken by the rate at which this encounter was developing, and was temporarily lost for words. Perhaps the minister interpreted this as obstinacy, for he now escalated his attack:

"So, forgive me for knowing that you were sent here to put on a flypast at our Independence celebrations. Forgive me too for pointing out that on this, the day of our nation's birth, Britain has effectively committed an act of war by sending you here with the power to destroy two major cities." Chipokwe glared pointedly at the Yellow Sun, whilst taking a deep and noisy breath. "While we're about it, you'd better forgive me for taking the trouble to offer you and your men our hospitality, which you seem keen to reject. Forgive me also if I appear to have jumped the gun – I expect your orders will drift along, perhaps forty-eight hours from now. Forgive me in the meantime for relaying your government's instructions, which seem very simple indeed." His delivery now changed to a slower speed and a more melodic tone, as if he were explaining matters to a half-wit for the tenth time. "One: unload the bombs and place them in a secure location until help arrives. I see you've unloaded one already. Good. Two: permit Zambian forces to guard the bombs, and defend them against all threats until help arrives from Britain. And Three: maintain a semblance of normality by performing the flypast with as many unarmed airworthy aircraft as you can muster at the scheduled time."

A handful of African policemen had pushed through the hangar's side door, attracted by the spectacle of a black man administering a dressing-down to a white. The speech also disturbed those aircrew who had still been asleep. One by one, they rose to their feet in a gesture of support for Creswell, their stance and expressions making it clear that they stood ready to share the consequences of the blame that the minister heaped upon him. Creswell attempted to lick his lips, but his mouth was dry and his stomach was empty. What wouldn't he give for a mug of tea right now? The seconds ticked away.

"Squadron Leader," said Chipokwe in a low, conciliatory tone, intended for his ears only, "This is unfortunate. I hadn't meant to take you by surprise. You and your men are clearly exhausted. I've relayed your government's orders. Why don't you brief your men on your position and give me your decision in five minutes? But we haven't got long. The sun is almost up. Soon there'll be hundreds of people about. We need to act quickly to shift that second bomb inside this hangar, so we can concentrate our defences around them both, not split our forces."

"You keep saying 'defend'. Defend against who...

whom? What's the threat?"

"Well, Zambia's neighbour to the south for one. I'm sure Mr Smith would love to embarrass your new Socialist government. Then there's our neighbour north of here. The border with Katanga is less than ten miles away. Imagine if Tshombé should get his hands on your bombs – or even worse – a raid by Olenga, Gbenye, Mulele – even Cuba! There's your threat, Squadron Leader. You're unarmed. You can do nothing. I'm here to protect these weapons until your stupid politicians and generals can remove them from my country."

As the senior officer, Creswell felt obliged to remain formal, not wishing to be the cause of further diplomatic offence. "Minister, thank you for your consideration. I'll take a few moments to brief my men as you suggest, and give you my verdict shortly." He felt that sounded too starchy. "But we're not a committee. It'll be my decision alone."

Chipokwe inclined his head toward Creswell, stepped back and, turning on his heel, walked the few yards to where Inspector Makondo stood. The aircrew moved forward, clustering in a semicircle around the squadron leader.

"Okay, you buggers," said Creswell. "We all knew we were in a jam, but here's how it looks now. I say 'looks' as I can't prove any of this. Chap over there says he's the Zambian Minister of Police. Here's his card." He passed the evidence to the first man on his right. If it was a con, it looked like a highly professional one.

"He says he's come from the High Commission, and that Maxted's got through. He seems to know about the accident, the bomb over there, the flypast and such-which. He's got armed backup and we can't even muster a pea-shooter between us. I imagine security's pretty awful here, so word about our predicament is bound to get out. If he's right about Maxted, help should be on its way from home, but we've got to reckon twenty-four to forty-eight hours before it gets here. He says there's a risk of a cross-border raid by Congolese rebels. There'd be hell to pay if those bastards got their hands on one of our bombs." Creswell paused to add weight to his remarks, noting the grave expressions on the faces of the aircrew. "On the one hand, if Chipokwe is a bandit himself, he could kill us now and just take the bombs. As he hasn't done so, it seems likely that his story is true. This means he's our best chance of keeping the bombs from falling into the wrong hands. I don't like it much, but it's my decision. I'm going to accept his offer. If I'm wrong, then apart from that silly sod, Purdham, there's only my head on the block. Any questions?"

The aircrew from the three Valiants appeared to ponder the matter. Jonesy spoke first. "So what's he want to do? Bring the other bomb in here and mount an armed guard over both of them?"

"Sorry, yes, I should have said. He's relayed some verbal orders, which he says are from Whitehall. That seems to be his plan."

Terry Hardaker spoke next. "I don't see as how you've got much choice, boss. But what a fookin' turn-up eh? The uranium what's in this bomb probably come from t' Congo in t' first place. We might've even flew over t' mine on us way in. Be a right fookin' bugger's muddle if they was to nick it back again. Can't have that now, can us?"

06:20; Shinkolobwe Mine

The two-axle Mercedes truck that Jonas had obtained at Jadotville stood ticking over with the rugged precision of a

Tiger tank. Its faded green cab and bulbous bonnet contrasted somewhat with the dull red and black of the front wings and mudguards. The sides of the cargo bay had been painted brown so that it was hard to tell where the paint patches ended and the rust began. The prized sacks of rock occupied the forward end of the cargo area. The *muganga* and a dozen Simbas had arranged themselves and their few possessions as comfortably as possible, next to the sacks. Rising above each side of the rear bodywork, six rusted iron stanchions curved inwards to meet in an apex above the truck's centre-line. Fixed to this arrangement, a canvas awning formed a tent of sorts that would at least promise some respite from the direct rays of the sun. Above the awning an empty rack, half a metre high, would once have been used to carry extra people, parcels, bales and assorted livestock trussed or caged. A generous coating of light-brown dust overlaid every surface.

Chan was pleased to have Jonas sitting with obvious pride at the wheel of this, the workhorse of Africa and the Middle East. Lately Jonas had appeared uncomfortable at having been in one place for too long. His face showed genuine determination and relief to be on the move. Chan hoped he was looking forward to the journey to China and what that might mean for his country.

Behind the Mercedes, Hwang sat in the passenger seat of a Dodge pickup of far less character. A further six Simbas were clustered in the cargo bay. The plan called for Jonas to lead the convoy on the descent from the mine to the main highway. There would be a better view from the truck's cab, giving early warning of any police roadblock, however unlikely.

Chan thrust his hands into his pockets and faced eastwards, shifting his weight from left leg to right and back again, stamping as he did so. He had emptied his bladder five minutes before, and was anxious to get on the road. He walked away from the Mercedes, head down, and spoke to Hwang. "You ready?"

"You asked me that five minutes ago. And five minutes before that. Yes, I'm ready."

Chan glanced to the east once more. "The sun will be up in a couple more minutes."

"Are you still happy about these savages?" Hwang jerked his thumb backwards over his shoulder. "We've come too far to risk getting our throats cut."

Too far, indeed. "If Jonas is happy, I'm happy. He knows how to handle them."

"You still plan to abandon them once we get to the border?"

"I think so. This is a dangerous country all of a sudden. I'd rather have some extra protection for a few days, than none at all." Chan nodded towards the Mercedes. "Getting Jonas and the samples to China – that's the important thing."

Chan and Jonas had discussed their escape route in considerable detail, trying to anticipate as many potential pitfalls as possible. Their plan was to drop down into Jadotville and take the road to Elisabethville, where they would have two choices, depending on the state of the Belgian-made roads. If the word was that the road to the northeast was still in good condition they would head that way, eventually crossing the Luapula into Northern Rhodesia, newly independent as Zambia. Then they would make for the southern end of Lake Tanganyika and charter a boat to take them and their spoils north to the railhead at Kigoma. With Tanganyika very much under the influence of the Zanzibar Communists, Chan felt assured of a sincere welcome in that country. If the state of Katanga's roads, rebels or the river appeared unreliable, they would head south and make a covert crossing into the Zambian copper belt, then drive the much greater distance around the Katanga pedicle to finish up, once again, at the southern end of the lake.

Anxious not to wreck the enterprise by driving the convoy into a ditch in the half-light, Chan kept the vehicles waiting until the sun had crested the horizon, the top edge of its disk shimmering like molten steel. Now, as the dawn brought Africa to life, and before the baking sun washed out all its fiery colours, he gave way at last to his desire to be on the road. With a double slap on the truck's left-hand door, Chan signalled Jonas to move off, before running back to the Dodge. Jonas inched the Mercedes forward, clearly taking care to get used to the weight of the truck in case its handling should have changed under the new and precious load. He built up speed, moving away from their camp, rolling smoothly over the levelled earth of their bush road, through the low scrub, heading for the macadam surface of the Union Minière road, a kilometre away.

Although Jonas and Chan were quite different characters, they both possessed a sixth sense for self-preservation that was always on duty. The narrow track might lead ahead, smooth and inviting, towards its junction with the main route to the highway, but it lulled neither of them into carelessness. Each had the instinct of the true professional soldier. Chan felt confident that as the truck built up speed, Jonas's eyes would be moving in an unconscious search pattern – over the bonnet, left verge, left middle-distance, horizon, right side, bonnet again, his mind never ceasing to address two fundamental questions – 'If I wanted to attack the convoy now, where would I do it from?' And 'If I get attacked right now, what evasive action will I take?'

From the Dodge, Chan saw Jonas slow down to creep round a right-hand bend. The trees and thorn bushes grew thickly here on their wide hilltop. As the bend unwound, the first proper view of the plain emerged. But, with the trail descending gently for a clear half kilometre ahead, Jonas brought the Mercedes to a halt. Obviously, something was not right. Chan halted fifteen metres behind the truck and watched as Jonas opened his door and swung out, standing as high as he could with one foot on the floor of the cab, one on the door hinge.

Chan trotted forward. "What's happened?"

Jonas switched off the engine and knocked the truck into gear to hold it on the slope. "Dust rising, see? Someone's coming." A moving, slanted wisp of dust drifted up in the middle distance, where the main Shinkolobwe road should be. He tilted his head to one side and listened.

"What do you make of it?"

Jonas screwed his face up in uncertainty. "Could be two jeeps, maybe three. Hear it? High revving – I'd say petrol not diesel. Police? Soldiers?"

Chan skirted around the front of the Mercedes and clambered up the right-hand side of the cab. He sat on the roof, cupping his hands behind his ears to catch the sound. There was no question. Jonas was right – it meant trouble.

"Come on – let's get back into cover. I'll get Hwang to reverse around the bend. You follow him and block the road with the truck, sideways on. Hopefully, they'll stay on the good road and just go straight on up the hill. If they turn off and come this way, they'll only be fifty metres from you before they spot you, so they'll be taken by surprise."

"Then what?"

"If they look official, you and the Simbas just blaze away at them. Shoot to kill. I'll take my Kalash as well, for safety, and run on ahead to see if I can spot them as they pass. Any that escape, I'll finish off as they retreat down the road past me."

Jonas was already climbing back into his cab: "Okay – let's move!"

Chan raced back to brief Hwang. As he grabbed the Chinese-made Kalashnikov from behind the driver's seat, his words brought a look of terror to his colleague's face.

"Enemy sighted, Hwang! Don't just hang about! Get into the driving seat and reverse a hundred metres back around the bend. Move!" Chan slammed the pickup's door and trotted back towards the Mercedes. Jonas was already reversing towards the Dodge, putting pressure on Hwang. Chan turned, ready to yell instructions at Hwang again if necessary, but his colleague was already in the left-hand seat. The Dodge bucked as he found reverse gear and engaged the clutch with more urgency than finesse.

Chan estimated that the dust plume had been almost a kilometre distant. But the advancing trucks had to cope with the way in which the road swept left and right, climbing steadily between long 180° bends. He reckoned he had to cover five hundred metres in less than two minutes. He broke into the pace of a quarter-miler. At least it was downhill. Thank the gods he was wearing proper boots this morning. He concentrated on his breathing. Now into a good rhythm he lengthened his stride, eating up the distance to where their side-road met the main route. He hoped to avoid a gun battle. The jeeps would emerge from the last hairpin bend just as Chan's side-turning was revealed. The chances were that they would speed past, heading straight for the mine.

Seventy metres to go – maybe fifteen seconds at this pace. He needed a good place to take cover, to check the jeeps as they powered past. Now he could differentiate between two engines – two jeeps – as they flew along to his left, behind the scrub. There! The perfect place! Five metres to go, dive across the drainage gully, rotate in mid-air, land shoulders-first on the clump of tussock grass, protect the weapon, keep rolling and come up on all fours, then lock solid behind the thorn bush. Don't move a muscle. Count in your head: 'and one and two and three and ...'

The whining four-cylinder engine propelled the first jeep past the junction and on up the incline. Two gweilos in the front, four in the back. Nobody looked to the side. These people were amateurs – no, not even that good. 'Four and five and six and...' The second jeep sped past. Only one person looked into the side-road, without apparent interest. But Chan could see these people were not tourists.

Jonas had been waiting in the back of the wagon with his weapon cocked, following the progress of the jeeps by ear. They were not coming closer, but seemed to be still surging uphill towards the mine. He jumped out of the truck and trotted forward on the inside of the bend, careful to keep in cover. Four hundred metres away a figure was loping uphill towards him in the centre of the road. From the clothing, height and with the weapon in hand, it could only be Chan. Jonas jogged back to the frightened Hwang. The poor fellow was clutching his assault rifle, clearly desperate to avoid using it.

"Chan's on his way back. I don't want a sound, so don't start your engine – we'll free-wheel downhill on the brakes and pick him up. Follow me."

Little more than a minute later, Chan, now panting, was squatting on his haunches against the front wheel of the Mercedes lorry.

"Twelve white men in uniform... Two jeeps... Looked

new... I reckon it's the Belgian Army... They all had FN rifles... They mean business; we've got to get out of here!"

"Okay, Chan. Jump up into the cab with me – we need to work out a new plan. Those guys will be after us as soon as they've talked to the miners. Hwang – you follow on. We'll coast downhill for another kilometre. Remember – don't start your engine before I do."

"The way I see it, Weifeng, the miners must have heard us talking about heading down the road to Elisabethville. They've no reason to keep quiet when the Belgians question them. Once a few cigarettes or a bottle of whisky changes hands, the soldiers'll be right on our tails."

Chan sucked his teeth, then gave an ironic smile. "Even the best of plans may fail to survive its first contact with the enemy..."

"So, what do you reckon?"

"Flexibility – that's the key. Do the unexpected. Once we hit the highway, we head north, then take the first road northeast to get off it again as soon as possible. It's the shortest way to Lake Tanganyika – maybe seven hundred kilometres. Avoid Zambia altogether."

Jonas took his eyes off the road and stole a glance at Chan. "We never planned to go that way. We wanted to get out of the Congo as fast as possible. Now you're saying we should stay in the country all the way to the lake. And another thing – we don't know what condition the road will be in."

"No – but with those people on our tail we've got to do the unexpected. Hitting the lake at Baudouinville looks like our best chance to escape, now."

"Baudouin. King of the bloody Belgians. It's time they re-named that town."

"Don't worry. They will. Have you got a better idea?"

"No." Jonas gripped the wheel harder and fixed a scornful glare on the road ahead. "Seems you were right. We might need the *muganga* and his men after all."

≈

Corporal Du Plessis's Land Rover burst on to the open area where the macadam surface gave way to graded mine tailings. The driver swerved left and braked violently, skidding to a stop. The recruits sprang out of the jeep with marked enthusiasm, obviously intending to make their first experience as potential targets as brief as possible. Four seconds later, Vermaak's crew launched on to the stage at 50 kph, accelerating and sweeping to the right. The element of surprise was in their favour, but Du Plessis knew how easy it would be to sacrifice it. In a mere twenty seconds at these speeds Vermaak would be over three hundred metres away. At that distance, over open sights, an enemy soldier became a small target. Even for an experienced marksman, this would make it difficult to provide accurate supporting fire.

Du Plessis's section had scarcely reached their cover positions before he was calling them back. In combat situations he always trusted Vermaak's judgement. His friend seemed to be pressing home his advantage, not stopping as they had planned. From his forward position he must have assessed the threat to be low. Du Plessis took a left-flanking approach and, a minute later, half-spun the jeep in a tight turn and a shower of gravel to face back the way he had come, finishing twenty metres from Vermaak's Minerva.

Vermaak had dispersed his riflemen to cover the four points of the compass. The two corporals gazed at the mine, trying to take it all in. A concrete ramp about a hundred metres long descended into the earth before them, shored-up with a robust rock wall leaning back some fifteen degrees from the vertical. At the far end of the ramp, a crater disturbed the flat surface of the concrete. The rusted steel reinforcing bars curved up and outwards around its rim. The rubble scattered to one side gave the impression that the crater had been caused by an eruption from the depths. Ranged around it, three or four un-armed Africans stood facing the mercenaries. Others stood close to a pile of yellowish rock half way up the ramp. The speed of Vermaak's arrival had achieved its objective. Du Plessis watched with amusement as each African's expression changed from shock to guilt.

"Hey, Johannes! Keep your rifles out of sight for a minute, man. Don't want to scare these guys even more." Then Du Plessis lifted a packet of cigarettes into the air, raised his voice and shouted to the Africans: "*Hey! Mes Amis! J'ai des cigarettes! Venez ici!*" But they showed no inclination to accept his offer. He tried a few words of Swahili: "*Mimi ni ndugu.*" He waved the cigarettes again. "*Unataka sigara?*"

"Friend, huh?" laughed Vermaak. "How long have you been a friend to Kaffirs? Bet you five dollars they'll come up here for me." Then he also hollered out to the Africans. "*Kuja hapa – sigara! Sigara!*"

"Ask them if anyone speaks French."

"*Unasikia Kifaransa?*"

The miners refused to move for Vermaak either. Du Plessis made a ribald comment about how Johannes's infamous reputation still appeared to be a sordid subject in that part of Africa. Then:

"Hey Danny! Come over here a minute." Du Plessis seemed pleased that by now Daniel knew enough to move forward with his rifle in hand, rather than the unwieldy radio. "Now you're learning. You seem a smart kid, Danny. What other lingoes do you speak?"

"Schoolboy French, Corp. A bit of Afrikaans, some Shona, some Swahili." Although Du Plessis had introduced himself as Jacobus, he could see by the way that Danny looked slightly sideways at him that the boy felt uncomfortable about using his name. Maybe he just needed more time to feel part of the unit. A bit of enemy action should help.

"We're in the same boat, then." Du Plessis turned to Vermaak. "Listen, Johannes. Danny and me are going down the slope for a bit of a parley with those guys. Keep us covered without making it look too threatening, will you? Don't want to frighten them, or we'll never find out what they know." But as he called Danny forward to walk down the concrete ramp with him, Du Plessis unclipped the flap of his holster as a precaution.

Half way down he waved to the miners. "*Hey, mes amis! Peut-on parler avec le chef?*" Then, as he and Dan neared the first of the Africans, Du Plessis held out the packet of cigarettes. This seemed to break the ice. The miners broke ranks and pressed forward, arguing with one another. Du Plessis tried to cool things down. "*Hey, hey hey! Attendez. Qui est le chef?*" A rather short gentleman, wiry, grey and given to a vigorous manner with his elbows emerged at the head of the melee.

"*C'est moi. Vous donnez les cigarettes à moi.*"

"Not so fuckin' fast, *mon ami. De l'information pour commencer, et alors les cigarettes.*" The corporal looked around and pointed at the crater. "*Qu'est-ce que vous cherchez dans cette grande fosse?*" The African rattled off a rapid expression at one of his minions, flapping his hand at the heap of yellow rock, waving him away. With his eyes on the cigarettes, the underling detached himself from the group and trotted over to the pile. He picked up a book-sized chunk and hurried back. He held it out to Du Plessis, who took it and immediately dropped it, amongst great peals of laughter and thigh-slapping.

"*C'est très lourd, monsieur le Capitaine, heh?*"

"Très bloody lourd indeed, monsieur le chef. Hey, Danny. Pick that up and tell me what you make of it."

Danny stooped to grip the rock, then whistled. "Phew! It feels heavier than lead." He dropped it on the ground again. "You say the major wanted us to bring back some samples from the mine? This'll be what he's looking for. I've never lifted anything as heavy as this – well, I suppose I mean 'dense', more than heavy. It must be the ore of some kind of really heavy metal. What do you reckon? Gold?"

"No, I shouldn't think so. I worked in a gold mine once, down south. Gold comes in narrow seams; you can see it glittering in the rock. If you crush the ore, you can see the tiny flecks of gold. This isn't gold."

"What about lead, or mercury? It's got to be a heavy element if you think about it. If it was light, like aluminium or something, a piece that size wouldn't weigh anywhere near as much as this stuff."

"Eh man – 'element'? Where d'you learn words like that? You really are a clever kid, eh. Maybe mercury, then. I had some mercury ointment once – that was yellow."

Du Plessis turned to the ring-leader. "*Hey, monsieur le chef... Qui veut acheter ceci?*" The African simply mimed the action of smoking a cigarette, making it clear that the mercenary's credit had run out. Du Plessis made a show of patting all his pockets, then put on a pantomime expression of sudden inspiration, clowning around to show that he was no threat to the miners. For their benefit he kicked the lump of yellow rock, then spoke to Danny in

French. "Hey, Danny. *Portez cette pierre à nos amis, et retournez avec plus de cigarettes.*" They seemed to understand and watched him go.

Having shown good faith in his willingness to provide more cigarettes, Du Plessis tried to elicit more information through small talk. Whatever the real value of the rock that Danny had carried off, the workers clearly saw it as worthless, having given it away. It was even less likely to be gold. In simple French, Du Plessis tried again to find out who was the customer for the yellow ore. But the miners remained polite, though non-committal, until Danny returned with the cigarettes.

For a third time Du Plessis asked his question, but now in return he received a mime. The head man made play of washing his face, then spoke the words '*manjano ganda*' with a smile.

"What's he saying, Danny?"

"I think he said 'yellow skin'. Maybe he means he's working for a Chinese boss?"

On hearing the word, the miners made encouraging sounds to indicate that Danny had made a good guess. They seemed to be greatly enjoying the game and keen to prolong it. The head man now took both forefingers and pushed up the outer corners of the skin around his eyes, placing the matter beyond doubt. "*Ndiyo! Mbili Kichina mwanaume. Chinois!*"

"Two Chinese men, Corp."

"That's what the major wanted to know... Let's see if they're still here... *Monsieur le chef, où sont les Chinois maintenant?*"

"*Partis.*" He pointed over the horizon in the direction from which the mercenaries' jeeps had come. His comrades joined in, indicating the same direction, their deep voices and rapid speech combining indecipherably.

"Une semaine? Un jour? Une heure?"

The African seemed to be enjoying the play-acting. He gesticulated downwards with his right index finger, whilst nodding with excitement.

"Aujourd'hui? À quelle heure?"

Nodding even more furiously, the African licked a finger-tip, pointed to the sun and drew an imaginary line in the sky back a little way towards the eastern horizon; no great way at all.

"Cheesus! They've only just gone. *À pied? En avion? Cheval? Camion? Quoi?*"

The African crouched and mimed the act of sitting at the steering wheel, whilst bouncing up and down and growling to imitate the sound of an engine.

"De quelle couleur est le camion?"

"Toutes couleurs – Rangi nyingi – kijani, kutu, nyekundu, nyeusi."

"Danny?"

"We're looking for two Chinks driving a rusty lorry. Green, red and black."

Du Plessis needed to know one more thing. He handed over another pack of cigarettes. *"Monsieur le chef... le camion... c'est parti à destination de...?"* But there was no reply, other than the universal Gallic gesture of a shrug accompanied by upraised palms and down-turned mouth.

Corporal Vermaak fixed Du Plessis with a piercing look. "There's no easy answer to this, is there?"

"No, man. But we can't just sit around wasting time trying to work it all out. The major's going to be pissed off if we lose the initiative here. I reckon we've got to get after these Chinkies now and work out a plan while we're on the move."

"Okay, I'll jump in the same jeep as you while we head

back down to Jadotville. We can work it out together, eh, man? You and me... Like always."

Du Plessis acknowledged that this seemed like the best way to get started, and called the small band of men together. "Listen up, you guys. I need two good drivers, now."

De Witt stepped forward. "I can handle a Land Rover." An athletic-looking Southern Rhodesian volunteered that he had also been driving jeeps since he was ten.

"Yah, right. That's settled. Johannes and me are going to ride in the back of this Minerva with Danny. We've got some messages to send. I want one armed man in the front and one in the back here with us. And I want the rest of you with your weapons at the ready, keeping a sharp lookout. We're looking for two Chinese blokes driving a rusty lorry, red, green and black. And I reckon they're keeping a better lookout than you bastards. How do I know that? Because the old Baluba over there says we've only just missed 'em. De Witt – you lead off; we'll follow. And you bastards in the back, you just make sure you don't let him race away so fast that you lose sight of us. You can bet your butt that if we get separated, we'll come under attack. *Verstaan jy*?" Everyone accepted the wisdom of sticking together. "Right, mount up!"

"Okay, Johannes. Here's how it looks to me. From what the old miner said, we've only just missed these Chinkies – agreed?"

"Yah, man."

"But we didn't bump into them on the road up to the mine, so I'm guessing they must have heard us come screaming up the mountain, and pulled into a side road to let us go past." Vermaak nodded. "That tells me they're aware of us. Maybe they even spied us and saw the weapons. But they must have guessed we'd find out about them just as soon as we had a word with the Baluba guys. So not only do they know about us but also, they know we'll soon know about them, okay?"

Vermaak's brow developed a slight furrow. "I think I'm with you so far, Jaco..."

"Now, here's the thing. Remember who flew us down here? That Colonel Leitner? If he isn't US military intelligence or CIA then you can call me a Kaffir. This is no training mission – we're here working for the Americans. And when it comes down to a choice, money doesn't matter to those boys, just results. They want us to bring back as much info as we can about what's going on down here. Remember they said to capture some prisoners if we could? Think, man. We've got the sample and some photos, yah. But there's got to be an extra stripe in it for you and me if we can catch these Chinks and bring one back to Kamina for questioning."

"Yah, keep talking."

"Think, Johannes. Whatever it was that those guys were digging out of the ground matters a lot to both the Chinese and the Americans, right?"

"No doubt about it, man."

"Now, if you're mister Fu-Manchu with a lorry full of that stuff, and your government's desperate to get their hands on it, and the Yanks want to stop you – well... when you get to the bottom of this hill, which way are you going to run?"

"I'd head for Elisabethville and make it south across the border as fast as my wheels could carry me, Jaco."

"And I'd catch you and give your arse a good kicking long before you got there."

Vermaak's face fell. "What's wrong with that, man? It's obvious – there's something about this rock that isn't kosher, right? 'Fu-Manchu' wants to get it out of the Congo *vinnig*."

"But he knows you're on his tail. For Christ's sake, we only came along that road yesterday. It's a fine road, but remember those long straight stretches? He knows we could spot him from miles away. And what about those long hills? He knows we're much faster in the jeeps, especially on the hills. Okay, he can still sneak off into the elephant grass or hide in a native village if he gets too panicky, but that gives us the chance to leapfrog him. Then we'd just set up road blocks and stop him that way. He won't go southeast."

For several seconds Vermaak stared ahead at De Witt's jeep weaving its way down the mountainside. He seemed reluctant to keep playing a guessing game that he could only lose. "What's your idea then?"

"I don't think he'll go to ground in Jadotville. Like we said, he wants to get out and he can't afford the risk of staying in one place. He daren't abandon the lorry. Once we find it, we've likely found him as well, see? And he won't head northwest towards the mines at Kambove and beyond. It's another long road – makes it more likely we'd catch him. And all the time he's heading deeper into Katanga, not escaping."

"Yah, man. But all you're doing is trying to second guess his double bluff. For us, this game's easier to lose than to win. Just cut the crap and tell me where you think he's going."

"He'll skirt round Jadotville and head north."

"Aw, Jaco. Don't make it so difficult. *Hoekom*?"

"Why? Well, first of all, he'll gamble we go with your first guess and head southeast. Second, the Simbas are killing whites up in the north, so he'll feel safer knowing we'd prefer to avoid the place. And it gives him the best chance to escape across Lake Tanganyika – it's maybe only fifty K wide. Once he's on the other side he's on friendly soil, gone for good."

"Yah, man – but the lake's got to be eight or nine hundred K from here. He knows we'd catch him easy."

"Which makes it a great double bluff, eh man?"

"You don't want to maybe split forces and send one jeep towards Elisabethville and the other one north, just in case?"

"Nah, these young recruits here are still green. Think of the casualties if a single jeep got ambushed. I don't want to lose you, man."

"Okay, but don't forget about this: The wet season's long gone. The Luapula and the marshes will be drying out. What if he makes a quick dash east from Elisabethville? He could be in Northern Rhodesia in no time." Vermaak had a point. Despite occasional evidence to the contrary, he was not stupid. Now it was Du Plessis's turn to look uncertain.

Even though the road was in good condition, the Land Rover swayed and bucked as the Rhodesian boy kept station with De Witt ahead. Hanging on to one of the Minerva's grab-rails, Du Plessis moved his feet further apart for more support. Maybe it was better for somebody else to make the decision.

"Anyway, we've got to go north to get back to Kamina. It's still the best bet. Let's see if Danny can get a message through and leave the final decision up to the major or Leitner, eh?"

On hearing his name, Daniel looked up at Du Plessis. The corporal had kept one eye on Dan's face during the conversation with Vermaak, and reckoned he had taken in the whole situation.

"Have you been listening in to those radio schedules I

gave you?"

"Yes, but there's been no messages for us."

"Okay Danny, let's get on the R/T. We'll give them a progress report and see what they want us to do about Fu-Manchu."

"Sorry corp' – didn't you know? This set's only got short range R/T, like for staying in touch between the two jeeps over a couple of miles. That schedule you gave me? The way it works is I've got to send long-range messages in Morse to this spy-ship, and then keep listening at the proper times until a reply comes through."

Nine

Saturday 24 October, 1964; 07:55
Ndola Airfield, Zambia

Following Chipokwe's ultimatum, Creswell's shoulders had drooped, as if physically weighed down by the burden that fate had laid upon him. He knew it, and hoped that nobody had noticed. What the men needed now was to feel confident that their man was still in charge. He filled his chest, and his shoulders opened out once more.

"Okay, lads; this is what we're going to do:" All eyes focused on him. "Noddy and I will stay here for a while to supervise off-loading the bomb from my aircraft, like Whitehall seems to want. Thinking about the display over Lusaka later today, I'm standing some of you down to go and take a rest break. For the flypast the two co-pilots will fly my aircraft. You two tanker boys will crew your own as before. I want Terry to stay here and look after the electronics, assisted by the armourer and the flying spanner. That means ten of you can go straight to the hotel for forty winks, shit, shave, shampoo and shower, but no alcohol, right? Flight crews need to be back here to get ready for the flypast – say three o'clock this afternoon. Any questions?"

"What about the flight-plan to Gan?"

"Thanks, Jonesy. Noddy and I will work on that while you're away."

"Roger, boss."

"Nobody else?" There were no takers. Creswell cleared his throat, then hailed Chipokwe.

"Minister! I'm ready to accept your offer. I'll release ten

of my men to go to the hotel, just as soon as we've agreed on how Inspector Makondo's policemen are going to mount guard." Chipokwe looked up, clasped his hands behind his back and wandered across in a nonchalant fashion.

"Guard duty, Minister," said Creswell. "What I recommend is this: No access for airfield personnel along the side of the hangar where you came in, or anywhere near the main doors at the front. And I want a perimeter established around both Valiant aircraft outside. From what I can see, you don't have enough men to do that, so the question is – how soon can you get more policemen or soldiers here?"

"I see, Squadron Leader. Thank you." Chipokwe turned towards Makondo who stood a short distance away with his squad. "Inspector! We're going to need more men on duty here. I suggest you make arrangements to accommodate ten airmen, and return as soon as possible with reinforcements." The policeman saluted the minister with parade-ground precision and, avoiding English, spoke to his sergeant in Bemba.

"Minister, Inspector – there's more. I need all four pilots and both navigators back here at three o'clock, to get ready for the flypast. You can fix that, can you?"

"Yes sir, baas," agreed Makondo. "I fix it from my HQ."

"Ho-o-old on a minute. If you're going off with my chaps, who'll be in charge of your men? I need to be sure they know what they're doing. Do they understand English?"

Chipokwe touched Creswell's forearm. "I'll look after that side of things."

And after a short hiatus while everybody sorted themselves into groups, Makondo led the party of aircrew away through the side door of the hangar. Though they were intent on taking a well-earned rest, there was clearly enough energy and morale remaining for some spirited banter aimed at the men left behind.

"Hey! You buggers," called Hardaker to his colleagues as they trooped off. "Boss said no drinkies, mind." No matter what the circumstances, it seemed that Terry Hardaker would always have the last word.

With the departure of two thirds of his detachment, Creswell's false dynamism descended again into a temporary lull. Hardaker and the other technicians stuffed their hands into their pockets and looked around, taking stock of their surroundings, searching for some tool or abandoned piece of equipment as a diversion from their bewildered feelings. Two or three of the remaining policemen left through the side door, presumably to mount guard.

Left to himself, Chipokwe began to pace around the hangar. After a while he crouched beneath the stricken Valiant's fuselage and gazed up into the empty bomb-bay. Next, he transferred his attention to the crew access door on the port side and peered into the cabin. His curiosity then drew him towards the Yellow Sun, though he refrained from prodding or patting it. He wandered away, using slow, deliberate, measured steps and he massaged his chin, clearly deep in thought.

At length, he stopped pacing and looked at his watch. "Squadron Leader?"

"Minister?" Creswell took a couple of steps towards him.

"Time," he stated, raising a finger to make the point. "Time is of the essence. It waits, as I understand it, for no man. Look, there's no telling how long it will be before Makondo returns with more men. I was just thinking...

Your orders say that you've got to unload the bomb before carrying out the flypast. But this bomb-bay is so low that an ordinary flatbed lorry wouldn't fit underneath it. So it's obvious we can't unload the bomb from the other aircraft without a special sort of trolley or something..." Creswell gave a polite grunt of assent. "...And it would be foolish to just lower the thing down and leave it lying out there in the sun." Chipokwe paused to allow Creswell to follow his thinking. "How about if we made room by towing this aircraft outside, then brought the other one in? Then we could unload the second bomb inside here, away from prying eyes. That way, both bombs would be secure and under cover, and the flypast could go ahead with two aircraft, not just one."

Creswell and Blyton faced each other. Chipokwe's unexpected suggestion had merit. Creswell raised one eyebrow. "Minister... I believe we were both thinking the same thing."

Ndola City

Makondo had been able to squeeze the ten RAF personnel, plus himself and four police guards, into two vehicles. Two of the guards were armed. The police Land Rover, being an open vehicle, was less cramped than the second vehicle, a twelve-seater Ford Thames minibus. It was therefore with mixed emotions that the aircrew greeted their arrival at what appeared to be a cement-rendered fort, rather than an hotel. It was a relief, particularly for those who had travelled in the minibus, to be able to unfold themselves and to fill their lungs to full capacity once more. However, it was not a relief for the crews when the police guards circled around them, making threatening movements with their rifles.

"Inspector! What is the meaning of this outrage?" It sounded inadequate, a powerless protest from a bygone imperial age.

"Please sah! I do not want to have to shoot anyone. Move inside, quickly please."

"This doesn't look like an hotel to me!"

"No sah," said Makondo, without apparent irony. "This is the jail." He made a signal to one of the guards, an assenting nod in the direction of the RAF officer. The guard struck the officer in the kidneys with the butt of his rifle. "Move inside, quickly please."

08:55; British High Commission, Lusaka

When Maxted arrived at the British High Commission, it was not in the condition that he expected to find it. There were signs of recent revelry, although, to be fair, the debris was being gathered up. He approached the front entrance, but was prevented from entering by a Royal Marine sentry who asked to see his identity.

"Certainly, Corporal. I'm Squadron Leader Maxted – RAF Ndola. I should rather hope the governor-general and Colonel Roberts might have been expecting me."

Roberts's name caused the Marine to lighten up a little. "Let's just see if your name is on the list, sir." The Marine consulted his clipboard. "You don't appear to be on the list, sir." He held it out for Maxted to see. "You know it's a Saturday?"

Over the previous twenty-four hours, Maxted had had other things on his mind. Whilst those events had not caused him to forget that this was the weekend, he declined to take exception to the Marine's polite reminder about what day of the week it was. However, since the taste of petrol had still not left his mouth, and feeling worried, tired, hungry and thirsty he was not at his most agreeable.

"Look, Corporal... I'm in the middle of rather a crisis, I'm afraid. I'm sorry we couldn't have arranged for it to happen on a weekday, but that's life I suppose. Mind you, it's lovely to stand here having a chat – glorious morning and all that. I rarely see a white face where I'm stationed, so I don't get anything like enough social contact. However, I rather fancy the governor-general will want to see me. So if I promise not to run off and try to sneak in through the bathroom window while your back's turned, why don't you just pop inside for a couple of seconds and make two phone calls. Press the red button or whatever you have to do, and tell His Excellency I'm here and will see him now. Then call the kitchen and get me a large mug of tea please, milk, no sugar, with toast and marmalade – I've been on the road all night."

"Only doin' my job, sir."

The High Commissioner-designate apologised to Maxted for the slight security obstacle that he had encountered, pleading the comfort and safety of the Princess Royal. It seemed fair to assume that she still lay asleep upstairs in the Blue Suite. Maxted, however, felt no rancour on this account. Security was effectively his business. He liked to see it working well. He formed the impression from the gentleman's tone that he normally employed a hearty voice, but that this was being kept very much in check to avoid disturbing Her Royal Highness.

"So you see, when young Hunter couldn't find Colonel Roberts, he came and found Sir Evelyn and me instead. Neither of us could understand your message, and when we eventually found Roberts, he wasn't in such good condition. By that time, the telephone had gone dead so we couldn't speak to you anyway. Still, you're here now..."

"Did anyone speak to the MoD last night?"

Though a first-class diplomat of many years standing, he failed to find a watertight answer to this question, staring for a few moments at Maxted through his heavy-rimmed spectacles. Maxted met his gaze with the rare confidence of a man who has successfully averted a nuclear disaster. The High Commissioner-designate's clipped, traditional moustache twitched and he smiled, giving the impression of a benevolent schoolmaster.

"Still, you're here now," he echoed, his voice tailing off. "We are where we are, I suppose. I'm happy to make this a top priority, but it's inevitable that I shall get drawn away by the ceremonies as the day unfolds. But I trust by then, you and Roberts will be on top of the situation... I suggest you both deal with the Deputy High Commissioner on this. He'll have more time than I will. I'll ask him to keep me briefed."

Maxted hoped his thoughts could not be determined from his face. "I suppose it's a long shot, but what do you say about trying to locate Air Commodore Purdham via the MoD?"

"I imagine it'd be faster if you knew which golf club he belonged to. It *is* a Saturday, you know."

09:50; Ndola Airfield

Chipokwe had invited himself into the cockpit of WP198, showing a boyish interest in the baffling array of knobs, dials, switches and levers. Although he made it appear that Flight Lieutenant Blyton had granted him a great privilege, there was nothing timid about the way he claimed the adjacent seat during the tow. He managed to control his fascination during the power-up sequence and when Blyton reached forward to the left-hand side of the centre console to operate the bomb door control switch, Chipokwe looked away, feigning a sudden curiosity with the console panel on his own side of the cockpit. With an initial whine and a final clunk, the bomb-bay doors closed. Once the aircraft had been towed outside, Noddy and Chipokwe transferred to the second bomber. The airfield tug manoeuvred it back into the hangar, leaving the broke-back Valiant standing next to the tanker aircraft. To all appearances she was still a pristine flying machine, a testament to advanced British aeronautical engineering. In truth, thirty-five tons of scrap metal.

The hangar doors stood wide open, with Creswell and Blyton standing together inside, a little way back from the centre. An ancient dust-sheet now screened the damaged Yellow Sun from view. The police Land Rover returned, followed by the minibus. Each executed a wide sweeping turn, and parked at the side of the hangar doors, not obstructing them. Makondo hopped out of the jeep. Chipokwe moved forward to greet him. They exchanged a few words, after which the minister clapped Makondo on the back. Both gentlemen seemed to be in good spirits. In unison, the two Africans lifted their heads, looking directly towards Creswell and Blyton.

Full daylight had already brought clarity to the landscape. Now, with that one look it seemed to Creswell that the two Zambians had taken on the manner of a pair of predators weighing up their prey, and in that instant Chipokwe's scheme became clear too. An expression of horror crossed the squadron leader's face. He turned away to hide his shock and hissed at his colleague, "Noddy! I need a word." Blyton still clutched a hammer, which he had been using to detach the tow bar from Creswell's aircraft. With slightly exaggerated movements and a louder voice than necessary, Creswell continued, "Just drop your hammer on the workbench and let's clean up a bit, eh?" Then he lowered his voice and whispered, "Follow me. This is urgent."

Conscious that his actions already looked suspicious, and uncertain of the amount of time he would have for explanations, Creswell began to hiss at Blyton as soon as they had walked the first few paces. "Noddy, I've dropped the most frightful bollock."

"What's up?"

"I haven't been thinking properly. Remember what Maxted said last night? He reckoned he ought to be able to make it to Lusaka by breakfast time. Well, that means he's probably only been there for about an hour even now. So Chipokwe's story is impossible. They could never have met at the High Commission. To have turned up here when he did, Chipokwe might even have left Lusaka before Maxted left here."

"Oh bugger! But how could he have known to come here?"

"I've no idea. I've been a prat, Noddy. I mean – it's classic Agatha Christie. Only we're not struggling to fill in a missing ten minutes here. The timing's a good six hours adrift and I never spotted it."

"Come on, boss. Nobody spotted it. We were all shagged out. We'd all been thinking about something else – if you remember." They reached the workbench. For effect Noddy threw his hammer on to the steel surface with something of a clatter. He picked up a handful of cotton waste, rubbing it across his palms and between his fingers, then turned to face back towards the hangar doors. Whilst Makondo directed his police guards in the act of closing the doors, Chipokwe was ambling towards the two officers.

"What do you reckon? What's Chipokwe's game?"

"Shhh! He's coming this way."

"Ah, gentlemen... A slight mix-up, I'm afraid. The Customs and Immigration people need to see your passports. I'm sure we can straighten it all out in a few minutes, if you'd just like to follow me."

"Minister, I was just wondering if you could clear something up for us." But the moment had arrived before Creswell had been able to rehearse his approach for luring Chipokwe into a verbal trap. The fellow was probably too cunning to fall for it anyway. "Er... how long do you reckon it would take to drive to Lusaka from here?"

"Well, it'd be faster to fly!" Chipokwe chuckled at his little quip.

"No, seriously. How long?"

"Well, it's two hundred miles you know, and the road can be dangerous. You have to be careful about passing even the slowest trucks. Traffic seems to wander all over the road. If you didn't take a break, you might get there in less than five hours – or it might take all day, especially if there's been an accident. Why?"

"Oh, well it's just that I can't see how you could possibly have met Squadron Leader Maxted, because he only left here around midnight last night. That means he wouldn't be in Lusaka before – say – five o'clock this morning at the earliest; and you got here around dawn."

"Did I say that? I'm sorry if I gave you that impression."

"So what's the explanation, Minister? You got here very quickly..."

"Your Squadron Leader Maxted is a very resourceful man. When he left here, he found himself driving past the main police headquarters in Ndola. Clever man. He stopped and used the telephone. The High Commission informed my government, and they sent me straight here." Chipokwe cocked his head on one side and gave a reassuring grin. "We probably passed on the road without even knowing it. Meanwhile, the authorities worked out what had happened and what to do about it. When I arrived in Ndola, I went straight to the police station and telephoned Lusaka. They filled me in with all the details and here I am. It's quite simple. You're right. I never met Maxted."

"But you said..."

"What I said and what you heard are possibly two different things. If you remember, when I walked in, you were fast asleep. It's not surprising if your memory of those first few seconds is different from what actually happened."

"You said you'd come from the High Commission."

"I *mentioned* the High Commission, that's true. But Zambia is an independent state now. I wouldn't have been sent here by the High Commission – I couldn't, in fact. Clearly my government and yours must have had contact at the highest level. As soon as they realised the importance of what was happening, they sent me here, like I said." Chipokwe shook his head. "But I would never have told you I'd come from the High Commission."

The explanation sounded very plausible. However, Creswell was unwilling to accept that his memory had misled him. He tried another approach. "But why – I'm sorry, I mean no offence – why did your government send the Minister of Police when this matter is so obviously a military matter? I should have thought it would be more appropriate to send the Minister of Defence."

"Oh, Squadron Leader, I do advise you to steer clear of politics. Believe me, you would not want Zambian soldiers trampling all over this affair. This way is better. I can keep things much quieter. Your government and mine were very determined on this point."

Frustrated that he had no credible counter-argument to Chipokwe's suspected lies, Creswell failed to prevent his distrust from spilling over on to his face, a factor that the minister could no longer ignore.

"My dear Squadron Leader..." Facing Creswell, Chipokwe spread his arms wide and splayed his fingers openly. A warm smile blossomed over his face. "I can't keep calling you by your rank. I introduced myself as Laurence – please call me Laurence – we're going to need to work together for a while yet, before this problem is solved. What do you say?" He held out his hand. To refuse to accept it would have been a declaration of war.

"Laurence... Call me Tony."

Chipokwe's smile mushroomed into a wide grin and he clasped Creswell to his left shoulder with one Savile Row-tailored mohair arm. "Let's go and sort out this matter about your passports, Tony." With his free hand he beckoned Blyton forward and, enfolding him under his other arm, he led the officers away towards the Ford Thames minibus.

Twenty feet away, Flight Sergeant Hardaker turned away and addressed the armourer. "I were standing right there when he said it. 'I've come from t' High Commission,' he said."

"And then there were three."

"Aye."

10:08; USNS Pvt. José F. Valdez, Cape Town Harbour

After the first few silent radio schedules, the communications technician had not expected there to be any activity on his watch. Hell – it was a Saturday! When the message came through, it was good Morse – easy to receive and not enciphered. Plain language was always more interesting than code.

```
REPORT SMALL SCALE LOCAL OPERATIONS
RESUMED STOP AM NOW IN POSSESSION OF
SAMPLE VERY HEAVY MERCHANDISE STOP
LOCAL WORKERS UNAWARE OF VALUE STOP
JUST MISSED CONTRACTOR STOP ASSUME YOU
KEEN CONSULT MR REDLAND BUT AM UNAWARE
HIS DESTINATION STOP CONSIDER UNLIKELY
EVILLE OR JVILLE OR ROAD NORTHWEST
STOP POSSIBLE REDLAND PLUS ONE
COLLEAGUE MAY HEAD EAST TO ZZZ BORDER
STOP BELIEVE BETTER CHANCE REDLAND
TAKES ROAD NORTH THEN TURNS EAST
DESTINATION LAKE TTT STOP AM HEADING
NORTH HOPING TO INTERCEPT STOP ROAD
SPLITS AT LUAMBO STOP QUERY MY NEXT
ACTION STOP NORTHWEST RETURN TO KKK OR
NORTHEAST IF SIGNS OF REDLAND STOP
AWAIT YOUR INSTRUCTION STOP
DUPLESSIS ENDS
```

The CT acknowledged receipt and signed off to Danny's call-sign. Standing instructions said that anything received from that station had to be relayed straight back out to Kamina. He spun the dial to re-tune his receiver to Kamina's transmission frequency for that date and time, then flicked to a different crystal, held the key down and tuned his transmitter to the scheduled calling frequency. The operator at Kamina must have heard the howl of the circuit going live, because he answered with that hour's call-sign after only the first signal.

The CT passed the message and got an acknowledgement, a 'QSL'. Since the message had ended with a request for guidance on whether the sender should return to Kamina or head into the bush in pursuit of this Mr Redland, he decided to keep monitoring the circuit in case there should be an immediate reply.

The CIA had equipped Leitner's transport aircraft as a flying radio station so, shortly after the *Valdez* message came in, a copy lay in his hands. But no matter how much he might have wanted to send a message straight back, authorising Du Plessis's patrol to pursue codename Redland, his terms of engagement were clear. As yet, Leitner commanded no troops of his own on the ground. The only armed Western forces were Hoare's mercenaries, under Vanderwalle's control. Any message to the patrol would need to arrive under Vanderwalle or Hoare's authority. For Leitner to forge a reply would have had profound effects.

"Well, you guys can see the signal. This codeword 'Redland' confirms it's a Chinese operation and this reference to a sample of 'heavy merchandise' suggests to me that they've been mining for uranium ore. There was only ever one reason to open up Shinkolobwe anyway, and that was it. Colonel Vanderwalle, Sir, I must request you to give permission for Du Plessis's detachment to pursue these two Chinese and, if possible, to take them prisoner."

Vanderwalle turned to face Hoare. "Major, there are ten recruits out there. None of them has yet seen combat. They signed up to join your force and are on... er... a training exercise. This is, I admit, one of the more unusual training exercises that I have seen. I believe it has now achieved its purpose. Would you give us your appreciation of the situation?"

Hoare recognised the role that the United States could play in his campaign. The C-130, of which he had none under his own command, could give him the ability to deploy his troops with great speed and surprise over long distances. He did not want to risk losing the good will that might make that possible. He could also see the extent of the bad blood between Vanderwalle and Leitner. Clearly, Leitner still viewed Vanderwalle as nothing but a uniformed grocer, and resented any need to partner with the man. Hoare decided his best approach was to try to act as a bridge that would allow the two men to meet in the middle, in support of each other's individual missions.

"Colonel Leitner, sir, you know very well the size of the job that I have to accomplish with the limited number of troops under my command. Losing ten volunteers and two experienced corporals would make rather a dent in those numbers. I've got a few reservations about your proposal. In my place I imagine you'd have exactly the same ones. Will you hear me out?"

"Sure, Major – go right ahead."

"Well, I've already told you my first problem – I can't afford to lose fighting troops on a side operation that doesn't contribute to achieving my objectives. The problem is that even if I were convinced that pursuing two Red Chinese should have a high priority, I can't replace those troops quickly. As you know, a week from today – November 1st – we start operations, beginning with the advance to Kindu. If those recruits don't join the first push, they'll be no use to me for the rest of the campaign. They won't feel part of it. They won't get the early experience and the old hands won't accept them."

Colonel Leitner had done a fair amount of soldiering of his own; he nodded.

"The second thing is practicality. This training exercise was only provisioned for the journey from Elisabethville to Shinkolobwe and then back to Kamina. Jadotville to Kamina is the best part of 300 miles, maybe just top side of three-forty when you add in the diversion to the mine. If my men take a detour at Luambo to chase these two Chinese, every mile they go means two miles less fuel in reserve. Pretty soon we're going to have a supply problem."

"I don't want to give you a worry on that score, Major. I can promise to air-drop whatever they need, wherever and whenever they need it. And fast."

Hoare was impressed with Leitner's initiative. No telegraphing for permission, no requisition slips, no bullshit from a fat quartermaster sergeant in regimental stores – just whatever it took to get the job done and no questions asked. "I hoped you'd say that, Colonel, and I'm grateful. But my other main reservation is over the quality of the intelligence. Du Plessis and Vermaak are my men, and I'd rely on them a hundred percent if and when the shooting starts. But they're infantry corporals, not intelligence officers. As far as I can see, there are half a dozen other perfectly sensible routes that the Chinese could have chosen and we've got no information about why Du Plessis thinks they've picked the one that says 'go north'. Although I don't suspect the rebels of being able to co-ordinate much of a classical campaign, if I permit this sideshow it plays into their hands. It's a gift. It draws some of my combat troops away. Tactically, maybe that's even what the Chinese intended."

"Thank you, Major. I can't disagree with anything you say. But we both know this Simba crisis is a proxy war. We think the people standing behind them are Cuban, and the people standing behind *them* are the Soviets or, more likely, Mao. So, whichever way you look at this, you're going to be fighting the Chinese a week from now. And why? Because this country in general, and Katanga in particular is the most mineral-rich slice of real estate on the whole planet. Independence struggle – baloney. This is economic warfare – possession and denial of strategic materials. This ain't no sideshow. This Shinkolobwe thing is the best example of what it's all about." Leitner timed the pause to perfection. At the point where Hoare was about to reply, the colonel spoke again. "Let me cut you a deal, Major."

"Okay, I'm listening."

"If Du Plessis gets to Luambo and there's no sign of Redland, he comes straight back to Kamina. But if he's guessed right, he carries on pursuing the Chinese. If that involves a detour away from the Kamina highway we allow him to run them down for up to forty-eight hours and re-supply him by air. Okay so far?"

"Keep going."

"Two days outbound detour, plus two days back to the road, plus at the most, a day and a half's driving from Jadotville to Kamina still gives Du Plessis a whole day spare to be back here in time for the push to Kindu. I say we get a *sitrep* out of Du Plessis after they've been on the side roads for forty-eight hours, and the three of us take a 'go/no-go' decision. If we decide Redland's trail has gone cold, we pull Du Plessis back. What do you say?"

"It's not the worst offer I've ever heard."

"You've got a good radioman out there, Major. If you ordered Du Plessis to send a report every six hours, we might even be able to co-ordinate some offensive air support and cut things even shorter."

Hoare needed some support of his own. He looked across to Vanderwalle. "Colonel?"

"We know what we've just agreed. Draw up a signal, Major, and we'll all sign it."

11:25; Ndola Airfield

With its now familiar scraping sound, the rusty iron side-door of the hangar opened, to admit Laurence Chipokwe and two armed policemen. The minister called out to Makondo in the local language. In turn Makondo gave an order to his men, some of whom moved to close off any potential avenues of escape. Chipokwe strolled towards that small group of men, the remnants of the flight crew. Inspector Makondo followed, an ancient Webley service revolver in his hand.

The minister spoke. "I regret the necessity of asking for your surrender, gentlemen, if that's not too old-fashioned a term. I'm placing you all under arrest. I'm afraid this means you must all be handcuffed. If you shout or try to escape, there will be no alternative, other than violence. I should like to avoid that." He pointed at Hardaker. "I'd like you to be first."

Useful as Makondo and his men had been, Chipokwe now viewed their presence as risky. The more the Inspector saw, the more complicit he would become. For both their sakes he wanted to avoid that. The fewer who knew the truth, the better.

"Inspector, I'm grateful for the help your men have given in arresting these people. The British had no right to send these men to Zambia with weapons of war. There are also irregularities with their passports, so they're here illegally as well. I think the best thing is for you to take these last three fellows away and put them in jail with their friends, until it can all be sorted out."

Makondo looked around, taking in the clean, white, low-slung aircraft and the curious great metallic object lying on the hangar floor. Chipokwe could tell that he knew enough to recognise a bomb when he saw one. It was what this sort of aircraft carried, after all. But the man was surely still ignorant of the nature of the bomb. Hopefully too, he knew nothing about the Chinese engineer who had followed Chipokwe's official vehicle from Lusaka.

"Yes sah, Minister sah."

"I'll stay here and see things through."

Makondo turned aside and formed up his squad of policemen, then marched the last remnants of the crew away to the waiting transport.

Chipokwe held out his arm with pride. "So, Mister Guo, here is the bomb ready for your inspection."

The railway engineer stepped forward and gently drew back the tarpaulin from the casing of the Yellow Sun. He stooped and opened his briefcase from which he extracted a clipboard, bearing a single page of handwritten notes. He then sat down on the concrete floor of the hangar, removed his shoes and socks and, taking a pencil from his briefcase, drew a wavy line through the first item on his checklist.

Chipokwe's eyes widened in surprise at the engineer's actions.

"A precaution," said Guo. "I don't have quite the right equipment, so I need to make sure the bomb isn't triggered by static electricity or anything like that." The minister's face registered shocked realisation at the perilous situation in which he found himself, followed by a degree of fear. "Don't worry – I have my instructions. We have just satisfactorily performed the first one, and survived." A Chinaman with a sense of humour.

Chipokwe attempted to regain a degree of control. "As you might imagine, Mister Guo, I can't read Chinese writing. I wonder if you'd just mind outlining your plan?"

"Certainly, Minister. It's very simple. First, I will inspect the bomb, all over. Then I will remove the side-plate and carry out the first proper safety procedure. There is some doubt over whether the bomb is battery-powered or whether there is a ram-air turbine..." He smoothed his hands over the shell of the bomb and over its blunt, dark grey nose, then poked the bomb with what seemed to Chipokwe to be a reckless contempt. "Perhaps the turbine is under here. It's like a little fan, with the blades driven by the flow of air as the bomb falls towards its target. It generates electricity. Whether it's powered by batteries or by a turbine, I shall have to disconnect the power source. Then I'll take as many photographs and measurements as possible and we can leave."

"Photographs? How? Surely it's too dark in here."

"I've brought plenty of flashbulbs."

"Is that safe? They're filled with magnesium, aren't they? They get very hot. Sometimes they explode."

The engineer was neither a physicist, a chemist, nor even a knowledgeable photographer. A worried look crept over his face.

Chipokwe reinforced his point. "We wouldn't want there to be an accident."

"I suppose my instructions *are* quite brief."

"Well," said the minister, rather unnecessarily, "you'd better be careful." And then with evident reluctance, "Do you need me to help?"

Guo shrugged and made the 'I don't know, but we'll see' face, before resuming his inspection. Within seconds he found damage to the two top-most tailfins of the Yellow Sun. He hunched over and stared at the hangar floor, then inched outward from the bomb. His aim seemed to be to divide up the hangar into sections and quarter the ground between the bomb and each of the hangar walls in turn. After a few moments he crouched on his haunches to examine two fresh holes chipped into the concrete floor and some equally fresh flakes of paint. He returned to the bomb and laid down on the floor, feeling underneath it with his fingers. A cheerful 'aha' signalled the fact that he had found a significant piece of evidence.

"Well, Minister. I think I understand the nature of the accident now." Guo got to his knees to explain. "The bomb is lying upside down. See these lugs underneath? That's how they hoist the bomb into the aeroplane. When the plane landed, the lugs snapped, the bomb broke free and when the bomb doors were opened, it fell out, tail first. That's how its tailfin got damaged. The plane's heavy landing must have dislodged the central section of the bomb's casing – see it's like two halves of a steel barrel – and it's also shaken out the bung in the actual explosive core of the bomb. The bung would be facing down, you see." He massaged the casing again. "Look – the hole is on the top now. If the plane had to go out on a bombing mission, the final thing the armourer would do would be to pull out the bung, catch all the ball bearings in a large tray..."

"Ball bearings? What are you talking about?"

"It's the failsafe mechanism. There are five hundred kilos of ball bearings filling the core of that bomb so it can't implode, even if the charges are set off accidentally. Once they've been emptied out, the bomb is live. The armourer then sets the airburst height on the radar fuse, winds up a clockwork motor..."

"A clockwork motor?"

"Yes. Then he re-fits the underside casing, and the aeroplane can leave."

"Incredible."

"Yes. See here... The armourer has even left his tools lying on the ground here after re-fastening the casing. Phosphor-bronze, too – that's good. I was worried about how to get these flush-fitting bolts out. See? Only special tools will fit them." The engineer checked his sheet of instructions and began to loosen off the bolts holding the panel in place.

"Mister Guo! Hold on a minute!" The engineer was just getting his fingers under one edge of the half-casing and about to heave the whole thing off. "Don't touch it. What if it's booby trapped?"

"Don't worry. Nobody would booby-trap their own atomic bomb. They wouldn't expect it to fall into the wrong hands for one thing. For another, there's always at least one booby on your own side who'll do things in the wrong order. Imagine that!"

But whether the bomb was or was not booby-trapped now became a matter of no consequence, for the casing half-shell was free and they both remained reassuringly alive. The minister helped Guo to place the steel clamshell on the ground, and the two men peered into the guts of the Yellow Sun with at least a temporary reverence. The engineer consulted his clipboard again, checked off a couple more of his instructions, then got down on his hands and knees for a closer look.

With the casing removed Guo could see that the innards of the apparatus were built around an alloy frame which consisted of two circular structures resembling cart wheels set fore and aft of the central casing. Stretching between them were several longitudinal bracing struts, to which the outer shell had been bolted. Mounted between the cart wheels was a spherical assembly, almost filling the air space within the casing. Several dozen regularly-spaced, saucer-like patches covered the surface of the sphere. Two cables issued from each patch and connected to the perimeter of a cylindrical object, the size of a wide, shallow cooking pot, fixed to one of the wheel-like devices.

Drawn, perhaps, by morbid curiosity, Chipokwe crawled alongside Guo but refrained from touching any of the bomb's internal components. As though he might be overheard, he whispered, "It's just like a giant football, isn't it? A football inside a cylindrical framework."

"Yes, I suppose it does look like that."

"Pardon me for saying this, Mister Guo, but I thought you were a railway engineer. Now you seem to be some sort of atomic scientist. Do you know how this thing works?"

"Only the basic details. There wasn't much time for me to find out a great deal. Apparently, a lot of small explosions happen at the same moment and bring about a huge chain reaction in the uranium. He tapped his clipboard. "But I've got some good instructions to tell me what needs to be photographed."

"I hope so. We don't want to waste any time. Your notes seem okay so far, don't they?"

"Yes – so far."

"How did China get this knowledge?"

Guo smiled. "First the KGB stole the plans from the British, then our people got a look at the Russian documents. That was when Khrushchev was helping us to build our own bomb. Later, he changed his mind. I don't know why." He passed a hand over his clipboard again. "These notes – they were dictated to me by one of our scientists who saw the plans. They're all he could remember about what was inside."

"An awful thing like this... It must be very sophisticated."

"I don't know... A simple idea in one way, but terribly complicated in another." Guo had been holding a screwdriver. He rested the tip on the concrete floor, leaned on the handle and turned to face Chipokwe. "That's why I'm here. A bomb like this – it's a very costly device, so the aim is to get the biggest possible explosion from it. They need it to go with a massive bang, not a squeaky pop. The

Americans and the British had to find the best mathematicians on the planet to work out a design to make that happen."

"I see."

"I'm a civil engineer, Minister. I do calculations every day, but the science behind a thing like this –" he pointed the screwdriver at the great sphere at the heart of the bomb, "– well, I wouldn't know how to start. I've just been told to get photographs of the things we're looking at now, and get out quickly."

Although he had professed a certain amount of ignorance, nevertheless Guo's instructions allowed him to keep up a conversation with Chipokwe. He explained that the sphere was hollow, with the outer surface constructed of explosive charges shaped over weapons-grade uranium. Then he pointed at the object that resembled a cooking pot.

"What you've got there is the firing switch. See how these cables are connected to explosive lenses on the outside of the sphere? When the bomb is triggered, they all go off at the same instant. Bang! It compresses the core. Critical mass. Chain reaction. Like I told you, the idea behind an atomic bomb is really quite simple, isn't it?"

"I've never had any reason to think about it." Chipokwe squatted next to Guo and peered into the cavity. "Interesting, though."

"The next instruction says to disconnect all the firing cables." Guo earthed his hands on the ground, took hold of an alloy bracing strut with both hands, released it and earthed himself again. With nimble fingers he proceeded to detach each of the cables, counting as he went; seventy-two.

Chipokwe rose and stood back, watching with growing curiosity as Guo disconnected the final fuse cables. Clearly, there was something on his mind. "It's not what I expected," he announced.

"What do you mean?"

"Well, this is supposed to be the ultimate top-secret weapon, wouldn't you agree? But it looks – I don't know – empty and ordinary. It's just a sphere in a drum with some cables attached. And it relies on clockwork, for heaven's sake. I mean, what do you suppose China's scientists are going to learn from the photographs? They won't tell you exactly how long the cables are, or what they're made of, or what explosive is used in these lens things."

Guo stood back and stared into the device. He seemed to agree with the minister's point. "Or the shape of the charges," he added. "Or how much uranium is inside the core, or what voltages are used – or anything, much."

"That's right," said Chipokwe. "Let me put a proposition to you,"

"We haven't got much time. I need to start taking photos."

Laurence Chipokwe was not exactly an instant evaluator. Things just had to take their time. But now he had analysed the situation and drawn his conclusions.

"The British aren't going to forget about what's happened here today. Once Lusaka finds out, this place will be crawling with government officials getting in the way. Troops, police, and soon British soldiers too, I shouldn't wonder. My career is over. Even though today is my country's first day of freedom, I can't stay to enjoy it." Chipokwe paused and gave Guo a meaningful look. "Too many people would work out what part I've played. I shall have to leave Zambia... Fast." Another pause. "So what I need is a way to stay alive. And a way to make enough money to enjoy life... into what we call a ripe old age."

Guo had started preparing his camera with the

flashgun attachment, but Chipokwe's announcement caused him to halt the operation. "I don't understand."

"Why don't we do something really worthwhile? See what you think of this: I watched what the pilot did when he moved this plane into the hangar. All the controls in the cockpit are labelled. It's the same inside the bomb-bay. Why don't I see if I can lower the second bomb? Then we could remove just the central sections of both bombs and crate them up to look like mining equipment or something."

Guo gaped, but Chipokwe's enthusiasm had taken hold. Now he was unstoppable.

"There must be other equipment under this grey cover too. You mentioned a radar fuse and a turbine or something. We could maybe even unscrew this firing switch and its cables. Those must be the really clever parts of the bomb. If we could remove those, and get them out of Zambia with the nuclear cores, well... China would be grateful, don't you think? They'd fix me up with a villa in a safe, warm country – Cuba, maybe – and enough money to live a good life."

The impossibility of continuing to live in Zambia and the implications of having to make a new life elsewhere seemed to strike Chipokwe. He became quieter, less idealistic, more rational. "That's what I'm depending on, Mister Guo. How quickly do you think we could detach those parts and get out of here with them?"

"Steal the bombs?"

"Why not? I've got nothing to lose now."

Ten

The nose in the air, the arrogant smile – clearly Chipokwe was feeling proud of himself. By remembering what he had seen Blyton do, and then manipulating the switches in the cockpit, he had managed to power-up the second Valiant's electrical systems and open the bomb doors. Using the ground-crew winch controls in the bomb-bay he had lowered the Yellow Sun to the hangar floor. During this operation Guo had dealt with all the bolts that fastened the nose and tail sections of the first bomb to its deadly middle. He had also unplugged the electrical connections linking the units. Together they tried to roll the tail assembly out of the way, but even getting the great cylinder to rock from side to side required considerable effort. They turned their attention to the centre section and tried to roll it, but it proved too strenuous a task for two men.

"Maybe it's already lying with its heavy side down," suggested Chipokwe, now an expert.

"Yes, but if we got it rolling, we might not be able to stop it so easily. We can't do this without help."

Chipokwe saw the part that he could play in solving the problem. "Mister Guo, I suggest that you stay here and unfasten everything that seems important. I'll take my car and find some casual labour, perhaps a carpenter as well, so we can shift the cores and build crates around them."

By mid-day Maxted had begun to feel light-headed through lack of sleep. This temporarily affected his judgment and emphasised the farcical stupidity of the situation. Roberts, who appeared to have nothing in his technical background to help him cope with the situation, extended the shambles by pulling rank and insisting that Maxted write out a short statement about the previous day's events at Ndola. Maxted played along with this bluster and officiousness, penning his summary in the hope that at least it might provide time-stamped documentary evidence for the anticipated court-martials. He also reasoned that if the colonel appeared slow off the mark, it probably had as much to do with a desire to keep his nose clean, as with respect for any standard procedure. After all, Roberts had probably lived his entire military life 'by the book'. But the whole idea was preposterous that the War Office could conceivably lay down a chapter in a service manual to handle the case when some poor chap arrived on foreign soil with a concealed atomic weapon and no means of taking it away again. Although tact and resourcefulness were required, tiredness and mounting frustration claimed the day. Pretty soon, Maxted felt himself slipping beyond acceptance of the ludicrous into the early stages of contempt. The time had come to be more assertive. He remembered his pet proverb: 'Assumption is the mother of all cock-ups'.

"I assume that we'll be able to speak to London on a secure line?"

"Afraid not, old chap. The scrambler gubbins has been out of action for a week or two."

Maxted gasped and cast his eyes upwards in an apparent appeal for divine intervention.

"No need to look like that, old boy," said Roberts. "Not my fault."

"Well, I'm just getting a bit pissed off with all of this. What do I have to do to get someone to take this seriously? We nearly had a nuclear disaster on our hands last night, and I should have thought that would have created the Jesus-Mary-Joseph and the effing donkey of a diplomatic incident. Now you're telling me we haven't got a secure way of shouting for help. I'd say I've got every right to look a bit grumpy. Haven't you even got some sort of government code book? So if I said 'Wimbledon' it would mean 'bomb' or something, then at least we could avoid saying 'broken bomber' or 'buggered-up atomic weapon' while the rest of the world is listening in."

Realisation that this whole affair was bound to result in a military inquiry dawned on Roberts's face. "No book of code-words that I know about, old chap... At least not for the techie stuff we need to pass up to HQ. We could always try sending an encrypted signal by telex, I suppose."

"Well, that'd be a start." Until they had made a plan, Maxted knew they were going nowhere. It might not prove to be the best plan in the long run, but as long as it looked like having a chance of success at the beginning, the important thing was actually to take that first step. "That half-page summary of mine – why don't you get one of the staff to cipher it up, then bang it out on the telex to London? Meanwhile we could call them on the open line and at least warn them they need to look out for it and de-code it pronto."

"Good plan, Maxted." It was a start.

12:55; Luambo, DRC

Du Plessis halted the small convoy on the southern

outskirts of town. Luambo had grown up beside the main highway linking Elisabethville with the capital at Leopoldville. The town had swollen to its current size because this was the point where the road to the northeast broke away – the road to Lake Mweru and onward to Baudouinville and Lake Tanganyika – if you could call it a road, that is. Du Plessis eased himself off the damp, sweaty surface of the horsehair-filled plastic seat cushion, climbed onto the bonnet, then stole a few more inches by standing on the spare wheel that was fixed there. There seemed to be quite a crowd of people ahead at the centre of town. The local market of course. He compressed his mouth into a tight slit, causing his breath to hiss as he considered the risks that he must take if he were to discover whether two Chinese had passed that way in a lorry. He already felt unwelcome here. That was it – apprehensive, like a tomcat that strays too far and finds itself in a dark and unfamiliar alley. He reckoned he was the equal of any man in Luambo in a fair fight, one to one. The trouble was that not only did these people detest the whites, not only did they outnumber his patrol on a vast scale, but they never fought fair. A simple gathering could so quickly change to a mob lusting for blood and scrambling for their machetes. That was not his idea of fair. Best to avoid provoking them. He glanced across at the fresh-faced recruits in Vermaak's jeep, sucked his teeth and called them to gather round.

"Okay men, you're going to need to keep your wits about you for the next fifteen minutes or so. We want to be out of here fast. If we stay any longer there's a risk that some Kaffir will fetch a gun and start taking pot shots. First thing." Du Plessis held up one finger. "We're here to get information. Anyone speak any Luba?" No takers. "Swahili?" Danny and two others held up their hands. "French?" The same people plus an extra two.

"Right then. When we get down there, keep listening all the time. If you hear anyone say anything that sounds threatening, sing out, and we'll be off like a rocket. If you think there's a chance that somebody could tell you anything useful, don't wait – ask them. Second thing." Du Plessis held up two fingers, keeping his thumb on the non-Churchillian side, facing inward, enjoying the obscenity. "Buckle your pouches, zip your zips, button your buttons and hang on to your weapon. These people will steal the skin off your teeth if you give them half a chance. Listen – your job isn't just to keep yourself alive, but right now to cover your mates on either side as well." Du Plessis felt there was far more that he could have said, but time was short. They would just have to do their learning on the job.

"Three." He held up a third finger the same way round as before, jerking all three upwards in a gesture that had no settled meaning. But they all knew what he was thinking. "These people may be pleased to see us, but I doubt it. Don't let them get too close, eh? Watch their eyes. Eyes tell you a lot. And if they start pressing in, keep a watch on what's happening at the back of the crowd. Look out for weapons. Anyone pulls out a machete and we're out of here. Anyone gets his filthy hands on your mate's SLR, don't wait – plug the bastard. Okay, my friends... Mount up!" As Du Plessis dropped back into his seat, he called out over his shoulder: "And don't let them see you're afraid." But all the same, he fingered the holster where his Smith & Wesson lay ready.

The two Minerva Land Rovers eased their way towards the centre of Luambo. Getting into a lively town was not normally a problem, as people were often engaged in their own business and only became aware of you once you had passed them. Survival today would depend on escaping before hard words could incite a fractious assembly into a hostile mob, bent on murder. Du Plessis and Vermaak knew enough to keep smiling and waving. By contrast the ten recruits had the air of being the appetiser course at a human sacrifice.

Du Plessis stopped a couple of yards short of the junction to keep his options open. Vermaak pulled up close behind. The sun had passed its zenith, but the day just carried on getting hotter. The majority of the market stalls lay in an open area west of the main road and opposite the turning to the lakes. For the most part, the buildings on either side of the road were all single storey huts with tin roofs. That was one less worry; the threat of being fired at from a second storey window would have made it even harder to watch for an attack.

As if a magician had conjured them up, small boys appeared, shouting and holding out their hands for *baksheesh*. People in bright colours surged around them, not yet pressing hard, mixed evenly between young and old, men and women. What did the eyes say? The women's eyes showed suspicion, not yet hate. The men looked at the rifles, firing covetous glances between the jeeps, the weapons and the recruits. Already the locals had an advantage – the young soldiers were scared witless. Some of the market's customers had been drinking, and not in all cases to quench their thirst. It was clear the mercenaries dare not stick around. Du Plessis would have to hurry.

"*Je cherche deux Chinois. C'est très important.*" He gave it a moment, but his words had little effect. "*Des cigarettes?*" They knew about tobacco well enough and he could see a flicker of interest. He could not decide whether they were genuinely ignorant of the French language, refused to use it because of the association with the Belgians or were keen to avoid displaying too much interest too soon. He disliked using his limited Swahili, but had little time and few choices. Searching for the words to begin a fresh opening gambit, he tried the *lingua franca*, rather than French. "*Mimi nataka mbili Kichina mwanaume.*" No reaction. His words had made them listen, though now they seemed to be gathering more densely around the jeeps. Keep looking at the eyes. "*Chinois – Kichina – manjano ganda* – which way have they gone? *A quelle direction sont-ils partis? Kichina kwenda wapi?*"

The throng pressed further in. Somewhere near the back, an African was trying to attract attention. He stood a head taller than the main body of the horde, shouting and waving his long arms. His words began to set off a murmur amongst the mass of people. Du Plessis could see from their elbows and the way the people at the front pushed back that some were getting anxious about the crush and wanted to move away. The native at the rear started pointing. Others took up the action, jabbing the air to indicate the building on the northeast corner of the road junction. A space began to open in front of the jeep's radiator grille. The circle seemed less intimidating, as if urging the party forward.

"Okay, let's be careful. Move ahead dead slow." Du Plessis motioned the jeeps forward about thirty feet then halted them again, still keeping the option to make a fast turn to the right or power straight ahead if the situation flew out of control. What was it that the people wanted him to see or do? It became clear that the group of townsfolk was excited about two males slumped against the wall of the corner building. They seemed to be asleep. An empty bottle lay on the ground, a square, clear glass bottle with a diagonal red label.

From the driving seat, Anton De Witt brayed his verdict. "Hah! Johnnie bloody Walker got here before us.

Two legless Kaffirs, Corp!"

Danny saw the point straight away. "Yes, but who gave them the money to buy the booze in the first place?" He faced Du Plessis and raised his voice above the clamour of the crowd. "Why do these people want us to see a couple of drunks? The only connection has got to be our mister Fu-Manchu. There's no other reason for them to show us these guys straight after we started asking about *Kichina*." Du Plessis acknowledged Danny's conclusion with a nod.

De Witt still failed to comprehend. "Well, they won't tell us much in that state."

Four or five women and the tall man with the long arms were struggling to raise one of the drunken Africans to his feet and to drag him forward to meet the soldiers. People had started shouting for cigarettes. Du Plessis opted to play it safe, hoping to delay any confrontation.

"Let's see, eh. Dole out a few fags, but keep their filthy paws out of the jeep." Du Plessis climbed onto the seat. "Hey Johannes! Keep 'em happy with a few smokes, eh man!"

One of the drunks was now alongside Du Plessis, his arms stretched over the shoulders of two women, his head lolling between them.

"This man's a Luba, not Chinese. And he's drunk! *Mtu hapa iko Baluba, hapana Kichina – Mtu iko lewa!*" The nearest ones began to look amused, not bursting with laughter, but sniggering like mischievous schoolchildren. The situation still looked innocent enough. The two women began to harangue the drunk, gabbling and gesticulating, slapping and pinching him, seeming to demand that he should wake up and tell what he knew.

Vermaak called out to Du Plessis: "Ask about the lorry, Jaco."

"Ya, okay. Hey! *Lori – nyekundu – kijani – nyeusi? –*

Kichina kwenda wapi? – Njia nini? And that's about my bloody lot."

It seemed unlikely that the drunk would respond to female coercion, but in a brief show of semi-consciousness his right hand fluttered at the shoulder of one of the women. Both women took this as a cue and began to gabble at Du Plessis, using elaborate gestures to indicate the road ahead to Kamina.

"*Wamekwenda njia hii,*" said one of them.

'They went this way, my arse,' thought Du Plessis. A section of the crowd joined in, inviting the soldiers to carry on past the junction and head north. With shouts of '*sigara*' others began to press in again, encouraged by the prospect of cigarettes being given away.

Standing on the seat of the Minerva, raised above the heads of the multitude, Du Plessis had been keeping one eye on a small, animated swarm of people a little way off, in the main section of the market. With alarm he noticed a sudden change. This menacing squall had started to roll in his direction. Had the word spread? Was this a mob attack, a human wave intent on dispatching him and his men, then stealing the rifles and the jeeps? The movement was not a general mixture of sexes, but solely male, stamping their feet, chanting and raising a cloud of dust. Time to go.

"Johannes – we're getting out. There's a riot boiling up. Anton, don't hang about man. If they won't move, run 'em down." De Witt sounded the jeep's horn and let out the clutch. Instantly the mood of the natives changed. Those closest to the Minervas were unarmed, but they beat on the bodywork of the jeeps, and tried to reach inside, shaking their fists and shrieking. It had happened so fast. Hanging on to the top of the windscreen with his left hand, Du Plessis lifted the flap of his holster and pulled out the Smith & Wesson. One shot in the air. A gap opened up ahead. An empty bottle arced over the heads of the brawl, smacked into the side of Vermaak's head and shattered. Blood ran down one side of his face, the flecks flying. Twenty miles per hour and accelerating hard in second gear, the engine screaming. Du Plessis turned and dropped into his seat. They should outpace the crowd, but now a gang of young men moved to cut off their escape. Choosing his aiming point with care, he fired a single shot into the thickest part of the affray where it came closest to the road. Several fell, tripping over their wounded colleagues, and the way was clear. Now they were drawing ahead of the mob by a healthy margin.

Four hundred yards clear. Du Plessis swivelled round and signalled a change of direction to the driver of the jeep behind, then shouted to De Witt. "Turn right here!"

"Corp?"

"Don't fuckin' argue. Just do it."

De Witt swung the wheel and the Minerva swerved down a side track bucketing over the rutted surface between the shacks. Dogs barked and leapt out of the way. Few people were about. Du Plessis presumed they were all at the market. Another three hundred yards gone and a wider track came into view, crossing their path.

"Turn right again!"

De Witt wrenched the jeep into a tight turn. "Corp, we'll be back in the square if we're not careful!" Du Plessis twisted round again and gesticulated to the other driver, signalling him to expect a left turn next. A wider road lay ahead.

"Turn left at that main road." De Witt slowed for the junction. "Keep your bloody foot down, man!" Looking to their right, a loosely spread-out rabble was loping along the road in their direction. The nearest man was still fifty yards away but, although he was not the only one holding a machete above his head, it no longer mattered. Du Plessis sank back into his seat, turned to De Witt and smiled. "Straight ahead please, driver. Next stop – Lake Tanganyika."

Two kilometres ahead, they halted to attend to the cuts on Vermaak's head. He sounded unhappy. "What d'you want to go and start shooting for?"

"The bastards were lying, Johannes. 'Fu-Manchu' must have paid 'em to say he'd gone north, to throw us further off the spoor. But he went northeast. I'm sure of it. The Kaffir bought himself a bottle of hooch with the cash and got wasted. Those women were trying to get him to tell us to go straight ahead, just to keep to their side of the bargain. The mob wasn't in on the deal and when they heard we were in town, they just came along for the fun of killing us and stealing the kit."

"You crack me up sometimes, you really do."

"Let's have a look at your bony old head, eh man?" And then: "Hey Danny, see if you can write out another signal to tell Leitner what we're doing."

14:45; Ndola Airfield

Chipokwe proved to be a good organiser. He had conscripted enough people and acquired enough rough timber to construct strong wooden platforms and raise both bombs onto them so that they might be lifted by a pallet-truck. The carpenter had then chocked the centre-sections, lashed them to the base and boxed them in, giving them the appearance of normal crated cargo. The overall impression was of a professional job that only wanted stencilled lettering to look fully authentic. However, for his plan to work, he and Guo needed to get the crated bombs away from Ndola without delay. An idea took shape in his mind.

Chipokwe had no time to waste. He rattled the handle of the office door beneath the all-encompassing and somewhat optimistic sign announcing these to be the premises of 'Copperbelt Air-Freight & International Air Charter Services (Inc.)'. The door was locked. However, the lean-to office, such as it was, lay in front of a corrugated iron workshop standing in line abreast with four others. He marched to the nearer end of the block and doubled back to the rear to see if anyone was at home. Two Europeans in blue boiler-suits looked up from their work as he appeared in their doorway. They looked hot and sweaty. They were also quite filthy from contact with an array of mechanical apparatus, which looked to the minister rather like an out-sized motorcycle engine spread across their workbench.

"I've got some urgent air-cargo to shift," announced Chipokwe, seizing the advantage. "And I wondered whether you gentlemen might be in a position to help me."

There was maybe fifteen years difference in age between the two mechanics. The elder eyed-up Chipokwe's mohair tailoring and spoke. "What is it, and what's the weight?"

"Er... Two cases of engine parts that I need to get to Kasaba Bay. I'm not sure about the weight – maybe a ton each."

"How big?"

"About six foot by four. We'd need a fork-lift to move them. I imagine you could borrow a fork-lift, couldn't you?"

"Yeah, but it's the weight... You said 'maybe a ton'. But if you're guessing and it's, say, a ton and a half each I couldn't carry both cases together. My C-47's maximum payload is just under two and three-quarter tons, but we're hot and high here, so it won't lift as much as that. Even two tons would be pushing it."

"How much to carry a single crate, then?"

"Well, if I said five hundred dollars, that might just cover it. But I've got some more questions. Who's your agent at Kasaba Bay?"

"I don't understand."

"Well, there's nothing but a dirt strip up there. No facilities. Certainly no-one with a fork-lift the last time I was there. So, it's no use me flying your engine parts to Kasaba Bay if we can't unload the crates when we get there. And," he said, waving his spanner in the general direction of the cylinder and valve assembly from a Pratt & Whitney Twin Wasp radial engine, "my aircraft's going nowhere until Monday, at the earliest."

"I see. Well, thank you gentlemen." Chipokwe grimaced at the rusty metal, with its substantial covering of grime and grease. "You'll excuse me if I don't shake hands." Then he turned around and set off to break the bad news to Guo that they were going to have to hire a lorry.

17:05; North of Kalundu, DRC

Late afternoon. After Luambo the day had gone well. For the most part they travelled through a country of open savannah, tall dry grassland and scrubby bush. Progress north was not rapid, but Du Plessis reckoned their quarry would be slower. He had imagined himself into the Chinaman's shoes. If, as suspected, 'Fu-Manchu' knew the strength of the mercenaries' patrol he would probably try to evade them rather than ambush them. Earlier he had assumed that the two Chinese were unarmed. But now he wasn't so sure.

A few miles back, Du Plessis had halted the patrol for a short break whilst passing a native who was walking towards them along the road. The fellow seemed inclined to be helpful. Perhaps it was the sight of all those rifles. They had asked him if he knew about a lorry – red, green, black and rusty. Yes, the man had seen it. Also one, if not two, yellow-skinned foreigners. But on the other hand, there were two lorries, not one, and not so far ahead. Vermaak seemed anxious to avoid the kitchen-Swahili conversation getting too complicated and had tried to settle a simpler question: how many men? But the native seemed reluctant to say. Most likely he had not known what answer would most please *bwana* – fewer Africans in the trucks, or more. Which was better? So he had compromised with a nice round number. Yes, there were ten Simba soldiers in the two trucks. The same number as *bwana's* soldiers.

Time for a lesson in reconnaissance. The road ascended a gentle incline ahead, but the crest of the ridge offered two chances for Du Plessis to foul up. He did not want to burst into view over the top of the hill and find himself at close quarters with the opposition lying in ambush. Nor, if the enemy was farther away, would he want to advertise his position by sky-lining over the summit, and giving them time to prepare for his attack.

Leaving Vermaak in command of the rest of the patrol, Du Plessis beckoned his colleague's Rhodesian driver to follow him on foot. Together they walked fifty yards forward of the Minerva jeeps along the dirt road before moving to the side, fifty yards away from it. Then, by degrees, the two walked onward, first stooping, then crouching, before dropping to their hands and knees and finally using a belly-crawl to reach the summit. Ten yards ahead, a thorn bush offered cover. They squirmed towards it. Du Plessis raised a pair of binoculars.

"Well, will you look at that!"

There was no chance that the Rhodesian boy could make out anything with the naked eye. Beyond about eight hundred yards, the shimmer of the rising waves of heat combined with the dust and haze to veil any detail. Even so, Du Plessis's field craft came into play as he lightly brushed the flies away from his face, to avoid making any sudden movements.

"Hard to pick anything out, isn't it? Here. Have a look through these." Du Plessis passed across the binoculars and the youth tried again. "Follow the road down in front of a line of low trees – from here they look like a hedge with a flat top. The road disappears left around the hill, see? Now go right two o'clock and it pops out again. Tell me what you see."

The driver took several seconds to bring his focus on to Du Plessis's target. "I see a lorry and a white pickup truck. The lorry is open, but it's got an awning rigged. It's mainly sandy-coloured, but I think the cab looks green, mostly. It seems to be sloping to one side. Have they had a puncture do you think?"

"If you ask me, I'd say they're digging themselves out of a ditch. They're caught in a trap. How many men, do you reckon?"

"You've got me there, Corp. I can't tell."

"Me neither," sighed Du Plessis.

Du Plessis and Vermaak had withdrawn a little way from the group to plan their next move. The Rhodesian boy was escorting two recruits at a time up to the ridge to keep them busy by learning how to keep a low profile, keeping a watch on 'Fu-Manchu' and giving them an impression of the ground ahead. It seemed clear that there could be a fire-fight later.

Vermaak spoke first: "I thought Leitner said he might be able to call in an air strike. That would soften them up a bit."

"Nah, man. I wouldn't know how to direct them in. They could end up mistaking us for the Chinks and killing us instead. Besides, it'll be dark in less than an hour, now."

"Which means we're on our own as usual, eh?"

"Yah, it's difficult. This is leopard country good and proper, so we can't keep a picket out on the hill all night, watching what mister Redland is doing. My guess is that he's in that hole till dawn at least."

"So how about a dawn attack? If it wasn't for that Chinkie, I wouldn't have taken a bottle on the side of the head earlier. It's time to take some prisoners, Jaco. Time to get even."

"Yah. I was thinking... How about if we pull back a mile or so now? Get some grub and check the weapons. The moon was up by about nine o'clock last night, so say ten o'clock tonight before she's any use to us. Only half a moon, but it'll be some help at least. You set off about ten o'clock, low revs, nice and easy. Pick your way round the ridge to the west and circle back to the road a couple of miles beyond 'Fu-Manchu'. Stay in radio contact. We'll creep over the ridge an hour before dawn, coast down the hill and get into position. Then we'll hit him from both directions just before dawn. Those Simbas down there won't know the first thing about a stand-to, so we'll catch the whole lot of them with their trousers down."

17:05; Ministry of Defence, Whitehall

No doubt Air Commodore Richard Purdham, expectantly

seated in the ante-room to the Secretary of State's chamber at the Ministry of Defence, wondered why his weekend had been interrupted. Perhaps he mused on a possible promotion to Air Vice-Marshal. From his calm and dignified manner, it appeared unlikely that he had given any thought to the possibility that he might have been invited along for a carpeting. The door opened and he was summoned inside.

"Purdham," said the rather handsome gentleman behind the desk, without using the air commodore's rank. "Let me introduce Inspector Dodd, Special Branch. Over to you, Inspector."

"Richard Gregory Whittington Purdham, I arrest you on the charge of endangering one of Her Majesty's aircraft in that on or about the nineteenth of October nineteen sixty-four you did conspire with others to remove arms and or equipment from store without due cause or authority, in contravention of Queen's Regulations and that such removal may be prejudicial to national security. You are not obliged to say anything unless you wish to do so but whatever you do say will be taken down in writing and may be given in evidence."

There came a dull thud as the air commodore's knees hit the floor, followed by a combined hissing and crumpling sound, then a final hollow thud as his head encountered an Afghan rug.

"Whittington?"

"Yes Minister, apparently," said Dodd. "In my book that makes him a Dick twice over."

"I must say, I found that a little disappointing. It fell rather flat in my opinion."

From the corner of the room, the permanent secretary chimed in. "Oh, very droll, Minister, very droll."

"Well, Inspector, if you'd like to cuff this chap, as they

say in the movies, get him along to Colchester Glasshouse and hand him over to the Military Police I dare say he'll sing like a linnet as soon as his head's better. May I suggest you take him out through the side office, in case your lads have picked up Sir Timothy by now..." Inspector Dodd accepted his cue. He knelt to clip a pair of handcuffs around the air commodore's wrists and took hold of the limp legs. He then towed Purdham out of the office by sledging the body and the Afghan rug across the polished parquet floor.

17:05; *The White House*

McCone and Cline sat in silence, allowing Bundy a few minutes to digest the signals that had come in from the *Valdez* during the day. These amounted to an unwelcome complication in the current situation. But Bundy was a powerful thinker.

"Mind if I use your phone, Ray?"

"Go right ahead, Mac."

Bundy dialled a number from memory. "Oh hi! It's Mr Bundy here. Tell me, has that telegram gone out to Kaunda yet – congratulations on Zambia's independence and so forth? ...Yes, sure, I'll hang on." Cline and McCone made polite pretence of re-reading the signals. "Okay, that's good. I want you to pull it and return it to me. There's something we need to add... And thank you too, ma'am... Yes ma'am, I do realise it's a Saturday."

"Nothing too sycophantic I hope, Mac," joked McCone.

"Damage limitation starts here, boys. I guess it won't hurt if Ambassador Engelhard doesn't deliver the President's warmest congratulations till Monday, but when he does, it's got to look like LBJ is the greatest friend Kaunda's ever had."

"So what went wrong with this scheme you cooked up with McNamara?

"We're still trying to make sense of an incomplete picture. What we *do* know is that Leitner's got a direct line to the Congo mercenaries and they're trying to run down the Chinese who've opened up the mine at Shinkolobwe. What we also know from traffic intercepted by the *Valdez* is that a different set of Chinese are trying to get a look inside this bomb that the British seem to have allowed to..." His voice tailed off with the realisation that they only knew that a Valiant bomber had had some sort of accident. The British High Commission in Lusaka clearly knew about it but everything else was based on supposition. There was no word on what the British intended to do. The one clear fact was that the Chinese wanted the Zambian police to arrest the RAF crews on any slender pretext and use the resulting confusion to photograph the workings of an obsolete nuclear weapon.

Bundy's pensive mood prompted Cline to begin summarising the situation. "Slick work from Mao. It's barely a week since China exploded its first bomb. Now it looks like they've not only cornered the purest source of uranium on the planet, but they're just about to get a free look inside a British H-bomb."

A sour expression appeared on Bundy's face. "This is goddamned serious. I'd say it gives Mao the sort of great leap forward he never could have dreamed about, three or four years ago."

"You mean weaponising his bomb?"

"Yeah, but not just that. If his guys get a look-in on this British fiasco, it could put him well on the way to building his own fusion bomb." The grim mood now affected all three.

Cline's wall clock ticked through a generous half-minute before Bundy's next move began to form itself. "Seems to me we can't just sit back here and pretend this is only a British problem. We need info, sure, but the fact is that the British did what they did because we got McNamara to put pressure on them. If that comes out, we'll bear some responsibility for what's happened. And we don't know enough yet to say whether what happened was plain ordinary stupidity or an accident."

"Okay, Mac," said Cline. "We'll see if we can get the low-down on what happened, but I'm guessing we need to do more than just that."

McCone had remained silent while Bundy and Cline had been analysing the situation but now he added his weight. "We sure do. But we can't lose sight of the bigger picture."

"How do you see it, John?" asked Bundy.

"All this started because we needed to get inside the consulate at Stanleyville. Now we've given ourselves a second problem and it looks like running away with us." Cline and Bundy wrinkled their foreheads and nodded in agreement. "If the Chinese save a month on weaponising their bomb, nobody's going to fuss too much about it. But if they save a couple of years on the road to an H-bomb, maybe even more, it's serious. And it's not only the British who'll suffer – it's all of us."

Bundy drummed his fingers on the desk, lifting his eyes upwards and sideways, his mind running through the options and their possible consequences. "Boys, I can't stress this enough. It'd be too easy to start sharing out blame here, but we can't afford that for two reasons. One, the British will clam up. And two, they'll make darned sure the finger turns right round and points at us. John's right. What we want to achieve, with or without help from the British, is to stop China making capital from stealing the west's nuclear secrets."

"And right now, we've hardly got anyone on the ground with freedom to act," said Cline. "LBJ can't make an open military move until after the election."

"So any plans to rescue the hostages," said Bundy, looking from one to the other, "plus what's in that safe," pausing again for emphasis, "still have to remain under cover."

The DCI cleared his throat. "Seems the only way we can act is to get a deniable team on the ground fast, Ray. We've got to assume the worst scenario where the Chinese get a look inside this British bomb. Our best hope is to foul up this second Chinese operation and stop the info getting back to Peiping."

Bundy remembered the other angle. "Have you managed to find Flick Ferguson yet? Seems to me if we could get him down there with a squad of your free Cubans it could make all the difference."

"There's been no word, John." Cline paused, then looked straight at Bundy. "Maybe if I check to see if there's anyone in the embassy at Lusaka who could take this on?"

"No dice, Ray," said Bundy. "The President needs to wage peace with Kaunda, not get caught out with a posse of front-line agents from Langley playing James Bond in his back yard. We need deniability on this operation – that means irregulars."

But still, Bundy had the feeling that they had overlooked something.

19:15; Kincaid Creek, Tennessee

A concussive thump shook the rowing boat and, for a moment, lifted it with its single occupant an inch or so out of the water. Twenty feet away a patch of water boiled white. Closer to the boat, the surface of the small lake vibrated like the skin of a drum, causing tiny droplets to sparkle and skitter in all directions. With practised dexterity the man removed a packet of cigarettes from the top pocket of his jacket and took a filter-tip between his lips. He returned the pack and, disregarding the remaining two sticks of dynamite, flicked a flame out of the Zippo lighter, drew in a lungful of smoke and heaved the sort of sigh that says 'all is right with the world'.

Presently the hunter dropped the cigarette into the water and used the oars to scull over to where a collection of dead and heavily stunned bluegill and rainbow trout floated belly-up on the surface of the lake. He netted half a dozen of the plump ones and slid them into a polythene bag. Then he rowed back to the short jetty and tied up the boat the way he had found it. Best not to upset the owner. Pocketing the dynamite, guided by the fading light of dusk and gripping the sack of fish, he hiked along the trail towards where he had left the pickup.

As the hunter eased the truck along the forest wheel-ruts and up towards his cabin, he had the impression that he was not alone. Maybe a black bear had paid a visit to his dumpster while he was away. Senses jangling, he climbed out of the pickup, loosening his jacket to make sure that he could get hold of his knife in a hurry.

Ahead, a figure stepped aside, away from the fly-screen door, keeping his face hidden in the moon-shadow beneath the overhang of the shingle roof.

"How's it going, Flick?" Twelve long yards and six shaky wooden stairs up to the porch.

"That you, Ace?" The hunter noticed that the visitor kept his right hand behind his back.

"Been sent to bring you in, Flick."

"Ain't goin' nowhere till the mornin'. Got me some fish to fry. There's plenty for two. You'll stay a while?"

"Figured you'd say that, Flick, so I brung this along." The visitor brought his hand from behind his back. He held an object at his side, where the hunter could see it. "It don't have to be this way." He began to raise the object, a stubby article, thinner at one end than the other. "We could leave now – no problem."

"The last guy who pointed one of those at me wound up with a real sore head. I'll stay."

"Well – if that's your final answer..." The figure stepped forward into the moonlight, held out the object in front of him, drew the cork and flung it into the bushes. "Your favourite sippin' whiskey, Flick."

"That's mighty civil of you, Ace. Just like old times, huh?"

"Old times? You still dynamiting fish?"

"Don't need no permit that way, Ace."

Eleven

Bundy sat up in bed with a start, his back and chest damp with sweat. At least now he knew what the forgotten factor that had been worrying him was. This was serious; there would be no more sleep for him that night. He needed a shower but the phone call had to come first.

"Hi, Ray... Yeah, sorry, I know. Something's been bothering me about this RAF bomb that we don't officially know about... Well, we've got to find out PDQ if it's a Limey warhead, or one of ours that we've given away under the defence agreement. That would make the hell of a difference to the way we need to play this, wouldn't you say?"

North of Kalundu

Du Plessis: Vermaak's mobile section was ready to set off but Jaco recognised that after the fracas in Luambo, the young mercenaries were certain to be afraid for their lives. He felt that he needed to encourage them, to remind them that they were the superior force and that they had right on their side. He wondered whether he could distract them from the coming danger with a simple motivational speech – kicking Chairman Mao out of Africa, a poke in the eye for Communism – that sort of thing. He also wanted to offer some soldierly advice based on his years of combat experience. But where should he start? Or finish?

Jaco's impression was that if an African waved a loaded AK-47 around, he rarely knew how to aim it, and would probably fire a whole magazine into the air, hoping to frighten off his attackers by noise alone. And the Simbas were the worst of the bunch. However, he realised that saying so might encourage recklessness among his men. He also had the wisdom to avoid second-guessing the effectiveness of the enemy based merely on hope and rumour. Finally of course, you could not teach a soldier how to be lucky. Some things just had to be learned the hard way. So he decided to content himself with a few hearty words and omit the handshakes and the empty comments about being okay or seeing them all for breakfast.

"Okay, lads – listen up." Five faces, liberally smeared with camouflage paint, turned towards Jaco. "Just pay attention to your corporal. Look out for your mates and remember what you've been taught. Johannes! Take good care of these men and don't forget to call in with regular radio checks. Don't go stopping any bullets, eh?" Jaco could have kicked himself for his offhand remark, which had really been aimed at his friend. The young mercenaries tried to look unconcerned. Well, what the hell! They had all volunteered. They must have been happy with the pay. Now for the conditions.

Vermaak raised his hand to acknowledge his friend's farewell. "You too, Jaco." Then he signalled his driver to move off. They had removed the tail-light bulbs from the jeep, so after thirty seconds it was impossible to track the progress of the Minerva when it braked. Five minutes later, the vehicle was both out of sight and out of earshot.

'No,' thought Jaco, 'You can't feather-bed your men for ever. It's time to forget about comfort and safety for a while and think about winning the fire-fight.' He crouched down beside Daniel to await the radio check.

Vermaak: By 02:30 Johannes judged that their parallel course had taken them beyond Fu-Manchu's truck. It was time to circle round. He had spotted a rough track to the right, leading up to a notch in the ridge. They took the trail and began to climb. There seemed to be plenty of time to take the proper precautions, so he disembarked below the ridge and led one of the mercenaries forward to check for signs of ambush. Seeing none, he sent the young man back to call the jeep forward, but ordered all except the driver and a rearguard to dismount and walk ahead with him, their weapons at the ready. They moved beyond the ridge for about half a mile before Johannes was satisfied that they were alone and he could let the section board the jeep again.

At around 03:45 they bumped down onto the Luambo road and soon sighted a village to the south, straddling the main road. Johannes guessed that the villagers would be used to the occasional vehicle passing through during darkness. But times were tense. He decided to give as little time as possible for the inhabitants to wake and attack them. The Rhodesian boy floored the accelerator and the party sped through the cluster of huts. Behind the stockades of sticks, stones and thorny branches, only the dogs barked and bayed in alarm at their sudden intrusion. The people remained hidden. A mile beyond the village Johannes ordered the recruits to dismount again. To keep the best lookout for enemy sentries, he planned to approach the objective on foot with the jeep bringing up the rear.

"Hey, Sparkie. Time to contact your mate. Get Danny to tell Jaco we've reached the road and we're heading his way now."

When the message came through, Du Plessis's party

adopted similar tactics for crossing the ridge. The young mercenaries walked forward, alert, but with the change levers on their rifles firmly engaged in the safe position. The blacked-out Minerva ticked-over in low ratio, cresting the rim and dropping back below the horizon as quietly as possible. And the impartial moon peeked out from behind broken cloud, favouring Du Plessis's section equally with any Simba who was both awake and vigilant.

Jonas: In the ditch-snared Mercedes lorry, Chan, Jonas and Hwang lay wedged in the vee between the tilted flatbed and the side panel. All three were awake. A leopard had been skulking around for almost an hour, its guttural voice hacking through their sleep. The constant call of the tree-crickets in the roadside bushes rasped against their senses, offering little hope of further rest.

"Hey, Weifeng! Are you awake?" hissed Jonas.

"Of course I'm awake..."

"I've had an idea. I reckon these Simbas would respect you a whole lot more if you managed to kill that animal – if they could see its tail hanging from your belt." Chan didn't reply. "What do you say? We could take a Kalash and see if you could get a shot at it."

"Well, I suppose so. Nobody can sleep with it prowling around out there, can they? How long to sunrise?"

"Maybe two hours from now – about a quarter to six, I should say."

"Come on then. Let's go hunting." Jonas moved towards the tailgate empty-handed. Chan already held his own assault rifle in his left hand and placed his right hand on Jonas's shoulder in gentle restraint. "Aren't you going to take your weapon?"

"Nah. If they even think I've set out with it, they'll assume I shot the animal, not you."

The pair jumped down from the lorry. Chan slung his assault rifle over one shoulder and they both looked up towards the section of hillside where they imagined the leopard had last been. The slope was a typical mixture of dry grass, scrub and loose stones, with the occasional rocky outcrop. Jonas led the way for about a hundred metres, treading as lightly as possible, trying not to disturb any loose grit that might make a sound trickling downhill. Although the stone chips might make only the most hushed murmur, if the pair meant to kill the leopard, they had to stalk it in silence. At each step he made sure that the ground was firm before letting his weight spread from his toes to the ball of his foot, then to his heel.

Jonas stopped, then squatted on his haunches, scanning for movement. He listened, hoping to hear the angry swish of the beast's tail or the rustle of grass brushing against its body as it slunk about in the dark. He had the sudden thought that this was a futile, if not stupid, occupation. Their quarry would already have worked out that the two men were on its trail. The animal would be hunkered down, watching them, relying on its markings to blend into the landscape, infinitely more patient than they were, waiting to seize its chance if the two hunters should split up.

"It's out there just in front of us – I can feel it," whispered Jonas. "You creep ahead. Careful now. I'll follow. Keep the rifle at your shoulder. You'll only get time for one shot. Make it count."

Chan gave Jonas a silent thumbs-up sign and moved forward. After ten metres he crouched again and motioned Jonas to come up to his position.

A hundred metres further up the slope the leopard lay flat in a shallow depression, watching them. From where it lay, it would also have had a good view of five more men to the south, stealing in silence along the road in the middle distance, pausing every few seconds to peer at a bush or into the ditch. But the animal must have judged the approach of two groups of men to be too risky. The creature sprang to its feet without a sound and bounded away to Chan's right. He saw it go. He raised his weapon and fired a snap shot after the retreating form. It was a fair shot, all things considered. The lack of light was a handicap but his directional aim was good. The bullet kicked up a puff of dust and a sprinkling of small pebbles five metres short, then ricocheted over the animal's back. In his haste, Chan had forgotten to aim high for the uphill shot.

To the east, a square metre of sky began to make that subtle change from tar-black to a deep inky blue. Africa was thinking about the new day.

The echo of the shot seemed to linger in Jonas's ears. "Never mind, Weifeng. At least we've chased it off. It won't be back. Come on. We could make an early start on getting the truck out of the ditch." And they turned to make their way back down the hillside in time to glimpse, four hundred metres away, five rifle-carrying men sprinting the last few strides towards an open-topped jeep and leaping aboard.

Chan gasped. He sprang down the hill for twenty metres, making for the partial cover of a low, weathered rock. Unarmed, Jonas realised he could not get back to the lorry in time to pick up his own weapon. He dropped into a crouch, then moved wide to his left, cat-like, seeking the cover of some low bushes. A nightjar burst up in front of him and flew a hundred metres away, churring over its territory, forced away from its chosen daytime refuge. Jonas cursed and pressed himself into the ground to shrink his profile.

Du Plessis: Single shot. AK-47. No-one had seen the flash, but each man in Jaco's section figured the gunshot had come from the hill above. If anyone had stopped to think, they would have realised that with no visible flash and no whip-crack as the bullet sped by, the shot had probably not been aimed at them. But Jaco couldn't take that sort of risk now. He realised that even if he and his men charged like rhinos it would take them at least ninety seconds to reach their objective – the trapped Mercedes truck, which lay directly below the place from where the firing had come. They could not afford ninety seconds. Nor did they have the time to co-ordinate their attack with Vermaak's. Unless they acted quickly, they would lose the element of surprise. The Simbas would be ready and the mercenaries would take casualties.

"Jump in! Hang on tight!" Jaco's men clung to hand and footholds on the Minerva for the short ride to work. He had less than thirty seconds to issue his orders. "Watch out for your mates. Just keep hitting the Simbas with single aimed shots and it'll all be over inside a couple of minutes." De Witt was driving. "Anton, stop when I say. You and Danny stay in cover behind the jeep and engage them from the front. Pin them down. You other three stick close to me! Danny – when you get a chance or if I get hit, call Johannes and tell him what's going on. Brake now!"

De Witt skidded the Minerva to a halt allowing Jaco and his men to leap out, then punched the jeep forward another fifty feet, stopped and rolled out to the right with Danny, keeping the body of the vehicle between them and the stranded truck.

Daniel: The clouds parted again and light from the half-moon dribbled over the scene. To his left, he could see that Du Plessis had spotted the Simbas under the Mercedes.

The corporal was walking forward with his three men, discharging his SLR from the hip, keeping the angle low, firing into the screaming. Danny worked the cocking handle of his SLR to load a round into the chamber. The unfired round previously in the breech whirled out to his right. A beginner's mistake. He had forgotten that his rifle was already loaded with one up the spout. One wasted, nineteen left. With his right thumb he flicked the change lever one click forward, from 'safe' to the position for single rounds, and was ready.

Beside him, De Witt selected his target. He leaned his left elbow against the spare wheel on the bonnet of the Land Rover, took aim at the lorry's fuel tank and pulled the trigger. A misfire? He pulled back the slide and released it to clear the weapon, then jerked the trigger again. Another misfire! He worked the slide three times in rapid succession, cursing as the brass cartridges arced away to his right, flashing gold in the moonlight as they toppled end-over-end and fell to earth. He took aim and pulled the trigger with the same result.

Danny realised De Witt's mistake. "Safety catch – idiot!"

De Witt slammed the change lever all the way to the end of its travel, pointed his weapon and hosed a burst of shots in the general direction of the truck. The muzzle of the SLR reared up, out of control, until he had emptied the magazine and was able to relax his trigger finger. Attracted by this fusillade, an accurate volley of aimed shots rattled out from above them on the hillside. The air suddenly became full of grey billowing dust as the spare tyre exploded next to De Witt's cheek. Anton flinched away with a cry, alarmed at becoming the enemy's first target.

This time Danny did see the muzzle-flashes. Kneeling beside the jeep's right rear wheel, he aimed high – two shots just above the flash. He waited for movement, straining to see whether he could pick out the form of a man in the moonlight. Yes! Just there. Before he had time to squeeze off another shot, the shape moved. The figure leapt to its feet and charged downhill, spraying the contents of his magazine towards Du Plessis and the boys. Danny followed him down in his sights, firing – crack, recoil, aim – crack, recoil, aim – crack, recoil... Pause. The assault rifle on the hillside had fallen silent. Keeping his finger on the trigger and the butt of his weapon firmly nuzzled into the crook of his shoulder, Danny lifted his cheek to improve his view of the dim pre-dawn target area. Nothing moved.

Du Plessis: The incoming fire from the hillside stopped but Jaco was alert for any return of fire from under the lorry. He still had three men at his side, so no casualties yet. He needed to press home their advantage but with Danny firing above his head and De Witt punishing the whole landscape, personal safety had to be the first priority.

"*Hou op met skiet!* Cease fire!" The firing stopped, but all was not silent. Jaco's hearing rang with a high-pitched tinnitus in reaction to the sharp bark of the FN rifle and the metallic clank of the self-loading mechanism. A low pulsing roar of adrenalin-fuelled blood echoed inside his ears. Somewhere between the two extremes he could hear harsh, bubbling moans coming from under the lorry. And somewhere the high-revving wail of another jeep.

Vermaak's section motored into view at high speed, keeping as far left as possible, to give the best view around the right-hand bend. When the driver saw Du Plessis's jeep he braked hard and stopped for two seconds to let Vermaak offload men to engage the front of the truck.

Then he moved his jeep forward again, blocking the road about fifteen yards from Danny and De Witt. They all hopped out on the same side as Danny.

Johannes shouted: "You okay, Jaco?"

"*Dit gaan mij goed.*"

"You might have waited, you bastard."

"Cover me. I'm going to have a look under the lorry."

"Aaah, don't bother having a look, man. Just roll a grenade or two under there."

"Don't forget we need a prisoner, eh? Let's just secure the position first. You and your men face out and watch the perimeter for a counter-attack. Danny! Watch the hillside." With two men to cover the under-side of the lorry, Jaco stepped forward. He was not impressed with De Witt. The guy had panicked.

"Hey! De Witt!"

"Yes, Corp!"

"Move your change lever to safe. Fix a new magazine. Pull and release the cocking handle. Change lever one click, to single rounds, *like you've been fucking taught*. Two rounds through the cab, two rounds through the side panel above the rear wheel. Now!"

"Yes, Corp!" De Witt fumbled for a fresh magazine and took aim at the cab. Another mistake: Jaco noticed the surreptitious movement as De Witt flipped up the rear sight. It must have been folded down for the whole action. The useless bastard took aim again and fired off the four rounds, as ordered.

"Okay De Witt, watch the hillside. You take centre and right. Danny cover centre and left." Two voices acknowledged.

Jaco stepped another two paces towards the lorry. "*Kom daar uit*! *Kuja kutoka hapo*! Come out, you brave bastards..."

And after something of a pause, from underneath the lorry there emerged, with understandable fear and in no great hurry, eight unscathed Simbas, six more walking-wounded and two with more serious flesh wounds who still managed to crawl out unaided. Jaco called his three followers forward, ordering them to lay the prisoners face down in the dirt and shoot the first one who offered any resistance. The low moaning continued from beneath the truck. He moved towards the rear wheel for a cautious look, hoping to present a difficult target to any die-hard with the strength and intention to use a weapon. There were maybe another six men in the ditch. He looked into the flatbed. One more man, clearly dead, Chinese, probably caught by De Witt's single shot. Not much use as a prisoner now.

Jaco walked over to one of the unharmed, spread-eagled Africans and gave him a kick in the ribs. With an expressive jerk of the head, he moved his rifle in an arc, beckoning – 'come this way' – and persuaded the Simba to crawl back towards the truck.

"*Trek hulle uit*. Pull them out. *Uwakokote*." The Simba scrabbled on his belly under the lorry for several minutes. He managed to extract two more men, one with a chest wound and one with a broken leg from a bullet above the knee. Then he dragged out four bodies.

"That old Kaffir on the road said ten. I make that twenty-two."

"I can count, Johannes." He waved his hand towards the Mercedes. "Plus this Chink in the back, here. I expect it was the other one who fired that first shot from up on the hill. Danny got him, I reckon. Get the lad to point out where he thinks he fell and take three or four men up there to bring him down. If he's still alive, I'd rather he stayed alive, eh?"

"*Ja, baas.*" Johannes slouched off to talk to Dan and appoint a few volunteers to search the hillside. He found Danny looking stricken. The young man choked on his words and was only able to point out roughly where he thought the soldier with the automatic rifle had fallen. "Take a drink of water, man. You'll feel better."

With the sky growing lighter by the minute, Jaco ordered a search of the Mercedes and the pickup truck. This produced a mixed haul, consisting of a quantity of immensely heavy sacks containing the familiar yellow ore, an assortment of personal possessions and five assault rifles. The assault rifles were of a similar pattern, but no two were exactly alike. AK-47s seemed to be reaching Africa from East Germany, China, the USSR and God only knew where else. At least they had space to take the captured weapons back to Kamina and get them out of circulation. However, the eighteen prisoners, two of whom were quite badly wounded, presented a problem.

While Johannes and his men were searching the hillside, Jaco jumped up on to the flatbed to check the dead Chinaman for papers. He found a pocket notebook that he decided ought to go back for analysis. And the guy was wearing a money-belt with over six hundred dollars in it. Spoils of war. The Chinkie would not need it now.

The single gunshot from the hillside came as a surprise.

As the search party came down from the hill a short while later, Johannes, carrying a sixth assault rifle, detached himself from the small group and signalled Jaco aside.

"You finished him off, then?" queried Jaco.

"Yeah, man. He was in a bad way; gut-shot. Bloody good shooting, though. That Danny's a real crack shot. Looks like the Chinkie took a bullet in the shoulder that spun him round, then the other one right through the guts from side to side. Babbling away in Chinese. Couldn't get through. No use even trying to question him. He'd have been dead in a few minutes anyway with a wound like that, so we photographed his head and shoulders for the major and I put him out of his misery."

"Did you search him?"

"Nah, he was a mess, man," said Johannes. "Blood and shit everywhere."

"Go back alone. If he's carrying any papers, I want to give them to the major. Check him all over. This other one had a money belt."

"How much?"

"Six hundred bucks, man!"

Johannes was not away for very long, but when he returned, he wore a huge smile. He winked at Jaco and made great play of handing over the few scraps of paper that he had found on the body. Then he waved his SLR at the Simbas who were still lying face-down in the road. "What d'you plan to do about this lot, Jaco?"

"No idea. We only need one or two. This guy for sure." Jaco indicated one of the prisoners who was rather older than the others and dressed more extravagantly. He sported a Hawaiian-pattern shirt, a pair of denim jeans that were rather too large for him around the waist, and a handsome leather belt holding them up. Hanging from the belt was a selection of items advertising his qualifications – a number of leather pouches that were probably best left unopened, and an impressive collection of animal fetishes, ranging from soft fur tails to mummified monkey heads and other unsavoury body parts. A pair of human ears – white – had been threaded on to the wearer's necklace amongst the fangs and polished bones. Jaco unsheathed his bayonet. Wearing an expression of disgust, he cut through the leather thong, taking care that he also left an accidental three-inch slice in the flesh covering the *muganga's* clavicle. He cast the necklace away. It was not a trophy he cared to possess.

"And maybe this young kid – he'll talk." A pause. "What's your record?"

"Thirteen."

"Okay. Let's get started."

Daniel: Danny watched, detached, as Du Plessis ordered two men to remove the *muganga* and the young Simba then tie them securely, one in each Minerva. No traffic had yet appeared on the road. Clearly the Katanga emergency made people nervous about travelling unless it was in full daylight. Meanwhile, Vermaak was engaged in a different exercise.

It reminded Danny of the process for picking members of a team. Vermaak strolled along the line of prisoners, each time nominating a player with a kick in the ribs, the shoulder or the leg. Under his direction the young mercenaries would then remove the participant and sit him in line, so that each new player sat close behind the fellow in front with his legs splayed either side of the man's buttocks. In time, the logic became clear – shortest at the front, tallest at the rear. The players were all roped tightly together to prevent a mass breakout, sitting as they would be if they were pillion passengers on some vast, invisible motorcycle. But there was only one team, not two – a team of sixteen Simba prisoners including the wounded.

Vermaak took out a notebook, found a blank page, licked his pencil and with great apparent concentration wrote the numbers 1 to 16 down the left-hand margin. As he did this, his tongue protruded from between his lips, the tip making small questing movements up, down and from side to side.

"Okay!" he announced. "We can't take all these gentlemen back to Kamina, so we're going to hold a little sweepstake." This sounded like a novel concept to Danny and his colleagues. One or two of the Simbas had begun to look quite wary, darting glances left and right, the whites of their eyes making a stark contrast against their ebony faces, beaded with sweat. "So if we make this big guy at the back number one and the little guy at the front number sixteen, who'd like to sign up for a number? Just ten Rand a go!"

Maybe this was what mercenaries did – took risks and gambled high stakes. But what was this game of chance all about? Anton De Witt must have thought it was time to redeem himself. He stepped forward first and swaggered along the line, then handed over ten Rand to sign up against number eight. By and by, Vermaak had collected eleven entries in his book.

"Now boys – just one little rule I should have explained. There's only going to be one winner and I still have a few blank lines left. This means if none of you wins the pot, I take it all, eh? So – last chance. Does anyone want a second line?" De Witt stepped forward again. "Feeling lucky, eh?"

"Give me number fourteen if it hasn't gone already, Corp."

A sudden piercing shriek came from Vermaak's Land Rover. "Aieeee! *Mai Mulele!*" This disturbed the Simbas, who attempted to turn round to see what had upset the *muganga*. Du Plessis ordered one of the young soldiers to keep the man quiet. Then he stood in front of the line of prisoners, filled his chest and stood to attention. He walked forward to the first man, delivered a kick to the thigh and, by example of standing erect once more, he got the man to sit up straight, then the next one and the next until they were all sitting at attention. But they were also murmuring rhythmically.

"*Mai mulele... mai mulele... mai mulele...*" It became a chant, resonant like a drum, a deeply grunted "*mai*" and a softer, musical "*mulele*".

Du Plessis moved away. The chant began to possess a hypnotic quality, so it was possible that nobody truly heard the single shot. But they saw the result, as life was ripped away from the Simbas in one violent instant.

And, seared on Danny's memory for all time, glowed the image of Vermaak, gazing without emotion along the line of burst, broken and blossoming skulls. Vermaak kneeling, his legs slightly spread, his weight balanced easily with the seat of his khaki combat trousers resting on the heels of his boots. His arms were stretched before him, a Smith & Wesson model 29 with a five-inch barrel, chambered for 44 Magnum ammunition clasped in a two-handed grip. A wisp of smoke snaked up from the muzzle. An age passed.

Du Plessis walked forward to the line. "All but two. Who's got number fourteen?"

Vermaak got up off his knees and inspected his book. "Looks like you, De Witt. You just won yourself a hundred Rand, son." Calmly, Vermaak walked to the front of the line, faced the two remaining Simbas, looked into their eyes and blew them away with a single casual shot. Elsewhere, Anton De Witt, bent horizontal from the waist, leaned against the front bumper of the Mercedes sobbing and puking, sobbing and puking.

"Okay boys," called Du Plessis. "Snap out of it. Let's untie these bastards and fling 'em in the back of their truck, eh? Quick's the motion, now. Chop chop."

Trembling and almost gagging in time with De Witt's retching, Danny leaned his rifle against the passenger seat of his Minerva. At least half of the recruits seemed to be in the same state as himself – moving slowly and mechanically, ashen-faced, sickened by the casual act of murder that they had witnessed but feeling powerless to protest about it. He tried to take a deep breath but his chest felt paralysed. Each exhalation was almost a sob but with every new gulp of air he found he could fill his lungs a little more than the last. With an act of willpower, he stepped forward towards the Rhodesian boy, Vermaak's driver, who had taken the arms of one of the bodies. Danny took the legs. Together, they swung the corpse into the back of the Mercedes lorry and their eyes met.

"Every one of them was a killer, Dan. You saw what the guy in the fancy shirt had round his neck. At least it was quick. Not like having your ears and your wedding tackle sliced off and bleeding to death."

So Danny and the others, minus De Witt, tossed the sixteen bodies from the road, plus the four who had died earlier under the truck, into the back of the Mercedes. Then they moved away to take refuge near their Minervas, while the two corporals splashed diesel fuel from a jerrican over the bodies and lit the pyre.

Once the blaze had taken hold, Du Plessis was ready to leave. "So, Johannes – you've beaten your record at last, eh? Let's get going, man. This place gives me the creeps."

"*Ja, baas.* We might need the rest of the day to find a way round Luambo. I want to be in Kamina when the next bottle comes my way."

The two Rhodesian boys looked back at the flames, with the curling plume of oily black smoke rising from the burning bodies. Startled weaver birds chirped in alarm, deserting their perches and taking refuge well away from the crackling, billowing ditch.

"Dan?" asked his companion. "What's '*mai mulele*' –

the words they were chanting?"

"Water of Mulele," said Danny, looking up somewhat morosely. "He's one of the rebel leaders. The witch doctor chants some sort of ritual over a bottle of water and sprinkles it on the Simbas before a battle."

"Holy water, eh?"

"Guess so. It's supposed to give them the courage of lions in war and turn our bullets into water, so they can't be killed." But the two young men were not such battle-hardened fighters that any sick comment about the spell's effectiveness could comfortably be uttered.

A pause, then a slow drift back to reality. "You fired the shot that killed the Chink on the hill, didn't you?"

"Well, not quite." Now wearing a blank, far-away expression, Daniel felt guilty. He had not been brought up as a killer. It was a reputation he preferred not to acquire or boast about. "I brought him down, that's all. Johannes finished him off."

"And that was bloody good shooting, too," crowed Vermaak, hearing his name. "That Chink goes down to you, Danny, not me. You probably saved Jaco's life – and half your mates." Maybe that was true but in the face of so much sudden and brutal death, Daniel, who only days before had assumed that he would not even be carrying a rifle, was having difficulty adjusting to the fact that he had taken a life. They were all killers now.

Du Plessis walked back to Daniel for a brief word. "Come on Kid; there's a first time for everything. Most people feel a bit low afterward – it's only natural. But when the chips are down, it's kill or be killed. That's how it has to be. You saved your mates' lives today. Tomorrow, maybe one of them'll repay the favour." He put a hand on Danny's shoulder and gently steered him towards the Minerva. "Jump aboard and code up a signal for Leitner, eh? Tell him we're on our way back. No casualties, two dead Chinks and we've got two prisoners and some bits of paper for him." Danny noticed that Du Plessis avoided mentioning the Simbas.

Jonas: When he saw Chan fall, Jonas felt torn between the need to get off the exposed face of the hillside and the needs of his comrade who lay groaning thirty metres away. As soon as the shooting stopped, he could tell that the situation was hopeless. The shouted commands had not been given in French, so it was obvious that the soldiers were not Belgian. They must be mercenaries then, and not so inexperienced as Chan had mockingly decided, only the day before. His party had been followed without knowing it and suffered a dawn attack without suspecting it. And who the hell could shoot like that? Maybe these weren't even the same people but, whoever they were, they couldn't be amateurs. He knew that once these guys had consolidated their position, they would be quartering the hillside to check for further bodies or signs of resistance. He needed to get away and lie low before the dawn advanced any further. The leopard had known the way to go. He would follow until he felt safe. There was nothing he could do for Weifeng now.

From way up on the hillside, Jonas looked down on the road, in full daylight. He reckoned he could count twelve mercenaries riding in the southbound Land Rovers; also two dark-skinned men, including the *muganga* in his colourful shirt. Because of the convex slope he could not see the Mercedes truck or the pickup, but it was pretty obvious where they lay, with the smoke rising lazily in the still morning air. At about his own level, the gentlest of zephyrs brushed the top off the dissolving plume of smoke and carried it away to the northeast. He imagined that somewhere in that dimly smeared twist of discoloured air Hwang's spirit drifted away to join his ancestors. In that moment Jonas resolved to complete his friends' work. His destination lay north and east, too.

When the mercenaries had passed out of sight, abandoning his caution, Jonas made his way back down to where Chan's looted body lay. Already the flies were sucking at the incapacitating shoulder-wound and the eviscerating injury lower down that would soon have proved fatal. The sound of the shots had burned into his brain forcing the inner soldier to re-appraise his enemy. Two ranging shots to panic Chan into breaking cover, then hitting the mark in the dark with two shots out of three. He looked down at the final, merciful bullet wound in the forehead. No rancour there or lack of proficiency, just a matter of courtesy – one professional had simply relieved the suffering of another.

On this stony hillside a burial was out of the question. Jonas squatted beside his comrade's body for a few seconds longer, while a prayer of sorts wandered through his mind. Then, fighting the urge to steal a last backward glance, he got to his feet and hiked down to the road. He needed to get there before any Congolese passers-by appeared.

The two trucks were totally burnt out, still smoking. Hwang's scorched body was indistinguishable from the rest. No useful possessions remained to be salvaged. What little Jonas owned he had lost, except for the contents of his pockets – a few dollars that Chan had not reclaimed from various local purchases. It was not a fortune. Although he had seen charred bodies before, he felt the spasms beginning in his throat, but his stomach was empty and nothing came.

He refrained from touching either of the trucks, which still radiated a great deal of heat. The sacks containing the yellow ore had all been destroyed by the flames. The cargo of rocks, now black with the soot from diesel oil, burnt human fat and seared flesh, had subsided into heaps. Breaking a branch from a nearby bush he hooked a chunk of the precious rock off the flatbed onto the ground. The rock was too hot to hold. He broke the branch again and split it to make a pair of Y-shaped crooks in which to carry his trophy away from the scene. Then he set off northwards along the road, true to his resolve, never looking back.

Within the hour, the landscape began to fall away before him under a shallow incline. A village came into view with a wide plain beyond and a distant view of blue hills. A party of local people was dispersed in the parched fields, tending the red-brown soil, picking over the last of the beans, the maize or the sweet potatoes, looking for something for the pot.

Jonas wondered who these people might be. Luba? Yeke? Maybe even Wanyamwesi? They appeared to be quite un-warlike. An old man, very old indeed, squatting by the roadside looked up as Jonas approached. Kiswahili seemed the best way to begin.

"*Hujambo!*"

"*Sijambo*," replied the ancient. "You are a long way from home, Stranger."

Jonas noticed that his eyes had turned blue and opaque. "Your hearing serves you well, grandfather. You can tell that I have travelled far. You are a wise man."

"Not so wise or full of life now, my son. I forget more than I remember and my balls have gone cold. Your voice says more about you than you suspect. I think you carry the hardships of the world on your shoulders."

Jonas stopped to consider how little he should say, or how much he should admit. "Did you not hear the guns in the night? Many were killed. Two were my friends."

"May my tears mingle with yours. I heard nothing. But these days I dream deeply and wake little. The young people heard the Belgians come through the village long before dawn, and they told me about the shooting. It was no surprise to me."

Jonas tried to change the subject. "What's the name of your village?"

"Welcome to Bunkeya, my son. Help me to my feet. We must see if there is any food to be had."

After finding a helping of millet porridge to stave off Jonas's hunger, the village elder invited him to walk for a while. Although the old man needed help from a staff, he managed to shuffle along in a purposeful way. He announced that they were going to climb a hill. He called it 'Nkulu'.

Because of its ever-present familiarity, Jonas had scarcely given a second thought to the rolling savannah, acacia scrub and distant ridges. However, the character of the landscape thereabouts was disturbed every so often by an isolated, steep, domed hill, not a natural aspect of either the plain or the mountains. Nkulu was one of these. A path led away from the village directly towards the hill, which stood alone, not too far away. But the old man was soon defeated by the gradient. He stopped several times to get his breath, started again and stopped within only a dozen steps. Jonas became concerned for the old man's well-being. He did not want to witness death again so soon.

"If you want to get to the top, I could carry you on my back..."

"I would not ask..." The old man panted a little before

resuming. "But there is something you need to understand – something I want to show you. With each new dawn I wonder if it may be my last chance to feel the glow of the sun over this land... Whether my heart gives out first or the light in my eyes, I will not have to wait too long now." So, Jonas hoisted the old man on to his back. As they climbed towards the summit of Nkulu, he reckoned the old man weighed no more than an eight-year-old.

Relaxing in the shade, Jonas looked out into the far distance. The land was baked to a dull, dusty ochre. Many of the bushes were leafless and only the taller trees bore any greenery. The rains would come soon and once again the landscape would wear its bright green mantle. By then he hoped to be thousands of miles away.

In time, when he had recovered a little, the old man spoke. "This morning, when we first met, I said that I was not surprised by the shooting. You never asked why. Do you already know the answer?"

"No, grandfather, I have no idea."

"Look around you. Do you see the walls and heavy stones? At one time, there were also poles that held up a roof, but the ants have eaten everything. Here at the top of Nkulu was once the palace of a powerful King. You have heard of Msiri?"

Jonas turned his head sharply towards the old man. "Msiri? Of course I've heard of him! You mean this is where Msiri had his *boma*?"

"I do. Let me tell you why I was not surprised to hear that all your friends had been killed. Bunkeya is a special place, for whatever is in a man's heart becomes a thousand times greater here. Even just to know about Bunkeya can make a greedy man ruthless. And its magic can turn a ruthless man into a brutal tyrant – a persecutor. Such men are all the same. No amount of riches can satisfy them. People say that Msiri was a merciless killer, but that's just a story that suited the Belgians. Their King Leopold was far worse. He sent three expeditions against Msiri before they were able to end his life and steal his lands. But Bunkeya took its revenge on them and many of the whites perished from hunger and disease as they tried to return to the coast." He shrugged. "So, when more white men came through Bunkeya last night with evil on their minds, fate was certain to have its way. It could only end in more killing."

"I think I'm beginning to understand," said Jonas.

The elder fixed him with a half-blind but sympathetic stare. "When I hear you speak, I hear a man with power in his grasp, but who is weighed down by his cares right now. Only remember – this is a special place. It can shape a man's destiny or his fate." The old man took Jonas's hand. "Promise me this: Before you leave Bunkeya you will know your own mind. You must be certain of what is in your heart and be prepared for where it will lead you."

"Though your eyes grow dim, grandfather, you see things clearly."

"And you, my son... You must learn to see not just with your eyes, but also with your mind. Think from your heart. See with your mind. I suppose there may be difficult days when you cannot easily decide which one to follow. But know your own mind. Promise me."

"I promise."

London

"All I know is, Sir, that I've got to deliver this to you in person."

The constable held out the envelope once again. Charles

Rook's curiosity only deepened. He wrinkled his brow. The envelope was certainly addressed to him. It looked genuine enough too, with the official letters 'OHMS' printed across the front. The words 'BY HAND' had been scrawled diagonally where a postage stamp would normally have been applied. He experienced a sudden aversion to opening the envelope at the front door of his apartment, in case it contained bad news from home.

"Come in for a minute, won't you?"

Charles eased one finger under the corner of the envelope's flap, tearing it into a jagged slash before he could extract the single page. He scanned the text at speed, fearing that the names of his father or mother or Daniel would leap out at him, but the whole thing seemed to be about Zambia. The nervous anticipation had had a strange effect, leaving him unable to undertake a proper second reading of the letter quite as calmly as he should. He tried again. 'Special knowledge of the region'... 'Local language competencies'. After his performance in front of the Commonwealth Secretary on New Year's Day he had felt that his card had been marked and his career was in a mess. But far from being a poisoned chalice, this looked like a great opportunity.

He wondered what was meant by the phrase, 'a fact-finding mission to Ndola.'

Twelve

Sunday 25 October, 1964
British High Commission, Lusaka

Because London had not dictated what Maxted's next move should be, Roberts had done the honourable thing and offered him a bed for the night. The two servicemen returned to the High Commission during the morning but Maxted was restless. Since the promised fly-past had not materialised, something had to be wrong. Not having heard from Creswell, he felt worried about the men, accusing himself of letting down his own side.

"Look, Lionel, I'm worried about the lads. I think I'll phone the tower and see if they can put me through to my office. Creswell or somebody ought to be manning the phone there." But Maxted's extension failed to answer. The tower told him there were still two Valiants on the pan, with no obvious sign of activity.

"I don't like it," said Maxted. "I shouldn't hang about any longer. I ought to get back and find out what's happened."

"Understood old boy. We can't sit around all day just waiting for London. You're right. You'd better deploy back to Ndola, so you're on the spot when the brass-hats get their fingers out." He scratched his head, clearly working it out in stages. "You'll need to stay in contact with me at HQ, of course. I'm afraid that means using open telephone lines. I'm worried about the lack of security though. Careless talk costs lives, as we used to say, so anything we *do* say needs to be in code. And like I said earlier – there isn't one."

"We'll have to invent one, then. Simple – you know, so

we can remember it without writing it down."

"I suppose we could..."

"An alias for each of the pilots... A codeword for the bomb..."

So, with the enthusiasm and cryptological skill of a pair of twelve-year-olds, they settled on players from the England soccer team, nominating the likes of Jackie Charlton and Gordon Banks, to stand for Maxted's colleagues. For chromatic simplicity they decided to call the Yellow Sun 'banana'.

Maxted waited until after lunch but with no word from Whitehall, he and Roberts felt pressure to agree the next steps. With no news, either, of any local difficulties at Ndola, they felt it best to take no chances. Maxted would go straight to the Country Club at Ndola and ring Roberts to let him know that he remained free, at least up to that point. Roberts would update Maxted with any new developments. If Maxted failed to make contact by the following morning, Roberts would press the diplomatic panic button.

Ndola Country Club

Dusk had fallen by the time Maxted arrived at the Country Club. Some of the members had spent an energetic afternoon engaged in a tennis tournament. A barbecue had been arranged to follow the tournament, which was intended to round off the Independence weekend in style. The whole event had been well-attended and since the tennis players had found the tournament thirsty work, the prevalent mood was already boisterous by the time Maxted located the club secretary to ask him for the use of his telephone.

After the standard wait, Maxted got through to Lusaka.

"Any news?"

"Not exactly, old chap. Our friends in London have got some fellows on standby to come out and lend a hand, but it's all a bit sensitive. Apparently, they've decided not to tell the local African chaps anything about it yet, but we can't put it off much longer. It's their territory, after all. I'm afraid it depends on you, rather. My boss wants you to go and take a look, then report back with the latest info before we decide what we should tell the locals."

"But I might be..." Maxted found himself on the verge of saying 'walking into a trap' but using words like that would alert any eavesdropper to a potential problem. He stopped himself in time. "Well, I'd need to be a bit careful. I mean, if the fellows in the er... local office have found out about it already, they could be quite upset. Explanations might take a while."

"Point taken. Why not just drive past and check for signs of panic? It's your patch, old man... You're entitled to be there. If it looks dicey, phone me and say so. If not, stick with the plan and check how Jackie and Gordon are getting on."

The members' bar had never looked so inviting, but Roberts's words shattered Maxted's vision of enjoying a quick beer. "I'll go and take a peep, then," he said with a sigh.

"Good show, old chap."

Groaning inwardly, Maxted abandoned the revellers to their festivities.

Ndola Airfield

When Maxted arrived at the airfield, he couldn't see any special security measures in place, no regiments of the Zambian Army or detachments of police on duty. He parked his Land Rover at the rear of the RAF hangar and stole around to the side entry, hoping to encounter friendly faces, but found none. Discovering the hangar's side door standing unguarded and slightly ajar worried him. He crept forward and crouched, then snatched a quick peek through the gap. What was there to be afraid of? The disabled Valiant gave him a reason to be there. Roberts was right. It was *his* hangar, for heaven's sake.

The hangar lay in darkness, creaking as the ironwork cooled and contracted under the gentle touch of the night air. He knew he needed to take a proper look inside. He grasped the door, lifting and tugging the angle-iron frame to avoid scraping the concrete pathway. The rusty hinge screeched, setting his teeth on edge and making the hairs on the back of his neck stand up. Maxted felt unsure about the new departure his career had taken. Creeping around an airfield in the dark for the second time in 48 hours was not why he had signed up. Being alone in the vast space of the aircraft hangar gave him an eerie feeling. Whilst he might not be so happy about the circumstances, they certainly stimulated his adventurous spirit.

He forced himself to enter. A stray eddy rattled the great double doors and disturbed the set of the corrugated roof panels. The noise startled him, driving barbed needles through his taut nerves. He shivered as if a river of ice had flowed through his spine. The panels chattered for a few moments, settling into new positions, still shrinking after the heat of the day.

Despite the fact that he knew something was wrong, Maxted had not really thought about what dangers might lurk within the cavernous space, now frozen into an ominous stillness. He stepped forward, sensing rather than seeing the nearness of the Valiant, feeling the aircraft's presence by the sound-shadows it left against the hangar's background murmurs. The toecap of one shoe kicked against an object, not heavy, that skittered away gently across the concrete floor. He waited until he felt that his night-vision was becoming more attuned, then shuffled forward, both hands outstretched in case he should collide with anything else unremembered. Maybe his memory was playing tricks on him but WP198 seemed to be in a different position from where he recalled it had been when he left. He half-rotated, hoping that the meagre illumination from the outline of the hangar door might reveal the Valiant in more detail. Everything was still indistinct; it was no better than being at the bottom of a mineshaft.

Maxted squatted on his haunches, feeling for his box of matches. Discounting the infinitesimal risk of detonating the bomb's explosive charge, he struck a match and held it above his head. The object that he had kicked away appeared to be a timber off-cut. Looking around, there seemed to be quite a lot of dunnage lying about. No people though, and the aircraft really did seem to be in a different place. The match flamed out.

More confident of his surroundings, he walked several paces forward and struck another match to be sure of his bearings. But what about the bomb? Striking this second match had been foolhardy, but now, so close to the aircraft, the stench of AVTAG made it reckless to consider a third. The boffins had designed the fuel not to explode in open air, but this was not the time to prove the chemists wrong. What he needed was a safety torch. Logically, there should be one on board the aircraft. He raised his hands to head-height, angled slightly ahead, and shuffled forward, feeling for the fuselage. But in the darkness, he blundered into an object that knocked his breath away, bruising his ribs and right hip. He cursed as his fingers traced out the shape of the bomb's tail fins, angled diagonally upwards, left and right. He must have strayed too far to the left. Maxted moved to the right, groping his way round the tail fin, feeling for the Valiant's fuselage. After locating the smooth, cold, curved panels, he crept forward again, his right hand in contact with the metal. Taking more care, he worked his way along until he brushed against the steps outside the cabin exit hatch. He grabbed the handrail with his left hand, stretched out his right and blindly quartered the darkness, hoping to avoid any further injury or surprises. With a puff of relief, he climbed into the cabin.

Maxted had no idea where the emergency pack might be stowed. Risking another match seemed inescapable. He held his breath and struck. Glancing around, he noticed a first-aid kit installed on the forward bulkhead, just above the cockpit entry. A torch with an orange plastic body was fixed in a spring-clip close to the pills and bandages. He pinched-out the match, felt for the torch and switched it on. A bright beam blazed out. Thank God for something in good working order. While he was inside the aircraft, he thought it might be a good idea to see whether the boys had left him a note. He searched, but rather than finding a message, he noticed the aircraft's engraved identity label above the navigator's position. Curious; this was not Blyton's aircraft, WP198, but Creswell's.

Stooping to return through the hatchway, Maxted climbed down to the hangar floor, then flashed the torch around, making a few quick scans. At first, he found the sight puzzling. Assuming that the torchlight was throwing up confusing shadows, he moved closer to the Yellow Sun before letting the beam play over its surface again. But puzzlement turned to astonishment when he realised that he was not looking at one bomb, but two. Well, not quite. He was looking at two tail-fin units, the gutted remnants of two nose-cones and a fair amount of sawdust. But the nuclear cores were nowhere in sight. Both Noddy's warhead that had caused all the trouble and, by the look of it, Creswell's, were missing.

He breathed in sharply with a hiss. "Oh shit!" he whispered.

Out on the dispersal pans, Maxted had no difficulty in locating WP198 and the tanker. In neither aircraft could he find human sign or scribbled note, or – an empty hope – the missing nuclear warheads. He felt quite baffled, unable to imagine what might have happened. The situation made him think of the *Marie Celeste*. A reasonable explanation would place the RAF crews in the same location as the warheads, guarding them tenaciously. It would also require a redirecting message to have been left with a trustworthy character, say, in the control tower. Without forcing an entry again, he could not check with the tower until morning. All other circumstances spelt trouble.

With a loose and empty sensation below the midriff, Maxted decided to return to the Country Club, detouring via the Victoria Hotel just to check whether any crew members had billeted themselves there.

Ndola Country Club

Maxted turned his back on the dwindling number of merrymakers and hunched over the phone. "Well, I've had a snoop around."

"And?"

This was all going to sound so juvenile. "You know all this started when we had a problem with Gordon's banana cargo?"

There was a pause, while Roberts caught up. "Er, yes."

"Well as you know, Jackie had a consignment, too." It seemed more stupid with every sentence. "So it was never really about solving a problem with one cargo, but both of them."

"I'm not going to like this, am I?"

"Probably not. You see, I haven't found either Gordon or Jackie or in fact any of the team down at the... er... docks, and if I might put it like this... those bananas... well, there's nothing left except the skins."

"Sorry – you're going to have to make this a bit more obvious for me."

"I don't know if I can. Maybe London could draw you a diagram, but all I can say is that the important parts – the tasty bits in the middle – well, they're gone. Looks like they've been stolen, Lionel." Maxted waited for a response from Roberts, but the man was clearly floored by his news. He needed a nudge. "Is your boss with you at the moment?"

"No," said Roberts.

"Okay. Look – here's what we do." Privately Maxted was furious. When would the bloody diplomats begin to take things seriously and show a bit of commitment? But there was nothing to gain and everything to lose by getting angry. "I'm knackered now so I'm going home to grab a few hours' kip. I'll set my alarm early and get back to the – er, docks for about six-ish, when the sun comes up. You tell your boss how urgent this is and get him to meet me on site. I need some help. There'll be plenty for me to do – trying to find out if anyone saw anything suspicious, looking for clues, taking care of security issues. Your chap needs to find Gordon and Jackie and handle the authorities. How's that for starters?"

"Okay, but what are we going to tell Kaunda? Sorry! I mean the African boss. Sorry. Oh bugger."

"Well, you could always try the truth. There's less to remember that way."

"I suppose there has to be a first time for everything."

Monday 26 October, 1964
Ndola Airfield

Refreshed by sleep and decked out in a clean uniform for his first meeting with the Deputy High Commissioner, Maxted sauntered into the main building at Ndola airport. He assumed that the official concerned would either arrive late or not at all. He proposed to leave a note: '*Send a runner to find me and I'll come as soon as I can.*'. It was therefore a pleasant surprise when the gentleman himself stepped forward with his hand outstretched.

"Squadron Leader Maxted?" An athletic-looking man of perhaps forty-five; dark hair, slicked down; quite a long nose, sharply angled; tasteful suit, well-fitted and wrinkle-free; spectacles with fashionable dark frames – he looked trustworthy. Maxted took the offered hand. "Best to use first names... Arouse less suspicion that way. Call me James, if you're comfortable with that."

Maxted agreed, but the gentleman's direct and business-like approach had knocked him slightly off guard. He expected stuffiness but observed the beginnings of co-operation. Not before time.

"Pleased to meet you, James. It's fine by me. Call me Pete." It seemed best to head for the main hangar, make an appraisal of the situation and agree an initial plan. For all the importance of planning, they were still without one.

But after half an hour in the hangar, James's smile had slipped away, although his manner still spoke of collaboration. Maxted suggested a joint visit to the tower to check whether any of the controllers was harbouring a message from Creswell or had any clues to his whereabouts. It would be a difficult conversation to have without hinting at a problem.

≈

"No, there's nothing for you, Squadron Leader," said the chief air traffic controller. "But a few minutes ago, we received a message for the Deputy High Commissioner to phone Lusaka urgently. He can use my office if he wants."

"Thanks. He probably won't want the operator listening in though."

"Let's see what we can do."

James was duly installed in the private office for his call to the High Commission but when he came out of the office, he was grim-faced.

"We need to talk, Pete." James thanked the chief controller over his shoulder and touched Maxted gently on the elbow to lead him away. "I've got some orders for you."

"At last!"

"No, this is serious. This whole thing is about to go into diplomatic overdrive. And London wants you back home. You've got to be on the first plane out of here."

"Come off it! That's bloody stupid. I'm the only one around here who knows what's actually happened. Okay, I'm no expert. I wouldn't normally know a single thing about this Yellow Sun bag of tricks, but I've seen it, touched it, nearly shit myself helping the boys to make it safe. I know what I'm looking for. I've got all the local connections." Maxted's eyebrows twitched, leaving the crease between them more sharply defined. "In fact, now I think about it, I'm pretty browned off about this. I don't have a guilty conscience. I'm not the prat who thought he could get away with landing two nukes here in Zambia. I'm one of the Johnnies who tried to pull the government's bloody chestnuts out of the fire!"

"Which may be exactly why they want you home – to give them a first-hand account."

"If I swan off out of here, the trail goes cold. We need to act now."

"Cold? Two or three hours from now I guarantee it'll start warming up. It'll be as hot as Hades before the day's out. Look – you've got no diplomatic protection. If Kaunda decides to arrest you, I can't stop him. That means London loses access to your account of things." James had made an important point. Maxted fell silent, contemplating the prospect of roasting inside a Zambian prison cell. "We can't take that risk. London reckons that the Zambians have taken possession of those two bombs and thrown your men into clink."

"Why would they do that?"

"It's not for me to say. But it's an absolute gift, isn't it? Think about it. Kay-Kay is suddenly the most powerful man in Africa. He's got two nuclear weapons to bargain with, so Britain would have to dance to his tune."

"That's not his style. Bargain for what?"

"I can't answer that."

"I suppose he might want protection from a slump in the price of copper. A bargaining chip against Southern Rhodesia?"

"Your guess is as good as mine." Clearly the diplomat was unwilling to comment.

"What about security against losing the rail link to the port at Lobito? Zambia's always wanted a route to the east coast for insurance."

"Britain couldn't afford to fork out for a tenth of that."

"Unless he's got us by the balls."

"Steady on... You could find yourself doing my job if

you aren't careful." This brought a smile to Maxted's face. "Look, I mean it. We've got to act fast on this. The High Commissioner's got an uncomfortable interview with Kay-Kay in a couple of hours – slotted in after the Americans, if you please. By that time, I want you out of here on your way back to London. It's orders, Pete."

Maxted was still reluctant. "I get your drift, but I'm beginning to think somebody other than Kaunda has got our bombs stashed away somewhere."

James cocked his head on one side. "Why?"

"No diplomatic protest – no police presence. Back at the hangar it's just an ordinary day. You've seen it – nothing's happening. Nobody knows anything – yet. If they did, the whole place would be crawling with police, soldiers, the bloody lot. If I were the High Commissioner, I'd go in with all guns blazing and demand to know where fifteen RAF airmen have been taken. I'd not admit anything about the nukes."

"You're saying London's guess is wrong?"

Maxted spread his arms wide, then gestured out through the control tower window towards the hangar and the two aircraft on the pan. "There's the evidence. The Zambians don't know anything about it yet. Spot the policeman. Nothing's different."

James looked Maxted directly in the eye. "I think you're right. That's what I told the High Commissioner ten minutes ago."

"What?"

"I'm sorry – I just wanted to get your view of what went on here. So that's the line you'll take when you get back to London?"

Maxted understood James's motive. His anger faded as quickly as it had arisen. "Sure."

"Look, we mustn't waste any more time on this. My

driver will take you home to pack a few things. Then you need to get out of the country, pronto. Once you're safely on your way, I'll start at the local police HQ and ask about the crews. But the longer we delay asking about the men, the more suspicious it looks. I want you gone, and fast."

"Okay, but just one thing. How do you expect me to get out of Zambia?"

"You're the chap with all the initiative, Pete. The best combination of speed and safety, I should say. I'd head south to Salisbury or Jo'burg to catch a Europe-bound flight. Maybe north to Nairobi if there's an earlier flight from here in that direction. Hire a bush pilot — whatever." Another idea struck him. "Maybe your safest plan would be to head for Mombasa and let the RAF get you home — I've no real preference."

"I didn't mean that. I'm going to need a pocket full of cash for buying last-minute flight tickets, aren't I?"

Northern Province, Zambia

After leaving the well-maintained northbound highway at Mpika, Chipokwe had more time to think. As the truck drew nearer to Abercorn, around twenty miles from the shores of Lake Tanganyika, they began to descend from the high plateau, fertile, farmed and green, with the distant view of grey-blue mountains. Right now, the Abercorn Road was as passable as it was ever likely to get. Dusty, rutted in places with deep wheel-tracks and at times suffering from a washboard surface that threatened to dislodge every tooth in his head, the pinky-brown laterite ribbon unreeled before him. The lowering grey skies reminded him that the rains were due soon. When they came, the roads would quickly turn to ankle-deep mud; in places it might even reach to his knees.

Irrespective of the season, the typical African will still attempt to drive such a road almost as fast as his vehicle can go, as witnessed by the occasional wreckage at the side of the road. Guo had, however, managed to convince the minister that with the cores of two nuclear weapons crated up and loosely lashed in the rear of the truck, extreme caution was required and any speed faster than bicycle pace should be treated as suicidal. Chipokwe, mindful that these weapons were his future meal ticket, was happy to indulge his new masters. He had also managed to piece together an outline of how he wanted matters to pan out, and needed to test his theory with Guo.

"I expect you're thinking we should just carry on across the border into Tanganyika?"

Guo took a few moments to consider. "I think it could be risky. We'd have to wait for clearance at the Customs post, and my passport is still in Lusaka. We don't have any proper paperwork, so probably the officials would want to see what's in the crates. Even if they couldn't tell what it was, it looks complicated. I don't want to seem rude, but to them that means it would also look expensive, so they'd certainly ask for a big bribe before letting us through." He paused to form his next thought. "Even if we got through, I'm certain the Tanganyikan police stop Zambian lorries every so often and ask for money. I know we could transfer the load to a local lorry, but we'd still be taking too many chances. Nobody knows we're coming, so there wouldn't be anyone to help us. We might not even get out of Zambia if the people at the border are already looking out for us. There's just too many problems."

Chipokwe was pleased. "That's exactly how I see it. But there's a port at Mpulungu. It isn't watched as closely as the road across the border. I'm hoping we can get the bombs out that way." However, he too had become cautious. "But I don't want to attract attention by driving straight in there. We really need somewhere to leave the lorry, go in on foot, have a look around and make sure the plan looks good."

"That sounds fine as long as nobody finds the lorry and you don't have to wait too long for a boat. The longer you have to wait, the more likely that the police will trace you." What Guo said was true. Chipokwe nodded and began to look pensive. Guo continued. "And you're the only one who needs to leave Zambia in secret. I've got to leave in the proper way, to avoid any diplomatic problems. Have you thought of somewhere we can leave the lorry?"

"No. But something will turn up."

About five miles further on from Abercorn, now heading west with perhaps only half an hour of daylight remaining, they noticed a weathered red and yellow sign at the side of the road. '*Kitongyama Mission*' it stated, pointing south. A narrow un-graded track, seemingly rarely used, veered away from the road, just two wheel ruts with a central spine of scruffy brown grass. No telegraph poles spurred off in that direction. As a potential hiding place, it appeared hopeful. Chipokwe steered left. The lorry bucked and lurched along the rough trail so he dropped the speed to walking pace.

After about a mile, with the sun sinking fast, they came to a fork in the trail. Nailed to a tree was another sign, pointing right. '*Kitongyama Leper Hospital*', it said; '*5 miles*'. Chipokwe stopped the truck. His first reaction was to retreat, wanting nothing to do with a leper colony.

"I don't think we should go any further," he said to Guo.

Guo did not understand. "Why not?"

"Leprosy. You know..." He hunched over the steering wheel and wheezed to indicate sickness, miming bandages and disfigurement as well as he was able.

"Ah, I understand. The wasting disease? People are sent away so they don't infect others, yes?"

"Yes."

"It's perfect. If *you* don't want to go ahead, neither will anybody else. What better place to hide? Drive on past the sign. We'll turn off the track after a few minutes, camp and figure out a plan."

Thirteen

The previous day's journey had exhausted Guo. After eating a few scraps, he and Chipokwe had fallen deeply asleep in the cab of the lorry. The overnight rest gave Guo's mind time to mull over their situation, with the result that the first lightening of the sky before dawn thrust him awake, churning with nervous energy. Chipokwe appeared to be brooding about his fate. Guo was conscious of their relative positions and did not want to appear to be taking command in case this offended the minister or affected his co-operation.

"Laurence – if you don't mind, can I tell you how it looks to me?"

"Carry on." Chipokwe flicked a hand in front of his face to brush away a persistent early insect. "Let's hear it."

"Thank you. I think it's like this. My embassy..."

The minister interrupted. "The Chinese People's Legation, you mean?" Status seemed important after all.

"Yes – the legation – well, they were only expecting me to return with photographs. They don't know that we've smuggled away the cores of both bombs." This was so far beyond question that Chipokwe merely gestured Guo to continue. "But with you gone, things can't have stood still at Ndola. By now the police must be looking for you, the bombs and pretty soon the lorry, though maybe not me. Not yet, anyway."

"I'd worked that out already."

"That means we need to get you out of the country as fast as possible."

"And you?"

"I need to get back to Lusaka."

"We covered all this last night. And the bombs?"

"All the initiative was with us yesterday. But today, everything that moves will come under suspicion. Travelling any farther with them is a big risk. We need to hide them."

Chipokwe eased out of his shell. "Okay. This much is obvious: The faster you get back to Lusaka, the better for both of us. Then maybe you can get accredited to Dar es Salaam and make sure your people over in Tanganyika are looking out for me." He shook his head. "But hiding the bombs? Where?"

"Well, Mpulungu feels too public. We can't just drive up, unknown, and expect to rent a private warehouse. People would be suspicious."

"So, what's your plan?"

"Bury them."

"Bury them?"

"Yes. If we get caught with the bombs, there'll be a huge diplomatic row, maybe even a war. But the authorities won't be expecting us to bury them and just walk away."

Chipokwe appeared doubtful, but clearly had no plan of his own. "Well, all right." He considered matters a little longer. "And I suppose we could still photograph the insides of the bombs before we do that... Like your people wanted."

"I'm sure it would work. The British won't know where to look... And they can't search everywhere. Eventually they'll give up and go home – but that'll give my people time to decide on the best plan."

"Yes, I can see that."

"Ferrying the bombs out by boat from Mpulungu may be the right answer but it'll be taken out of our hands. My people may decide on a better way out."

"Okay," said Chipokwe, opening up a little more. "I can see that too. Your people will want to take control. And I can see the difficulty of finding a secure place above ground to hide the bombs. But..." Chipokwe waved his arm at the two crates lashed to the lorry's flatbed. "...Without a crane and a bulldozer or something, how are you going to lift the bombs off and drop them in a hole?"

"If we can work out a way, would you be happy to go along with it?"

"I haven't got a lot of choice, Mister Guo."

Guo could see that an engineering solution was required and that Chipokwe was no engineer. The first problem would be to get the crates off the lorry. He needed to find out what kit they had available. It didn't take long to make an inventory. An incomplete set of spanners, a bent screwdriver, a hammer, a shovel, a knife and the rope that secured the crates to the flatbed. Nothing else. The lorry had a spare wheel but no wheel-brace or jack.

The ghost of an idea shimmered into Guo's head. He climbed on to the flatbed and began estimating how much rope had been used to lash down the crates, concluding that there could easily be fifty metres of line. From his higher vantage point, he scanned all around.

"Hey! Jump up here, Laurence and I'll show you what we're going to do." Chipokwe did as he was told. Guo gazed out into the distance where, about half a mile away, two large trees stood. "We'll drive the truck over to those trees and hope to find a strong branch, maybe three metres off the ground. Underneath it we'll dig a hole big enough for one bomb. If it's a really strong branch we could make the hole big enough for both. We fix one end of the rope to the front of the flatbed, pass the free end over the branch and tie it back around the crate. If we've measured everything carefully then drive the lorry away slowly, when the rope goes tight, the crate should slide towards the back of the flatbed and finally slip off and hang above the hole. Reversing the lorry will lower the crate into the hole –"

"– That's a big 'if'. What if the rope snaps?"

"It'll work – you'll see. Then we do the same with the second bomb, fill in the earth over the top, remember which tree we used so we can find it again, and leave. Simple." After a few moments a further thought occurred to him. "In fact, after we've photographed the insides of the bombs, if I use my camera to photograph the tree and the background from all four sides, we can be even more certain about where we've buried them."

The ex-minister glanced down at his expensive shoes and tailoring. Clearly, he realised they would never look the same again. "I'm not sure I fully understand. It sounds risky. I can't picture it."

Guo knew he needed to convince Chipokwe. He retrieved his clipboard from the cab and sketched the lorry in profile, the tree and the arrangement with the rope. They both looked at the drawing in silence for a few moments.

"It's not quite right, is it?" admitted Guo. "The length of the line is absolutely critical. If we make it too long or if the rope stretches, the crate could swing off the flatbed and crash into the side of the hole."

"Or the rope could snap, like I said. We've only got one chance."

Guo paced back and forth for a few minutes, turning the matter over in his mind. "You're right, Laurence. Here's a better idea: The crate's too heavy for two people to push it to the end of the flatbed so we'll anchor the rope round the tree trunk and fix the other end to the rear of the crate, like I said. Then we drive the lorry forward slowly and let the rope drag the crate right to the end." Guo turned to face Chipokwe. "When we're ready to hoist it, the critical thing will be to find a way to shorten the rope and keep the tension in it. When the crate swings free, it mustn't get damaged." Guo dropped to his knees, crawled under the lorry and felt around near the spare wheel and the exhaust system, emerging with a smile. "What we could do is pass two loops of rope over the crate so we've got a four-strand rope, not just a single strand. Then we'll remove some of these brackets and clamps from the exhaust pipe, and use them to grip the separate strands above the crate. Then we pass the free end over the branch like before and fix it to the front of the flatbed. We'll be able to take up all the slack using another clamp. It's even simpler than I first thought."

"I'm still worried that when the crate slips off it could swing around and crash back into the lorry or the sides of the hole."

"No – trust me. Once we've got the crate right to the end of the flatbed, we can use the exhaust clamps to shorten the rope to the ideal length so it just swings a little."

"I suppose if you're sure it'll work..." Then, with resignation Chipokwe added, "Best make a start while the morning's still cool." With only one shovel it was going to be a long hot process, but at least they could take turns digging and resting until the job was done.

During the morning they encountered tree roots, so it was mid-afternoon before they had hacked through them and dug a serviceable hole. By early evening, fly-blown and finger-blistered, burial duty was complete. They spent a second night in the cab of the lorry, planning to make an early start at dawn. Guo would drop Chipokwe on the outskirts of Mpulungu, then turn around and head back to Lusaka, perhaps abandoning the truck within reach of the capital and taking a bus for the rest of the way.

Chipokwe had used the word 'port' to describe Mpulungu, but the term was open to interpretation. The place boasted one or two short, rickety jetties and a modest concrete wharf. This provided about a hundred feet of frontage, allowing the occasional ferry or small commercial craft to work its cargo. Mpulungu was simply a large fishing village, the native boats launching from the stony beach to take advantage of the plentiful variety of fish in Lake Tanganyika.

At one end of the wharf, on the door of the customs-house was pinned a note. It consisted of a page from a spiral-bound shorthand pad, about five inches by seven and was hand-written. The fact that it had not blown away was due to the commitment of the writer, who had secured the note to the door with at least a dozen drawing-pins. The message was brief:

BACK

IN

SEPTEMBER

Chipokwe was now unrecognisable as a former government minister. His trousers would not have been permitted within a hundred yards of Savile Row. Covered from head to foot in red dust and with his shoes scuffed beyond recovery, he smiled and turned away to see about buying his passage to Kigoma. Black clouds had begun to gather over the lake. A squall was visible in the distance and the dust at his feet swirled as occasional puffs of breeze drifted ashore. The season's first real rainfall was about to arrive.

Sunday 1 November, 1964
Ndola Airfield

Flick Ferguson had arrived at Ndola by road, late on Saturday afternoon. Noticing the tight security at the airfield, he had driven straight past and doubled back into town to track down the market. Although the item he wanted did not seem to be on offer, there was always someone willing to run an errand for a dollar. Without bothering to haggle about the price demanded by the Indian merchant, money changed hands and within the hour he became the owner of a freshly-tailored blue boiler suit. He left the market in search of an hotel.

Dawn on Sunday found Ferguson dressed in an olive-green shirt and slacks, clipping the wire of the airfield perimeter fence, peeling up the tongue of netting and squirming through un-noticed to blend into the deep early morning shades. It would have been pointless trying to bluff his way airside by a frontal approach past the armed police guards. Under the circumstances he did not anticipate any weekend laxity on their part. His early start meant that he would have at least a couple of hours to kill before people, other than a fresh shift of British MoD policemen, arrived to start their day. He decided to fill a portion of that time by burgling some of the sheds and workshops occupied by air-cargo firms and the like, in the hope of stumbling upon a piece of information worth his attention. He slipped the blue boiler suit on over his green outfit and moved towards the rear of the buildings.

Within half an hour, Ferguson had forced the metal window latches at four of the premises. To gain access to the remaining one, he had lifted one end of a top-hung rolling door off its track and squeezed inside through the gap. His portable Geiger counter worked well when he tested it against his luminous watch, but in none of the sheds did he find any unusually high traces of radiation. That made it unlikely that the nuclear cores from the British bombs had passed through as air freight unless they had been loaded directly onto a cargo plane. In fact, he could see only one aircraft that could have transported the material at all, a C-47 that stood in the morning sun with the port engine cowling removed. It was obvious which company owned the machine from the profusion of air-cooled cylinder units and valve gear that he had found spread across the work-bench in the shed belonging to Copperbelt Air-Freight International. He decided to retreat to a vacant storage shed, and wait there to see if anyone arrived to open up and start work on the dismantled engine.

Over the years Ferguson had grown quite resigned to lying in wait, but in all that time he had never found a good way to overcome the desire for a strong cup of hot coffee. When the craving arose on a stakeout, there were only ever two alternatives. In the majority of cases, like today, you simply had to put up with it. By 9:45 in the morning, it had begun to look as though Sunday was truly a day of rest for everyone but him. His best bet appeared to be to march out of the airfield in his blue overalls, offer a cheery greeting to the soldier on the main gate and sneak in again on Monday. He was on the point of giving up when a fellow of about thirty, dressed in an oil-streaked boiler suit, passed the window. Ferguson rose to his feet and glided through a communicating door between the rear of the storeroom and the front office, ready to exit via a window if the mechanic began to unlock the rear door of his hiding place. But all was well. With a lucky one-in-four chance, the mechanic walked past and unlocked the C-47 workshop. Ferguson decided to give him precisely six minutes in the hope of finding him half way through making the first coffee of the day.

It was clear that, for some, Sunday in Zambia counted as an ordinary day. Ferguson put on an upbeat tone, calculated to inspire the mechanic into showing more benevolence than perhaps he felt.

"Howdy, fellah."

"G'day, mate."

"Smells good…"

"It's only Pommy Maxwell House instant shit. It's all you can get out here. You're welcome to a mug-full if you can find a clean one. What can I do for you?"

"Thanks – much obliged." Ferguson looked around for a clean mug but was compelled to choose the cleanest dirty one. He turned the mug upside down, shook it and handed it over. "As long as there's nothing living in it." He grinned. "I always say it's the coffee that counts, not what you drink it out of." This seemed to be the right thing to say, because the mechanic grinned in return.

"Haven't seen you round here before, have I?"

"Passing through."

The mechanic pointed at Ferguson's outfit. "Looking for a job?"

"Looking for a guy. Thought he might have been through here – maybe tried to charter your C-47 out there." Ferguson reached into his breast pocket and pulled out a photograph. He looked down at it to make sure it was the right way round, then offered it to the mechanic, watching his face for a reaction.

The Australian's eyebrows twitched up and he pushed his lips forward a little. Ferguson didn't want to appear too anxious for information and stayed in conversational mood. "You're right about this coffee, buddy. But I'm grateful all the same."

"What's he supposed to have done?"

"His name's Laurence Chipokwe. He's a junior government minister. Or was. But he's been missing for a week. That's maybe all he's done. Does he look familiar?"

"See those MPs out there?" Ferguson glanced politely through the open doors at the MoD policemen and nodded. "They're looking for him too. Seems like a pretty big manhunt for a bloke who's most likely shacked up in the bush with a bit of rough, if you know what I mean."

"What did you tell 'em?"

"Me? Nothing, mate. Pommy bastards. There's some rumour they're an advance party supposed to set up a temporary base for a photo-reconnaissance flight, due in a few days. But I don't buy it."

"Why not?"

"Something fishy. Too many questions. Then there's the snooping."

"Snooping?"

"They've been checking over a few of the aircraft with some box of tricks. Wired up with a gizmo on the end of a pole. Saw 'em giving our C-47 a quick look."

The gizmo sounded to Ferguson too much like a Geiger-counter for him to want to risk asking any more questions and making the Aussie suspicious. He needed to slow things down. If he appeared to be pumping the mechanic for information, the fellow would more than likely clam up and confine himself to talking about nothing more controversial than the weather. Ferguson glanced idly at the carbonised valves and piston heads that lay on the bench. He began to fiddle with an aluminium cooling fin assembly, ingrained with oil and dust. After thirty seconds he put the object down again and took another sip of coffee.

"You've seen him, haven't you? Chipokwe, I mean."

"Yeah, I've seen him but I wasn't going to tell the Pomms that. They've got no authority here any more. Looked like more trouble than it was worth, 'specially as it seemed to be the Military Police doing the asking. Interview after interview, witness statements, appearance in court – small outfits like us can't afford to waste time with that kind of shit. What's he done to deserve all this fuss? No bullshit. I mean what's he really done, right?"

Ferguson glanced over his shoulder. "Well, if anyone asks, you didn't hear this from me, okay?" The mechanic assented and moved closer as Ferguson lowered his voice. "Seems like he may have made off with most of the country's gold reserves."

"No way, mate!"

"And the theory is, if he was looking for a quick getaway with a couple of tons of looted bullion, he might have come sniffing around for an aircraft to charter."

"Yeah, the bastard was here a week ago. Well-dressed, spoke like a public school Pomm, but I knew he was flaky. Didn't like him a bit. He was in a hurry – wanted to go almost right that second, but he didn't even know what the shipment weighed. Anyway, we had this engine in pieces so we couldn't have ferried him anywhere." The mechanic fell silent and thought for a moment. "That'd be right. If he'd just nicked all that gold, he wouldn't know how heavy it was, would he? We couldn't help him. Sent him packing."

"Did he say what the shipment was?"

"A couple of crates of engine parts, I think. The bugger wanted us to fly him to Kasaba Bay, up north."

"Hmm. Heavy cargo – good cover story." Ferguson still felt sensitive about rushing matters. He swilled his coffee round in the mug and stared at it for a few seconds. "Kasaba Bay – that's on Lake Tanganyika, right?"

"Yeah, but there's no gear up there to handle air cargo. Not unless you take it with you."

"So he was trying to get out of the country, d'you reckon?"

"Too right, mate. Don't suppose I'd want to stick around in the same circumstances." They made a few minutes' small talk about radial aero engines, the heat, Africa, the bloody flies and the bloody British before Ferguson made a move to be on his way.

"Thanks for the coffee, pal." Ferguson took his mug over to the kettle and threw the dregs into the sink. "Say, what are all these RAF bombers doing here?"

"Oh, they came in just over a week ago as well. Story goes that one of 'em burst a tyre on landing and the local fuzz took the crews away in dribs and drabs and stuck 'em all in jail. The word is they only let them out yesterday. A week in clink for a heavy landing – it's a flaming liberty. This place'll be just as bad as the Congo in a couple of years... Guaranteed."

"Nothing to do with young Chipokwe, then?"

"No way, mate."

Ferguson smiled. So far, the true story had not leaked out.

Victoria Hotel, Ndola

Room 205 rattled to the sound of a portable typewriter as

Charles Rook compiled his preliminary report from the scraps and jottings that he had accumulated over the previous two days. It was all very inconclusive. With commendable honesty Charles had attempted to dispense justice even-handedly, exonerating the RAF crews after their brief but brutal incarceration. He even forgave Inspector Makondo, whom he suspected of simply obeying orders given directly by a government minister. But new facts were hard to come by. As a final act he began to compose a one-page management summary.

```
The junior Minister of Police, Mr
Laurence Chipokwe, continues to be
unaccounted for, together with the
central sections of two British
nuclear weapons.  It should be noted
that the arrival of these devices in
this country places the United Kingdom
and Zambia in breach of the nuclear-
free zone (NFZ) undertakings of UN
General Assembly resolution 1652 of
1961 and the NFZ protocol of the OAU
as agreed at the Cairo Heads of State
Conference on 21st of July, this year.
Should the truth become known, the
extent of political reaction in Zambia
or the OAU cannot be over-estimated.
```

Because he had been sent to Zambia as an Africa-specialist rather than an economist, Charles was tempted to explore other avenues too. Having earlier flagged the suspected involvement of the Chinese, he now moved from informed guesswork to downright speculation and summarised what were, for him, their two most likely motives.

```
Objective 1: Since the Chinese and the
Cubans are thought to be inciting the
rebellion in the Democratic Republic
```

of the Congo, a strong suspicion
should be entertained that one or both
bombs have been or are being
transported to the Congo, perhaps to
Stanleyville, to render inadvisable
any international attempt to rescue
the western hostages.

Objective 2: A lesser possibility lies
in the potential theft of the devices
by Chinese agents intending to remove
them to China for dis-assembly, either
to copy the design, or for other
experimental purposes.

Charles finished by considering the possible routes taken
by the bombs on their way out of the country. He then
rounded off the report in the official style and sealed the
top copy into an envelope to be despatched to the military
signals unit at Ndola for enciphering and transmission to
London. His particular whirlwind of activity was dying
down, at least temporarily, so he figured it would be
reasonable to try to place a call across the border to speak
to his parents. Hopefully they had heard encouraging news
from Danny.

Cairo Road, Lusaka

Jonas had stayed in Bunkeya longer than he intended. The
deaths of two people, with whom he had crossed half a
continent and whom he thought of as friends, had affected
him more than he expected. The old man never asked him
to disclose his secret purpose, and Jonas never confided in
him, but the few days' respite allowed Jonas time to re-
think his options. Going onward to Baudouinville, not
knowing whether the mercenaries would return, would be
too risky. After all, the two burnt-out trucks still faced

northeast and little else lay in that direction that would call for twenty Simbas and two Chinese to be driving along with a ton or more of uranium ore. Whoever was in command of the mercenary force might decide to investigate further if his intelligence service was on the ball, placing any travellers beyond Bunkeya under suspicion. In fact, traffic bound for the northeast had become sparse, far outweighed by the number of trucks passing through in the opposite direction containing people, complete with possessions and livestock, fleeing the excesses of the Simba rebels.

Jonas had spent two days in the back of trucks, in company with refugees, before crossing the Congo border into Zambia. His throat was dry and his clothes were dusty. He knew that he smelled powerfully of goat. His transport now drew to a halt just beyond the junction at the centre of Lusaka where the north-south Cairo Road crossed the main east-west road. But this was where he felt he had to leave. Although the road ahead led directly to Salisbury and onward into Mozambique, reaching the coast at Beira, Jonas was without a valid passport and needed to act cautiously. Attempting to cross Zambia's frontier with Southern Rhodesia felt too risky. To be carrying a strange, heavy yellow rock would make matters worse. His plan was to hitch a ride to the east, where the road ran parallel to the Mozambique border, and then walk across it by night. Once there, his command of Portuguese would allow him to blend in. At Beira he would head for the port and try to contact a communist cell that might put him in touch with Chinese officials... Or he could always wait for a Chinese cargo ship to arrive, and hope to stow away.

USNS Pvt. José F. Valdez,
At Sea; Bound for Luanda, Angola

In addition to paying special attention to British diplomatic radio transmissions from Lusaka, the *Valdez* had become aware that an RAF signals detachment had begun operating from Ndola, and so was monitoring those circuits too. When the Ndola transmitter tuned up, a junior CT was waiting for it. As the RAF telegrapher sent out the five-character code groups, the CT copied them down, and when the schedule was finished, he took the signal to the cipher section. Charles Rook's message was decoded within thirty minutes, summarised by an intelligence officer within the hour, flagged as ultimate priority and put on the top of the stack for re-transmission to Washington.

Victoria Hotel, Ndola

Flick Ferguson paused in the doorway of the Victoria Hotel bar and admired the fake Tudor panelling, cricket team photographs and gold-lettered honours boards that reminded the British in Africa of their homes and former schools far away. The outmoded décor contrasted somewhat with the lion skins and buffalo heads adorning the upper part of the walls. Set into the ceiling a slowly-turning punkah fan squeaked, un-noticed by the regular drinkers. He strolled forward to the bar, where a black steward, smart in his starched white monkey jacket, raised his eyes from the glass that he was polishing and with a respectful 'Sah?' invited Flick to name his refreshment.

"I'll have a beer." This, however, was not sufficiently specific for the steward, who reeled off the list of beers available, none of which, apart from Guinness, he had ever heard of.

"Try a 'Tusker' – that's what I'm drinking," said a voice from the bar-stool next to him. The stranger extended a hand towards Flick. "I'm Charles. You're American, aren't you?"

"Hi, Charles." He took the hand and shook politely. "Yeah, I sure am. Folks just call me 'Flick'." He turned to the steward. "Give me a Tusker and another one for my friend here."

The conversation ebbed and flowed around the benefits of drinking the local brew, the heat of the day and other small talk. In a while, once each was feeling a little more confident that he would not inadvertently offend the other's sensibilities, the talk turned towards their separate reasons for being in Ndola. Flick's purpose in Zambia was not something that he would ever openly admit to, but being a practised deceiver it was easy for him to concoct a story about being an oil man on leave from Houston who had flown over to bag some hunting trophies. He turned to admire the mean-looking head of a buffalo on the wall. It bore a proud spread of horns, anchored to its skull by a thick helmet of solid bone.

"I'd like to get me one of those." They tossed the subject around for a few more minutes.

After a while, something in the way that Charles's attention kept drifting towards the bubbles rising in his glass began to suggest to Flick that his companion was holding back some melancholy secret. Having nothing better to do, and aware that Charles was probably a drink or two ahead of him, Flick bought another round and determined to uncover the hidden problem. "So what brings you to these parts, Chuck?"

Charles looked down at his beer, then up at the rows of bottles arranged in front of the full-length bar mirror. Flick could see that he had not focused – it was displacement activity. The guy was stalling for time – either thinking how to begin or thinking up a lie. Flick waited for a sign that might tell him which option he would choose.

Charles stroked the side of his nose with his right forefinger. "Oh – I'm an economist." For the first time he seemed to notice a bowl of nuts on the bar. He reached forward and took a few, then moved the bowl in an unconscious way so that it rested between them. "Been sent here by the World Bank to write a preliminary report on the Zambian economy."

"I guess that was your typewriter I could hear, then? Next door to me. Just bashing away all afternoon."

"Sorry. Yep."

"Zambia trying to get a loan or something?"

"Well, I can't say too much, but you could guess most of it. It's all pretty obvious."

"So – no loan?"

"Not my decision. Zambia may be relatively rich for an African nation, but the whole economy depends on copper. Trouble is, they can't smelt the ore without power from Kariba and coal from Southern Rhodesia, so the new independent government here has to be polite to the old white colonial government over the border." There seemed no hurry. Charles paused to let this information take root, twisting his glass, idly wiping away the beads of condensation with one finger.

"But they need the world price of copper to stay high," he continued. "If the price falls, they're done for. And the country's land-locked. To export their copper, there's only two choices – south to Beira, through Southern Rhodesia again, or west by rail."

"There's a railroad heading west, then?"

"Yes, but relying on that – well, it'd be a huge gamble. It'd mean valuable refined copper travelling a couple of hundred miles through the Congo – bandit country – then another eight hundred on the Benguela Railway to Lobito Bay." Charles fingered the condensation on his glass again. "And what if the Russians make Angola their next target, or Castro interferes – or even the Chinese? See the problem?"

"There must be better ways to make money. I guess there's no route to the east?"

"That's what Kaunda wants – it's his pet project. Him and Nyerere want to build a railway from the copperbelt to Dar es Salaam. It's been talked about since the war, but no African economy could afford it. Neither can Britain. How about the United States?"

"I hear there's copper in Canada," said Flick. "Doesn't sound like a good reason for Uncle Sam to build these guys a new railroad."

"That's my point. Not to mention all the local problems – hunger, disease, politics, Russia, war... Too risky."

"Building a railroad takes years. Isn't there a highway?"

"Only a dirt road," said Charles. "The rains will be here any day now. You'd never believe how deep the mud gets. Everything just squelches to a halt."

"Sounds like a few too many 'buts' to me."

Charles showed no desire to expand on his negative conclusions, so the conversation became trapped beneath this impasse and petered out. But Flick could see that although Charles's thoughts had floated far away, there were signs that he had been fabricating his story. Why? What had kept the guy busy on his typewriter? Was he indeed an economist, like he said, or something else – perhaps a con-artist? Maybe this was an attempt to sell shares in some mythical mining company to a gullible American? Flick smiled. If so, the guy had chosen the wrong sucker. But it could be something much more devious and interesting.

Flick mused about Charles's report. Getting sight of it shouldn't be too difficult. He shut out the sound of the punkah and allowed the lull to creep along undisturbed. Taking a swill of Tusker, he put the glass down on the bar an inch or two closer to Charles to disturb his introverted thoughts.

"I wouldn't want to depend on getting *my* exports out through the Congo. They reckon there's trouble brewing."

This brought Charles round. "You're telling me... My brother, Daniel... He's there right now."

This didn't sound like a lie. "Doing what?"

"Search me. Humping a radio around for Mad Mike and his mercenaries, I think. He's only a kid – he's supposed to be at university in London, not risking getting his head blown off. Right now, he might only be a hundred miles away from us, but it might as well be a million. I wish I could just whip across there and drag him back before it's too late. You can imagine what it's doing to our parents."

Flick remained silent, waiting to see whether there would be more, but Charles merely uttered a 'tut' as if he felt he had gone beyond the accepted code of *sang-froid* that governed the conduct of Britons abroad.

"Mothers, eh," said Charles. "Always worried about something."

The dismissive words seemed at odds with what Charles had said before. Was he too distracted, not concentrating on what he was saying, or was he trying to cover something up? Flick's mind was made up. He needed to take a quick look round Charles's room.

"Guess so. How'd your brother get mixed up in that sort of trouble?"

"No idea. One minute he's sitting in his room fixing radios and listening to Morse code, and the next minute he's signed on with a load of maniacs to recapture the Congo. Beats me."

"Is he any good at fixing radios and sending messages and that kind of thing?"

"He's clever, Flick – a natural."

"Well Chuck, it seems to me that if he's as good as that, the mercenaries will have figured out they need to keep him in one piece. They'll realise he's too valuable. As long as he survives, he'll make a sackful of dollars out of his little adventure."

Charles seemed to want to latch on to the hope of Dan's safety. Some of his despondency disappeared as he looked into Flick's face.

A rare hint of pity crept into Flick's voice. "Look, my friend. What we need right now is a steak and a couple more beers. It's on me. The company's paying. Why don't you go and book a table in the dining room? I'll be back as soon as I've paid a visit to the bathroom. Then you can tell me all about the big game in this part of the world."

Having excused himself, Ferguson headed briskly for room 205 and eased the Yale latch aside using a strip of thin, flexible plastic that always lay in his wallet. There, next to Charles's Courier typewriter sat a signed carbon copy of his report. Flick scanned through it quickly and left the room. So... Charles was no World Bank economist, but finding him had been a lucky break. And it was interesting that the British still had no firm idea of where the two nuclear weapons had disappeared to. Charles appeared to suspect that Stanleyville was a fair guess, but with a prize like that in Chinese hands, Flick would have bet a World Bank economist's salary that this Foreign Office analyst had got his guesswork in the wrong order and the bombs were now bound for China by way of Tanzania.

And something else had fallen into his lap. Maybe

another piece of luck, but Charles's brother, Daniel, sounded useful. Furthermore, he was right there on the spot.

Washington

Ray Cline felt that he owed it to Flick to be on immediate call for the first few days after the agent's arrival in Africa. With Flick, things often moved fast. Somebody needed to be on hand to make decisions – or sometimes to rein him in. So, Cline had decided to spend Sunday in the office and maybe catch up with a couple of things. And of course, if Flick turned over a promising rock or two it would be good to hear what had crawled out from underneath.

Ray had spent some time worrying over a despatch, sent earlier by Flick after learning that Chipokwe had tried to get to Kasaba Bay with some interesting air cargo. The trouble was that if Flick knew it, it might not be long before others found out too. If Chipokwe was at large with two nuclear weapons, they would make a handsome prize – a prize worth fighting for. This left him trying to second-guess what steps the opposition might take to make themselves the permanent owners of the two British nuclear weapons. He had begun to sketch out the various scenarios when his train of thought was disturbed by the arrival from the *Valdez* of their intercepted flash transmission from the RAF signals unit at Ndola. So – the British were tying together Chipokwe and the Chinese. There was a strong chance that the Chinese had got hold of the missing bombs already. You couldn't afford to underestimate Mao's boys. He picked up the phone.

"John, I've just had word. The Limeys seem to think there's a chance the Chi-coms have already got their hands on those nukes."

"Any chance of re-capturing them?"

"Too early to say. My guess is negative on that."

"Where do the British think they are now?"

"Top two guesses – and I mean guesses – are: one, headed for Stanleyville, and two, back to China by way of Tanzania. Right now, I can't figure out which one would be worse."

"Where's Flick?"

"Zambia – Ndola. Probably only a couple of miles from where the British signal was sent."

"We'll have to depend on Leitner to look after the Congo scenario. Put together a signal to brief him. How soon can we get Flick mobile and headed for Tanzania?"

"Eight hours ahead, John. He's probably sleeping, but I'll send the signal."

"You'd better get word to Bundy, too, and we'll toss ideas around tomorrow morning."

Tuesday 3 November, 1964; 17:25
Johnson Ranch, Johnson City, Texas

Bundy knew by the way the President's puffy red eyes had come to rest on the photograph of his favourite beagle that the man had no more to give. The election had drained him totally. Through pain and lack of sleep, Johnson's capacity to give his attention to anything new had sunk to bedrock. But win or lose, America expected one final thing of the man: the end-game at the Driskill Hotel in Austin and later at the State Capitol. Although Bundy figured there was no point in detaining him, he had misjudged. There was clearly a fraction more on the President's mind.

"Mac. Whichever way it turns out today – well, tomorrow, business just carries on. No let up, till January, right?"

"That's so, Mr President."

"And the Pentagon and the generals in Vietnam don't need any hand-holding from me for a couple more days?"

"I guess not."

"But two things... Stanleyville. The generals aren't on top of the hostage situation yet?"

"The Joint Chiefs don't have a firm plan right now, no."

"And I guess there's still no admission from Prime Minister Wilson or any word about tracing those Limey bombs?" Bundy shook his head. His wordless reply and the disappointment on his face were enough. "You know, Mac... we're going to have to fix both those things ourselves. Tell DCI McCone I want action. No delays. I want a briefing on Saturday."

"Yes, Mr President."

Fourteen

Scarcely had Dan and his colleagues returned to Kamina before they were air-lifted to Kongolo to form a mechanised column with the objective of fighting their way north to liberate Stanleyville. Within four days, under the command of Lieutenant-Colonel Albert Liegeois, Hoare's 'Stan Column' had taken Kibombo, against weak resistance. Before fleeing into the bush, however, the retreating rebels had murdered three Europeans. Naturally, this enraged both the mercenaries and the Belgian regulars. Assuming he had the advantage, Liegeois pressed his fired-up troops forward towards Kindu, overcoming a number of roadside ambushes and taking the town the following day. Air support provided by Free Cuban pilots, flying obsolete American combat aircraft, proved decisive. In Kamina, Vanderwalle had not calculated on such rapid progress.

Sitting in the abandoned telephone exchange, Hoare was able to follow much of the conversation in French between Liegeois and his headquarters. He gathered that Vanderwalle wanted Liegeois to consolidate the position. Liegeois protested. It was imperative to forge onward to Stanleyville. Hoare could see why. Up country, many Europeans still needed rescuing. His troops had freed numerous hostages and discovered many others already butchered. Following this, for some reason the mercenaries had found it impossible to take many prisoners alive. Cooped up in Kindu, discipline might start falling apart. But Vanderwalle had another small matter to discuss.

Liegeois turned to Hoare. "I need to detach one of your signallers, Mike."

"Why?"

"A favour to the CIA. They need a good Morse man – somebody with no American connections. They want to operate a secret monitoring station in the hills west of Lake Tanganyika. Intelligence reckons Castro's about to send in a battalion of regulars."

"I need good radio operators too, Albert."

"The Americans are paying for our air support. We can't really refuse."

"Is Leitner behind this?" Liegeois nodded. "He can have Schmidt, then."

"He wants Rook."

"Rook? He can't have Rook. Not only is he the best signals man I've got, but he's the kid who killed that Chink in the dark from a range of three hundred yards. If I ever need a sniper, I've got one already – Rook. I can't decide whether to call him 'Marconi', 'Cat's-eyes' or 'Dead-eyed Dick'. He can't have Rook."

Monday 16 November, 1964
Kivu Province, DRC

"We're just too thin on the ground, Danny," said Flick. "I need you to stay here –"

"– Up in the rain clouds."

"At least you'll be safer here than where you were before." Clearly, after only a few days in his new mountain home, Danny saw only inconveniences and did not yet appreciate the life-preserving advantages of not being on the front line. "I've got a job to do in Stanleyville for a few days. You and the boys just keep listening out for signs that the bad guys are building up their forces over there."

"And the other thing?"

"Moving the bombs?"

"Yep. If this isn't a wild goose chase, I think they're running out of options, Flick."

"How so?"

"Well, you can see for yourself." Danny flapped a hand at the overcast sky. "Now the rains have come, if they try to get the bombs out by road, they'll get bogged down. Their best option is to ship them to Kigoma, then by rail to the coast at Dar."

Ferguson shook his head. "Maybe so, but we can't risk snooping around the docks at Kigoma for weeks on end, or in the railway yards. And we haven't got anybody local, less obvious, who could take it on right now."

"If you say so. But I've been thinking about that, Flick. Lend me your notebook for a minute." Ferguson opened his notebook at a fresh page and passed it across without a word. Danny talked as he sketched. First, a crude drawing of a railway train pulling a couple of wagons across the page, from left to right – from west to east.

"Now, what your people want to know is not only if they go, but when they go. What about this? What we need is a sensor and a recording device, so we can detect the bomb remotely." He drew a lightning bolt coming out of one of the wagons. "Radiation." Flick nodded. "We could detect that with a sensitive Geiger counter, buried in the track ballast, just under the surface." Danny scribbled a square ahead of the train and shaded it in "If your people could set this up near the track, somewhere quiet, maybe twenty miles east of Kigoma, hopefully they could scan every eastbound train, and no need to hang around the docks. But whoever they send, he needs to stay hidden, so nobody on the train gets suspicious. That's where this comes in." He drew a curved line from the shaded box, attaching it to a bigger rectangle in which he showed a cylinder with a wavy line running across it.

"This thing is a bit like a barograph," continued Danny. "Normally it turns a complete circle once a day and an inky needle records the changing air pressure as the drum with the graph paper moves round. What we need is the guts of a barograph with the cog ratios changed so it turns a complete circle in only about twenty minutes. Except it's not going to be recording air pressure any more, but radioactivity." He tapped the paper with his biro. "There must be a way to stick an amplifier here in the middle to make the Geiger signal big enough to give us a read-out. Then a way of moving the pen up and down, so it's effectively just a voltmeter with a pen attached instead of a needle. The operator sets the thing running when he sees a train coming. And when the bombs pass over the top of the counter..." With his biro he added a jagged spike in the middle of the wavy line. "He gets an indication on the trace."

"Yeah... So he knows the bombs have passed and on which train."

"Yep. Maybe even which part of the train. If the operator was hiding behind some rocks or something, watching the needle, he might even tell which wagon triggered the spike."

Flick grinned. "I reckon that might just work."

"Could your people fix up something like that and get it out here really fast with somebody to operate it?"

"That's what they're there for. You know what, Danny? You're a smart kid. I think you may just have solved one of our problems."

Danny let the lashing rain subside to a gentle patter before venturing out of the tent. Though the camp was only five degrees south of the equator, the temperature at over seven thousand feet was bitter during the frequent rainstorms. He gazed out to the east, but the rain clouds obscured the lake. On a clear day you could look right across to Kigoma, forty miles distant and maybe a vertical mile lower in altitude. But today, under slate-grey clouds, the mist obscured everything farther away than a hundred yards in any direction.

A burst of Spanish chatter erupted from the open door of the US Army so-called 'surplus' radio truck. The direction-finding loop aerials on the roof twitched a few degrees to either side before the operator could be certain where the signal was coming from. With a hiss and a crackle of static the transmission subsided into silence again. The Free-Cuba radio operator appeared at the door.

"Only a radio test, señor Rook. His boat hasn't moved from Kigoma." Lake Tanganyika could be treacherous enough in any season. The current crop of squalls would prevent Castro's speedboats from ferrying arms or guerrillas across the lake until there was chance of a calm, dark night. If things went well and they were lucky, Danny might be able to call down an air strike from one of the CIA-sponsored *Makasi* pilots.

A couple of hours earlier, Flick had radioed-in. Although he had accomplished his mission at the US consulate in Stanleyville, and although the vast majority of the hostages had been rescued, it seemed his luck had deserted him. True, Langley had approved Danny's idea, knocked together a prototype bomb-detector for a field trial and shipped out a mark-one version with an agent in less than a week. However, so far, no eastbound trains appeared to be carrying detectable quantities of nuclear material. Flick had no resources to widen the search, so with the whole Congo basin and now the Great Rift as their target, they needed a breakthrough.

Danny glanced at his watch. Two hours forty before his next radio schedule with the *Valdez*, and another 'no activity' report to send. Hitching his belt and holster up above his hips again, he strolled off to answer a call of nature, leaving the barefoot Cuban teasing out a couple of troublesome jiggers from between his toes.

Sunday 20 December, 1964
Institute of Atomic Energy of the Chinese Academy of Sciences, Beijing

"So, Engineer Guo," said the white-coated scientist, speaking in English for the benefit of Chipokwe. "You and our honoured guest have done well. Your photographs do indeed seem to show a British nuclear weapon – two indeed – as we expected when the news first came through of the accident at Ndola." He turned to acknowledge a military man seated at the circular table. "Marshal Nieh has asked me to add the congratulations of the People's Liberation Army." The academic shuffled his papers for a moment. "What a pity that the devices are not, even now, here in the Institute." Was this a rebuke for lack of initiative when the bombs first came into China's hands – a reprimand for lack of determination? The words stung Guo for a moment until the scientist closed his hands together in front of his chest, as if about to pronounce a blessing or utter a prayer. But instead, he began to clap.

Taking this as their signal, the soldiers, atomic experts and Party officials in the room did likewise, wreathed in smiles. The academic moved to where Chipokwe was sitting and patted him warmly on the shoulder, to the ex-minister's obvious delight. Chipokwe acknowledged the applause, bowing his head and smiling in return. The assembly redoubled its applause and the People's smiles grew wider still.

"Comrade Guo," said the general. "This man will be nothing but trouble. We cannot set him up with a palace and harem of his own as he seems to require. Word will quickly leak out and we shall be condemned."

Guo inclined his head but said nothing beyond a thoughtful 'mmm'.

"He is of almost no value to us... But of course," the general added with a certain chill, "at the moment, no-one can be certain that he's here in China."

As a relatively lowly engineer, Guo felt unsure what further part he might have to play. The ensuing pause, following the general's icy words, prompted him to fill the silence by underlining his own loyalty. "It's an honour for me to have been of service to The People."

"Indeed so." The general placed his forearms on the desk, brought his hands together and interlaced his fingers. "We have your photographs, so I'm sure we can very easily find the spot where the bombs are buried, just as I presume you intended." Long before the pair arrived in Beijing, Guo had already realised how poor Chipokwe's bargaining position was. He wondered when the African would work it out for himself. Some slight evidence of these thoughts must have appeared on his face. "What are you thinking, Guo?"

"Well, Comrade General, it's only that it was something like ten days after he and I parted company before we met again in Dar es Salaam. I hope he trusted me enough not to be thinking about … er, insurance…"

"Are you suggesting that perhaps Chipokwe could have returned with a crew of African labour, dug up the bombs again and then re-buried them somewhere else?"

"We have to consider it. On the other hand, time was short. It would have been difficult to organise and hard to keep secret. But it's still a possibility."

"It seems neither of us feels we can trust him completely, then."

Guo chose his next words with care. "He *is* a western-oriented politician, after all."

"Ex-English public school."

"The very people who have placed China in the position we are now suffering. Someone like Chipokwe might not naturally play fair… or show his whole hand to us."

The general sat back and smiled. "Which is why, once interest in this matter has died down, we shall be sending you back to Zambia with an African graduate from the academy at Nanking. You will take him to where you buried the bombs and confirm to me that they're still there. If they are, he will organise a guard for them until we can safely get them out of the country. You will then return to Dar es Salaam to report on the state of East Africa's railway network."

"Is Mister Chipokwe coming with us?"

"No. He will stay here. He may live like a prince until we decide whether we need him or not."

Thursday, 4 February, 1965
Ministry of Defence, London

The secretary of state for defence and his permanent secretary were closeted together, engaged in a last preprint reading of the final draft of the Defence White Paper – the *Statement on the Defence Estimates 1965*. In one week's time the cabinet would be asked to approve the document.

Being a distinguished ex-soldier with a strong sense of loyalty, the minister took no pleasure in wielding the axe, although in the case of the Royal Air Force he was beginning to feel some justification.

"Paragraph one-four-nine," said the permanent secretary.

The minister had underlined the words about the entire Valiant fleet being withdrawn from service due to metal fatigue. The words reminded him of the incompetence that had led to the Ndola incident. "No further comment," he replied, in a monotone.

Together they moved from the subsection on equipment to the topic of administration. They dealt with the Royal Dockyards and the Royal Ordnance factories and came at length to the subject of surveying.

"Paragraph one-seven-five."

The minister looked down at his copy where heavy circling, underlining and several angry exclamation marks revealed his feelings. Photographic reconnaissance aircraft had undertaken surveys of Zambia, Southern Rhodesia and Bechuanaland. His tone altered as he growled the words: "No further comment."

"Quite... I imagine the RAF must feel very embarrassed about not being able to locate those two bombs, Minister. It seemed like such a good idea at the time."

"And to think they screwed another seven hundred and twenty thousand quid out of me for that idiotic idea. Astounding!" The minister gasped in frustration, running his fingers through his already disordered hair. "Well, that's their last chance... Madness! Finding the bombs by detecting increased levels of radiation from the air. Absolutely potty. Some of those people couldn't find a fanny at the Folies Bergère."

One week later, the minutes of the cabinet meeting showed that the cabinet 'took note, with approval, of the Statement on the Defence Estimates, 1965'.

Saturday 24 April, 1965
Kivu Province

For no particular reason, the thought occurred to Danny that he had been a nominal mercenary now for six months. However, barely a month of that had been spent as part of the fighting force. For most of the past five months he had been sitting in the clouds on top of his mountain, relaying intelligence signals to the *Valdez* and trying to keep the radio equipment working in the midst of the most oppressive humidity that he had ever experienced.

Danny's Free Cuban colleagues were generally a committed bunch of people, although enforced exile made them prone to bouts of the blues. On these occasions their professionalism faded away and they became distinctly morose. They attempted to dissolve these moods with white rum, though with limited success. There was little that Danny could do about the binges except join in for good form, try to pour away more than he drank, feign intoxication as soon as seemed reasonable and weave his way back to his tent to sleep it off. He had developed a useful technique of wandering into the jungle a little way, where he would throw up as much of his stomach's contents as possible, then return to his tent for a Hershey bar before turning in. So far, the Cubans had not rumbled this deception, which also allowed him to maintain the sober level of service that Flick expected.

A month before, Danny had written to his parents to let them know that he was well and that because he was not operating on the front line, he was not in great danger. He knew this was not strictly true but he felt he owed them some encouragement. He had only given his letter a fifty-fifty chance of getting through. So far, he had not received a reply. He hoped the violence had not spread and that nothing awful had happened to his family.

The radio operator ambled out of the truck with his head bent forward. He gripped a single piece of paper with both hands and stared intently at the message as if reading it for the first time, even though he had scribbled the note only half a minute before. This apparent respect gave temporary significance to the scrap – an example of what the team at the listening post had come to know as a 'Simbagram'. He entered Dan's tent and spoke.

"Have we heard of anyone code-named 'Tatu' before? It's not quite the same as the Spanish word for 'tattoo' and the sense was different – it was used like a name."

"What about the accent?"

"Same as before – Cuban-accented Spanish."

"Let's have a look." The operator passed the message across. Danny's Spanish had improved from zero to commendable in those few months. "Well, it's the first I've seen of anyone with that name." He thought for a moment. "*Tatu* sounds like Swahili for the number three. It looks to me more like the alias for a third Cuban fighter, particularly as we've already come across *moja* and *mbili*. Probably someone quite important." He read through the transcription again. The code-words seemed amateurish. But unless a message came through in clear, Danny's unit was not allowed to act on supposition.

"Did it come from the same direction – Kigoma?" The

Cuban nodded. "Okay, better code up the conversation and bang it out on the circuit to the *Valdez* – see if they can make anything of it."

But the act of enciphering the message, transmitting it, deciphering it on board the *Valdez* and then interpreting the embedded intelligence took almost three hours. During that window in time, Tatu's launch glided unmolested across Lake Tanganyika and Number Three landed in darkness at the small, isolated fishing village of Kibamba on the western side of the lake.

≈

Friday 28 May: Robert W Komer of the National Security Council staff sent a memo to McGeorge Bundy saying that President Kaunda had cornered Averell Harriman at the Addis Ababa conference. Kaunda had warned that Zhou Enlai was due in Tanzania within the week and was going to offer to build the railroad to the coast. Komer informed Bundy that Kaunda had pleaded for a Western counter-offer 'to keep the Chicoms out of the heart of Africa'.

≈

Tuesday 29 June: At Bendera in the Democratic Republic of the Congo, mercenary forces recovered the bodies of two rebels. One of them was wearing a pair of underpants bearing a label that established their origin to be 'Hecho en Cuba'. The other was carrying a Cuban passport and a notebook naming an international revolutionary, fighting in the Congo under the code-name 'Tatu', whose whereabouts had been unknown for many weeks.

Thursday 1 July: Before flying home from Heathrow Airport after the Commonwealth Conference, Simon Mwansa Kapwepwe, the Zambian Foreign Minister answered a question from a member of the press. The minister denied that there had been any offer from China to build a new TANZAM railway although he was grateful that Britain had offered to pay half the cost of surveying the route.

≈

Saturday 13 November, 1965
Kivu Province

Flick had long since returned to God-only-knew-where, leaving Danny in nominal command of the Free Cuban listening post. For some while, Danny had felt unsure of who he was working for. Was he an honorary Free Cuban, an irregular CIA operative or a solitary outpost of Hoare's mercenary army, overlooked or abandoned? True, Coca Cola, white rum and other essential supplies kept arriving, so he wasn't entirely forgotten; he just hoped he was still getting paid.

Radio intercepts from Tatu and his followers had recently become more frequent, more curt and more discontented in character. The direction-finding equipment indicated that Tatu had turned to the east and was moving back towards Lake Tanganyika. It could only mean that the Cuban revolutionaries were in retreat.

≈

Saturday, 20 November: Disheartened, sick with dysentery and severe asthma, Tatu, with the remainder of his band of Cuban fighters, evaded the patrol boats, slipped away from Sele, on the Congo shore of Lake Tanganyika, and escaped to Kigoma. Whilst the rest of his irregular troops returned to Cuba, Ernesto 'Tatu' 'Che' Guevara made his way to Dar es Salaam for treatment. He lived there under cover for some time to write an account of his time in the Congo.

≈

Sunday 21 November: The United Nations Security Council passed Resolution 217, implementing a trade embargo against the Smith regime in Southern Rhodesia. The Resolution was passed by ten votes to nil; France abstained. Since Zambia had always obtained petroleum products from the refinery at Umtali in Southern Rhodesia, and because the embargo included oil, this left Zambia needing to obtain its supplies from elsewhere.

On the following day, orders for new oil drums were placed at Mombasa. Space was chartered to bring fuel by rail from there to Dar es Salaam and onwards via the Tanzanian central rail line to Kigoma and thence by barge to Mpulungu.

≈

Friday, 26 November, 1965, Leopoldville, DRC

Lieutenant General J D Mobutu, President of the Republic, thanked the Belgian ambassador who retired with great dignity from his office leaving him alone with his shorthand secretary. Mobutu leaned back in his padded leather swivel-chair and sighed. He held a single sheet of paper, folded in half, which he swished through the air to open the fold. The preamble declared the document to be a summary of accumulated intelligence reports, forwarded by courtesy of the President of the United States of America.

Mobutu had waited a long time for this news. A great smile spread across his glistening face. He would read the document again and again for the pleasure it would bring. 'Tatu' had fled. The Simba rebellion was over.

Mobutu laid down the note, paused to collect his thoughts, then turned to his secretary to dictate a letter of thanks.

«*Lettre... au Colonel Hoare, Durban, Afrique du Sud... Mon cher Colonel... C'est avec un sincère et profond regret... que je vous vois quitter cette terre congolaise... que vous servez depuis bientôt deux ans...*»

The mercenary war in the Congo was won. It was time for the Wild Geese to fly home.

Sunday, 28 November, 1965
Kitongyama, Zambia

"It doesn't feel like a whole eight months since I was here," said Guo. A half-remembered proverb hovered at the back of his mind. "Time is like water in a stream – it trickles away..."

"...And when it's gone, it's gone for ever. I know. You're sure this is the right place?"

"It's the right place." He pointed up to the overhanging branch. "See the two marks where the rope rubbed through the bark when Chippy and I lowered the crates into the hole."

Guo stood with his hands on his hips, contemplating the area below the branch. Instead of the expected low mound of earth that he and Chipokwe had left, the ground was now slightly saucer-shaped. This discovery added to his fear that in those few days Chipokwe had returned and dug up the bombs. For weeks, Guo's mind had constantly played on the consequences for himself if Chipokwe had indeed squirreled away the two bombs in some unwise attempt to guarantee his future. The thought made his pulse gallop and left a churning feeling in his guts. He knew what Jonas thought about it – that with the ex-minister now effectively a prisoner on Chinese soil, the man would have to be insane to believe he could hold China to ransom.

Jonas seemed to understand. "Look – if the bombs have been moved it's not your fault." He lifted two shovels and the Geiger counter from the back of the Jeep and switched on the detector. "There's certainly a lot of radioactivity here. Let's hope it's the bombs and not just leftover contamination." He handed a shovel to Guo. "Come on. Let's get digging."

In a matter of minutes, they exposed the woodwork on the tops of the crates. "Feeling better, now?" said Jonas through a wide ivory grin.

Guo sat on the ground, puffing up his cheeks and wiping his forehead. "Let's wait until we can see inside."

Jonas took a crowbar and levered off one of the top planks. Although neither crate had collapsed, in nailing the top surface together a slight gap had been left between one or two of the lengths of dunnage. Jonas prised away a second and third plank, then leaned over to peer into the void. Guo stepped forward, now panting, his eyes wide open. Jonas withdrew his head and turned to face Guo. He tightened his lips and shook his head. Guo fell to his knees with a cry, but Jonas simply rolled away, covering his eyes and laughing with delight.

"It's okay, it's okay. Take a look!"

Guo scrambled towards the hole and let out a whoop. Over time, loose soil had seeped through into the cavity, possibly helped by the rains. But, joy of joys, there lay the core of the first bomb, resting on a thick carpet of half-dried mud.

"You gave me a shock."

Jonas laughed again. "It was worth it. Are you going to stop worrying now?"

"Not yet. You see all that mud? We ought to try to scoop it out. It's still damp down there. What if it rusted all those ball-bearings into a solid lump?" Guo could see that Jonas understood, but the African had not bounced straight back in agreement. "What do you think?"

"Listen – I don't want to get a fatal dose of radiation. I'd rather hire a gang of labourers when the time comes. For now, I vote we nail the planks down again, shovel earth back over the crates, then go away and buy some tarpaulins. We'll come straight back, uncover the crates and spread the tarps over them to stop any more earth trickling inside."

"I'm not sure. I'm glad Chippy didn't move them, but..."

"I know it's urgent," said Jonas. "But we might have to go through another rainy season before Beijing works out a way of transporting the bombs to China. If we had somewhere to store them – I mean, totally secure – I'd say we should do that, but right now they're safest where they are."

"Maybe you're right," said Guo.

"You'll contact Beijing?"

"Yes – as soon as I can. I wouldn't want to be Chippy a day or two from now."

"No. I wouldn't trust him. Once a traitor, always a traitor – that's what I say."

"No doubt he'll disappear like a thousand others."

Jonas stood up, planted his shovel in the loose earth and leaned on it for a few moments, clearly searching for the right words. "Just think of him as a petty-bourgeois casualty of imperialist war-mongering in the People's struggle to assert their fundamental rights."

Guo found it hard to decide whether Jonas was being serious.

Fifteen

At leisure on Saturdays, Charles had grown used to a detailed reading of *The Times*.

He harrumphed over the report from Addis Ababa where members of the Organization of African Unity had given Britain an ultimatum: Crush the Smith regime in Rhodesia before December 15th, otherwise African states would break off diplomatic relations with Britain.

Charles anticipated that the Prime Minister would not be greatly moved by their threats. Anyway, it was impossible. The commonwealth secretary was still deadlocked with President Kaunda over stationing British troops in Zambia. Kay-Kay had not yet forgiven Britain for the Ndola affair or for failing to make an offer to build the railway to Dar es Salaam. Denied a bridgehead through which to land troops, the OAU deadline was farcical.

He wondered whether anything had leaked out about the real reason why the Valiant aircraft had been grounded at Ndola, and the disappearance of Chipokwe. The policeman, Makondo, was a weak link, of course – and anyone in the first few hours who might have helped to crate-up the bombs' central sections. Although security in Africa was a joke, if rumours of missing nuclear weapons had reached members of the OAU, it could easily explain their threats. The last thing those gentlemen wanted was the possibility of the weapons turning up in Southern Rhodesia.

Things seemed to have quietened down in the Congo.

Charles's gaze drifted up from the newsprint as his thoughts turned to his brother. Was Daniel even still alive? Would he ever see him again? The mercenary war had ended, but there had been no news or relief for the family. He had kept an eye open for any opportunity to intervene discreetly, but with no clues as to his brother's whereabouts he was powerless to influence matters. The worry of it all had made his parents ill.

Reading on through *The Times*, Charles raised his eyebrows on discovering that Lockheed had demonstrated an air cargo operation that lifted 6,000 gallons of diesel fuel from Dar es Salaam to Ndola and returned with twenty-three tons of copper ingots. There was also a summarised cost analysis showing how many aircraft would be required to airlift Zambia's whole annual copper production to the coast. Charles snorted at the figures.

Just below the item about the airlift lay a short report filed the previous day by the paper's correspondent in Dar es Salaam. A convoy system was being set up. Fuel in oil drums would be brought by rail from Mombasa to Mikumi in Tanzania and loaded on to lorries. Cargoes would be restricted to five tons to avoid damaging the Tanzanian roads, which were acknowledged to be poor. (Charles raised his eyebrows in mock surprise at this shameless overstatement.) Ten lorries at a time would then ferry petroleum products to the Zambian border, a journey of 450 miles, returning with copper for export. With road transport at the mercy of the weather and the highways repair budget, Charles estimated the road would be wrecked within the first week.

The articles only confirmed what he had been saying for eighteen months. The telling difference between Harold Wilson and Ian Smith was that the first was an economist and the other was a fighter. In a practical sense, without

Smith lifting a finger, the UN sanctions that were intended to strangle Rhodesia would strangle Zambia a lot sooner. 'And,' thought Charles, 'it'll set the whole of Africa baying for our blood.'

Sunday 12 December, 1965
Dar es Salaam, Tanzania

Guo stood in front of the lorry's warm radiator grille, patting the chromium-plated symbols with approval – M•A•N Diesel 415. The cab, bonnet and front wheel arches had received a recent coat of glossy white paint. Someone had stencilled the words 'ZAMBIA FUEL AID' in black on both cab doors. Sandwiched between some thirty steel oil drums, the cargo deck held half a dozen railway sleepers, a quantity of freshly-sawn whitewood, a chain block and two stout poles. The whole kit was tightly bound together with half-inch steel wire and lashed to the truck in shipshape fashion. But only two of the drums contained oil – a supply of diesel fuel to keep the truck moving. The others were three-quarters full of water, making the weight for the sake of appearance.

The lorry's owner, an Arab merchant, looked out of place in his Chairman Mao suit. He pressed the self-starter. The engine spun, whistling and coughing into life, before settling into a comfortable rhythm. From the rear of the truck, Jonas nodded as the initial puff of black exhaust fumes dispersed into the morning air. He sauntered to the front of the vehicle, smoothing his hand over the bodywork.

"How's she sound?" asked Guo.

"No rumbling, so I don't think the big-end bearings are worn." Jonas cocked his head on one side, listening for several seconds. "I can't hear any piston-slap either. No squeaky water pump or blowing exhaust. I think she's good." He flashed an appreciative expression at Guo. "Do you want me to take her for a quick test-drive?"

Guo shook his head, then turned away, feigned a cough and spoke out of the corner of his mouth. "It's a matter of trust. He's hoping for more business." The owner jumped down from the cab and invited Jonas to climb into it. Guo handed over an envelope of cash, which the owner accepted with a bow, making no attempt to count it. They exchanged a brief conversation, then shook hands. Jonas climbed up into the cab.

"He says the convoy won't get going until Wednesday," said Guo.

"I told you they wouldn't be well-organised. It should be easy to stay well ahead of them." Jonas gripped the steering wheel and leaned forward a little, as if anxious to leave. "And easier to get through Mikumi in the dark, before any local officials are awake."

Guo reached up to pass a forged bill of lading to Jonas, consigning the bogus fuel to Mpulungu. "Good luck, Jonas. I'll see you soon. And thanks for everything."

Once beyond Mikumi the plan called for Jonas to divert off the road about ten miles short of the border and wait until the convoy started to trickle past. With luck it would be quite strung out by then. This would allow him to tag along somewhere in the middle. By the time the convoy reached the border, the ten official trucks could easily have become nine or fewer. They expected the vehicles to be waved straight through the customs post and, even if by some miracle eleven vehicles appeared where only ten were expected, Guo figured that Jonas would be long gone before the eleventh driver was asked to justify his arrival.

Wednesday 15 December, 1965
Bulawayo Road, Southern Rhodesia

"Hey! Stop the car." Danny twisted round in the rear seat of the Hillman taxi. "Reverse up to that woman." The Lebanese taxi driver, no doubt out of respect for his tyre tread and brake linings, slowed to a gentle stop. Sanctions had been running for a whole month. People said that motor spares and fuel would be harder to obtain. Everything would have to come by road from South Africa now. He began to reverse. Danny wound down the window.

"Miriam?" The woman stopped and turned her head, seemingly astonished.

"Massa Daniel? Is that you?"

He climbed out of the taxi and with joy clasped his arms around the old Shona woman. They seemed to reach further round than they had before. "What are you doing out here? Why aren't you back at the farm?"

"Mister Rook and your Mamma sold the farm, Massa Daniel. Gone away."

Joy turned to anguish. "What? I don't understand." The reasons for returning – the pillars that had supported his whole life – eroded in an instant, crumbling into nothing more substantial than a heap of sand.

Miriam sniffed. "New man only want the land and a couple of the farm boys. He got no use for us old folks. New man promise your Daddy to look after Noah and me, but..." On her head she had been carrying her belongings, the pathetic bundle wrapped in a blanket. She lowered it to the ground, looked down at her bare feet and changed the subject. "Praise the Lord you're safe Massa Daniel."

"Don't worry about me, Miriam." God! This was so unexpected, and so unjust. In that instant, Danny's throat felt choked with dust. His vision shrank, tunnel-like. He drew in a great gasp of air, an instinctive reaction to his anger and the sudden pounding of his heart. The sound of rushing blood filled his ears along with the echo of his own words, disembodied, as if from a distant room. "Where are you going?" Another gulp of air, then, "Who's going to look after you?" In seconds his vision began to clear, and his heartbeat to settle. Clearly Miriam had no idea where to go or what to do. Her chin and bottom lip quivered and her agèd blueing eyes started to glisten. The remote voice drew closer and he heard himself say, "You'd better get in the car with me."

"Hey – is not a good idea – you know that," grumbled the taxi driver. "I can't take her."

At least the fellow had not driven off and abandoned them. "Can't or won't?"

"I got plenty other customers to think about."

"How much?" The driver sat silent. "Nobody's going to see you out here." Danny gestured towards Bulawayo, the direction from which they had come. "How much to take us to that village we passed six or seven miles back?"

"Dollars?"

"Yeah – dollars."

"I'll do it for twenty."

Danny's nostrils flared. "You'll do it for five."

The taxi retreated in a cloud of dust, leaving Danny standing beside his canvas rucksack and the heavy kitbag full of possessions. He called out to the house.

"Mum! – Dad! I'm home." A hundred yards away, two Africans sidled out of their shacks and stood looking over at him. They made no move to come across. Silence. He raised his voice and called again. "Hey! Hello! Anyone home?"

Distant sounds of movement came from within – then a muffled order, sharp, not in English, maybe a command to a guard dog. Presently a man appeared behind the fly-screen door. Danny could see that he was dressed in khaki, with a holstered handgun dragging down the belt at the right-hand side of his shorts. A heavy calibre job. The man opened the door and stood on the stoep in the shade. He seemed to feel no threat from Danny.

"What you want, son? There's no jobs going here."

Danny smiled and shook his head. "No, I don't need a job. I'm Daniel. I was hoping to find my parents at home." The man failed to latch onto the clues. "Er... I live here."

He thought he heard a mocking nasal puff from the man – not quite a sneer, but far from welcoming. With his eyes shaded beneath his wide-brimmed hat, Danny had had a few seconds to assess the man. Red face, unreceptive, short-cropped ginger hair, a slight paunch and an accent from a long way south. He reckoned the guy was perhaps just top side of fifty. Two large dogs moved closer behind him.

"Not any more, kid."

"I don't understand... May I ask who you are?"

"De Vries. I own this place now. Bought it off your folks six months ago, lock, stock and barrel, legal title, everything fair and square."

"Oh." Danny's voice sank. "I see." He removed his hat and fiddled with the brim.

"How come you turn up here and don't know a thing about it?"

Danny bowed his head as if to acknowledge his sudden lower status, then looked up again. "Sorry, sir. Been away – up north."

"Zambia?"

"Congo." He sucked in his cheeks. "We moved about a

bit. I guess the mail was worse than we all thought." He tried his best to look crestfallen. "I wrote to tell them I was okay. Well... a couple of times, anyway..."

De Vries shifted his feet, making his stance a little less aggressive. He glanced down at the military kitbag and the webbing backpack. A flash of understanding, perhaps tinged with respect, flickered across his fleshy face. "Kill any Kaffirs?"

Danny nodded without expression. The man grinned.

"Any idea where my parents are now, sir?"

"Your old man said something about heading for Australia... Maybe New Zealand."

"Didn't they leave word for me – a letter or anything?" De Vries remained silent. "What about my books and my radio stuff?" Danny suspected the fellow had sold them. He tried again. "Isn't there a trunk or any boxes? Something with my name on?"

Danny watched the man's face. Shifty. There was something he wanted to avoid saying. There – the glottal double grunt of denial and a slight shake of the head to reinforce the negative message. De Vries swallowed. So that was it. He hadn't trusted his voice when taken by surprise and compelled to respond with an unrehearsed lie. A wordless rumble was easier, then the swallow to ease the tightness in his throat. Danny knew that, if necessary, his mother would have climbed off her deathbed to leave a letter for him. And this two-faced bastard had chucked it out along with the rest of his things.

"Oh, I see. Nothing, then?" Danny set his mouth to show disappointment.

"Got any folks anywhere else?"

There seemed to be no point mentioning Lizzie. "Brother in London."

"He's best getting out of there, eh man? Wilson and his

English commie bastards are fucking up a good country there as well as here."

Danny had already taken in the situation. Fifteen months gone and the place had become shabby. His mother's flower beds were brown and shrivelled, the fields too.

"Worst drought for years," said De Vries, as if this would excuse the fallen standards. He paused for a moment, then added: "I reckon that'll be Kaunda and his witch doctors over the border." It was a poor attempt at humour but he grinned again. Bad teeth.

Danny hung his head for a second. "So, it's a wasted trip." Then he brightened up. "Any chance of a lift back to Bulawayo, please sir?"

"You really have been away a long time, haven't you? There's a fuel shortage now, son... Umtali's nearly run dry. I'm driving nowhere if I don't have to."

Danny peered back down the road, then lifted his gaze to meet the man's eyes. "Looks like I've got a long hike back to town. Would the lady of the house be kind enough to give me a drink and maybe a spare bottle of water, please sir?"

"No lady here, son. Drought or no drought though, I guess I can spare you a bottle." Without inviting him to step into the shade, De Vries turned away to fetch the water. Danny put on his hat and watched as the fellow tramped along the passageway. One of the dogs stood up – a ridgeback. With a breed like that to back him up, there was no need for the guy to show any courtesy. Yes, that would be why the two farm boys had stayed away from the house instead of coming to say hello. His father had never treated his workers that way. Danny wondered how long they would take it.

De Vries soon returned with the promised bottle and

295

some water in a smeared glass. Danny touched his hat in thanks and drank from the glass to slake his thirst. He took a few moments to buckle his belongings together, then he swung the burden on to his back, waved farewell to De Vries and without another backward glance set off to return to the Bulawayo Road. Ahead of him the farm track sloped gently down towards a dry watercourse, rose slightly on the other side, then dipped again. Once the second dip had safely hidden him from sight, Danny turned to make sure that he was not being followed, then stopped. With this drought, if there were any big cats or hyenas around, he guessed they would be hungry. He stopped to unpack his gun.

A mile distant, a familiar rocky outcrop stood up above the surrounding bone-dry bush-country. He remembered the times he had spent there with Noah. He remembered Miriam's singing and how the Shona children came to listen, and how much it had all meant to him. Now grown, today those same children hadn't the courage to even call out to him.

Danny was sure he could find what he wanted over there amongst the rocks.

De Vries was late to bed. Danny waited until all the lights had gone out in the main house, then gave him a further twenty minutes before approaching the barn from behind the cover of the African workers' huts. He found keys in the ignition of both the Land Rover and his parents' Morris Traveller. He turned the keys. Each petrol gauge showed more than half full. He pocketed the set from the Morris and waited for another agonising twenty minutes, before emerging from the barn with a pair of his father's pliers in one gloved hand and a cotton shirt, gathered and knotted into a bag, in the other. Gliding barefoot over to where the telephone cable entered the house, he cut through the wires. Next, he crept up onto the stoep and, with considerable care, tipped out the contents of the shirt-bag in front of the fly-screen door.

De Vries awoke to the sound the Land Rover's starter motor and the roar of its engine as the vehicle burst into life, followed by the angry barking of his dogs. Grabbing his gun, and clad in only his underpants, he flung open the door and stepped forward as the vehicle sped past. He raised the gun and closed one eye to aim, but failed to notice where he was about to plant his foot. Though sluggish in the cool night air, the sturdy, four-foot-long puff adder, its body as thick as a man's forearm, struck instantly, injecting its venom into his calf. He fell, dropped the gun, cursed and rolled onto his side. The reptile hunched and rippled away, caterpillar-like, seeking a hiding place.

Danny dropped the other set of car keys on the far side of the riverbed and set off to recover his pack two miles ahead, resolving to seek out Miriam again. He should offer to take her to her own village, or at least leave her with some cash. This was no place for him to stay now, or his childhood nurse or the snake-charmer gardener, either.

Thursday 16 December, 1965; 19:35
The White House

Cline thanked the caller and put down the phone – the President's meeting with Prime Minister Wilson had ended. He looked around for something to hold, picked up a folder containing the day's despatches from Vietnam and headed for the water-cooler.

The thick carpet deadened the sound of Bundy's approaching footsteps, but Cline's sense of timing was more than equal to that. With his eyes buried sightlessly in an assessment of the build-up of Soviet anti-aircraft missiles around Haiphong, he gave a twitch, acting surprised as Bundy's hand descended gently onto his shoulder.

"Hiya, Ray. What's tonight's scuttlebutt?"

Cline brandished the despatches and snorted gently. "Best thing is that Crosby reckons we're going to get a white Christmas." He looked up and, affecting slight concern at Bundy's careworn expression, nodded in the direction of the cabinet room. "Tough in there, was it?"

"You said it, Ray. That's some devious son-of-a-bitch."

"Still no admission about those missing nukes, then?"

"Naw – the trail's gone cold. The main thing on his mind was trying to get LBJ to help enforce this oil embargo – bankroll him. He's made a few half-assed moves with some tired old Limey flat-top to make it look good, but you can see he isn't serious."

"Sending out the Royal Navy to make the oil embargo stick... It'd make a good cover story if he really was trying to get those bombs back under control, though."

"So why not be honest about it? He nearly drove LBJ crazy in there. Trouble is, this guy doesn't understand how to play ball."

"Pudd'nhead Wilson, eh?"

"Yeah. Just like the book. Nobody wants to do business with him."

"At least Pudd'nhead kinda came good in the end."

"I can't see it happening this time, Ray. Frankly, I don't see why we need to bust our asses trying to dig him out of the shit."

≈

Guo had taken almost a week to travel to Mpulungu. There he met the gang of Tanzanian soldiers who had arrived in plain clothes over a period of days, by ferry and fishing boat. Now, the squad stood ready for action under Jonas's command, with Guo supervising the engineering. The decoy oil drums containing river water had been rolled off the lorry in a haphazard way. The whitewood lay in a random heap, ready to reconstruct crates around the two bombs. The railway sleepers were close at hand, whilst the wooden poles had been erected as shear-legs with the aim of lifting the bombs out of their wooden coffins. Guo was leaving nothing to chance. They had lashed the shear-legs together, textbook-fashion, guyed off on each side and supported with a length of half-inch steel cable looped around the tree.

The soldiers had shovelled away the covering of earth, peeled away the tarpaulins and removed the dunnage that formed the lids of the underground crates. Now it was time to haul out the bombs using the chain block slung below the apex of the A-frame. A steady drizzle had begun to fall, soaking everyone, bringing cold and misery despite the need for rain.

"This place," Guo called to Jonas. "I hate it. First the dust; now the rain."

Jonas laughed. "And nothing in between, right?" He picked up a rock and flung it at a rough, irregular earthen pillar twenty metres away, now streaming with water. "Then there's the termites." He laughed again as Guo scowled. "You ready?"

"Heave away!"

Guo felt that lowering the bombs into the pit using lorry

power had worked so well before that it made sense to lift the first one out by the same method. As it rose clear of the pit, the soldiers slid the sleepers underneath, to prevent it from falling back. Then they hoisted it higher, so that the men could construct the base of a new crate on top of the baulks of timber. With the base constructed, the bomb was made fast upon it and raised once more, while the soldiers refilled the pit with earth. They removed the sleepers last of all, enabling the lorry to reverse underneath the apex so that the bomb could be lowered onto the front of the cargo deck. The M•A•N drove forward again and two chippies set to work building the crate around the bomb, while the other four, with a better understanding of how to go about their work, started moving the shear-legs over to lift out the second bomb. By and by, the rain stopped and everything began to bake dry again.

When the job was complete, Jonas produced the metal stencils from under the driving seat, together with a brush and a tin of black paint. With a certain artistry he worked away, branding each crate as containing copper ingots and consigning it to a mythical buyer in Singapore. He was certain that it would fool the border officials.

Guo looked across at Jonas. "At last," he smiled.

Wednesday 22 December, 1965
Dar es Salaam

Dar es Salaam harbour falls neatly into two halves: the northern part between East and West Ferry Point and the southern part, south of Ras Makabe – Southern Creek. After no more than two miles, the creek becomes un-navigable to anything larger than a canoe. It finally branches out to the southeast and southwest into tidal mangrove swamps. A little way before the mangroves take over, on the western bank lies a slipway, out of sight of the main port, screened by a bend in the creek.

In the cool of the morning Guo stood on the slipway, resting a hand on the front wing of the truck. Jonas leaned his buttocks on the front bumper, taking a little weight off his legs. They had drawn up their lorry beside a steel-tracked crawler-crane. The African crane driver started jockeying with the controls, trying to raise the jib, not apparently making a very good job of it. A rapidly-burning cigarette stuck out from the corner of his mouth. Perhaps the smoke was getting in his eyes for every half-minute or so there came a squeal from the winch-brake, a burst of revs from the crane's diesel engine and a menacing shudder from the jib.

Loosely moored alongside the slipway lay a craft of sorts, half barge, half lighter, not a square inch of which retained even a flake of paint, being taken over entirely by rust. The gang of African boatmen bickered amongst themselves, waving their arms and shouting at the crane driver, jumping from the lighter to the slipway and back again for no apparent reason.

"Are you sure these people are going to be able to manage it, Jonas?"

"Relax. It's their job... They do it all the time." Jonas glanced over his shoulder at Guo, who seemed worried. "It's not difficult. Just two straight lifts – lorry to lighter – simple."

"That's easy for *you* to say. If they foul up, I'm a dead man."

Jonas saw the point. Now not quite so secure in his opinion, he eased himself off his perch, walked ahead and stopped with his hands on his hips. "Hey, hey hey!" The boatmen stopped arguing. Jonas rattled off a few phrases in Kiswahili that caused the accusations to break out again amid cries of '*Fedha, fedha*'. He turned to Guo. "They want more money."

"I just want my consignment out of here. Pay them, Jonas. It'll be quicker than shooting one or two of them... All the same, I'd be tempted."

The boatmen continued squabbling. "Hey," interrupted Jonas again. "Okay, okay. *Mimi kulipa*. I'll pay."

This news broke the short strike and the Africans swarmed off the lighter up onto the lorry's cargo deck, manhandling the crane's heavy spinner and forcing the hook under the rope strop of the first crate. The winch screamed as the crane driver started to take up the slack. Guo leapt forward in alarm, frantically crossing and uncrossing his arms.

"Stop him, Jonas! Too fast. He'll upset the lorry. He'll snap the wire!" The driver released his lever, stopping the winch with an abrupt metallic jolt that caused the crate to swing, then slip back onto the flatbed, which made the lorry lurch from side to side and buck like a mule. The men standing next to the second crate staggered. At the same instant, a harsh clunk, like a sledgehammer on granite, made Jonas suspect that the impact had damaged the lorry's leaf-springs. The Africans shouted a fresh chorus of accusations at the crane driver who returned the abuse with his own brand of insults.

But along with the lorry's fractured suspension, this demonstration also shattered Jonas's tolerance. He rushed towards the crane, shouting, ordering the driver out of the cab. The driver refused. More money changed hands until the driver's greed was satisfied and he ambled a short distance away, sullen-faced, carrying his cigarettes.

The crane's brutal controls proved difficult to tame. With his new-found responsibility, Jonas broke into an immediate sweat as, with the first crate again swinging in the air, he slewed to face the barge. He needed to lower the jib and raise the load at the same time to extend out over the craft. Guo had moved to the edge of the slipway and was darting concerned looks between the cab, the load and the grey-green ooze over which it was suspended. Two Africans aboard the lighter gave wild signals about where to position the crate but Jonas only felt relief to have landed it in one piece. Skill played no part in it.

Guo turned to face the crane, wearing a look of utter dread. He passed his sleeve across his forehead, tried to catch Jonas's eye, puffed up his cheeks and blew.

"You don't know how lucky you are," muttered Jonas, his words lost under the grinding throb of the machinery. Total mayhem and one more crate still to load.

The motor vessel *Liang Hong 7* had started life in the early 1950s as a French-built, Dutch-owned general cargo tramp steamer, and had descended through Greek, Panamanian and Cypriot registry until the point where her mainland-Chinese owners had to be careful about the ports she visited. If any respectable maritime safety agency had asked to see her certification or details of the latest survey, there would have been an embarrassing silence.

On that day *Liang Hong 7* swung between tide and breeze, shackled by the anchor chain to a buoy in the northern part of the harbour. With her bows pointing vaguely out to sea, the port side of the vessel faced towards the passenger pier, the adjacent cathedral, and the other bustling sights of Dar es Salaam's waterfront. Towards midday, a rusty lighter approached the vessel on the less public starboard side. The ship's derricks had already been rigged at number three hold to work cargo 'over the wall', and it was scarcely twenty minutes later that two whitewood crates had been taken aboard, stowed below deck on the centreline, lashed down for the voyage and the hatch covers dogged down, ready for sea.

Only fifteen minutes after that, the *Liang Hong 7* was flying a 'P' flag and calling on the radio for the pilot. A freshly-plotted great circle course to the Sunda Strait lay marked out on the chart table. The waypoints and pencilled calculations were pinned up next to the chartroom clock. But after leaving the Sunda Strait and its smoking volcano behind, she would not be heading for Singapore as the stencil marks on her new cargo suggested. Her destination lay further north, into the South China Sea: Canton for orders, maybe Shanghai, maybe Tsingtao.

Monday, 3 January, 1966
Salisbury, Southern Rhodesia

Danny stared into the bathroom mirror with a certain degree of gloomy regret. With thumb and forefinger, he pressed the flesh under both eyes so that the lower lids curled away from his eyeballs. A different phrase would be required to describe what had once been the whites of his eyes. He leaned forward and stuck out his tongue, to discover that a coat of yellowish rind had grown over it. Looking around, his bathroom was not altogether wholesome. The overall effect, as distant scenes of debauchery trickled back into his memory, only worsened his headache.

A chance acquaintance had invited him to a New Year's Eve party. Somehow, it had all seemed like such a good excuse for celebrating the anniversary of his country's independence. The illegality of its declaration had counted for nothing. Popular defiance in the face of British measures to starve out the country only increased the fervour of the merry-making. But that had been three nights before. What had happened since then? He turned the tap, to run some hot water into the basin so that he could start the repair process but something, perhaps the sound of running water, made him feel light-headed. He swayed, felt the rush, crouched over the W.C. and retched. The immediate muscle pain across his stomach told him that he must have spent a considerable time straining in the same way over the past three days.

After a wash, Danny felt slightly better but a fresh wave of nausea made him groan. He sat on the bed until the feeling had passed. Rationality slowly returned. He figured the best thing would be to treat this as a reminder of his own weakness, to suffer the headache until it was gone and to swear a New Year's resolution about avoiding further self-indulgence. Surveying the wreckage of his bedroom, his last bonds to Rhodesia began to dissolve. True, Southern Rhodesia was his native country, but with the farm sold, his parents potentially in New Zealand, Charlie in London and Lizzie – well, God only knew where Lizzie might be – he realised that the place held few ties for him now. His adventure was finished. It was a reckless thing to have done in the first place and only by luck had he survived.

Mike Hoare had told them that they fought in the cause of freedom. Surely that was so? He had seen the wanton slaughter carried out by the Simbas. He had seen death at first hand and been the instrument of delivering it to others. He had known comradeship and valued it no less for the fact that his colleagues were mercenaries. At the time, he had quickly understood that the important thing was watching out for one another and following orders.

Yet he had also waged a second secret war, kept his own counsel and learned to shoulder responsibility. He resolved to exercise some of it now and head for London as he should have done, sixteen months earlier. He began to gather his belongings together.

Up-ending the kitbag and rucksack over the bed, he attempted to separate his possessions into piles to make it easier to fold them up and pack them away. At this point it struck him as odd that although he had only used one of the drawers in the dressing table, they were all open. The obvious suspicion hit him a moment later. He found his wallet in a corner of the room – empty. He could not recall throwing it over there. Although the discovery made him suspect that he had been robbed, making his chest flutter as his mind flew to the worst conclusion, he tried not to get worked up about it. If the modest amount of money was gone, then getting it back again seemed a futile hope. A painful lesson was forcing itself upon him. But there was worse yet. Where was his gun?

Danny's mind now sprang to a different set of conclusions as he searched frantically for the Smith & Wesson. If he failed to find it, he could not report it stolen. He had crossed from South Africa with the weapon concealed in his kitbag. He had not declared it or registered it under his name. This was serious. The ammunition was gone, too. There seemed to be only one course of action: pack up, check out, visit the bank and get a seat on the next train to Jo'burg as quickly as possible.

Anyway, if he needed to, he knew now how to get hold of another gun.

Thursday, 13 January, 1966: 23:30
Shanghai Pilot Station, People's Republic of China

The vessel's short-lived name of *Liang Hong 7* had been daubed over with another temporary identity and the buff funnel painted red in amateurish disguise. From the latitude of Canton, the People's Liberation Navy had shadowed the ageing vessel without detecting any threat from British warships anxious to ask for their bomb back. Accordingly, the Chinese had taken the decision to head for a large port with good facilities rather than run for cover. Their low-key plan had worked. Neither the British nor the Americans seemed to have any intelligence about the secret cargo stowed below, in number 3 'tweendecks.

Sixteen

Flight Lieutenant Longhurst, predictably 'Shorty' to the whole of 37 Squadron, mooched out of his meeting with the boss and went to find his navigator. He thought it best to start in the officers' mess.

"What've you got planned this weekend, Sandy?"

Alexander Baker had learned to approach such questions with suspicion. He rested his snooker cue between the brass lip and polished woodwork at the centre pocket. "Weekend in Paris, I'm afraid. It's a pity none of you married chaps can come along. Good job you popped round and interrupted me though... Reminds me I need to get a shower and shave before the flight." He made as if to leave.

"How many times have I heard that one?"

"You shouldn't have asked. Suppose you just tell me what I'm doing this weekend."

"You know the rules – no talking shop in the mess. Come on. Let's go and find somewhere quiet."

"No joking, Sandy. There's a straight line from here to Downing Street on this one. The boss wants us to deploy to Port Reitz and do a few proving flights... Keen to see whether we can operate search missions over the Mozambique Channel." Like many old RAF hands, Shorty still called Mombasa 'Port Reitz'. It was one of those traditions that seemed to have more to do with keeping ignorant newcomers in their place than providing any useful information.

"Any chance of a safari up country, at all?"

"Come off it. What do you think?"

"Searching for what, then?"

"Ostensibly, tankers heading for Beira. The Rhodesia pipeline starts there. They want us to be the air component of the oil blockade."

"Oh." Sandy hung his head a fraction before it occurred to him that Shorty had implied another matter, too. "You said 'ostensibly'. There's something else isn't there? What's the real reason?"

"Official Secrets Act. Two of our nukes are missing. Intelligence reckons they might be on their way by sea to China. They want us to find them."

"You're having me on." But Shorty stood, stony-faced. "Seriously?"

"Seriously." Shorty watched as his navigator's jaw dropped, waiting for the shock to sink in and his wandering eyes to re-focus. "You didn't sound too keen about enforcing the oil embargo..."

"Well, it's just that I've met some good blokes from Rhodesia over the years. Great flyers, great sports... Smith was a bit of an ace himself. Spitfires, I think. Doesn't seem quite right to be trying to spoil their party." Sandy angled his jaw as if chewing a lump of tough meat. "That's not all. You realise Beira is probably so close to our maximum range that we couldn't do much good anyway."

"Orders is orders, matey. Whitehall doesn't have too many other options."

Friday, 28 January, 1966
Mombasa, Kenya

Shorty Longhurst was a logical thinker. For him, there

could be no wrong findings following a proving flight. You either proved that something worked, or that it didn't. If the concept could not be proved the first time, the right thing to do was to re-design any sub-standard elements in the process and try again. After a whole series of negative results, and provided you had not done anything stupid, you called the boss, told him that the boffins were wide of the mark and would they please have another think. Not your fault. Which was why he was feeling aggrieved to be listening to a tirade from the squadron boss.

The problem was that the Avro Shackleton's range was a whisker short of two thousand miles. Beira was just under a thousand flying miles from Mombasa. You could get there. By the skin of your teeth, you could get back again. But you could only loiter in the area for a few minutes before it was time to fly home.

"It's got to work. The squadron's whole reputation is on the line."

"It half works," said Shorty. "We not only kept watch over the whole perishin' shipping lane from Port Reitz to Beira on the way down, but on the way back too. It's just that we can't get further than Beira or spend much time down there without winding up in the drink on the way home."

"Anyway, what do you mean – it half works?"

"What I say – the other half doesn't work at all. Searching for lost nukes on the high seas is next to impossible. For all I know, we could fly right over one and never know it. That latest box of tricks never made a sound... You can't tell if it's bloody working or it isn't."

"You've got to give me some sort of hope, Shorty. Fact is, our stock's pretty low with Denis at the moment and 'no-can-do' just isn't an option if we want to stay in business."

"Well, I don't like to put it this way boss, but the Fleet Air Arm could manage the Beira problem very nicely. You've got HMS Eagle cruising about off Dar es Salaam right now. Matter of fact, we gave them a low pass at fifty feet today to say hello. If she steams south and pootles around outside Beira, their Gannet anti-sub jobbies will be able to plot all the shipping north and south, night and day, round the clock, rain or shine…"

"Give it a rest, Shorty."

"Well, with the greatest of respect, my shacking-great fuckle-bomber won't do what you're asking. I still say this is a job for the Navy."

"But what you don't seem to understand is this: HMS Eagle needs about ten days in port for every twenty days she spends at sea. Once Johnny the Greek and his tanker pals understand that, they'll wait till the Eagle steams back to dry dock and then turn up off Beira like flies round a dung-heap."

"Send another flat-top, then. Send the Ark Royal. Turn and turn about."

"Denis is quibbling badly enough about the cost of one carrier and a couple of frigates as it is. That's why he called us in. He's hardly going to take kindly to being told he needs to send two carrier groups, now is he?"

"Received and understood. I've got all that. But listen – I can't keep repeating this – if we need some useful time over the target, Beira is effectively out of range from Mombasa. And because it's my range that's the problem, the solution is simple. Get me closer. What about Tanzania?"

"Tanzania? No chance. Chairman Mao is bigger than Chairman Wilson there at the moment. They don't want to know us."

"Okay. Obviously South Africa and Mozambique are

out. Both the Seychelles and Mauritius are too far away. So it seems there's only one bit of land left – Madagascar."

"You've spent too long in the sun, old boy."

"No, I'm not joking. Temporary plan." Longhurst looked the squadron leader in the eye and tapped a finger on his desk. "Tell Denis to get one of his carriers patrolling the southern end of the Mozambique Channel in case Smith tries to out-fox us by coming from the Durban direction. We'll patrol the northern end and keep tabs on everything coming in from the Red Sea and the Gulf. Meanwhile, he sends his diplomats round to ask for landing rights in Madagascar while me, Sandy and the crew brush up on our French."

"And what? Once you're set up at some jungle airstrip, the carriers go home?"

"That's it boss. I can reach my target from west coast Madagascar. I'll have spare fuel so I don't have to bugger off home straight away. And if we spot any blockade-runners, we'll call in a frigate."

"Hmmm... You might just be on to something there, Shorty."

"And don't forget. You need to get the teckies to think again about their nuke-detector."

Thursday, 17 February, 1966
Foreign Office Building, King Charles Street, London

"What do you know about Madagascar, Rook?"

Lewis-Williams was his usual peevish self. Charles knew that the best approach was to answer the question without responding to the mood. For instance, pointing out that the country had acquired a new name would only irritate the stuck-up bastard.

"Er... Used to be a French colony. Been independent for

five or six years, I think." Charles cast his mind back, trying to remember something – anything – from the Foreign Office briefing files. "Wasn't there a problem in the war because of the Vichy French, or something? The original inhabitants aren't Bantu so they speak a non-African language. And didn't I read that the experts reckon there could be huge deposits of titanium ore?"

"Thank God for somebody who knows something at least, instead of less than sod-all. All I've heard so far is folks rambling on about bloody lemurs."

Charles decided to say no more. 'L-W' had the reputation for being unimaginative, short-tempered and for descending into un-diplomatic language when under stress. Also, the fellow badly wanted what he regarded as his rightful gong. He had focused his ambition on a CBE in the New Year's honours list, then got nothing. His strategy seemed to be to demonstrate leadership by bullying the people below him. But there were two particular things he seemed unlikely to ever understand. First, that his management style made tasks go a whole lot more slowly, and second, that the lack of positive results probably pushed his decoration further beyond reach, at least for another year.

"Come with me, Rook."

No 'please' about it. Charles got up and followed. "Where are we going?"

L-W made him wait a few seconds for the reply. "Flap on." He seemed to realise this was not enough. "Briefing at four."

Charles recognised a few faces from the Commonwealth Relations Office as well as the Africa people from the Foreign Office. He also noticed some naval uniforms. The permanent secretary was away in Washington again.

Deputising, Galloway, an official from the Middle East desk, called the meeting to order. It was standing room only.

"Now apparently, Commonwealth Relations have heard from unofficial sources that for the last few days, oil has been reaching Rhodesia over the Limpopo at Beitbridge. At this morning's cabinet meeting Bottomley raised this as a suspicion, but the PM took it as an established fact and was somewhat – ah – disappointed, shall we say, not to have been told about it before." Galloway lifted his eyes and gazed around the room with a smile. "We don't know how much oil, how often, whether it's crude in rail tankers, diesel in road tankers, or a few drums strapped on the back of a donkey cart. But the PM is cross and he wants everyone to pull their socks up." This was an unusually light-hearted introduction. "So I'm establishing five different working groups and giving each syndicate just twenty-four hours to come back here with a briefing paper to be passed via myself to the PM." One or two people looked at their feet, no doubt hoping not to be nominated as a group leader.

Galloway continued. He spread the fingers of one hand, ready to check off his requirements. "I want verifiable facts. If you haven't got facts, then I want best estimates supported by a percentage reliability. I want Rhodesia's oil stocks and daily consumption figures today, and future estimates in one week, two weeks, four weeks, eight weeks and three months." He folded over his first finger. "Also, I want proper strategic assessments of the Smith regime's economic and military position in those timescales." Two fingers down already. "If Smith is getting oil, I want to know how much and where from." Three down. "I want a proper assessment of the mood in the OAU and the same on the other side of the fence in South Africa and the

Portuguese territories." Four. "And finally, I want to know how many British companies may be disposed to break the sanctions and in what ways."

It was clear that Galloway had not finished. "And just in case any of you think I'll be sitting on my posterior doing nothing, I shall take charge of stepping up a number of diplomatic initiatives." He then revealed the names of the syndicate heads and waved a sheaf of papers in the air. "Come and collect your instructions, gentlemen. I want you back here with your results in exactly twenty-four hours." Several of those who had been contemplating their shoe leather breathed again. "Nobody leaves here without knowing who he's working for and what's required of him." In a pointed flouting of the 'any questions' convention he then added, "That's all. Get on with it, please, gentlemen."

Charles wondered which task force he had been allotted to.

Lewis-Williams nudged him on the elbow. "Follow me." The fellow thrust his way to the front of the room with Charles tagging along behind until they came before the speaker. "Sir... Um... Sorry, we're a bit short on Madagascar experts. You made a good choice in asking for Rook though." He leaned closer to Galloway and muttered from behind his hand. "I got some good work out of him recently during that hush-hush Ndola business."

Galloway turned and smiled. "Ah, good man!" Charles wasn't quite sure whether the praise referred to himself or 'L-W'. "You can leave Rook with me now, Michael. I'll take it from here."

"Very good, sir." Lewis-Williams bobbed and backed away.

Galloway drew Charles into a corner of the room as the delegates dispersed; he looked Charles up and down. "I asked for you especially. I'm aware that you know all about the Ndola fiasco and why we sent you there. I need someone who's already in touch, doesn't need to ask too many questions, knows Africa – that sort of thing. The problem is that the kit that went missing – you follow?" Charles nodded. "Well, it's still missing. Apparently, the RAF has invented some sort of special gadget and flown over half of Africa with it, but they still haven't found the, er... merchandise. Now they want to use the excuse of the Beira patrol to deploy aircraft to watch for the damned things being spirited away by sea."

Galloway compressed his lips into a straight line, drew a noisy nasal breath and allowed his eyes to stray towards the ceiling. Charles waited, wondering whether a party that had lost something so vitally important might not always be able to think clearly enough to find it again. Perhaps Galloway was having similar thoughts; a moment later, he broke free of them.

"That's the situation. Now for your mission. The RAF needs an airbase that's closer to Beira than Mombasa. We're putting together a team to negotiate with the Malagasy government for landing rights. We're hoping to find a suitable airfield over there. I need you to be a member of that team. Could you be on a plane right after tomorrow's meeting?"

Charles nodded. "Yes sir." It would get him away from Lewis-Williams for a few days, the rat, with his blatant attempts to take credit where none was due. Maybe he would even have a few hours to swot-up from the Malagasy country file.

"Good man!"

≈

Naturally, the meeting was being conducted in French. Charles was managing to follow about three words out of four. From the look on the face of the squadron leader from Aden, he was managing rather less. The Malgache minister had agreed with the British consul that his country had a duty under the Security Council resolution to assist in bringing down the illegal white settler regime. He declared he would be enchanted to see an RAF presence if the chosen airfield was suitable.

'Damned right he would,' thought Charles. The spending power of several hundred thirsty servicemen leaving their money in the local economy would delight many a government official.

But the minister just had one final thing to say. "I trust that you gentlemen realise that my country has a defence agreement with France. I cannot allow foreign soldiers or airmen to be stationed here without their agreement."

"Well that just about puts the tin lid on it," grumbled the squadron leader, later. "This'll go right up to De Gaulle, and all we can expect from him is a big fat «*Non*»." He shook his head as if the seeds of a fitting comment had started to take root in his mind. "That's the trouble with Frogs."

"What?"

"They're slippery and you never know which way they're going to jump."

"Except for De Gaulle," said Charles. "He's always predictable."

Flight Lieutenant Blyton glanced at his watch and noticed that the programme of interviews was running a good twenty minutes behind schedule. He derived no great pleasure from the bright sheen of his toecaps or the ruler-straight crease of each trouser leg. To calm his nerves, he reached towards the low coffee table where a week-old copy of *Flight International* lay. There, in the brief section on world aviation news, Noddy Blyton learned that Dan Air had just purchased two Comet 4s from BOAC. The aircraft would be handed over in a few weeks' time.

In that instant he knew that he no longer wanted to waste his time trying to impress a bunch of sour-faced brass-hats who only had limited space available for converting new pilots to fly the Argosy transport aircraft. There would be no fun in flying the Argosy; it was too small and too underpowered to have much effect when set against the Lockheed Hercules.

There was no point in fighting for a flight-deck job in the RAF any longer. After that business in Africa, his career was blighted anyway. Here was his chance to get out of a dead-end, dead-man's-shoes job and get in on the ground floor of the air charter market. Let some other desperate oaf take his place. The Comet and the Valiant were of a similar size. They both used the same Rolls Royce engines in a similar configuration. How could flying holiday-makers to the Costa Brava possibly be any more demanding than flying nuclear weapons around?

And then there were the hostesses. He tore out the page and stuffed it in his pocket. He planned to enjoy the coming interview after all.

Friday, 11 March, 1966
Ministry of Defence, Whitehall

The secretary of state burst out of his chair. "He said WHAT?"

The Grade 3 had just returned from the French embassy, having received disappointing news from the lips of the air attaché. Over time, he had become accustomed not only to foreign intransigence but also ministerial outbursts. He stood his ground. "Well, I rather think Maurice was embarrassed to have to repeat it, although I don't believe it loses much in the translation. He said '*Les Anglais sont seulement à la recherche d'une excuse pour acquérir une autre colonie. Si nous les laissons faire, ils ne quitteront jamais.*'

"Meaning?"

"Meaning that the air attaché has gone back on the agreement we reached, Minister."

"Not that! Your translation!"

"I understood him to imply that Britain is simply looking for an excuse to acquire another colony, Minister. His fear is that once we get in there, we'll never leave."

"This has got De Gaulle's malicious fingerprints all over it."

"Yes, Minister."

The permanent secretary stepped in. "Minister, I would, of course, much prefer to give diplomacy another try but I don't think there's time for that now. I rather think we've got as far as we can with Monsieur le Président."

But Healey would not leave it alone. "This vindictive attitude of his – it even came up in Cabinet last December. I can scarcely believe the way he acts sometimes."

"He's seventy-five now. He's not going to change."

"Change? The ungrateful bugger's getting worse. Whenever he gets some sort of rebuff, like this latest one from French voters, somehow it's all Britain's fault and he lashes out." Healey's voice leapt up an octave. "At us!"

"Well at least it's not a flat refusal."

The minister snorted. "Deluded, paranoid, senile bastard."

"Quite possibly, Minister."

The Grade 3 tried to drag his minister back to the subject. "We still have their list of conditions, Minister. Remember, they haven't actually denied us permission to use the airfield at Majunga."

Healey clenched his fists, took a deep breath and slowly exhaled. "Is this Majunga place the right spot? I mean, can the Shackletons operate efficiently from there?"

"I believe we can always rely on the service to make the best of a bad job, Minister. I understand there was one airfield a little closer to Beira, but nothing like so well suited as Majunga."

"But the old bastard has killed it stone dead, hasn't he? Just look at this list of conditions: No night flying, no more than three aircraft, no fighters, no armaments of any kind and this one... Well, it's just spiteful. There's no other word for it."

"Yes, Minister, I fear so." *'Pas de bâtiments permanents.'* No fixed accommodation. Living in tents on a baking hot tropical airfield was not going to be popular with the lads from 37 Squadron.

"Right – we've got no option, then... Approved. Sign up and pass the word, eh?"

≈

Deafened by the cockpit noise from four Rolls Royce Griffon engines, Flight Lieutenant Longhurst waved a gloved hand to attract the attention of the co-pilot sitting to his right. If he had simply spoken over the intercom, without warning that he was going to speak, the chances were that the co-pilot would not have heard him.

"Need a leak, Dodger. Look after her for a few minutes, eh?"

"Roger, Shorty. I have control. Piss off then."

Longhurst scrambled out of his seat and squeezed into the main body of the fuselage where the crew sat absorbed in their various tasks. He stopped first at the chart table. Fixed above it, an engraved plastic sign bore the words 'Routine Attack Navigator'. He plugged his intercom-jack into the spare socket. "How long to the last known position, Sandy?"

"Nineteen minutes, skip."

Next, he moved to the ASV radar operator's position. "Anything?"

"Just coming up now boss, I think. Say sixty-five miles and about four or five degrees right of our current heading. Give me a couple of minutes to do a plot." Shorty trooped off to the khazi. His digestive system was letting him know that it might be better to go easy on the local Majunga brew for a while. Other than that, he felt a whole lot happier now that his aircraft had been fitted with new auxiliary fuel tanks. He returned to the ASV monitor.

"That'll be him all right, boss – there's nothing else around. He's barely doing five knots, roughly northeast. I really needed a longer fix, though."

Shorty re-inserted his jack plug and spoke to the crew.

"Okay lads. We'll do a fast run up his arse – sorry, up his wake – at fifty feet and skim his port side. See if we can catch him napping – hopefully scare the pants off him. I'll fly figures of eight at two hundred feet so both observers can have a good look and shoot a couple of rolls of film. Radio silence until we reach the RV. Then we'll give HMS Plymouth a shout and let the boys in blue know what's what."

"That's her right enough. T2 configuration, twelve to fourteen thousand tons, wheelhouse amidships, engine-room aft, goalpost mast on the forecastle, loaded down to her marks. *Joanna Five*, busy going nowhere. Certainly not Durban where she's supposed to be heading."

No members of the ship's crew had appeared on deck to gawp at the aircraft flying low overhead. This was so far out of the ordinary that the vessel's clandestine motive seemed beyond doubt. "Up to no good – guilty as sin. Okay Sandy – give Sparkie his position, course and speed so he can bang it off to the Navy."

Monday, 9 May, 1966;
Mozambique Channel;

"Shorty, ASV here. One contact bearing left, zero one nine degrees, forty-eight miles. Heading approx' oh-three-five degrees true, speed twelve knots."

"Roger, coming left now. Give me a new course to cross his wake five miles astern and we'll take a butchers. Sonics and NBC on standby, please."

Twenty-one minutes later the Shackleton roared past the lone Iron Curtain merchantman at a hundred and forty knots, flew a desultory pattern around the vessel, fired off nothing more harmful than a few token shots from a camera and logged the instrument readings.

"What do you reckon? Was that an East German funnel or Chinese?"

"Thought it was Polish, myself."

"NBC... Any sort of a flicker on that gizmo of yours?"

"Nothing, Shorty. Clean as a whistle."

Longhurst turned to his co-pilot and mouthed, 'Don't know why we bother looking'.

Dodger shook his head from side to side, following this with a right-handed gesture to denote futility. He mouthed the words, 'Gone already'.

Lip-reading was an important skill for Shackleton crew. And of course, Dodger was absolutely right. Both Yellow Sun bombs were long gone.

From somewhere in the main cabin a voice piped up, "Anyone fancy a cuppa and a bacon sarnie?" A chorus of approval rang around the intercom system. When this had died down, a different voice could be made out, singing the Shackleton theme song to a familiar melody made popular during the nineteen-forties. Soon others joined in.

"...With four Griffon engines and flaps on their wings,
Bless all their pistons and their piston rings.
Though the bomb load they carry is small,
Three fifths of five eighths of fuck all.
You'll get no enjoyment from coastal deployment
So cheer up my lads bless 'em all."

"Oil temperature warning on number three."

"What was that about piston rings?"

Angola

Sunday, 13 March, 1966
Muangai, Moxico Province, Angola

Antonio da Costa Fernandes, eyes closed as if in prayer, waited for the operator to ring back and connect the call. The four others present in the room sat in silence. All seemed touched by the hand of fate, aware that this was a solemn moment. They had agreed upon a joint leadership. When the telephone bell sounded, breaking into their meditations, each man was jolted by the surprise. Da Costa Fernandes reached forward and took the call.

"Is that you, Brother Savimbi?" He nodded at the reply and tilted his head to strike an appropriate pose. "Then I am delighted to inform you that the committee has agreed upon a name for our movement. If you will accept the honour and share the role with me, you and I are to be joint leaders of the *União Nacional para a Independência Total de Angola.*"

For the benefit of his colleagues, Da Costa Fernandes angled the telephone receiver slightly away from his ear. The revolutionaries strained to hear Savimbi's response. With a tinny crackle the earpiece proclaimed his decision.

"I feel privileged by the revolutionary committee's confidence in me. My destiny is written on my heart and I am proud to go wherever it leads me. I accept the commission to work with you, Brother Antonio, at the head of UNITA. Long live a free Angola."

≈

Saturday, December 24, 1966; 23:15 local time
West Bank of the Kasai River, Moxico Province, Angola

Jonas Savimbi had been there before. He stood with his Chinese-made AK-47 slung over his left shoulder, offering encouragement to the hordes of armed men who were surging west from Dilolo, just across the Angola-Congo border, their hearts full of patriotic zeal for liberating their country. He needed as many of his soldiers as possible to see him, their leader, before he re-joined his own platoon. The men needed to know he fought beside them, at the front, not in a second wave or from behind a desk.

It would be Christmas Day in a few minutes. Nobody would be expecting an attack. The main force would enter the border town of Teixeira de Sousa and mount a dawn attack on the Portuguese police and army barracks. It would be easy – a crucial blow in the fight for freedom. While the others were attacking the barracks, Jonas's small guerrilla unit intended to blow a hole in a section of Benguela Railway Company track, and perhaps a bigger hole in its finances and willpower.

Jonas adjusted his beret, a vital symbol – Ché wore a beret He hurried forward to re-join his men as they crept into position. He gave the signal to attack. "Viva UNITA."

People's Republic of China

The chief scientist had maintained a close watch on the activities of his junior comrades. Virtually every square centimetre of the British Yellow Sun had been measured, photographed and made the subject of a technical drawing. No nut or screw was unfastened before a discussion had taken place to establish what the technicians hoped to achieve and to assess the risks involved. They logged the angular rotation each time they operated a screwdriver or spanner. They documented the whole process to the extent that, once dismantled, many items were weighed, measured, drawn or photographed all over again. In this fashion the Chinese put together what was effectively a methodology and a set of construction drawings for the Yellow Sun that were more detailed even than those sealed under lock and key in the cellars of the Ministry of Defence in Whitehall. With scrupulous attention to detail, every section of the device was dissected and then, to prove that the assembly details were correct, put back together again by a different member of the team.

"Comrades – we shall now see how clever you have been at re-assembling this atomic weapon. Once you have inserted all the steel balls for safety, we shall transport it to Lop Nur and test it. If the weapon fires successfully then not only will you have proved yourself as a team, but we shall also have valuable test data for calibrating the yield of our own copy of this bomb." The team members looked a little nervous. Nobody knew what really happened to those who fouled up at the Institute, but there were rumours.

It had to work.

Monday, 9 May, 1966; 15:20 local time;
Lop Nur Test Range, Xinjiang

The atomic energy institute had directed that the rebuilt British Yellow Sun be tested by erecting a steel tower, hauling the device to the top and setting it off. This was, after all, what they had done with their first test explosions. But the generals had a different idea. They wanted the pressure fuses and intriguing clockwork devices to be tested too. They were convinced that the mechanisms were of low reliability and could be improved upon. The result of their demands was that a delay of several weeks occurred during which dummy bomb casings were built, tested for accuracy in free-fall and tested again to ensure that the new timing and pressure fuses were reliable. There was really only one choice of aircraft. The licence-built Tupolev Tu-16 had already been used to air-drop a home-grown Chinese weapon.

A cloudless, bright blue sky arched above the cold, dry desert. At 15:28 a lone Tu-16 appeared over the test site and dropped a pattern of smoke flares to test for wind shear and to measure the potential drift from forty thousand feet, right down to ground level. Then at 15:51, aircraft serial number 50671 flew back into sight, approaching the range from the northeast, its con-trail the only blemish in the heavens. A fresh coat of white, anti-flash paint had been applied to the underside of the aircraft. The ground-based remote film and television cameras locked on to the aircraft with ease. Over a 100-kilometre radius the surface network of temperature and pressure sensors began to log local conditions and feed the data back to the command centre.

At 15:56 the Tu-16 released the Yellow Sun, some thirty thousand feet above the test range. The pilot felt the lurch as the bomb fell away in a parabola towards the aiming point. He banked the aircraft in a steep turn to port to reverse his course and put as much distance as possible between his aircraft and the plummeting bomb. The observer in the tail gunner's compartment set both cameras recording and struggled out of his cell to take refuge in the radiation-shielded central section of the fuselage. The crew put on their dark glasses.

After twenty-eight seconds the bomb reached terminal velocity. Twelve seconds later, the first pair of pressure fuses operated, deploying the parachutes. The bomb descended for a further two minutes, after which a second pair of pressure fuses triggered the firing switch to deliver the electrical current to seventy-two detonators simultaneously. Thirty-six explosive lenses fired in perfect synchrony, and a blinding white light blazed above the target point.

Wednesday, June 21, 1967
Beijing

The British Chargé d'Affaires, Mr Donald Hopson, had not been invited to the ceremony at the airport, welcoming President Kaunda to the People's Republic. In line with most of China's relations with Britain at the time, this was a political snub. On a normal day Hopson was far too diplomatic to have considered gate-crashing the occasion, but on that day the circumstances and the commonwealth connection made it necessary. Acting under orders to make it look good, Hopson managed to get pushed around and slapped a couple of times by Chinese officials before being ordered to leave the airport. For the ex-commando major, the whiff of conflict was satisfyingly reminiscent of old times. Naturally, he protested against this gross discourtesy and returned to his Residence, confident that he had delivered what was required. Whilst he had not even got close to President Kaunda, he imagined that Kay-Kay would get to hear about what had happened. If it reminded the President that he was falling into the hands of a bunch of untrustworthy ruffians, Britain's purpose would have been served.

That evening, at the official dinner, Doctor Kaunda was engineered into the position of having to congratulate the Chinese Premier on the success of The People's nuclear test conducted a few days earlier.

Zhou Enlai waved a dismissive hand to indicate that it was really nothing at all. From practised ease, born of a thousand such political meetings, he found no difficulty in restraining all outward expression of pleasure or satisfaction. However, some seven seconds later and with precise diplomatic timing, Mr Zhou looked Kaunda in the eye and, leaving no room for doubt that the two events were somehow linked, said. "I really think you should get your railway now."

Kaunda sat open-mouthed.

Zhou then added, "Because the commercial banks – not to mention the Bank of England – seem somewhat cautious, perhaps we might also make an interest-free loan to your country and Tanzania. I imagine the officials ought to be able to draw up the documents in eight or ten weeks... Then we can make a formal announcement."

United Kingdom

Charles drifted awake, aware that something was wrong but unable to recall exactly what had disturbed him. He lay still, listening, and then he heard it again: sobbing. The sound seemed to be coming from Danny's room. He rolled over to check the time on the bedside alarm clock, blinking until he was able to focus – 3:05. Maybe ninety minutes before the pre-dawn light of midsummer's day began to flood the city. He sat on the edge of his bed and twitched the curtains. The glow from the streetlights meant it was never dark in this city. Not properly dark. Not like home.

There it was again, a cry like the whimpering of a frightened puppy. The night had been warm. Charles shambled out onto the landing without bothering to put on his robe and slippers, then laid his fingers lightly on Danny's door. His brother was moaning. A nightmare? Now fully awake, Charles felt the kindest thing would be to wake Danny and break the dream. He shuffled forward and laid a hand on his brother's shoulder. It was moist and clammy.

"Danny... Tsst! Hey, Danny, wake up. You're dreaming." Charles shook the shoulder, then flinched in shock as his brother spun on the mattress and sat up with a shudder. "Hey, it's okay. You were having a bad dream. You're okay Danny." His brother's eyes flashed wide open but whatever he was seeing, it wasn't Charles. Charles reached out his hand again and rested it on Danny's shoulder. "You're safe now," he said. "Nothing to worry about, kid."

Danny blinked a couple of times and seemed to recognise where he was. He sank back onto his pillow with a husky exhalation. "Thanks Charlie," he said.

"Bad one?"

"Yeah." He filled his lungs and sighed again. "Congo."

"D'you want to talk about it?"

"Not really."

"D'you want a mug of tea and *then* talk about it?" Danny lay still. At least he hadn't rejected the second offer. Charles took it as acceptance. "We're both awake now. I don't expect I'll get off again. Go and splash some cold water on your face and come downstairs."

"I don't know what you went through, kid, but I've read a lot of stuff they couldn't print in the papers. Can't have been much fun. Isn't it about time you got it off your chest? Tell Charlie, eh?" Charles gave his brother a warm smile. "Charlie fix it?"

Danny reached both hands forward across the pine table, clasped the mug, closed his eyes and huffed through his nostrils. "I killed a man."

Four words. Charles searched for something to say. There was too little information, so the seconds ticked by as he tried to think of a response with as little potential for inflaming the situation as possible. "If you hadn't done, would he have killed you instead?"

"His shots had already come pretty close, so yes. He could, easily."

Charles knew enough to avoid sounding like a parent but it hadn't prevented the thoughts rising into his mind. '*You didn't have to become a mercenary. What did you expect?*' and '*Are you going to get in trouble for it?*' He settled for, "So it was kill or be killed, then?"

"Yeah. It was supposed to be a training exercise. I'd

only joined up about six weeks before. Signed on as a radio operator but they made me carry a rifle as well." Charles nodded. "They sent us down south to recce a mine in Katanga."

"A mine? Why a mine?"

"Well, it certainly wasn't for gold or copper."

"What then? Diamonds?"

"No, not diamonds – not coal or tin – something far nastier."

"Uranium?"

"Right," said Danny. "The biggest, most productive uranium mine of all time."

"You're talking about Shinkolobwe?"

Danny nodded. "We were told the Belgians had shut it down but it seems a Chinese advance party had come along on the quiet and opened it up again. They'd dug up some sample material and set off with it. I suppose they were taking it back to China for testing. We'd only just missed them so we chased after them, a couple of hours behind." Danny paused and took a sip of tea. "Had a nasty incident in a place called Luambo. One of the corporals was forced to fire into the crowd – probably killed three or four with a single shot. The other corporal got hit on the head by a bottle. I was glad to get out of there. It was a skin-of-the-teeth job, Charlie."

"Let me guess... That's when you caught up with the Chinese?"

"That night. We were going to take them by surprise – a dawn attack. But they must have had a sentry up on the hillside. He started shooting and nearly killed the chap next to me. But I never stopped to think – I just reacted. Like being back home and getting caught in the open – you know – having to take a snap shot at a hyena or a rhino or something."

"Only this time it was a man."

"Yes, but put yourself in my position. It's pitch-dark. This bloke that's doing the shooting is a good two-fifty yards away. I only fired off about four rounds but I hit him with two."

"Dad taught us well." The words spilled out naturally. Having uttered them, Charles felt pleased, hoping they might help Danny to feel better about the incident.

"Only he didn't teach me to kill *people*. It makes me no better than they are."

Charles still wanted to make Danny forget the whole thing, or at least feel less guilty about it. "I know the rebels did some nasty stuff," he said, remembering the pictures he had seen and the reports he had read. "Ritual murders, cannibalism." A gory curiosity overcame him. "Did you stumble across anything like that?"

Danny hung his head and nodded.

"...Only natural to feel upset in the circumstances, then." For a moment Charles forgot that he had offered to listen, forgot that he should be counselling, not holding the stage. "I got sent out to Ndola about the same time," he said. "Bit of trouble with the Chinese there too. You shouldn't feel so bad about it. They're cropping up all over Africa now."

His observations had interrupted Danny's flow, causing him to clam up. Staring at the tabletop, Danny picked up a teaspoon and began to work a small spillage of tea into a spiral.

Charles saw his mistake. "Sorry, kid." But the thought was too powerful not to voice. He wondered how much Danny knew. "Do you reckon my Zambia-Chinese and the one you killed could have been part of the same crew?"

"Ndola, you say? Doing what?"

"Oh... They were supposed to be working out how to

build a railway through Tanzania to the coast."

"Supposed to be," said Danny with a dismissive laugh. "No Charlie, I didn't mean *them* – I meant *you*. Why did they send *you* to Ndola?"

"Just financial stuff... And a bit of local knowledge, I think."

Danny put down the teaspoon and reached forward to engulf the mug in both hands again. The pause continued just a fraction too long for Charles's comfort. As brothers the family bond felt close enough for Charles to worry whether Danny had instinctively seen through his deception.

Danny changed the subject – a possible sign that he was either rattled or knew more than he cared to say. "Did you get to see Mum and Dad?"

Charles shook his head, his mind racing. "Too little time," he said. What could Danny possibly know? This was the first time he had disclosed any details about his mission to Zambia. Danny's brief mention of uranium and then his own comment about Ndola had opened things up for both of them. Could there have been a link between Chipokwe in Zambia and the illegal miners that Danny had encountered in Katanga?

"No. I guess not. There's never enough time."

"Anyway," said Charles, "they were half-way through selling the farm. I couldn't have faced going back."

"No. I know what you mean."

Charles's thoughts hadn't left Ndola. He knew that the missing bombs never turned up in Stanleyville, the way he had first suspected. What if his second guess had been correct and the Chinese had managed to smuggle them out? And what if Danny had been involved somehow? He needed to do a little fishing.

"Look," said Charles. "When I said 'supposed to be', you

jumped on it. What do *you* think the Chinese were doing in Ndola?"

"Like you said. The railway, obviously."

Charles might once have agreed, but Danny's reply came way too quickly. "Obviously," he said.

"Nothing's changed. Unless Zambia can get the copper out, the country will go broke. Smith's got Kaunda by the nuts. The roads turn to mud for half the year, so a new railway is the only way."

Charles forced a pause, appearing to ponder for a moment. "You're probably right. I still don't understand how China or Zambia or Tanzania could afford it, though. But that's a different thing." One more try: "So you don't think my Chinese and yours were connected?"

"Shouldn't think so," said Danny. "No sign of my miners ever setting foot in Zambia."

Charles needed another decent pause before he could comfortably get back to Danny's bad dream. Then: "Nasty experience you had, anyway. No wonder you had a nightmare."

"That wasn't it."

"Sorry?"

"It was what happened after I shot their sentry."

"Oh, sorry. Do you want to tell me about it?"

"Well, this corporal, the one who got hit by the bottle... The plan was for him and a jeep-load of the lads to outflank the Chinese. A pincer movement, you see? Him from the north and us from the south. Catch them just before dawn. Anyway, the corporal's section had taken a wide detour and doubled back through a settlement called Bunkeya..."

Charles stiffened. "Where did you say?"

"Bunkeya. Later I found out some big chief had his kraal there, back in the eighteen-hundreds. Msiri, I think he was called. Murderous bastard; killed people just for sport."

"Bunkeya?"

"That's what I said. Anyway, this corporal – we all thought it was down to the bash on the head – but once we'd captured the position and the shooting had stopped, he was just gung-ho. Steaming. Bloodthirsty. And he just lined up all the prisoners..."

"Bunkeya?"

"Yes, Charlie. Bunkeya. Are you listening or what?"

United States of America

Norris Bradbury had stayed late in the office. There was always a reason to stay late, but the trick lay in knowing when to quit and head home. Only this was not a time to be heading for his fireside. The Chinese had carried out another test at Lop Nur the day before. The USAF had captured samples from the upper atmosphere and jetted them across the Pacific for analysis. He had asked not to be disturbed until the physicists had come up with an answer.

A tap at the door. "Doctor Bradbury, sir?"

"Yeah. Come right in." It was amusing how everyone always put on a clean white lab coat before coming to see him. "What have you got for me?"

"A big increase in Iodine 131 in the jet stream, sir. There's some thermonuclear material in the debris, too." The young physicist brushed his forefinger under his nose and sniffed. "It looks pretty certain they're confirming their design principles for a two-stage device."

"But they haven't quite gotten from A to H yet, then? How long, do you reckon?"

"I'd say give it six months, sir. None of the boys can believe just how fast those guys are moving with this." He handed over the chemical analysis, the list of isotopes and a half-page of notes for Bradbury's approval as a briefing for the President.

"Thanks, son. Anything to add – any questions?"

"Well, unless you can tell me how they keep coming up with all the right answers, sir, first time, every time, I guess not."

"Just have to be patient. Maybe we'll find out one day. Could be this Sino-Soviet split is just a load of baloney and they've been working together all this time..."

"Yeah, maybe." The physicist sounded doubtful. "Will there be anything else, Doctor Bradbury, sir?"

"Not for today, son."

Of course, Bradbury knew exactly why the Chinese were making such swift progress from atomic fission to fusion. He pulled open the middle drawer of his desk and although he was familiar with what they said, he took out two further analysis sheets. On top was the data for the British Yellow Sun. The second sheet was datelined 'Lop Nur; 9th May 1966'. He laid the analysis of the previous day's test alongside the other two data sheets. With ninety-nine percent certainty the cores were stated to consist of uranium 238, enriched U-235, but no plutonium. Like three peas in a pod; mix them up and you couldn't tell the summaries apart.

He picked up the telephone and dialled a private number. Telling the President should be a job for the chairman of the Atomic Energy Commission.

Sunday, June 18, 1967
Los Alamos National Laboratory

When word came through that there had been yet another Chinese nuclear test, one look at the ominous seismic data was enough for Bradbury to call his people together to work on the Sunday. Eventually there came a knock at his door.

"So, what have we got?"

"It's a big one, Doctor Bradbury, sir. Maybe just on the top side of three megatons. We reckon a multi-stage thermonuclear device with U-235, U-238 and lithium-sixdeuteride."

Bradbury already suspected the worst; this confirmed it. "And out of interest, do you know how long it took them to get to this stage?"

"Not straight off, sir – but I'd guess around three years."

"Thirty-two months, son." He paused. "Do you know how long it took us?"

The young physicist cast his eyes up to the ceiling and appeared to think for a moment. "Must have been six or seven years, I guess, sir."

"Ivy-Mike test, November fifty-two. Best part of seven years four months. That's eighty-eight months." Bradbury kept his eyes directly on the face of the young man. "Something to think about, huh?"

Wednesday, June 21, 1967
The White House

Bundy, Cline, McCone, Bradbury and Foster needed something to lift their spirits. But nothing on the table in front of them was going to do that.

"I guess this whole thing is going to affect the way we need to conduct the war in Vietnam," said Cline. The others looked at him without any real expression. "With a fully-fledged nuclear power next door, I mean."

"They'll already have started working on ways to increase the yield," said Bradbury.

"Then there's relations with Taiwan, of course," added McCone.

"Yeah, the Generalissimo," said Bundy. "I wouldn't want him squeezing my balls."

Bradbury brought them back to home territory. "How do you think the President's going to take it when we see him?"

"Got a few things in the pipeline," said Foster. "Have to limit his options... Tell him we need to speed up that extra budget appropriation."

Finally, Bundy again: "What really worries me is where the blame's going to fall if the Chi-coms decide to make political trouble with that second British bomb..."

THE END

Glossary

Aldermaston	Village in Berkshire, England; site of the UK Atomic Weapons Establishment (formerly the Atomic Weapons Research Establishment)
ASV	Anti Surface Vessel (also Air to Surface Vessel) i.e., a radar system
AVTAG	Aviation Turbine Gasoline [Aviation fuel, a.k.a. JP-4]
BOAC	British Overseas Airways Corporation
Boma	[Swahili] Similar in meaning to '*Kraal*' (see below) but usually associated with tropical Africa, and with extra fortification
C-47	Twin-engined cargo aircraft, a.k.a. the DC-3, or Douglas Dakota, dating from 1941
C-130	a.k.a. Lockheed 'Hercules'; four-engined transport aircraft dating from 1954
CBE	Commander of the [Most Excellent Order of the] British Empire
CFB	*Caminho de Ferro de Benguela* [Benguela Railway]
CIA	Central Intelligence Agency
Colchester Glasshouse	
	Military Corrective Training Centre, at Colchester in Essex; used (in this case) to house in custody any serviceman who is awaiting the investigation of a serious matter
COMISH	United States Military Mission (Congo): An American technical mission aimed at improving Congolese logistical capabilities
Cranwell	RAF Cranwell, Lincolnshire; UK cadet training college, leading to commission as RAF officer
CT	Communications Technician
DC-6	Four-engined passenger/cargo aircraft dating from 1946
DCI	Director of Central Intelligence

dee-eff	(i.e., D.F.) Radio Direction Find-(er/ing)
DRC	Democratic Republic of the Congo
DSO	Distinguished Service Order
FN	*Fabrique Nationale de Herstal* [Belgian Arms Factory]
FOD	Various definitions (e.g., 'Foreign Object – Destroy' or 'Danger'). RAF maintenance hangars will always have a bin, labelled 'FOD' into which all waste should be dropped. This even extends to nuts and bolts that might slip out of a technician's fingers. In aero-engineering, once anything has fallen to the floor, it is FOD and must not be re-used. Therefore, FOD is another term for 'rubbish'.
GMT	Greenwich Mean Time
h.f.	High Frequency (radio) [3 to 30 megahertz]
HQ	Headquarters
HMS	Her Majesty's Ship
JCS	Joint Chiefs of Staff
JFK	John Fitzgerald Kennedy [US President]
K	Kilometre(s)
KGB	*Komitet Gosudarstvennoy Bezopasnosti* [USSR Committee for State Security]
Kraal	[South African] A traditional South African village of huts surrounded by a fence
Langley	Langley, Virginia; CIA Headquarters
LBJ	Lyndon Baines Johnson [US President]
M•A•N	*Maschinenfabrik Augsburg-Nürnberg* [German truck manufacturer]
MoD	Ministry of Defence
MP	Military Police(man)
MPLA	*Movimento Popular de Libertação de Angola*
NASA	National Aeronautics and Space Administration
NATO	North Atlantic Treaty Organisation
NBC	Nuclear, Biological and Chemical [i.e., forms of warfare]

NCO	Non-Commissioned Officer – Sergeants, corporals and equivalent
NORAD	North American Aerospace Defense Command
Northwood	UK military HQ, northwest of London
OAU	Organisation of African Unity
OHMS	On Her Majesty's Service
PDQ	Pretty damned quickly
Peiping	(a.k.a. Beiping / Peking) – a US courtesy to the Nationalist Chinese. The name remained in use by the US government until the late 1960s. The People's Republic of China adopted the name 'Beijing' in 1958 to refer to their capital city.
PM (the)	Prime Minister
Pongo	Derogatory term for the British Army
QSL	International code of signals: 'I acknowledge receipt of your message'
RAF	Royal Air Force
R/T	Radio Telephone/Telephony
RV	Rendezvous
Sitrep	Abbreviation for 'situation report'
SLR	Self-Loading Rifle
Stoep	[South African] An open, roofed platform or veranda in front of a house
T2	A particular design of tanker originating during World War Two
TANZAM	Tanzania-Zambia Railway [later 'TAZARA']
Tembo	Swahili word for 'elephant'
UNITA	*União Nacional para a Independência Total de Angola*
USAF	United States Air Force
USNS	United States Naval Ship
W/T	Wireless Telegraphy
Wideawake	[Wideawake Airfield] RAF Ascension Island, operated jointly with the USA

By the same author

...Colonel-Doctor Yu shepherded the delegation towards the block-built structure in the corner of what had come to be known as The People's Museum of Atomic Warfare.

'The People', however, knew nothing of their museum. Indeed, it was rare for visitors of whatever exalted military or political altitude to drop by. Until faced with the device, most people had difficulty believing that it even existed, yet these three had come solely to see this particular exhibit.

With a sweep of his arm, Yu indicated where the officials should stand, ranged in a semicircle in front of a pleated velvet curtain. Shifting to his left, he flicked a switch. A glimmer of orange light dribbled in streaks down the grey wall where the folds in the curtain hung away from it.

With a brief bow and a flourish, he drew the curtain aside.

COMING SOON FROM THE REAL PRESS

The Real Press

Come and have a look at our full range of books at
www.therealpress.co.uk

You can also download your free book at...
http://bit.ly/RemainsoftheWay

Printed in Great Britain
by Amazon